IN THE WASH

A Fenland Mystery
Set in the Time of King John

By Diane Calton Smith

Published by New Generation Publishing in 2020

Copyright © Diane Calton Smith 2020

First Edition

The author asserts the moral right under the Copyright, Designs and Patents Act 1988 to be identified as the author of this work.

All Rights reserved. No part of this publication may be reproduced, stored in a retrieval system or transmitted, in any form or by any means without the prior consent of the author, nor be otherwise circulated in any form of binding or cover other than that in which it is published and without a similar condition being imposed on the subsequent purchaser.

This book is a work of fiction. People, places, events and situations are the product of the author's imagination. Any resemblance to actual living persons is purely coincidental

Front cover image used with permission of St Peter and Paul's Church, Wisbech.

ISBN: 978-1-80031-744-4

www.newgeneration-publishing.com

New Generation Publishing

In memory of my dear mother, Janet Mary Calton who, right from the beginning, encouraged me to write.

Also by Diane Calton Smith:

Fenland Histories:

A Georgian House on the Brink (2015)

(Winner of a Cambridgeshire Association for Local History [CALH] Award)

Webbed Feet and Wildfowlers (2017)

Plague, Flood and Gewgaws (2019)

Fenland Mysteries:

Quiet While Dollie Sings (2016)

The Quayside Poet (2018)

West Door of St Peter and Paul's Church, Wisbech (with kind permission of the parish church)

ONE

Morning, Monday 10th October 1216

The king was late.

High above the keep, grey clouds scudded across the troubled sky and a gust of wind set the flags and pennants spinning in a wild, agitated dance.

Rufus of Tylneye came to a halt as a couple of red faced cooks staggered past with a huge wooden tray of pies they were carrying between them, on their way from the bake house to the kitchens. They almost collided with three acrobats, loose tunics covering their colourful costumes, who were going through their routine for later. The near collision caused some of the pies to fall from the tray on to the freshly laid earthen surface of the bailey, making the entertainers shriek with laughter.

The cooks swore at them, kicking in frustration at the remains of their wasted pies, but were silenced as the constable's deputy, Sir Giles of Ely, bustled importantly past. His expression was, thought Rufus, a curious mixture of pride and apprehension. Everything in the castle appeared to be ready, but there was so much at stake. There always was with a royal visit.

Up on the castle walls, men-at-arms patrolled and kept a look out. It had to be soon now.

'Boy!'

Rufus groaned inwardly as he turned towards the portly little man who had trotted out of the office behind him. 'Boy, where do you think you're going? I need you in here. The king comes here today, remember.'

As if he could forget. Obediently he fell into step with his master the chaplain and said nothing. He had needed a short respite from his desk in the oppressive office with its rush lights, scratchy quills and the noisily sniffing Oswy. The rest of the castle was vibrant with anticipation and excitement, and just for a moment he had wanted to feel part of it.

'I need that report finishing,' Father Leofric was reminding him. 'What did you think you were doing? It's not like you to wander off, especially on a day like this.'

Egbert and Oswy were sniggering behind their high, sloping desks as Rufus took his seat.

'Call of nature, Father,' he muttered contritely. Which was partly true.

He dipped his pen in the pot of ink and frowned. He'd have to make some more ink soon; the supply he had made a week ago was already running low. It was a part of his job that he didn't enjoy. He found the repetitive long soaking and boiling of the hawthorn bark, just to produce a small quantity of black ink, extremely tedious. It annoyed him how wasteful Egbert and Oswy, the other two clerks, were with the stuff, forever scratching out mistakes and having to start again, to the disgust of Father Leofric.

The chaplain's gruff manner and high standards were generally respected and Rufus knew that the elderly priest was well disposed towards him. This was probably due to his accuracy and his good hand, also to his Latin and French being of a high standard. The trouble was, he acknowledged, the better you were at a task, the more you were landed with patching up everybody else's mistakes.

Rufus of Tylneye was glad of his education, however. Since the age of ten, he had been tutored by his parish priest, learning Latin and French with surprising ease, even pleasure. As the second son of the lord of a small manor near Elm, he was not, at least not yet, required to play an active part in overseeing the manor's demesne lands, and so he had been sent to train as a clerk with the castle chaplain in Wisbech Barton.

With his lack of height and slight frame, not to mention his studiousness, he was the complete opposite to his older brother Ralph, who was muscular and athletic. Ralph excelled in riding and hunting and, at least in that respect, was shaping up for his future role as lord of the manor.

Both boys had been blessed with red hair, as had their parents, despite the colouring being quite rare elsewhere in the district. Their mother's was a paler shade that shone almost blonde in the sunlight, while their father's was an unabashed flame red. So sure had they been of their second son's ability to sprout the family's signature hair colour, that they had christened him Rufus.

Like his father and brother, Rufus had grown to be handsome, but unlike them, he was unaware of it. He had always been quiet and modest, but his worst character flaw, so far as his father was concerned, was his painful inadequacy on horseback. He had never learned to ride well. The lord of the manor had despaired of his younger son, threatening him with a life of needlework with the womenfolk of the manor. In the end, though, when Rufus reached the age of sixteen, he'd been packed off to work as a clerk with Father Leofric and no more had been said about his shortcomings in other matters.

And now, after three years of diligence, Rufus was about to witness a royal visit. King John was to honour the Manor of Wisbech Barton with his presence.

But he was late.

TWO (Present Day)

Rex Somebody

'So 'ow many should I put art, Monica mate? Shouldn't think many'll turn up, like.'

'At least twenty, Bertle. It's Rex Monday's first meeting and he's expecting a good attendance.'

'Too full of himself, know whatta mean?'

Monica Kerridge looked up and smiled. Bertle Bodgit's bulky form was filling her office doorway. His bushy eyebrows and short brown hair looked even more unkempt than usual tonight and his broad, honest face was looking at her indignantly, expecting a reply.

'But he's a *paying* too-full-of-himself person, so we have to prepare the room properly. We need the business.'

Monica went back to her work and left Bertle to set out the chairs in reception. Even from her office, she could hear him muttering and cursing to himself. The Poet's House Museum was doing a little better these days. As curator, with her small group of staff and volunteers, she had fought off many problems in the past and had worked her way through countless difficult seasons. Now at last, with new ideas they were reaching a wider public. Letting out parts of the museum to various local organisations for events, such as tonight's meeting of the newly formed Wisbech Heritage Society, was one good idea that was bringing in much needed funds.

There were a few townspeople, even a couple of the trustees, who disapproved of the idea. After all, the museum was meant to be dedicated to the life and work of the Georgian poet, Joshua Ambrose. The museum was even housed in the Wisbech home he'd grown up in, so to many people it felt wrong to use it for other purposes. But they needed the money. In order for the museum to survive, it was sometimes necessary to tread on a few toes. Besides, where was the harm in allowing a historical society to use one room twice a month?

Monica was still working on her laptop when Archie put his head round the door. He'd come straight from work and still wore his pea green fleece with the golf club logo, his office uniform as she called it. It didn't do much to enhance his looks, which were too sober in their neat, dark haired and green eyed way to benefit from such a lurid colour.

'Will they need coffee when they arrive?'

'I suppose so,' she replied. 'It'll make people feel welcome.'

She smiled to herself as he disappeared into the small kitchen behind her office. Sometimes she could hardly believe her luck that he was still with her. Archibald Newcombe-Walker, the man she'd met more than a year ago on holiday in Dorset, had remained in her life despite their various differences. He'd even sold up in the Midlands and moved to Wisbech, just to be near her. But she wouldn't hear of him moving in with her. That would be too much, too soon. Monica had always found it hard to trust, and that included her own emotions, as well as other people.

By the time she walked into reception, Bernadette, the museum's receptionist, had arrived and Bertle had fallen asleep on one of the chairs in the front row.

'Coffee's ready,' called Archie cheerfully.

'It'll be stewed by the time they get here,' grumbled Bernadette as she flicked her long, raven hair over her shoulder. 'You shouldn't have made it so early.'

She had never liked Archie and didn't see why she should start giving him any leeway now.

'What's tonight all about, anyway?' he asked.

'It's a new group called the Wisbech Heritage Society,' replied Monica. 'They're trying to get a few people together to learn more about local history. I'm quite interested, actually. I might stay and listen tonight. How about you?'

'Might as well,' replied Bernadette, though Monica had been talking to Archie. 'Nothing else to do, but I don't like that arrogant bloke who's running it. That one on the council. What's his name? Rex somebody?'

'Rex Monday, yeah that's him,' joined in Bertle, opening one eye as he awoke from his doze. 'I remember when he was an office boy in that 'lectric firm darn by Tesco's. He's on the council nah and reckons the town owes him a favour like.'

'Rex Monday?' queried Archie with a laugh. 'Is that *really* his name? As in 'Rex Mundi'? That's Latin for 'king of the world'! Can he be serious? I wonder when he made that up.'

'Well you'd better keep your educated opinions to yourself,' muttered Bernadette. 'The king of the world has just arrived.'

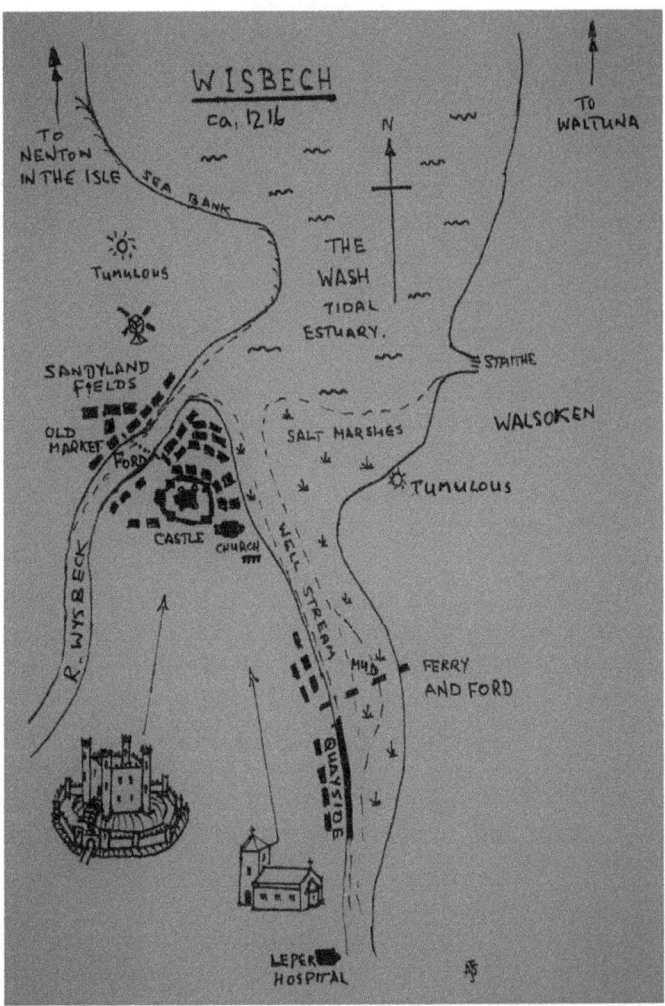

Sketch Map of Wisbech c.1216

THREE

Noon, Monday 10th October 1216

They could be heard long before anyone caught sight of them. The tread of more than a thousand hooves, as the king and his escort approached in one great body along the castle dyke road, was thunderously loud. Yet even that was drowned by the deafening roar of the crowd gathered by the gatehouse.

Though it was true that King John did not enjoy the greatest of popularity generally, his subjects in this region were loyal. It must have gladdened even his infamously frosty heart to be welcomed by so many Wisbech and Fenland folk.

Father Leofric had, at the last moment, allowed his clerks to climb to the top of the wall and watch the spectacle. They had been afforded but a brief glimpse of the king, cloaked in fur trimmed scarlet and riding at the head of his escort of barons and knights, before they'd had to scurry back down the steep, narrow steps within the thick curtain wall. They had managed to descend just in time to see the first men-at-arms as they rode through the gatehouse into the castle bailey.

The clerks weren't the only ones fleeing from sight. Two dogs had hastily been finishing off the remains of the earlier dropped meat pies before dashing into an alleyway between the buildings.

'Pity,' remarked Egbert. 'I felt like scraping up those pies for myself. I'm that hungry!'

'Quick, out of sight,' barked Father Leofric in Rufus' ear.

With Egbert, Oswy and the chaplain, Rufus slipped into the dark chapel. From the bailey they heard a few shouted commands and then there was a hush that fell like a curtain across the castle grounds. From the confines of the sightless chapel, its one narrow lancet window set too high in the wall to allow any view of the bailey, Rufus could only listen and imagine.

In his mind's eye he saw the tall and stately castle constable, Sir Hugo de Wenton, the slighter figure of his deputy, Sir Giles of Ely, and the imposing seneschal, Sir Milo Fulk. All of them were surrendering their pomp for a moment, sinking to their knees before a greater authority. Even the bishop, Robert of York, was bowing his head in respect for this earthly power.

'Perhaps we can eat now?' muttered Egbert sulkily. Dinner, usually served before noon, had been delayed due to the king's late arrival.

'Don't be disrespectful boy,' growled the chaplain in an undertone. 'We are honoured by the king's presence and he is doubtless hungrier than we are. His journey will have been long and arduous.'

From outside came the sound of movement again and Rufus guessed that the king was being accompanied into the forebuilding which led to the keep, the heart of the castle. He would then be shown to the chambers prepared for him on an upper storey.

'From Bishop's Lynn?' queried Oswy. 'Long and arduous?'

The look Father Leofric gave him was brimming with impatience.

'Yes, boy. And before that he rode over other, far greater distances. The king travels a great deal. The distance from Lynn is nothing at all on a swift horse, but for much of the journey the king will have accompanied his baggage train, which moves very slowly. It's thought that the journey had to be split across two days due to the effect of the recent floods on the roads. I believe they set up camp overnight on the far bank of Wiggenhall Eau, close to Crabbe House Priory. They've left the wagon train behind now, of course, but it's likely his grace accompanied it as far as the eastern bank of the Wash.'

'I've heard that he doesn't like to be parted from his precious wagons,' observed Oswy by way of reply.

'That's enough cheek, now get back to work.'

They returned to the office and had hardly settled before Father Leofric was sending one of them off again.

'Rufus, this quarterly report is to go to the bishop. Make sure it is handed safely to his chief clerk. You'll most likely have to search for him; who knows where anyone is on a day like this?'

Rufus tucked the sealed scroll inside his scrip, the small leather satchel attached to the long hanging girdle around his waist. He had been working on the castle's quarterly report for most of the morning, setting out interminable rows of figures for the bishop's scrutiny, and would be glad to see it delivered and out of the way for another three months.

The cold October wind almost knocked him backwards as he rounded the corner. It blasted its way down the alley between the office and the chapel, tossing into a frenzied tangle the brightly coloured bunting strung between the buildings.

The king would by now, he assumed, be resting in his chambers, duly soothed and attended after the rigours of travel. The two hundred barons and knights accompanying him had all been housed within the extensive castle buildings and the principal houses of the town, but the hundreds of men-at-arms, the ordinary soldiers who made up the great majority of the escort, had been obliged to set up camp in the New Market. Already, their tents would be filling the open space near the confluence of the town's two waterways, the great Well Stream and the smaller Wysbeck River.

The castle's best chambers had been ready for days, their floors covered with sweetly scented herbs and rushes, the high beds almost disappearing under the plumpest goose feather mattresses and finest perfumed linen sheets. This information had reached Rufus courtesy of Goodwife Elizabeth, who had heard it from one of the chambermaids.

The manor of Wisbech Barton was bursting at the seams. The bishop, the great Robert of York himself, had graciously consented to vacate his rooms in the keep so that the king's grace might occupy them. The bishop had taken humbler lodgings for the night, though there was nothing second rate about the fine house in which he was now ensconced. Close by the church dedicated to Saints Peter and Paul and overlooking the Well Stream, the handsome house would probably have suited the king himself.

The constable and his deputy had moved into small chambers above the gatehouse. They were perfectly adequate, it was said, but inclined to be draughty when the wind blew from the north, as it was doing today. All the town's stables had been requisitioned for the visitors' horses and temporary stabling had been erected by the Wysbeck.

In his search for the bishop's chief clerk, Rufus headed first for the castle steward's office. In the shadow of the high curtain wall and tucked between the carpenter's workshop and the smithy, the steward's office seemed forever hidden from the sun and totally lacking in cheer. Today it was bereft even of its usual bustle, occupied only by a single bailiff perched on a high stool and peering at a long list of names and figures. He was one of the steward's officers who were responsible for overseeing the manor's estates.

The bailiff was clearly too busy to take any notice of Rufus who had to do a lot of coughing before the man condescended to look up from his work. He pointed a careless thumb towards the door in response to Rufus' enquiry.

'They'll all be in there,' he grunted. 'In the Great Hall.'

Lost in his thoughts as he made for the towering stone keep, Rufus failed to notice at first one of the young under-cooks who was leaning, hot and tired, against the bake house wall. When at last Rufus spotted him, the lad gave him a grin, showing his crooked teeth.

'All ready for the great feast, then, Eustace?'

'Ready and waiting, as we have been for most of the day,' the under-cook complained, 'but still we must wait, it seems, for the king's grace to take his bath.'

'His bath?'

'Oh yes. The king, weary from his travels, must sink his bones into a warm tub before appearing at the feast prepared in his honour. You should have seen it, though, Rufus...' Eustace appeared to forget his frustration for a moment as he warmed to his story. 'I was watching, keeping out of the way, mind, from that door there,' he explained, pointing towards the kitchens. 'No sooner had the king acknowledged the steward than he was demanding a bath be readied for him. His own bath tub, which he carts everywhere, is still on his baggage train, I hear.

'You should have seen the panic in our esteemed Geoffrey the Steward's eyes! That old bathtub in the stores hadn't seen the light of day for who knows how long! After all, none of us bother much to use it, do we? All cobwebbed and filthy, it was, so the chamberlain had to organise its cleaning, carriage to the king's chambers, its filling and perfuming, all in time for when his grace had climbed the stairs and was ready. I've heard the king even has a special robe for when he undresses to take his bath. Of all the nonsense!'

'I must go, Eustace,' Rufus grinned. 'I have to find the bishop's clerk and the cook's hollering something. He doesn't look happy.'

Rufus made himself scarce as the cook, a large, heavily sweating man in his middle years, advanced on the under-cook, shouting and waving a ladle. Eustace bolted indoors to tend the dishes he was meant to be finishing. Perhaps, hoped Rufus, it was a sign that they might eat soon.

The bailiff had been right about everyone being in the Great Hall. The place was teeming with people. Visitors and castle personnel alike were gathered in impatient looking huddles. The bishop's chief clerk, though, was not hard to find. He stood aloof and alone, his disapproval of the rabble around him etched on his noble features. He accepted the scroll from Rufus with a cool nod of the head, leaving the clerk free to wander back to the office and await his dinner.

Like Egbert, he was ravenous. It had been a long time since that morning's bread and ale.

FOUR (Present Day)

Polite Applause

'It really is most gratifying to see such an excellent turn out for this, our first meeting of the Wisbech Heritage Society at the Poet's House Museum. I am hoping that we meet fortnightly after this, then see how things go. Shall we keep to Thursday nights? What do you say, everyone?'

Rex Monday scanned his twenty-strong audience. With his considerable height and broad shoulders, his neatly trimmed steel grey hair that framed a clean-shaven and confident face, he commanded and usually received respect. His clothing was invariably of the kind he considered appropriate for his role in the town and tonight's immaculate Harris Tweed jacket and silk tie striped in muted shades of beige were among his favourite items.

He was waiting for some kind of positive response, but most of his attendees were hedging their bets, waiting to see what this meeting was like before committing themselves to more. He finally received a few vague grunts which seemed to satisfy him.

'Doubtless, you will all have read my, ah, rather lengthy email, but I shall recap briefly. My idea was that a group of like minded people formed a society to explore some of this area's rich history and, judging by how many of you have turned out on this chilly October evening, it seems you share my enthusiasm. But perhaps,' he added with a smile, 'your attendance has more to do with those three magical words...'

'Like 'free light refreshments',' quipped someone at the back. There was a general smattering of laughter.

'Ah, most amusing. No, I was referring to those three little words which are practically guaranteed to earn one a response; 'King John's Treasure!' '

'So,' interrupted Bertle, 'are we looking for the treasure, or what?'

'Ah, Mr Collins, isn't it? Albert?'

'Yeah, but call me Bertle. Everybody else does. Bertle Bodgit of 'Bert'll Crack It', local handy-man, 'lectrician and plumber. And me work's better than the name suggests, like.'

Everybody laughed but sadly no one contradicted him on the quality of his work. Monica used the interruption to look around the room and see what sort of reaction Rex was receiving. Mark Appledore, Operations Manager at the nearby National Trust's Peckover House, looked bored to tears. There were a few people from the Wisbech and Fenland Museum and a couple Monica knew from other local groups. None of them looked particularly enthused.

'Ah, yes. Bertle, we shall certainly be looking into the matter of lost treasure, but I believe it would be infinitely more satisfying to study the whole subject. In particular of course, we must look at King John's brief sojourn in Wisbech, shortly before or during which he allegedly lost items in the Wash.'

'Then we can look for his treasure,' concluded Bertle with a nod. 'Count me in, then.'

'Ah, yes, absolutely. During the course of our research, we shall be looking at where the king's baggage train is likely to have met its sad fate, as well as what the allegedly lost treasure consisted of. I propose we look at what evidence there is, as well as past research. Then, just for the fun of it, we can get out there with metal detectors!'

'Nah you're talking!' grinned Bertle.

'Now, regarding my own role, I propose to lead our meetings, unless, of course, anyone has any serious objections. I hope you consider my work in local government adequate experience for such a role. So,' he continued, leaving no time for comment, 'to start with tonight, I would like to introduce a dear lady who is going to tell us about her research on the life of King John, for which she has received a number of well deserved awards. I trust you will all be as inspired by Mildred Winterbottom's talk as I was. Over to you, then, Mildred!'

Polite applause rippled through the thinly spread audience as a very serious and bespectacled lady took her place before them. Mark Appledore yawned noisily in the back row. Monica winced.

It was nearly ten o'clock by the time the staff and volunteers at the Poet's House could start clearing up. It felt like much later.

'Archie didn't help matters with his suggestion for a name for the project,' Bernadette said as she loaded the dishwasher. For once, she seemed to approve of his behaviour.

'I only said 'See Wisbech and Die',' Archie retorted. 'After all, that's what King John did, didn't he? It's not my fault if Rex has no sense of humour. And Mildred Winterbottom's talk went on a bit, didn't it?'

'To be fair...' began Monica. Bernadette groaned.

'Oh come on, Monica, why do you always have to be so *fair*?'

'Well, the first part of her talk was quite interesting,' she persisted, 'but I agree that five dozen slides about King John's rebel barons, complete with coats of arms and family trees, was a bit excessive.'

'I'm still yawning,' added Bernadette.

'Rex needs to lighten up,' said Archie as he brought another load of dirty coffee cups into the kitchen. 'Two and a half hours, most of which was taken up with Mildred's slides, was deadly. Someone needs to tell him, or no one will come next time. And that would be a pity.'

'Aw, come on,' giggled Bernadette. Monica raised her eyebrows. This was the best she had seen the pair of them getting on together.

'No really,' he insisted. 'Old Rex has some good ideas and I wouldn't like to see this whole thing flop before it gets started, but...'

'But,' said Bertle as he came in to wipe his hands on the tea towel after stacking the chairs in reception, 'he's too full of himself, know whatta mean? There's no helping a bloke like that.'

FIVE

Afternoon, Monday 10th October 1216

Rufus sat in awed silence, taking in the scene around him.

The spacious Great Hall was lit with more than a hundred beeswax candles, all specially made by the monks of Ely. Their glow mellowed the faces of the multitude of diners and cast strange, moving shadows on the huge wall tapestries, seeking out the silver threads and making them gleam more brightly.

With the rest of the assembly, he had waited in the draughty forebuilding while the king took his seat at the high table on the dais of the Great Hall. He had continued to wait while the salt in its elaborate silver server was uncovered and the king's bread was set before him, then while the cup bearer presented the king's hand washing bowl, so that his grace might dip his hands into the scented water and dry them on a crisp linen cloth.

Rufus and the others had also washed their hands, but had been obliged to line up to do so at the bowls in the ewery before filing silently into the Great Hall to take their seats. With Egbert and Oswy, he had found himself seated at the very back of the hall, on one of the long tables at the farthest end from the dais.

From this lowly position, he had a surprisingly good view of the king who was seated on a huge and elaborately carved oaken chair beneath a canopy at the centre of the high table. The canopy, which depicted the three golden lions of England on a deep red background, had been embroidered in honour of this occasion by the castle seamstresses. Rufus wondered whether the man occupying the seat beneath it had even noticed the fine needlework and whether he spared a thought for the many weeks of labour the canopy had taken to produce.

The man Rufus saw was hunched and weary looking. Even from a distance, the face framed by the neat beard and chin length dark brown hair looked lined and sallow, dark shadows etched beneath the eyes. If he was refreshed by his bathing, it did not show. On his head he wore a plain gold circlet; his 'travelling crown', as Oswy had put it earlier, risking a cuff round the ear from Father Leofric. Over his richly embroidered tunic of scarlet and blue, the king wore a fur trimmed cloak of the deepest purple Rufus had ever seen. Yet despite this grandeur, King John of England looked exhausted and low in spirits.

The king's face remained expressionless as his meat was cut and tasted for him. He nodded as the cup bearer returned with a golden goblet of wine, bowing low as he presented it to the king. The wine too was tasted, checked like everything else for poison in case an attempt had been made on the king's life.

Seated on either side of King John, Robert of York, the Bishop of Ely, and Sir Hugo de Wenton, the castle constable, looked tense. Though it was doubtless an honour to receive the king, entertaining this rather awkward royal guest must have been a mixed blessing.

Walter Bottreux, Baron de Prys, one of the king's most loyal supporters, was also seated at the high table, as were his lady Audrey, Mattilda, the constable's lady, and Sir Milo Fulk, the seneschal.

The seneschal was appointed by the bishop to keep the king's peace in the region known as the Isle of Ely. Since ancient times, for reasons long steeped in the past, the Isle had enjoyed certain liberties. No county sheriff had any authority there, leaving the Bishop of Ely free to appoint his own officers to oversee the law courts and carry out other duties. The most senior of them all was the seneschal. His role was much like that of a sheriff and his authority was as great.

Within the Isle of Ely was situated the Wisbech Hundred. This administrative area, with its eastern border defined by the Well Stream in Wisbech and stretching as far as Guyhirn to the west, Tydd St Giles to the north and Upwell to the south, had at its heart the great castle of Wisbech Barton. The seneschal, though his headquarters were in Ely, was often seen at the castle, his business on behalf of the bishop bringing him frequently to its gates.

Apart from the two ladies at the high table, the female presence in the company was small. The Queen, Isabella of Angoulême, had not accompanied her husband on his latest exhausting progress around the country and few of his escort of barons and knights had brought their ladies. The country was troubled and divided, and even in more peaceful times, travel was uncomfortable and dangerous. Few gentlewomen, given the choice between overseeing their lord's estates and spending long weeks in the saddle and under canvas, would hesitate in choosing to stay at home.

Walter Bottreux, Baron de Prys, was known to have received land and favours in plenty from the king as rewards for his loyalty. His land, as a result, was widespread over Lincolnshire and Cambridgeshire, as was his power and influence. He was said to be one of the few men in England who could keep the king in good cheer. His baroness, the Lady Audrey, whose home was situated in reasonable proximity to Wisbech, was one of the few ladies to have accompanied her lord to the feast. She appeared to be taking no pleasure from the experience, though. Seated at the opposite end of the high table from the baron, she looked cool and aloof, not once favouring him with a glance.

Rufus knew this because he couldn't take his eyes from her. Her beauty was like nothing he had seen before. Though her hair was covered by a short veil, Rufus could see that it was arranged in coils on each side of her face. Small wisps of fair hair had escaped the fine linen folds of her veil and touched the creamy skin of her long neck. Her face was slim, dominated by strong brows and lively chestnut coloured eyes. Now and again, she exchanged a few words with the seneschal, Sir Milo Fulk, who sat beside her, rewarding him with the smallest of smiles. The man was handsome; no doubt about that. With his dark hair and strong features, his height and broad shoulders, he looked capable of sweeping any lady, fine or otherwise, off her feet.

'Don't make it too obvious,' remarked Oswy. Rufus grinned.

Little about the banquet appeared to please the king, even though the cooks had taken such care to prepare his favourite food. As each sumptuous dish was presented to the high table, King John looked ever more downcast. When the royal misery appeared to reach its peak, Rufus saw the Baron de Prys lean past Sir Hugo de Wenton, who was seated between him and the king, and address a remark to his grace. John's mouth twitched, clearly enjoying the baron's wit, though there was something sour about the exchange, as if they were sharing a joke at someone else's expense.

At last, dishes for the other tables began to arrive. The highest ranking guests, seated at the ends of the long tables nearest to the dais, were served the same quality of dishes as at the high table; grilled sole in almond sauce, quail, roasted venison, beef and mutton.

For everyone else the fare was simpler, but still generously spiced or sweetened with honey, even with the sugar the king was said to love so much. Placed before the clerks and other lower ranking castle staff were communal mess dishes of spiced rabbit and mutton stew.

Egbert eyed the rabbit longingly, attacking the food as soon as it was polite to do so. He speared a chunk of meat with his knife and placed it on his bread trencher to cut up. Others simply grabbed the meat with their hands from the huge dish and put it straight into their mouths. The mutton stew had to be spooned on to the trenchers, an action which left trails of greasy gravy across the white linen cloth. The hall was noisier now, the company relaxing to eat and drink as they became less mindful of the kingly presence at the end of the room.

'Come on, Rufus, dig in,' chided Egbert, his mouth full of rabbit and wiping the grease from his chin. 'Got to feed that clever head of yours.'

Rufus laughed and took some of the stew for himself. It was good. The thick, creamy sauce awakened his taste buds and reminded him how hungry he was. He chewed in silence while the chatter went on around him, wiping his mouth on the long napkin that lay across his and his neighbours' knees and drinking cider from the communal cup.

'Specially brewed for the king,' Oswy commented as he received the cup from Rufus. 'He loves fine wine, but it seems he favours cider too. If you ask me, though, this stuff could have done with longer in the cask.' He gave a mighty sniff and wiped his nose on his sleeve.

'Tastes all right to me,' muttered Egbert as his turn came for the cup.

'Everything tastes all right to you,' pointed out Oswy.

The table cloths, now well and truly stained with grease and sauce, were removed from the tables as the dishes were cleared. New cloths were swiftly laid. The high table, Rufus saw, had already been reset with faultless efficiency, the king hardly appearing to notice.

There was then a hush as a procession of cooks made their graceful entrance, the first carrying a magnificently decorated roasted swan on a giant platter. The white feathers had been reattached to the roasted bird, its flightless wings outstretched, their tips painted with gold leaf. There was an audible intake of breath from the company as the lavish dish was presented to the king. The cooks dropped to one knee in a well choreographed full bow, a steady grip maintained on the precious, heavy dish.

The king nodded, a faint smile flickering across his weary features. The bishop made a remark which must have been amusing since it produced elegant peals of laughter from his fellow diners.

'Very impressive,' acknowledged Egbert as he gazed at the swan, 'but I'll wager we don't get a look in.'

'Surely you're not still hungry!' objected Oswy with another raucous sniff. 'You've eaten enough to last you 'til St Martin's, and there's another course yet.'

And there was. Messes of spiced beef and good white bread were now placed before them. There were also quinces in honey, another mutton dish and platters of raw peaches. The fruit had been grown in a riverside orchard, lovingly nurtured to bring it to ripeness for the king's feast. The peaches were served raw, which was apparently how the king liked them.

'Won't catch me eating them,' complained Oswy. 'Uncooked fruit's bad for the stomach. Gives you the belly ache. Everybody knows that.'

When the company was well fed and mellow from cider and wine, the three acrobats arrived. The men Rufus had seen rehearsing in the bailey earlier made their colourful entrance, turning cartwheels in the impossibly small space before the dais then juggling with skittles that flew faultlessly into the air between the three of them. The king looked mesmerized, Rufus noticed. Or had his eyes just glazed over from all the food and drink?

Their acrobatics successfully performed, the entertainers, with hardly a chance to catch their breath, knelt to sing. Their song was a delightful three part composition which was new to Rufus' ears, its harmonies joyous yet somehow soothing. The men sang well and their audience was captivated, transported by the beauty of the music. Dark sweat stains were spreading beneath the arms of the performers' bright costumes. The colour there had already faded, the vegetable dyes unable to withstand too much exertion.

The king applauded with surprising vigour when the song came to an end and he turned to the constable with something akin to a smile. The performers took their bows and departed to what must have been a satisfying volley of cheering and applause from the whole company. A buzz of conversation then rose to fill the hall, everyone remarking on the performance and few of them noticing the stranger, the messenger who had entered and was bowing before the king. While Egbert and Oswy continued to extol the skills of the entertainers, Rufus' attention was fixed on the messenger.

He saw the king gasp and clutch his throat, as if the man had assaulted him. John tried to rise from his seat but collapsed back into it, his legs refusing to support him. He had turned even paler than before and now the other occupants of the high table were listening and reacting too.

King John managed at last to stand, leaving the table with laboured, stumbling steps as the whole company rose to its feet. The constable and seneschal drew the messenger aside and questioned him while the company watched in silence. They knew trouble when they saw it.

Because Rufus and the other clerks were seated at the back of the hall closest to the doors, they were among the first to leave. Rufus found himself out in the cold bailey, the blasting northerly wind a shock after the warmth of the hall. He turned away, heading towards the office, then realised his way was blocked. Before him stood the tall and muscular form of the Baron de Prys and the short, slight one of the king himself.

Neither man appeared to have seen him. He shrank back against the wall and tried to edge away, but not before he heard the king utter three distinct words.

'Just find it.'

Perhaps he'd imagined it. Perhaps it was just the cider and his vivid imagination. Later, he would question that many times.

'Come boy, away with you,' came Father Leofric's whispered voice from behind him. He followed obediently, allowing the chaplain to lead him and the other clerks through buildings and across passages to arrive by a longer route at the chapel. The calm of the darkened building was a welcome relief.

Outside, the dusk was already gathering.

SIX (Present Day)

Nothing Important

Early mornings in the museum were usually quiet, especially towards the end of the season. Monica used these times to catch up with her administration and there was always plenty of it. Since they had started to open the Poet's House for broader use in the community, the curator found her workload had increased significantly.

It was worth it, though. Only a year ago, the future of the small museum dedicated to the Georgian poet, Joshua Ambrose, had been in serious doubt, but now, with local groups making more use of the place, things looked far more certain.

Her view through the office window was never very inspiring, but at least on that Tuesday morning the wheelie bins and Mrs Paynter's fence next door were cheered by the late October sun. One of Mrs Paynter's three cats, known collectively as the Smutties since they were all grey and practically indistinguishable from each other, was sitting on the brown bin. As Monica watched, the Smutty lifted one dark paw as if to wave at her, but then began to clean his face, licking the paw and using it like a flannel, washing his cheeks and forehead with total concentration.

A key rattled in the lock of the front door and within seconds Archie was standing in front of her desk, wearing his golf club fleece as usual. He had been working as a secretary at the local club for a few months now and seemed to be enjoying it. He would have preferred to work in one of the town's museums, but jobs like that were scarce and at least this one paid the bills and kept him in his flat on South Brink.

'Not at work?' she queried with a smile.

'I need to be in by eleven,' he replied, perching himself on a corner of the desk, 'but I thought I'd call in and ask whether you'd like to go somewhere on Sunday? Perhaps we could drive to Hunstanton and have some fish and chips on the seafront?'

'Lovely idea!' she enthused, knowing that encouraging Archie to eat anything other than fish and chips would be a waste of breath.

His phone cheeped and he removed it casually from his pocket. He glanced at the text that had appeared on the screen and a whole catalogue of emotions seemed to pass over his face. His smile faded as his mouth hardened and his brow furrowed and yet, throughout this transition his eyes appeared to shine ever more brightly.

'Problem?'

He looked at her, blinking, confused, as if he'd forgotten she was there.

'Oh, no. Nothing important.'

'Really? Doesn't look like it.'

'No, truly it's nothing.' He gave her a weak smile. 'Anyway, I'd better get to work. I'll see you before Sunday, of course.'

'Yes, I hope so. Will you...'

But he had gone, the front door clicking shut behind him.

SEVEN

Nightfall, Monday 10th October 1216

'All of it?'

Oswy paused with his pen in the air, remembering just in time to lower it and prevent a blob of ink falling from the nib on to the letter he was writing.

'Nothing is known for certain,' replied Father Leofric gravely, 'but the messenger's news is said to have brought the king little hope. His baggage train was extensive and the tides ill-judged. We all know this part of the Wash, the estuary, can be crossed safely if the tides are correctly observed, but such heavily laden ox wagons would have been moving very slowly. With bad timing, they could have been cut off by the tide. It is to be hoped that the first wagons reached the Lincolnshire side in safety, but for those in the centre and at the end, there can be little hope.'

'Many will have drowned , then,' concluded Rufus quietly.

'There can be no doubt of it. There were hundreds of men accompanying those wagons and most of them will have perished.'

'The king certainly seemed to have been struck a mighty blow,' remarked Egbert, his podgy face sorrowful.

'Indeed he had. What is more, he had only just ordered the shipping of supplies from Wisbech to his troops stationed in Grimsby. He had engaged the services of local shipmen and they were ready, awaiting their cargo. It is likely now that some of the supplies he was to send have been lost to the sea.'

'Good thing we'd finished eating by the time the news came,' observed Oswy, his sharp features peering out of his oversized linen cap. 'Would have been a terrible waste of food if not.'

'I told you before, boy; show some respect!'

Oswy was very fortunate to be in the charge of such a tolerant churchman. Anyone else would have landed him a blow about the ears.

The stout office door opened suddenly, letting in a gust of cold wind that lifted parchments from the desks. The castle constable entered the room, bringing to an end all idle conversation, and the chaplain and clerks stood, bowing their heads. Though he still wore the over tunic bearing the manorial arms of Wisbech Barton, Sir Hugo de Wenton looked far from festive now. His fashionably bobbed brown hair was windblown and untidy about his troubled face.

'My lord king has taken to his bed,' he began immediately. 'His life is not considered to be in danger, but he is unable to travel in person to the site of the tragedy. He has sent the Baron de Prys in his stead. The baron has already departed, even though there is little he can accomplish now that the daylight has gone.

'I have given my word that the dead will be buried in a respectful and timely manner and that the incident shall be fully investigated. The bishop has charged Sir Milo Fulk, the seneschal, to take charge of this matter. Sir Milo is of the same mind as I, that our efforts will be better employed in the morning, but tomorrow other responsibilities claim me and I must send my deputy. I would ask you too, father, for your assistance. The priests of St Mary's in Waltuna and St Katherine's in Newton in the Isle will doubtless be grateful for your help in such tragic circumstances.'

'Of course, sir,' nodded the chaplain. 'The king will expect to attend Mass in the chapel tomorrow morning, so I will ask the priest of St Peter and Paul's to take my place here.'

'Good. And you will need a clerk. Someone you can trust to keep proper records. I don't need to tell you how serious this is; a tragedy of such proportion on our doorstep! The king will need full reports at regular intervals, so it is essential that we are able to provide them.'

And presumably, thought Rufus as he recalled the scene he had witnessed earlier, his grace will be anxious to know whether we have 'just found it', whatever it is.

And that's when he noticed that the chaplain and constable were eyeing him speculatively.

'Excellent,' concluded Sir Hugo. 'I hope you understand the seriousness of this task, Rufus.'

He made some reply, something that came out in a muddle. He sounded ridiculously nervous. He understood all right, but he did not want the job.

EIGHT (Present Day)

Foggy Horizon

Monica had hardly seen Archie all week. In itself, there was nothing unusual about that. He had moved to Wisbech from the Midlands the year before, but that was about as far as things had progressed. They could hardly be said to be joined at the hip and since he'd started working at the golf course, she'd seen even less of him.

So why did this week feel so much worse than usual? She had heard nothing from him since Tuesday morning when he'd received the text he'd been so cagey about. Even now, as they drove through the fog into Norfolk on Sunday morning, their normally easy conversation was strained.

The main road skirted Sandringham, the woods on either side of the road dark and watchful, holding on to pockets of mist and promising no respite from the conditions. Monica tried her hardest to lighten the atmosphere, commenting on the thickening fog that seemed to intensify the nearer they came to the coast. Her chirpy little comments sounded false and foolish, even to her.

Archie hardly responded. Whether he was unaware of her attempts at conversation, or merely indifferent to them, she couldn't tell, but her spirits were sinking fast. They drove into Hunstanton in near silence, parking the car close to the green.

'Shall we walk on the beach?' she ventured. 'It's still murky, but not that cold. Come on!'

He grunted something and stepped out of the car, pulling on his black puffer jacket. It suited him a lot better than the golf club fleece.

The tide was out, the sea an invisible presence behind a blanket of fog. There were few people about, just the occasional dog walker who let their animals off the lead to race and spray their madcap way through the pools left behind by the sea. Monica laughed aloud, despite Archie's silence, watching the dogs as they charged into the water to retrieve balls or just for the joy of it, returning to their owners dripping wet and encrusted with salt and sand.

'Monica, I...'

She had been smiling, watching the dogs, but now her face straightened.

'Monica, I think I should mention...'

'Yes? Whatever it is, spit it out. This tension is really getting on my nerves.'

'I heard from Jemima this week.'

'Ah. The text that was nothing important.'

'Well, it wasn't, but I've had others since.'

'Saying what?'

They had stopped walking. They had reached a wooden breakwater, one of the sturdy fence-like structures that stretched from the concrete sea wall behind them towards the distant sea. Monica sat on the damp wood, her fingers brushing limpets and gelatinous seaweed.

Jemima. Apart from the basic facts concerning Archie's divorce from her, Monica knew nothing about the woman. He preferred not to talk about his ex-wife. They had been parted for several years now and her name was hardly mentioned.

'She needs to see me. Or rather our old solicitor does.'

'Why?'

'She had an aunt,' he went on rapidly now, seeing Monica's puzzlement, 'a nice old lady we visited often. Aunt Lizzie had made us both executors of her Will and it appears she never changed it. Jemima is the sole beneficiary; I wouldn't have expected anything else, but Aunt Lizzie died last week and I must act as her executor...'

'So that means you...'

'It means Jemima and I have to deal with Aunt Lizzie's estate. We have to apply for probate, clear her house, sell it and dispose of her other assets.' He sighed. 'This is the last thing I wanted, Monica. Not only will it bring back memories of things I'd rather forget, but it'll mean a heap of responsibilities I haven't the time for.'

'You'll have to go over there fairly soon, then.'

'Thursday. To see the solicitor and find out what's involved. But I'll be back that evening and see you at the Heritage meeting, let you know how it went.'

She nodded. It couldn't be helped. These things happened. It would just be a case of clearing the house and a lot of paper work. Maybe she could help, get the job done faster.

At least she knew now what all his silence had been about, but it made her no less uncomfortable.

Especially since Archie was staring at the foggy horizon with, unless she was greatly mistaken, a sparkle in his eye.

NINE

Morning, Tuesday 11th October 1216

They departed immediately after early Mass. The priest of neighbouring St Peter and Paul's had officiated, leaving Father Leofric free to make his other arrangements. The king had not, after all, attended Mass; by all accounts he was too sick to rise early.

The chaplain, with the deputy constable Sir Giles of Ely, the seneschal Sir Milo Fulk and the young clerk Rufus, set off from the castle bailey. The northerly wind that had chilled them for the last few days had calmed at last, leaving a cold, overcast morning. Rufus, well aware of his limits as a rider, had taken loan from the stables of a gentle natured rouncey he had named Arnulf. He was a good choice of horse for the boy, Father Leofric considered; an animal of bolder temperament might have caused him considerable problems.

The party of four passed through the gatehouse, over the lowered drawbridge and followed the dyke-side road towards the small church of Saints Peter and Paul. Worshipers were filing in through the south door, their usual early Mass delayed this morning to allow their priest time to fill in for Father Leofric at the castle. A few elderly folk were making their way from the almshouses at the eastern end of the churchyard. These simple yet sturdily built dwellings had been a gift from King John a few years before and housed a dozen or more of the town's poorest and most ailing souls. Such acts of charity had increased the king's popularity and were examples of the benefits that could reward a town for its loyalty.

The road angled itself around the perimeter of the churchyard before rising to the top of the high river bank, where it followed the Well Stream out of town towards the manor of Welle.

Milo had already sent his sergeant-at-arms and a small patrol of men to Newton in the Isle in Lincolnshire, on the western bank of the Wash. Newton was close to the point for which the king's baggage train had been heading when it made its disastrous crossing. The seneschal's investigation would therefore need to continue there after he had finished in Waltuna on the eastern bank. The sergeant was to keep order in Newton until Milo arrived.

The water in the Well Stream was high that morning, the brown tidal swell lapping against the muddy banks. At low water the party could have forded the river, but now they would have to take the ferry.

The door of the ferryman's hut creaked open as they arrived. Smoke from his hearth fire was making its lazy way through the thatch of his tiny dwelling as the small man presented himself to the travellers with a cheerful bow. In his homespun brown tunic, hood and hose, he blended almost to invisibility against the subdued shades of the river in the dull morning light. He rubbed his hands energetically together to warm himself.

'I regret I can take only one man and a horse at a time, my lords. The boat is willing, but unstable if I overload her.'

The seneschal nodded and indicated that Sir Giles should go first. The castle's deputy constable was an agile man of short stature, a man who seemed always to be brimming with nervous energy. The others watched as he dismounted and led his horse on to the long, low boat.

Shaped a little like a punt, the ferry had sides high enough to enable it to carry a load, but both ends were sloped to allow its passengers to embark easily from one bank and disembark on the other side. The ferryman leaped with practised ease on to the boat and thrust a long pole into the depths, manoeuvring the vessel into the channel and going with the current, reaching the far bank a little downstream but without apparent difficulty. Rufus was sent over next, doing his best to hide his reluctance. The experience was not new to him; if he hadn't been prepared to use ferries at high water he would never have travelled at all, but the combination of water and horses left him far from comfortable.

The seneschal paid the ferryman once they had all crossed, the little man smiling and bowing and depositing the coin in the purse hanging from his belt. Then they were riding away, on through the manor of Walsoken with its brood of thatched cottages huddled around their mother church of All Saints. Beyond the village, the road meandered between spinneys of willow and alder and marshy areas fringed with saw sedge, towards the eastern bank of the Wash.

Once again, the road climbed to run along the top of the sea bank. Floods, despite the continuous effort that went into maintaining sea defences, occurred with alarming frequency. The winter brought the worst conditions, when the most ferocious storms sent waves crashing over the high banks to flood village, town and pasture. Time after time, the misery caused by such severe weather was measured in the loss of human life and of livestock.

Even on the landward side of the bank, the ground was marshy, swathed in a seemingly endless sea of reeds and grasses. In places, glinting between the rustling stalks, the silvery water of a shallow pool could be seen, the grey, indifferent sky reflected on its surface.

'With the tide being in,' Rufus could hear the seneschal saying to the deputy constable as they rode in front, 'there'll have been no chance as yet of recovering any of the bodies. The first low tide following the disaster would have been just after midnight; too dark to do any useful work. The next low tide is due shortly after noon, so work cannot start in earnest until then.'

'And then this matter must be concluded as quickly as possible,' the deputy replied. 'It concerns me that the castle should be involved in this mess and the sooner it is dealt with and finished, the better.'

Rufus frowned to himself as he listened, glancing at Father Leofric who rode beside him. The chaplain appeared not to have heard, being lost in his own thoughts. To Rufus, Sir Giles' view of this tragic loss of life as merely a potential stain on the castle's reputation, seemed cold in the extreme.

Engrossed in such thoughts, it did not seem long to Rufus before the hazy smoke from the rooftops of Waltuna could be seen on the horizon. Gradually, the individual shapes of the small, squat houses came into focus. In the overcast conditions, their dun coloured wattle, daub and thatch appeared almost a part of the earth itself, as if they had sprouted quite naturally from the ground. Most of the homes were surrounded by neat wicker fences that kept in a few chickens or a pig, but there was no sign as yet of any villagers.

The road approaching the village was badly flooded in places and the horses had to tread their way around the worst of the water. In dryer areas, where the narrow field strips were drained by the long, straight ditches threaded between them, newly sown wheat and rye for next spring's bread making were starting to show. Branching off from the main road were tracks leading to the village's numerous salterns, the production sites for most of the region's salt. Closer to the sea bank, the grass grew healthily, providing good grazing for most of the year for the manor's sheep.

The church of St Mary was small and timber-built, yet for all its modesty it managed to serve two parishes. Father Anselm the priest walked wearily out to meet the riders. He looked like sleep had evaded him for far too long and his manner, as he beckoned a group of lads leaning against the church fence to take the visitors' horses, was agitated.

Milo watched Merlin, his sleek grey palfrey, being led away with the other horses as the elderly, portly priest collected his thoughts.

'My lords, this is a grim business,' began Father Anselm. 'The water level has at last fallen enough to allow the villagers to go out and begin their search. Goodwife Percy will attend to the bodies of the poor souls as they are recovered from the mud. You'll find her by the sea bank. It is going to be a long and painful process.

'A few boxes and other items are also being brought up from the estuary. The Baron de Prys made it perfectly clear on his arrival yesterday evening that the recovery of goods is of equal importance to that of men.' The priest's look of disapproval and distaste showed what he thought of the baron's priorities.

'The baron informed me that his orders came directly from the king,' he continued. 'The tide was in while he was here, of course, so nothing could be done to recover anyone or anything, yet still he and his men were suspicious. They were ruthless in their questioning of the villagers, accusing them of hiding goods from the baggage train, even though there had been no opportunity to do so.'

'Were they looking for anything in particular?' asked Sir Giles.

'They did not say, my lord, but they searched every house in the village, even ransacked the church. The most brutal of the men appeared to be in the service of one of the knights. He wore the de Prys arms, the Tower device seen so often in these parts. Yet for all their threats and violence, they left empty handed. Everyone here fears their return. When we heard you approaching, we thought at first...'

'That the baron had returned? No, father,' replied Milo. 'Fortunately, he will have left for Lincolnshire with my lord king by now. We may not see him for a while.'

'Let us hope not,' said the priest.

'I suspect the knight you referred to,' said Sir Giles, 'is Edward of Hagebeche. He is known not to be too particular about the company he keeps. I assure you, father, our business here is merely to investigate how this tragedy occurred and to help where we can. We shall not be here long, but shall need accommodation for tonight before crossing into Lincolnshire at tomorrow's low tide.'

'The Lamb Inn has room for guests and will gladly accommodate you, my lords,' smiled the priest, no doubt pleased to hear of their anticipated departure. 'Then tomorrow, the guide will take you across the estuary.'

'If he was the same guide as was responsible for seeing the wagons across yesterday,' remarked the seneschal, 'I shall need to speak to him as a priority.'

'He's expecting it,' nodded Father Anselm. 'He is miserable with guilt and shame and yet he made no error. I clearly heard him telling the men-at-arms leading the baggage train that they could make their crossing, but only if they set out immediately. He explained there was no time for delay, that the tide would soon turn. He pressed them to set out straight away, but they took their time, Sir Milo. They were so very slow in making a start. A wheel had come loose on one of the wagons and a repair had to be made. When at last they started to cross, the river bed looked dry enough, but by then there was little time.'

'Did the guide warn them again?'

'Most certainly he did. He told them their delay was inviting danger, that some of their wagons might not safely reach the other side.'

'How did they respond?'

'The men-at-arms did not take kindly to his advice. They had orders from the king and had to make the crossing that day in order to meet his grace the following morning. They declared the ford dry and that they knew their business. They began to cross, but the baggage train was so very long. Never in all my days have I seen such a train of wagons, oxen, horses and men. Perhaps with God's grace the first wagons made it across, but as for the wretched creatures in the centre and at the end, there was no hope at all.'

Rufus was still thinking of the priest's words as the seneschal and deputy constable went to speak to the villagers. With the chaplain, he was taken by Father Anselm to the section of sea bank near the church. Here stretched a line of bodies that had been brought up from the muddy estuary. It was a terrible sight.

Many of the dead were still clothed in the mail shirts of men-at-arms, their heavy armour having afforded them no chance of withstanding the sudden surge of water. Their bodies would have been dragged down, then left behind by the retreating tide. Others, probably wagoners, still wore their heavy travelling cloaks and hoods of rabbit fur. Some of the bodies had been found caught up against the banks of the deep creeks that cut across the bed of the estuary. Being trapped in this way, the bodies had resisted being carried out to sea with the outgoing tide, but many others would have been swept away and would never be seen again.

Rufus' job was to record as much detail as he could about each body. None of the men's names were known, all of them strangers to the region, so any hope of identifying them would lie in what he wrote down. He had to record details of their clothing, hair colour, eye colour where possible, their shape, size and any distinguishing features he could make out. As he knelt on the grassy bank beside the first body, he knew he faced a hopeless task and had to fight an almost overwhelming wave of nausea.

He took a clean roll of parchment and his ink horn from the scrip hanging from his belt and carefully removed the stopper from the horn. The first body was that of a young man about his own age, his once straw coloured hair thick with mud, his waxen face grimy. Leaning the parchment on the low, make-shift desk Father Anselm had provided, Rufus wrote down as much as he could before moving to the next body. As soon as his recording was completed for each individual, Goodwife Percy and her team of village women began to prepare the mortal remains for burial, wrapping each body in a woollen shroud. Later, the dead would be taken by cart to the churchyard, ready for burial the next morning. Already, Father Leofric was helping the priest to prepare for the event.

And so the work continued throughout that long, harrowing afternoon. As more and more bodies were brought up from the mud, they were added to the row by the sea bank. By the time the tide turned and the search was abandoned, there were sixty-three bodies there; a very small number compared to the many hundreds of men who had accompanied the baggage train.

When Rufus had finally completed recording the dead, he had to move on to the heap of broken boxes, chests and barrels that had been retrieved from the mud. Sir Milo himself came to help him with this task, breaking open what was left of each container so that Rufus could list the contents.

From what Father Anselm had said, the Baron de Prys had shown far more interest in goods than in the dead. This information was urging Milo to find out what might be hidden amongst the debris. Rufus' records, insisted the seneschal, would be more accurate if they included everything, goods as well as bodies. There was little worth recording, however. There were a few trinkets, but most of the chests contained nothing but wet linen and ruined food. Still the men worked on, until every last barrel of grain and chest of clothing was listed.

As he worked, Rufus spared a thought for the oxen and horses, all the poor, confused creatures that had been swept away by the incoming tide. Wherever their bodies were washed up, they would inevitably be left to rot. The dead men were at least being treated with respect, but it was clear that the authorities were more interested in goods than in the men and beasts who had served the king.

Because the king's men would understand his priorities, wouldn't they? They would know that his first thought on hearing of the catastrophe was for an object, rather than for his men.

For surely, his whispered words to the faithful Walter Bottreux, Baron de Prys concerned none of his subjects, but an item. Rufus, whether or not he had heard correctly, could not forget those words,

'Just find it.'

TEN (Present Day)

A Long Suffering Way

'He's gone then.'

'Yes, well, don't sound so pleased about it. Anyway, he should be back tonight.'

Bernadette and Monica had arrived early that Thursday evening for the second meeting of the Wisbech Heritage Society. They had already set out the chairs in the museum's reception hall and had prepared the coffee machine for later. Bernadette was making a point about Archie's habit of making the coffee too soon and letting it stew. And she was really going on about him and his trip to Leamington Spa.

'Of course I'm not pleased,' she retorted, 'but I can see you're far from happy about it. To be fair, though, he had no choice, did he? But ex-wives can be dangerous creatures. I'd be very careful if I were you...'

'Bernie, Jemima left *him*, not the other way round. She went off with some shiny suited bloke from Birmingham. Apparently, she thought Archie was too boring. She's hardly going to lay on the charm for him now, is she? They'll just sort out the paperwork, sell the house, and that'll be that.'

'And Bob's yer uncle,' came Bertle Bodgit's voice from behind them. He was talking to Sally from the bank, perhaps trying to impress her with his plumbing expertise. 'Nah, I told him. You'll never budge it like that. You'll need sommat big and heavy, so I got me big plunger art like and gave it a big heave and art came all this...'

Sally was giggling, asking a few questions in a quiet voice, then Bertle's voice sounded out again.

'See, I've always done the plumbing, 'lectric, handy man stuff sortta thing for the Poet's House and this year I started as a volunteer too, like. Me and the missus have split up and me boy'd rather be art with his mates than with his ol' dad, so I thought to meself, why not do a bitta volunteering like? Monica's me ol' mate and was glad to have a bitta muscle when it comes to moving things abart. Also, I like all this *King John's Treasure* thing...' he added, trying to sound like what he'd call a posh bloke on the telly, 'so I bought meself a metal detector, sortta thing and I'm gonna have a go once we know where to look...'

Monica and Bernadette forgot their own discussion, even their differences for a minute as they tuned in to Bertle's far more interesting conversation.

'Certainly has a way with women,' smiled Bernadette.

Rex Monday had been pacing about, pages of notes in hand, ever since his arrival half an hour ago. As the seats began to fill and the starting time of seven-thirty drew nearer, it became obvious that, despite everyone's doubts, attendance had miraculously increased since the first meeting. It must have had a lot to do with the reports in both the Fenland Citizen and Wisbech Standard. The words 'treasure' and 'King John' had worked their usual magic.

It was equally obvious that Archie was not going to make it to the start of the meeting.

'Good evening, everyone,' enunciated Rex at precisely half past seven. 'It is most gratifying to see so many of you here and...' he paused in a long suffering way as Mark Appledore from Peckover crept in thirty seconds late and found a seat in the back row. '...I am sure all of you are as keen as I to continue with the intriguing subject of King John and his baggage train.'

''Ere 'ere,' agreed Bertle loudly from the second row, 'so let's get on with it!'

ELEVEN

Morning, Wednesday 12th October 1216

Even with the help of a guide, Rufus found the experience of crossing the Wash while the tide was out extremely disconcerting. The sight of so many drowned bodies the day before had given him little hope for his own party's chances of survival.

They had spent the night at the Lamb, the four of them sharing the inn's single guest room, situated directly beneath the eaves and accessible only by ladder. The seneschal and castle deputy had been able to share a proper bed, complete with linen sheets and woollen blankets, but Rufus and the chaplain had had no choice but to bed down in the straw.

Rufus was used to it. For him and for most young people, these were perfectly normal sleeping arrangements, but the chaplain had long since moved on to finer things and found the situation extremely uncomfortable. He had complained bitterly about his aching, stiff limbs and the poor meal which had greeted them as they descended the rickety ladder in the morning. Stale bread from the previous day's baking and a lump of hard cheese washed down with weak ale had not been a promising start to the day. It was even worse than the thin pottage served after their labours the night before, but at least then the bread had been fresh.

They had been obliged to wait until midday before the tide receded again, allowing them to make their crossing. The morning's high water meant there could be no further recovery of bodies or goods, but by then it hardly mattered. All the villagers were saying the same thing; there was nothing more to find. Anything not already recovered from the mud had either been swept out to sea or had reached the far bank.

The seneschal had hoped to spend some of the morning in questioning the guide, but the man was away on an errand in the next village. There was nothing suspicious about his absence, the innkeeper had assured Milo. The guide's work often took him away from home, but he could always be relied upon to return when needed in Waltuna. In the meantime, the visitors had no choice but to wait and swallow more of the inn's terrible ale.

As predicted, right on time, the guide had come to find them, but even then there had been no opportunity for questions. They had had to set out immediately, the mounted guide leading the four men and horses over the high sea bank. Rufus had watched the guide as he surveyed the seemingly endless stretch of estuary bed that lay before them, in order to select the best way forward. Following them all on foot were two short and muscular assistants carrying a number of long wooden planks.

There was little conversation as the party followed the guide across the first part of the estuary. At first, the going was fairly good, the mud having been covered with a thick layer of gravel. This path soon came to an end, though, and the guide began to probe the ground before them, using the long pole he carried across his horse's back. Having decided on the best way forward, he pressed on, followed by the others over the algae and eel grass that grew on the regularly inundated mud. At first glance, this growth looked almost meadow-like, but the impression was deceptive. This was treacherous terrain which had to be traversed carefully.

One of the most troublesome aspects of their crossing was having to negotiate the numerous steep sided, muddy creeks that cut across the estuary. Some of these creeks were so wide and deep that the horses were unable to cross them unaided and planks had to be used as bridges. The guide's assistants would muscle in at these times, laying their wooden planks across the creeks and drawing them up again as soon as everyone was across.

The travellers' horses were nervous about stepping on to the planks and Rufus had a hard time in urging Arnulf across. Each small crossing, once it was done, felt like a major achievement.

Every time they came to a simpler part of the crossing, Milo used the opportunity to question the guide. The man confirmed what the priest had told them earlier, that he had warned the baggage train leaders not to cross once their time to do so safely had run out.

The seneschal continued his questioning once they had reached the far side of a particularly wide creek.

'When the baggage train leaders decided, against your advice, to set out across the estuary, did you still agree to act as their guide?'

'No, my lord. As I explained to the Baron de Prys, after the leaders had delayed the start of their crossing, I advised them to await the next day's low tide. When they ignored my advice, insisting on setting out there and then, I refused to guide them. I thought that might change their minds, but they went anyway. Now it seems I shall hang for it.'

'Hang?' Milo almost barked the word. 'Why say such a thing?'

'My lord de Prys made it clear that the responsibility for the whole catastrophe lies on my shoulders.'

Milo frowned, saying nothing for a while. The vegetation that had, up to that point, covered the estuary bed was becoming sparser, leaving the central channel as a sculptured waste of mud flats. The tides had shaped the mud into bulbous, other-worldly shapes that were both massive and perilous. Only the wading birds, the curlews and godwits, seemed at home here, their long bills probing the mud for shellfish and worms.

At this stage of low tide, the silty soil beneath the horses' hooves was firm enough to support them, but everyone was aware how quickly the surface would become hungry, sucking mud once the tide turned. The water would rise rapidly in the creeks, swelled by the surge of the sea as it rushed into the estuary, cutting off the path of any travellers and trapping them in an instant. There would be no chance of escape, even for men able to swim. Everyone and everything would drown.

'But you must have told the baron of your advice and refusal to guide the baggage train across.'

'Yes, my lord, just as I'm telling you. I told him I'd agreed to guide the train at first, but only if it set out straight away. But the leaders of that train didn't listen. They insisted on crossing, guide or none. They were to meet the king the next morning on his way from Wisbech and he'd expect them to be awaiting him in Newton in the Isle. I suspect they feared disobeying the king more than drowning, but I must live with what happened for the rest of my days, few as those days may be.'

'Nonsense!' exclaimed Sir Giles, who had been listening with great interest. 'It is perfectly clear that you have nothing to answer for.' He nodded with satisfaction. There was no intrigue here; of that he was certain. The matter could swiftly be dropped and soon forgotten.

Milo looked irritated by the interruption and turned back to the guide.

'The error appears solely to lie in the decision of the men-at-arms leading the train,' he considered thoughtfully. 'No matter what threats you received, the common law of this land treats all men fairly. Do not fear; you will not hang for other men's misjudgement.'

The guide nodded uncertainly, continuing to wear his worried frown as he led them forwards. He couldn't help wondering whether the king might yet have other ideas about who was to blame for such enormous losses.

The far bank could at last be seen in the distance and before long eel grass was coating the mud underfoot. The party continued on its methodical way between and across the creeks and soon they were climbing the gravelled path towards the top of the bank.

They were safely across and Rufus could scarcely hide his relief. The coins Milo took from his purse and handed to the guide, already mounted again and preparing to return to Waltuna, looked well in excess of the required fee.

The seneschal looked as relieved as any of them to be back on solid ground.

TWELVE (Present Day)

Soft Sword

'What we should do before moving on to anything else,' Rex was announcing to his audience at the Poet's House, 'is to look at the background to King John's visit to Wisbech in 1216.

'His seventeen year reign had been a troubled one. The country was still at war with France, many of his barons were standing against him and his quarrel with the Pope...'

'Yeah, like you said last time,' muttered Bertle who was chewing a toffee in the second row, 'but why...'

'If you could just bear with me, Mr Collins, ah, Bertle. Because of his quarrel with the Pope he and his country had been excommunicated from the Church. And then of course there was the trouble with his barons...'

A few people were beginning to fidget, exchanging a few whispered comments, things which Rex considered very ill mannered. He paused pointedly and stared at the worst offenders before continuing.

'You see, the English wool trade was booming, making the aristocratic landowners, even the sheep farming monasteries, very rich. But John taxed them to the hilt to pay for his never-ending military expeditions. One must be fair about this, however. His brother King Richard I had left the coffers somewhat depleted, but the people blamed John for it all. There is nothing like tax to make a leader unpopular!'

Rex paused for a reaction and a few polite smiles reassured him that some of his audience were still listening.

'Then, to cap it all, in 1214 John suffered serious losses against the French, including Normandy...'

'Soft Sword,' interjected Mark Appledore, who was slumped so far down in his seat that his long legs and red socks emerged from under the chair in front, battling for space with the feet of the woman who sat there.

'Indeed, Mark. King John became known as Soft Sword because he failed to recover the lands he'd lost. The barons were becoming ever more troublesome, their rebellion resulting eventually in the Magna Carta which was duly sealed in 1215 at Runnymede in Surrey.'

'Lot of good *that* did,' muttered someone who kept their head down.

'Well it did and it didn't,' pondered Rex aloud. 'The charter set out some firm principles. For example, from then on the king had to seek agreement from his barons and leading churchmen before imposing taxes and no one could be jailed without a proper legal reason.

'It has to be said, however, that the king was not unpopular with everyone. The people of Cambridge, King's Lynn and Wisbech, for example, remained loyal to him and he favoured the towns in several ways. There were also some barons who stayed supportive...'

A hand shot up.

'Yes, Ena?' Mrs Cross, one of the group's more senior members, hesitated before speaking, as if having second thoughts about her question. 'I was just wondering how King John favoured Wisbech, and...I think you said Cambridge and King's Lynn?'

'Ah, yes, that's right, my dear. Well, he granted Cambridge the right to hold an annual fair; it's still held today and known as Midsummer Fair. As for King's Lynn, John confirmed the charter granted by his brother, King Richard, which had given the town commercial freedom. King's Lynn, or Bishop's Lynn as it was then, did well out of it and provided John with ships and sailors. Here in Wisbech, John continued the exemption from tolls on markets and fairs originally granted by Richard and provided a number of almshouses for the town's poor. These are thought to have been built on the eastern side of St Peter's Church, roughly where the flats, appropriately called King John's House, are now.'

'I see,' replied Ena. 'Thank you.'

'You are welcome, my dear. So now we come to John's journey to King's Lynn and Wisbech in 1216. He had been engaged in fighting his rebel barons, succeeding in lifting the siege of Windsor Castle, amongst other feats. By the time he reached Lynn, he must have been exhausted from all the fighting and travel on horseback.

'No one can be sure of the precise date of his arrival in Lynn. According to which historian's version you read, it was somewhere around the eighth or ninth of October. He was welcomed in the town, where he feasted and rested, and then he, his escort and baggage train, probably with more than two thousand men in all, left King's Lynn for Wisbech.

'The route would have been slow and difficult. Most of his entourage would have travelled with the baggage train. This enormous, heavily guarded train would have progressed very slowly, the laden wagons pulled by oxen. Strong, but not exactly famed for their speed.

'Therefore, the king and an escort of two or three hundred men, including his most faithful barons and knights, would have parted from the wagons at some point along the route and ridden on their swift horses to Wisbech. Different sources put this arrival in Wisbech between the tenth and twelfth of October.

'The slow baggage train was left to take a short cut across the Wash. Remember that the Wash came much further inland then, as far as Wisbech. The Well Stream and Wysbeck River that flowed through the town opened into the estuary which was part of the larger body of the Wash. The wagons were probably expected to cross the estuary and meet the king on the other side the following day as he rode up from Wisbech.'

'Yeah, but where...'

'Patience, Bertle, patience. The big question is, of course, where did the baggage train make its crossing? There are several theories and all the possible routes have been well trodden by treasure hunters over the years, all of them hoping to find a priceless remnant of King John's hoard.

'What I propose, dear people, is that we take one theory at a time, over the course of the next few meetings, and discuss each one in full. Then, by all means, let's get out there and look at the lie of the land...'

'And get the ol' metal detectors art!'

'Indeed, Bertle. Well let's take a break. The coffee is percolating, if my senses do not deceive me. Let us enjoy some of Monica's beautiful cake and coffee, then reassemble for more of Mildred's fascinating slides.'

It was only then that Monica remembered promising cake. She'd forgotten all about it, being too distracted by Archie's continued absence.

Was he home from Leamington yet?

She had even forgotten to buy biscuits. She darted into the kitchen where she managed to scrape together a few half packets of custard creams and broken chocolate digestives. She piled them on to a plate and carried them into the hall with an apologetic smile.

They would just have to do.

THIRTEEN

Afternoon, Wednesday 12th October 1216

Rufus' heart sank as he saw what awaited them on the Lincolnshire side of the Wash. The peaceful village of Newton in the Isle, with its placidly grazing sheep and cluster of homes around the small church, had suddenly been thrown into utter confusion by the catastrophe in the estuary.

The bodies recovered during the previous day's low tide were lying by the south wall of St Katherine's Church. There were more bodies here than in Waltuna; at first sight eighty or more. Sir Milo Fulk and his party led their horses between the small homes of wattle and daub, glancing at the wicker enclosures where chickens scratched contentedly in the dirt. For the birds, and for the pigs in the sty, nothing had changed.

Father Dunstan, the tall and thin priest of St Katherine's, came promptly out to meet the seneschal and his party. The village's principal resident, the knight Stephen de Marisco, he explained, was not currently at home, or he would have been the first to greet them.

The manor of Newton in the Isle, like that of Wisbech, belonged to the Bishop of Ely, but the de Marisco family held a considerable amount of land in the area. Some of that land was in nearby Tydd St Giles, where the knight kept a larger and more comfortable home than the one in Newton. He therefore had little need for the fine looking residence which Father Dunstan took them past on their way to the church. It was a pity, thought Rufus, as he looked admiringly at the neat buildings framing the courtyard. There was no sign of life, the shutters dark and unresponsive.

At the church, Milo was joined by his sergeant-at-arms and the men he had sent to keep order in Newton until he arrived.

Though the priest's bony physique looked incapable of any serious endeavour, he moved with purpose and vigour. Summoning a couple of boys to see to the travellers' horses, he led Sir Giles, Rufus and Father Leofric into the church. Milo remained outside in discussion with his sergeant and it was clear from the seneschal's grim expression that he was receiving little in the way of good news.

The priest closed the church door behind them and sat with his visitors on the bench by the south wall. It was definitely colder inside the church than out, thought Rufus as he pulled his cloak more closely around him. Father Dunstan didn't appear to notice. Despite his obvious weariness from the last couple of days, he launched willingly into his account of the recovery of bodies and goods from the estuary.

Some of the wagons, he explained, thirteen in all, had made it safely across to the Newton side. The men accompanying those wagons had spoken of the disaster that had befallen their comrades travelling behind them. Sturdy wagons, mighty oxen and strong horses had become stuck in the softening mud, then swept away with scarcely a warning. Men, beasts and carts had been tossed about in the surge of water like sticks and straws in a stream.

He continued his account, Father Leofric interrupting him now and then with a question and Sir Giles making regular dismissive comments. Rufus let his attention wander as his eyes explored the simple beauty of the church.

Like most village churches, St Katherine's was small and solidly built of limestone. There were massive rows of columns on the north and south sides, each of them crowned with capitals of crisp chevron carving and cloaked in shadow. The only light to relieve the darkness stole in through the narrow unglazed windows in the thick walls or spread in a gentle glow from the candles on three altars.

The High Altar dominated the rounded apse at the eastern end, its lights twinkling in the dim recess and caressing the wall paintings with a glow that was almost magical. The colourful scene depicted there was of the Flight into Egypt, its human and animal figures eerily lifelike, the donkeys appearing almost to move in the flickering candlelight. Other wall paintings around the church showed the Nativity and one Rufus was less certain of, its many curiously shaped animals perhaps representing Noah's ark.

The priest was still in full flow when the door creaked open and a head peered around it. His face broke into a broad smile.

'Time to eat, my lords! You cannot commence your labours on empty stomachs. We can continue to talk while we eat.'

Rufus could not have agreed more. However strong his repugnance for the job still to be done, his hunger refused to be suppressed and his stomach was growling. As they emerged from the church, he glanced at the damp and broken barrels, chests and other debris that had been heaped up against the wall. He knew he would be required to move on to them once he had finished documenting the bodies. It was all going to take a long time. Darkness would be falling by the time they left, and that was assuming everything could be completed in one afternoon.

Once Milo had rejoined them, they were ushered into one of the houses by a smiling elderly goodwife. They bent their heads as they stepped through the low doorway and were immediately engulfed by wood smoke from the fire that burned within its square of hearthstones in the centre of the room.

'Please sit, my lords,' the woman said pleasantly and they perched themselves on the two wooden benches that faced each other across the fire. By sitting, they had dipped below the layer of smoke which now hovered above their heads and they were perfectly comfortable. The men were used to keeping below the smoke line in this way; most homes had a similar central fire arrangement. Only in castles where the keep had more than one storey, was the hearth set against a wall and a chimney used to take the smoke away from the room.

'My sergeant informs me that the wagons which survived the crossing have already left the village,' said Milo tersely, holding out his bowl so that some of the goodwife's fragrant, steaming pottage could be ladled into it.

'The wagoners would have had no choice,' replied Sir Giles loftily.

'Very true, my lord,' agreed the priest. 'The men had orders from the king himself. They were to meet his grace as he travelled from Wisbech. They were not at liberty to await your arrival, my lord seneschal, but they were questioned by your men about what happened in the estuary.'

'Fortunately, that is true.'

'I was there when the king arrived,' continued Father Dunstan as he spooned pottage into his mouth. 'I had been down by the sea bank, the tide having reached its low point again. Your men were helping too, as were all the able bodied men of the village, and we had started to bring up the bodies. Word reached us that the king was approaching, so your sergeant and I hurried back.

'We arrived in time to see the king and his escort riding into Newton. Together with the goodwives, children and elderly folk who had remained here while the others were down by the estuary, we witnessed his grace's reunion with what remained of his train. He looked gravely ill. He was riding, but appeared barely fit to do so. Whether his malady stems from his terrible losses or from some other cause, can only be guessed at. He and the sad remains of his once magnificent baggage train are now on their way to St Mary's Abbey in Swineshead.'

Milo nodded, dipping his bread into his bowl. It was good bread and the pottage was excellent. Compared to the previous day's miserable fare, this was thick and meaty and well flavoured with herbs.

'There was so little left,' continued Father Dunstan. 'I saw what cargo remained as the wagoners were securing their loads, ready for departure. There was nothing but clothing chests, meagre food supplies, tents and blankets, oh, and a huge wooden tub of some sort. That thing needed a whole cart to itself!'

'The king's bath tub!' Rufus couldn't stop himself exclaiming with a grin. 'Despite all that was lost, that thing survived!' He expected a reprimand from the seneschal or the castle deputy and was surprised to see the faintest glimmer of a smile on Milo's face. The anticipated disapproval came instead from Father Leofric, who sent him a warning look.

'Thank you, Father Dunstan,' Sir Giles was saying. 'Now we must press on with our work.'

Rufus finished his food and stepped outside, thanking the smiling woman who took his bowl and spoon. While the seneschal and castle deputy went to inspect the pile of broken goods by the church wall and Father Leofric began working on the burial arrangements with Father Dunstan, he walked over to the long line of bodies.

He looked at the first body, his heart sinking all over again. His task would become no easier, he knew; he would just grow more accustomed to it. Setting up the desk provided by Father Dunstan and charging his pen with ink, he unrolled the long parchment he had started on the day before and began to write in small, neat letters. He noted down the victim's dark hair and disturbingly open, staring brown eyes. The lad looked no more than fifteen years old. Rufus swallowed his sorrow and carried on.

As he had predicted, darkness was falling by the time they took their leave. The original party of four, now accompanied by the sergeant and his five men-at-arms, set out along the sea bank to Wisbech.

'I am glad to say our work here is done,' Sir Giles was stating to the seneschal as they rode along. 'The dead will all soon all be buried with enough respect to satisfy even the Archbishop of Canterbury. Your clerk has completed his records and you, my lord seneschal, can submit your report to the bishop. Let us hope this sorrowful event will soon cease to be connected in men's minds with our castle in Wisbech Barton.'

Milo left a lengthy pause before replying.

'My report to my lord bishop will no doubt satisfy you, Sir Giles, since our investigation discovered nothing more sinister than human error and arrogance. Fear not, the blood of the many hundreds of dead men will leave no stain on your castle walls.'

After that, no one spoke for several miles.

A half moon did its sporadic best to light the way, but hid for most of the journey behind great banks of cloud that all but shrouded the stars. The sergeant and one of his men rode at the front, carrying torches that cast wild, looming shadows on the bank top shrubs and across the narrow road. Sir Giles and Sir Milo rode behind them, with Rufus and the chaplain following. The four remaining men-at-arms rode at the rear, providing more than enough security against any dangers lurking along the way.

Below and to their left, where the torchlight flickered on the murky waters of the estuary, they could see that the tide was turning, the water beginning to rise. Hopes of recovering more bodies faded with each high tide; anyone and anything still lost was likely to remain so.

The dark road along the top of the sea bank offered few landmarks. For Rufus, there was nothing to see but the backs of the riders in front and the surge of water below.

Everyone in the party was armed, though Rufus carried only a small knife, more suitable for eating with than for defence. Sir Milo, Sir Giles and the men-at-arms, however, always carried swords at their belts and the knife attached to the chaplain's girdle was capable of inflicting a serious injury. In those lawless days every man needed to be armed. As hard as the seneschal worked to keep the peace in the Isle of Ely, there were always poor and desperate souls who, through poverty or other misfortune, lived outside the law. No man could be sure of his safety when travelling along a dark path miles from anywhere.

Rufus was glad when at last a few familiar sights greeted his searching eyes. The party had descended from the bank-top road and was passing the fields of Sandyland, the wide cultivated area to the north of Wisbech. A few shacks leant against each other at the side of the road, their patched up fences well known to him. Then, rising out of nowhere in the torchlight, like a great, tall beast throwing its arms about, loomed a strange and massive shape.

'By God's nails, what is *that?*' His blasphemy earned him a loud tutting from the chaplain.

'That, boy, is a clever device for grinding grain to produce flour,' he replied crossly. 'It is newly built and I suppose your reluctance for travel has kept you in ignorance of it. I hear such things are appearing all over the place now.'

In front, Sir Giles was laughing at the clerk's lack of knowledge.

'You are looking at the future, boy,' he said. 'Would you rather your mother and other women folk spent the rest of their days grinding a few grains between stones?'

Rufus considered it unwise to remind the deputy constable that his father was a knight and his mother the lady of a small manor, that she was burdened by no such laborious tasks herself.

'Indeed not, sir,' he muttered instead as they passed the giant structure. It had what appeared to be four enormous arms that turned slowly in the breeze. The effort was producing a low, creaking, groaning sound, as if the thing were in pain.

'The structure is known as a windmill and those are its sails,' Sir Giles went on, speaking loudly over his shoulder. 'They turn in the wind and, by means of an ingenious mechanism, drive great millstones which grind the wheat.'

'Ingenious indeed,' acknowledged Rufus. Before long, they were entering the Old Market.

This was thought to be the oldest area of town, a settlement long before the Conqueror had come to these parts, and the Old Market's simple buildings were in total darkness. Not a single light showed from behind a shutter as the party made its way between the houses and down to the ford. The moon had disappeared completely by then, leaving them to find their way down the river bank in the fading torchlight.

Even at high tide, there was never much water in the old Wysbeck River, so fording it was not difficult. They climbed the bank on the other side and rode quietly through the open court towards the castle drawbridge.

Mercifully, it was still lowered. The constable must have been confident of their return that night.

FOURTEEN (Present Day)

Switched Off

Still there was no word from Archie. Monica hardly ever bothered to carry her phone around with her, usually forgetting where she'd left it and missing practically every call. That Friday morning, however, it was tucked securely in the pocket of the old, tatty fleece she always wore for cleaning.

She was meant to be dusting Joshua Ambrose's bedroom, but wasn't getting very far. The weather outside was dull and cold, offering no inspiration, and she was feeling quite miserable enough without its gloom.

She had always done most of the museum's cleaning herself. It kept the bills down and she accepted that, as curator of such a small Fenland museum, she had to do bits of everything. Gardening, dusting, loo cleaning; they had all become part of the job that went with the paperwork and management of the place.

Joshua's bedroom had been the previous year's Poet's House project and still it pleased her. She and her small team had transformed the unused box room, believed to have been the poet's bedroom, into a proper representation of his personal space. There was something about the small room with its few, simple furnishings that attracted her and almost allowed her to believe that something of their Georgian poet remained within its quiet walls. Joshua was known to have spent long weeks at a time there during his periods of illness.

She moved her feather duster along the small mantle ledge, carefully moving the candle stick and the few books placed there. Now that November had arrived, the museum opened only at weekends, and even then attracted few visitors. In December, however, they would have their pre-Christmas special event. Visitor numbers for the few opening days of this event had gradually been increasing, people returning year after year to enjoy the seasonal programme which included everything from readings of Joshua's poetry to children's trails around the house.

She needed to think of a theme for this Christmas, something which would attract plenty of visitors. She ought to start working on it soon.

The house had to be kept open to visitors as much as possible and new attractions helped to bring people back for further visits. Joshua Ambrose's popularity, even two hundred years after his death, was quite uncanny. Monica never ceased to be amazed by the following this minor Fenland poet continued to have. People from all over the world had been known to visit, just to soak up the atmosphere of his house.

Opening Joshua's bedroom had been a popular move, but there was still plenty to do. Her next project would involve the old kitchen in the basement. The dark but spacious room, currently used for storage, had once been the warm and welcoming heart of Joshua's boyhood home. As soon as Christmas was over, and the museum closed for two months, work on the kitchen would begin.

Fortunately, it looked like it wouldn't be expensive. The old kitchen just needed opening up and new life breathing into it. The storage boxes and bags of things long forgotten would be taken out and everything given a good clean. The original dresser and table were still there, saved by the fact that both had been too large, heavy and unwieldy to be removed. They were damaged and stained, but Bertle Bodgit had assured her that they could be made to look the part. She wanted to believe him.

She ought to be down in the cellars now, she reminded herself, having a look at what needed to be done. She should be speaking to the trustees, planning work for January, but she couldn't motivate herself. Not with that silent phone in her pocket.

She sat on the small, wobbly chair in the corner of Joshua's bedroom and stared again at the phone's blank screen. Nothing. No missed calls, no texts. Archie had left the day before for Leamington Spa and a two o'clock meeting with the solicitor. He'd seemed certain about returning that evening and seeing her at the Heritage meeting, but still he wasn't home and she'd heard not the slightest thing from him.

When he'd failed to turn up at the meeting she'd tried to ring him, but his phone had been switched off. This morning, when still she'd heard nothing, she'd sent him a text. There'd been no reply. She was getting seriously worried.

Once again, she found the contacts list on her phone and touched the usual number. She waited in resignation for the automated voice to inform her, as usual, that the device was switched off. Instead, to her surprise, the phone began to ring. And ring and ring, unanswered.

Then, from downstairs, two flights of stairs away in her office, the museum's land line began to ring.

FIFTEEN

Friday 14th October 1216

The elderly cockerel was still in fine voice after years of strutting about the yard and Rufus stirred with a groan. Opening one reluctant eye, he could tell it was still dark outside; the thin line of sky usually visible between the shutters and the wall was still undefined. The room was completely still, Oswy and Egbert snoring gently on their mattresses in the straw. It wouldn't be long, though, before Goodwife Elizabeth came bustling in to make up the fire in the central hearth.

Rufus had come to live in the lodgings run by Jerome and Elizabeth when he'd left home to work for the castle chaplain. It was a pleasant place to stay, the couple being hard working and expecting the same from their small body of servants. With their daughter Agnes, they had a small separate dwelling across the yard, leaving the single roomed building for the use of the three clerks who lodged there.

Rufus was too comfortable on his mattress by the banked up fire to move, but move he must. The hessian mattress filled with bedstraw was perfectly adequate to sleep on, provided that he remembered to shake it out well each morning. His mattress and rough blanket of undyed wool made up all the bedding he needed.

With an abrupt movement, he forced himself to get up, brushing the straw from his long linen shirt and plodding over to the trestle table in the corner. He scooped up handfuls of cold water from a large tub and washed his face, wetting as little else of his shivering body as he could get away with, and drying himself hastily on the old cloth that always hung there. Already, he could hear Goodwife Elizabeth and her daughter Agnes in the yard, talking to the chickens as they fed them. The goodwife told everyone that talking to the birds made them lay better, but Rufus suspected it had more to do with her being a kindly soul with a fondness for all creatures.

By the hearth, Egbert and Oswy were still snoring, their noses barely visible above their blankets. Both had piled extra straw over themselves for warmth and the shock of cold early morning air always seemed a greater penance for them than for everyone else.

'Come on, you two, the goodwife's on her way!' Rufus tried warning them. There was no response.

He shrugged and began pulling on his breeches, tucking his shirt into them and tying them securely around his waist. He pulled his woollen tunic over his head, glad of its warmth, then reached for his hose.

The door was thrown open without ceremony, disturbing the dust and waking Oswy with a fit of coughing.

'What's all this?' the goodwife chided. 'Let's see some life in here!' She strode over to the shutters and pulled them open. The old oaken shutters screeched in their usual protesting way, letting in billows of cold, damp autumnal air. It was enough to wake even Egbert, who came to with a groaning curse and eyed the room and its inhabitants with a scowl.

'There'll be no more of that,' the goodwife snapped and from behind her came a giggle. Young Agnes stood there, hiding her flushed and rather spotty face behind her hand as she stole a look at Rufus. He gave her a curt nod and she scurried over to the fire to help her mother. Elizabeth was kneeling beside the hearth, working to bring the slumbering fire back to life, adding more sticks from the fireside basket.

Behind her, Oswy and Egbert stood up and shook the straw from themselves, making their way to the corner to wash. Rufus sat on the bench farthest away from the window to finish dressing, pulling on his hose. He secured them above his knees using the long cords attached to the top of his breeches. He stood to let his tunic fall to its full length. As a young clerk, he still wore a short tunic which just about covered the tops of his knee hose. On truly cold days he frequently wished for advancing years and the longer tunics worn by older men.

Finally, he fastened his long leather girdle around his waist, attaching his scrip to it and securing it all with a loose knot at the front. Goodwife Elizabeth glanced up at him from the fire and smiled briefly before settling the heavy water pot on the glowing embers. She was a tall woman in her middle years, as handsome as she was kindly, with smiling brown eyes. Her hair, as far as Rufus could make out from the small strands that strayed from under the linen caps that she and all other women of her class always wore, was of the same dark colour.

'Help yourself to ale and bread, lad. I should hurry before your two companions eat it all, if I were you.'

It was a timely warning. Though dressed only in their crumpled linen shirts, their faces still damp from a cursory encounter with washing water, Egbert and Oswy were already seated at the table by the door and greedily tucking in. It didn't seem to occur to either of them to wait until they were dressed or to leave much for Rufus, but their behaviour, as always, was thoughtless rather than mean spirited. Egbert greeted Rufus with a grin as he shoved another piece of bread into his mouth.

'What kept you? Early bird gets the worm and all that, remember.'

Rufus didn't bother to reply, helping himself to a crust of bread and a piece of cheese and filling a cup with weak ale from the tall, earthenware jug. As the mother and daughter left them to eat, Agnes lingered by the door and smiled shyly at Rufus. He nodded again, feeling irritated. Oswy gave a snort of a laugh.

When Egbert and Oswy had finished dressing, the three clerks made their way from the lodging house on the bank of the Wysbeck River, past the already busy workshops in the New Market, to the castle gatehouse.

'What's going on?' queried Egbert as they made their way over the drawbridge. Rufus was about to ask the same question. Even before they had reached the bailey it was clear that something was happening.

A stranger was there on horseback, a messenger, judging by the swift courser he was riding. Geoffrey the Steward and a few of his bailiffs had gathered round the messenger and were soon joined by Father Leofric and the castle constable, Hugo de Wenton.

The messenger departed, leaving the constable, steward and chaplain in discussion. As Father Leofric caught sight of his three clerks, he signalled for them to follow him into the chapel.

The chapel felt even colder than usual that morning, the damp clinging to the stone and hanging in the air like an ill tempered mist. It was relieved only by the single candle that burned on the small altar.

'We have received ill news,' Father Leofric began. He gestured for them to sit and they lowered themselves on to a bench against the north wall, beneath the single, narrow window. They peered curiously at the elderly priest, waiting for him to enlighten them. 'The king is perilously sick. He was staying at St Mary's Abbey in Swineshead on his way to Newark Castle and the brothers have sent us word of his grace's declining health. They tell us that he was so weak by the time he took leave of the abbey yesterday that he had to be carried on a litter.'

'It'll be all that cider he was putting down himself at the feast here,' observed Oswy carelessly, adding an almighty sniff to give his statement emphasis.

'I have told you boy, time and time again, that your ill judged remarks will get you into trouble. Have some respect. Though...' Father Leofric expelled a long sigh and joined his clerks on the bench. '...it is said that he is so weak from sickness of the stomach that he can hardly stand. The malady is thought to have been caused by something he ate or drank, perhaps worsened by long travel. Whatever a man's status in life, whatever his wealth and comforts, moving constantly from place to place, putting down rebellions and scarcely knowing the warmth of his own hearth fire, cannot be good for his well-being.'

'Was it...' Rufus began, then thought better of it.

'Yes, boy?'

'Well, father, as Oswy said, the king was drinking a lot of cider at the feast in his honour. It was very new. We thought ourselves it was unready for drinking. And those peaches...they were grown with such care in the walled gardens by the river, it being known they were favoured by his grace, but to eat them like that without cooking! It is well known that raw fruit is bad for the stomach, especially if not fully ripe.'

'You're right there,' agreed Oswy. 'I didn't fancy them at all. Needed a good stewing, if you ask me.'

'There is no suggestion,' growled Father Leofric, clearly regretting having shared his thoughts with his clerks, 'that the king's sickness results from his time here. And you had better stop those wagging tongues of yours, lest you get us all into serious trouble.'

'But now that I think of it,' said Rufus, 'the king was ailing even before he came to Wisbech. He looked grievously sick, and that was before the feast began.'

'It is not known when the king's malady began,' replied the chaplain, 'but by the time he reached Swineshead Abbey it seems he was ill indeed. Despite the care of the good brothers, his health declined further. The abbot appealed to him to remain at Swineshead, to allow him to recover his health, but the king insisted on travelling to Newark. With his grace having to be carried on a litter, I fear the journey will be slow and difficult. We must pray for the king. He is in sore need of our prayers.'

'And we'd better add a prayer for ourselves,' muttered Egbert, 'that it wasn't our cider and peaches that made him sick.'

SIXTEEN (Present Day)

Jemima's Aunt

Monica had just reached the top floor of the museum again, after answering the phone downstairs, when the doorbell rang. She sighed heavily, grumbling under her breath as she started down the two flights once more. She finally reached the front door in time for the fourth assault on the doorbell.

'Monica, mate! Had a spare minute and thought I'd come and look at that job, sortta thing, like you said to do, like.'

'Afternoon, Bertle,' she managed to smile. 'Come in then.'

The grubby door that led down to the cellars always grated on the stone top step and today it set her teeth on edge. Her head ached.

Bertle bounded cheerfully down the narrow, dark steps ahead of her, arriving at the bottom to snatch at the hanging light cord. A sickly, pale illumination filled the narrow passageway that led to the old wine cellar at the front of the house and to the long abandoned kitchen at the back.

They turned left and entered the kitchen. Like the wine cellar, its windows were set high in the wall. The cellars were situated partly below ground level, depriving both rooms of any sort of view of outside. The cold damp of the kitchen made the place even less welcoming and the high, cobwebbed, grime coated windows, partly covered by broken wooden shutters, did nothing to help. Monica found another light cord and gave it a tug, allowing another energy saving bulb to add its mean glow to the proceedings.

'Wouldn't fancy working darn 'ere for long,' commented Bertle. He paced about a bit, poking around in the corners. He came at last to a standstill, rubbing his stubbly chin thoughtfully. 'Floor's not bad, all things considered. Walls need a bitta plaster.' He moved a pile of boxes aside and squeezed his rounded belly between the upturned table and the dresser. 'Woodwork's not bad either, though there's a bitta rot on a few of the skirting boards...want me to do the 'lectric and all?'

'If you could, please, Bertle. Have a good look round and send me a quote and I'll see what the trustees say.'

She watched idly, lost in dismal thought as he made his way around the mouldering room, moving piles of junk out of the way and doing a lot of grunting.

Archie's call, when at last it had come, had been anything but reassuring. He was still in the Midlands. He and Jemima had driven from the solicitor's to Aunt Lizzie's house in Kenilworth, and that was where Archie intended to stay for the weekend.

There was so much to do, he had explained. They needed to freeze Aunt Lizzie's bank accounts and stop her direct debits and insurance policies, but they were having trouble finding the necessary documents. They had spent the rest of Thursday hunting around the house for the missing paperwork and it seemed their search had highlighted how much needed to be done before they could sell the house. In the end, Archie had decided to stay for the night, continue working on Friday and over the weekend, if necessary.

He could achieve so much more if he stayed for a few days, he had continued to explain to Monica, his voice soft and endearing. Bernadette would have called it wheedling. He and Jemima had decided to leave the furniture in the house when it was put up for sale, but thought the ornaments and 'clutter' should be cleared. Jemima's aunt hadn't left the house in too bad a condition, he said, and it was no penance for him to lodge in the back bedroom while they started to clear the house.

Aunt Lizzie had a lot of clutter, apparently, and a lot of clutter needed a lot of clearing. He hoped Monica would understand. His boss at the golf course was fine about him taking an extra day's leave, he pointed out. Perhaps he expected her to follow his example.

'Nah trouble, mate,' Bertle interrupted her thoughts. 'I can get started after Christmas and get the place ready for your new season in March. Bob'll be your uncle, like.'

SEVENTEEN

Tuesday 18th October 1216

'Dark as night out there.' Oswy shut the door behind him with a loud thud, rubbing his hands vigorously together. 'Cold too. The devil's own weather.'

It was almost as dark as he claimed. Though only just past midday, there was barely enough light coming through the narrow, unglazed window above Rufus' desk to allow the clerks to work. The shutter was folded hard back against the wall, letting in more cold than light, and still it felt more like twilight than midday. The clerks were having to work by rush light, an unusual necessity for so early in an October day.

Father Leofric looked up from his labours and frowned. In the distance the low growl of thunder could be heard.

'I need this letter taking to the messenger at the gatehouse,' he said as he pressed the heavy wooden castle seal on to a pool of hot wax to secure the document he had prepared. All three clerks looked up, waiting to hear which of them would be chosen for the job, each of them hoping it would be someone else. 'Rufus,' the chaplain confirmed at last, 'it had better be you. You're less inclined to burden me with a detailed weather report on your return.' He shot an irritated glance at the shivering Oswy. 'The messenger will be waiting to take this to my lord bishop in Ely.'

Rufus stood and took the letter, ignoring his smirking colleagues, and unhooked his cloak from the recess by the door. Once outside, he was glad of the respite.

But the weather was strange indeed. There was an amber hue to the brooding sky. The wind came in gusts; damp, cold blasts that tore at the flag high up on the keep and almost blew the linen cap from Rufus' hair. He wrapped his cloak around him, but then the wind dropped again, leaving an eerie stillness. As he made his way past the smithy, a shaft of brilliant, coppery sunshine pierced the clouds. He stopped and looked up at the sky. Behind him, the mature willows by the Well Stream, their tall, topmost branches just showing above the castle walls, caught the sun. The trees, the last of their autumn leaves hanging pale and insipid, shone in that moment like ripened corn. Rufus stood transfixed by the sight, the golden tree vibrant against the background of advancing thunderous cloud.

It was all over in an instant, the wind returning to shake the willows out of their daze, and Rufus continued on his way. A clap of thunder sounded, far closer now. The massive, iron-dark cloud was almost upon them.

The messenger was waiting for him by the Mote Hall, the large building next to the gatehouse. It was at the Mote Hall that the Assizes were held. Every six months, the judge and his entourage arrived with great pomp and ceremony before a jury was selected and the Assizes took place. The desperate souls tried in these law courts, for crimes as serious as murder or treason, usually ended up on the gallows.

Spending his days in such close proximity to the Mote Hall and all its misery, Rufus was only too aware of the consequences of crime.

Keen to be on his way, the messenger took the letter and was gone. His ride to Ely would not be an easy one. As Rufus started back towards the office, a fork of lightning speared the sky somewhere over the far side of the Well Stream. It made him think of Marshmeade, his home manor. He knew it was about time he paid his family a visit.

He reached the office just as the first fat drops of rain fell. He closed the door quickly behind him, saving his fellow workers from the fierce gust of wind that scattered leaves and debris across the bailey. Father Leofric looked up and nodded.

'Well done, boy. I suspect my letter will make slow progress while this storm rages, but you have done your part.'

As if in agreement, a great clap of thunder sounded overhead and Oswy let out a whimper. Egbert giggled nervously. Lightning followed immediately, striping the room through its narrow windows in a moment of violent illumination.

The clerks had stopped writing, poised for the next crash of thunder as the heavy rain poured from the thatched eaves and formed a temporary moat around the small office building.

'Is this an omen, father?' asked Egbert in a small voice.

'An omen, boy? Surely you don't listen to such superstitious nonsense! If God needed to tell us something, I'm sure he would find a better way of doing it than broadcasting across the whole shire by means of a thunder storm! Get back to your work, boy. There's plenty of it to do.'

But the chaplain had wandered to the window closest to his desk, as if mesmerised by the storm.

'Even so,' he murmured to himself. 'This freakish weather will do no good to anyone. Take that as an omen if you will.'

EIGHTEEN (Present Day)

Little Yellow Bird

Archibald Newcombe-Walker stood in the office doorway on Monday afternoon, having used his own key to enter the museum.

He was smiling too easily, talking too much, yet all he said was so very reasonable. At least the cat seemed to believe him. Smokey, or perhaps it was Smudge or Sooty, had jumped off the chair by the window where he had been dozing and was now weaving around Archie's legs in joyful greeting.

'...so I dropped all the bank and credit card statements we found into the solicitor this morning and drove straight home....ah, hello Smutty,' he smiled, bending down to stroke the cat's silky grey back.

Like everyone else, Archie had long since stopped trying to tell apart the three cats belonging to Mrs Paynter next door. Their collective name of Smutty was used all the time in the museum now.

Monica nodded, straight faced as he went on talking, keeping her replies to a minimum.

'...and dear old Aunt Lizzie had so much *stuff*, Monica. Covering every surface it was; china things, wooden things, collections of Snoopy in spacesuits, on kennels, with that little yellow bird...'

'Woodstock. I hope you kept the Snoopies.'

He grinned, perhaps feeling encouraged.

'I don't know. Jemima took it all. It belongs to her now. We removed all the personal effects and the pictures, ready for when the house is put up for sale. That alone took ages, but we still haven't started emptying cupboards and they are all *stuffed*, Monica. It is going to take *weeks*.'

'Yes, I suppose it is.'

'And even looking for the insurance documents and utility statements took hours. Jemima's aunt didn't just have one folder for everything, oh no, she had bits here and there, all over the house, but eventually we found what the solicitor needed. Now he can get on with that part of things, you know, stopping her policies, applying for probate etcetera.'

'Yes, I suppose he can.'

'Monica,' he snapped suddenly. 'What's the matter? You're behaving like I've been away on a stag weekend or something. I had to go and do this job. Do you think I wanted to? I spent four nights sleeping on damp sheets in a long unused back bedroom of a dead person's house and living off dodgy takeaways from the place round the corner. It seemed a better option than making the four hour round trip each day.'

'I suppose it was,' she admitted, straightening up in her chair. Put like that, it was very reasonable. 'But I wish you'd let me know on Thursday instead of letting me think you were coming home that night...'

'Why? Because we have such a close and loving relationship? Monica, I hardly *see* you these days! I moved over here to be with you and yet you continue to hold me at arm's length. I know I said I hoped to be back on

Thursday night, but quite honestly, I thought you wouldn't care one way or the other!'

Smutty, who quite clearly disapproved of such disharmony, had backed away from Archie and was leaving the room. Archie was still looking angrily at Monica, his composure shattered.

'I'm sorry,' she said at last, feeling it was better to apologise and restore some sort of peace. 'Maybe I had no right to demand to know where you were, but I was truly worried. It seemed like forever before I heard from you and it didn't help that you were with your ex-wife.'

'Ah, dear Jemima!' His voice was still angry, bitterness shaping each word into crisp, staccato notes. 'Well, if it eases your mind, she and I get on no better now than when she left me. She is blissfully happy, apparently, with her new husband. Having to share executor duties with me is the last thing she wants. She made that abundantly clear.'

Perhaps that was his real problem, Monica thought.

'Poor old Jemima!' she commented sarcastically, and didn't like herself for it. She was trying hard to snap out of her crossness. 'Come on,' she added in a brighter voice, 'I know you have to get back to work, but come and look at my new project first.'

She forced herself into something like cheerfulness as she led him down the narrow stone steps to the dilapidated kitchen in the basement. As she passed him in the narrow passageway he reached out to hold her. She gave in for a moment, letting him wrap his arms around her and giving him a brief kiss, but she moved away as quickly as she could. It didn't feel right.

There was still something uncomfortable about all this, a feeling that she hadn't been told everything. She couldn't just collapse back into old, easy ways. Not yet.

She pulled on the light cord and began to tell him her plans for the kitchen.

NINETEEN

Noon, Friday 21st October 1216

Rufus had never seen the Great Hall so crowded. Even at the king's feast, when the hall had been furnished with trestle tables and filled with visitors and castle personnel, it had seemed nowhere as full as this. Today, all the tables but for the constable's own on the dais had been dismantled; the trestles and boards were stacked against the walls, leaving plenty of standing room for the people who poured in.

The constable Sir Hugo de Wenton had sent a mandate around the manor of Wisbech Barton that all townspeople should gather in the castle's Great Hall at noon. Now, with predictable obedience, they were arriving. Soon, they were all gathered there; the miller, the smith, the stonemason, the husbandmen who farmed the land, the carpenters, dykers, tanners, weavers, fullers and many ordinary labourers. Most of the labourers were villeins, humble souls whose lot in life placed them at the bottom of the feudal chain. They had few rights and no option but to provide their labour free of charge when required by the lord of the manor on his estates. These manorial acres were known as land held in demesne.

The lord of the manor of Wisbech Barton was the Bishop of Ely, but it was not he who addressed his people today. He had many other manors in the Isle of Ely and could not be everywhere at once. It was the tall and authoritative figure of the castle constable, therefore, that stood on the dais before the people, waiting with a sober expression while the last few stragglers squeezed themselves into the back of the hall. Rufus noticed Goodwife Elizabeth, her husband Jerome, young Agnes and their three servants standing by the entrance. Agnes had already sought him out with her eyes. He caught her looking and she blushed a dark shade of pink. He gave her another of his cool nods and hoped she would look away.

'It is my solemn duty,' began Sir Hugo de Wenton, 'to inform you of the passing of our lord king two days ago, in the early hours of the morning. We received word today that he passed from this world while residing at Newark Castle. May the Lord have mercy on his soul...'

He paused as a shocked murmur rose from the people in the hall. Most of them were crossing themselves, looking suitably mournful.

'Church bells will be tolled in this manor and throughout the Isle of Ely. I ask you all to offer prayers for our lord king's soul. Masses will be held in our own chapel and at the church of St Peter and Paul's...' he paused again as the crowd's muttered reaction swelled, reaching its crescendo and almost drowning out his voice. His deputy Sir Giles of Ely bellowed a command for silence, allowing him to continue.

'The king leaves a nine year old son, soon be crowned, by the grace of God, as Henry III of England, Lord of Ireland and Duke of Aquitaine...' Again, the crowd's response rose in a wave, rendering the constable's last words inaudible, but his announcement was all but done and he let it rest.

Rufus was speechless as the news sank in. He was looking at the constable on the dais, but in his mind's eye it was King John who was there, seated beneath the canopy with its three lions of England. Rufus could still see the king's pinched and humourless face as he endured what must have been a painful occasion. The signs, even then, that he was seriously unwell, were there. And now he was gone.

'I knew that storm was an omen,' Egbert proclaimed darkly as they began to make their way through the crowd and out of the hall.

'It most surely was,' agreed Oswy. 'That storm was three days ago, when the king lay dying at Newark. No wonder it was so fearsome; God was giving his warning that the king was on his way to...'

'Purgatory,' finished Egbert with a knowing nod. 'He'll have to serve his time in purgatory like the rest of us. Perhaps, though, because he was so rich and acted sometimes with charity, such as when he granted our manor its almshouses, and because he has so many bishops praying for his soul, his time in purgatory might be shortened.'

'Maybe,' considered Oswy, 'but what was it that hastened his departure from this life? I still blame that cider. It should have been left longer in the cask, and as for all those raw peaches, I never saw fruit so readily consumed in its uncooked state! I suppose the king's liking for such things was his undoing in the end.'

'I'd keep quiet about it, if I were you,' put in Rufus. 'If Father Leofric hears you, you know what he'll say, and it won't do to put suspicion in people's minds. True, the king ate here, but first he feasted in Lynn. Later, after leaving Wisbech, he must have eaten at Swineshead Abbey...'

'Ooh yes', agreed Oswy with a knowing look, 'and you know whose abbey *that* is, don't you?'

'No, whose is it?' asked Egbert eagerly, as if all the suspicion about Wisbech's hospitality were not gossip enough.

'I'll tell you then. Robert de Gresley is the lord of Swineshead. You remember? He was one of the barons who revolted against King John the other year...'

'Swineshead Abbey is in the Baron de Gresley's hands?' asked Egbert. 'Well, he may have rebelled at one time, but then the king granted him land, so surely he was back in favour?'

'Perhaps,' continued Oswy, not wanting to give up, 'but there was more trouble between them, even after that. The king confiscated the land he had granted him, so there can't have been much love remaining between the king and his baron. I suspect...'

'Don't be ridiculous,' said Rufus. 'You're making something out of nothing and you'll come to grief if you carry on like that.'

The three clerks had made their way through the crowd and had reached the bailey. The bells of St Peter and Paul's were already tolling their solemn tidings across the manor.

'Well, I suppose we'd better pray for the old boy's soul,' said Oswy with resignation, 'though many will be glad to see the back of him.'

'I should keep that opinion to yourself too,' said Rufus, though he couldn't help smiling. 'Come on, we'd better go to Mass. You know what Father Leofric's like when he's kept waiting.'

The townspeople were making their way out through the gatehouse and around the castle dyke to St Peter and Paul's, but everyone who worked in the castle was heading instead for the small chapel next to the clerks' office.

Rufus caught sight of his old friend Eustace the under-cook and made his way through the crowd towards him. His chubby face was as pink as ever. Rufus couldn't remember a time when the lad hadn't been flushed from his labours over the kitchen's huge fires.

But there was time only for a quick greeting once they had squeezed inside the crowded chapel. Mass had begun.

TWENTY (Present Day)

Medieval Geography

'Yeah, but what I wanna know,' interrupted Bertle, 'is when do we get art there with the metal detectors?'

'We'll come to that in due course,' continued Rex Monday. It must have been the tenth interruption he'd had to put up with that Thursday evening since beginning his introduction to the third Wisbech Heritage Society Meeting. He was beginning to suspect that he was wasting his time with these people. Outside on Nene Quay, a lorry rumbled slowly past and he extended the pause to allow the sound to fade away.

'Now, as I was saying, there are many theories concerning King John's final journey from Norfolk, through Cambridgeshire and into Lincolnshire. The route taken by the king and his baggage train, what his 'treasure' consisted of, even the dates on which all this took place, are far from certain. Some say he arrived in Wisbech on the tenth of October 1216, others say the twelfth. But the greatest debate concerns the route taken by the baggage train over the Wash.

'Remember how different the medieval geography was to ours,' Rex continued, then paused to check that everyone was still listening. One of the volunteers from the nearby Wisbech and Fenland Museum had closed his eyes. Someone in the back row had knocked a cup over and was attempting to mop up the spilt tea with a tissue. Somebody else was yawning loudly; probably Mark Appledore from

Peckover. Rex gave them all a disapproving look before carrying on with an expression of long suffering.

'Wisbech, as we clarified earlier, was on the coast in those days, the Wash coming much further inland than today. When the tide was out, the Well Stream estuary, which formed part of the Wash, could be crossed in certain places, but the timing had to be right because mistakes could lead to disaster.

'As the tide receded, huge mud flats would have been exposed, great masses of sticky mud. Anyone hoping to cross the estuary needed the help of an experienced guide and even then extreme caution was necessary. No matter which crossing point was chosen, deep creeks and gulleys that were formed by the ebb and flow of the tides had to be traversed. Such obstacles took time to overcome and of course speed was of the essence. There was only so much time before the tide changed and anyone still crossing was likely to be swamped.'

'You'd choose the shortest way across, then,' pointed out Mark Appledore. He was slumped down in his seat at the back, as usual, his long coat draped like a cape over the floor behind him.

'Well, yes, Mark. You'd think so, wouldn't you? It always surprises me how many historians, even modern researchers, favour the longer crossing points as the route taken by the baggage train. But we shall come to that later. What no one seems to dispute is that the king must have parted from his baggage train at some point on his journey. The train, thought to have been at least a mile long and consisting of more than a hundred heavily laden ox wagons, would have moved extremely slowly. The king and his escort of around two hundred barons, knights and men-at-arms, however, would have been riding a variety of horses which were capable of much swifter progress; palfreys and rounceys most likely.

'At certain stages of their progress around England, the king and his escort would have left the slow baggage train behind and ridden ahead. This is what is believed to have happened as they approached Wisbech. The king probably accompanied the train as far as the sea bank, then left his wagons to cross the estuary while he and his escort rode to Wisbech. He is thought to have spent the night at Wisbech Castle before travelling into Lincolnshire the following day, expecting to rejoin his train on the far side of the Wash.'

'Must have been a bit of a blow for him, then,' someone at the back quipped.

'Indeed. As everyone knows, most of the train never made it to the other side. The tides were somehow misjudged and disaster struck. At first, as the tide began to come in, the mud would have become increasingly sticky, sucking at the animals' hooves and causing a few hold-ups. Unnoticed at first, the steep sided creeks would have been filling with water. A few horses or oxen may have lost their footing on the banks. Then, before they had chance to react, water would have surged in, trapping men, animals and wagons. Men-at-arms in heavy coats of mail would have been dragged down in the water and even less heavily burdened men would have stood little chance.'

'Blimey,' said Bertle. Others murmured their agreement. At last Rex had their attention.

'I propose that, starting from tonight, we look at the different theories concerning the route taken by the train across the estuary, as well as what that train was likely to have been carrying. Also, I thought it might be interesting to look at buildings, ruined and otherwise, in the local area which date back to John's time. It would help to give us an idea of the landscape he would have known. Would anyone like to work on that?'

Monica nodded and Archie looked at her curiously.

'Really, Monica? Haven't you enough to do already?'

'Yes, but this is part of our local history. It's important.'

'Indeed it is,' beamed Rex, as if to his star pupil, 'but before we get on to that, let's start looking at the various theories concerning the estuary crossing points. I propose we begin with the most popular theory, that of Walpole Cross Keys in Norfolk to Long Sutton in Lincolnshire. But first, we'll take a coffee break and then I'll get my map out.'

'Hell!' muttered Bernadette. 'I've forgotten to switch the coffee on.' She started towards the small back kitchen in a hurry. 'Hold on a minute, will you?' she added in a louder voice. 'Archie, don't just stand there; come and hand some biscuits round or something.'

At least this time the coffee wouldn't be stewed.

TWENTY-ONE

Afternoon, Friday 21st October 1216

'It couldn't have been the peaches,' protested Eustace as they left the chapel after Mass. 'Why is everyone talking about the peaches? I prepared them myself and they were nicely ripe and soft. We were told his grace liked them uncooked and they were truly fit for a king! The husbandman had brought them up to the castle that morning. He'd grown them in a sunny walled corner of his orchard by the river, had been tending his trees all summer long, determined to produce late ripening peaches for the king's visit. I tell you they were good, Rufus. I wanted to eat them myself.'

'Then ignore the comments. If you ask me, all that cider he put down himself would have given him more serious problems. Gave us all a mighty headache and stomach gripes, so who can tell what it did to the king?'

'So I suppose the next thing,' continued Eustace, 'will be the brewer being landed with the blame. He told me himself that half the stuff he'd produced wasn't ready because he'd not been given enough notice. He'd have been better prepared if he'd had the castle's order sooner.'

'No one is to blame. And the seneschal is safely home in Ely. If there were the slightest suspicion about our feast, don't you think Sir Milo Fulk would have ridden back here as fast as his horse could carry him? If he, who represents the law in the Isle, has no concerns about the peaches or cider, why should anyone else?'

'That doesn't stop the idle tongues wagging.'

'It's just foolish gossip. Don't react and it will soon be forgotten. We have a new king on the throne now. There will be new problems, new matters to resolve. The old king's death will no longer be given a thought.'

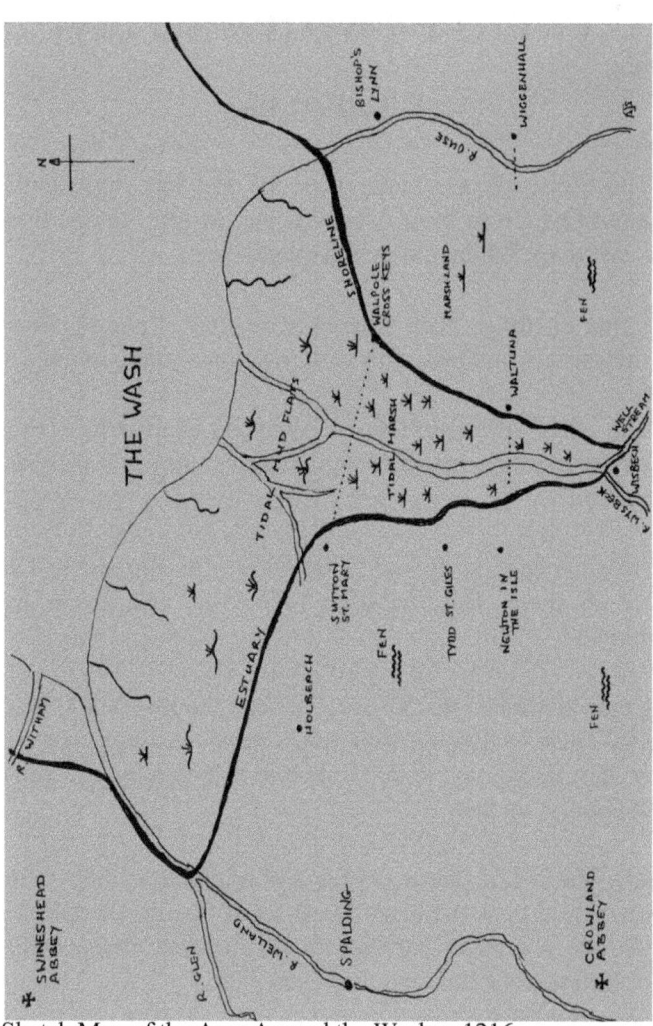

Sketch Map of the Area Around the Wash c. 1216

TWENTY-TWO (Present Day)

A Trifle Long

'These biscuits are better than the last lot, Bernadette,' called Ena Cross from over near the tea urn, 'not as fusty as last time. Where did you get them?'

'Come on folks, back to your seats, if you please. Bring your coffees and teas with you,' Rex was calling in vain.

'The other lot weren't fusty,' objected Bernadette. 'They were expensive, meant to be delicacies; they had lavender in them.'

'No wonder then. Bound to be fusty with ingredients like that in them. Best to stick to custard creams, in my opinion.'

'Come along people...ah yes, you lead the way Mark. Jolly good...that's right...oh dear, never mind. Just put your cup on the floor, my dear. I'm sure Monica won't mind mopping it up later...'

Satisfied at last that everyone had returned to their seats, Rex folded back the blank top sheet of his flip chart with a flourish. The chart wobbled on its stand, but all eyes were focused now on the map displayed there.

Marked in black was the modern coastline stretching west to east, from the River Welland to the Great Ouse. At a significant distance inland, the medieval coastline was marked in red. The area between the old and new coastlines was dotted with little grassy symbols to indicate salt marsh.

It was clear from the map how salt marsh had claimed the areas which in King John's time had been part of the Wash. Wisbech was shown at the bottom of the map, at the southern end of the estuary. The blue spot marking the town looked like a droplet of water leaking from the bottom of the funnel-shaped coastline.

'So you see how very different the geography was in John's time,' said Rex. 'The village of Sutton Bridge didn't exist then and there was no road or bridge either. Water covered that entire area. The A17, of course, was constructed many centuries later and even the road which preceded it was built hundreds of years after John's time.

'In 1216, if you wanted to travel from Bishop's Lynn, the name of which wouldn't change to King's Lynn until the 1500s, into Lincolnshire, you'd have to go all the way to Wisbech, then up through Newton in the Isle and Tydd St Giles. Or, you could cut across the estuary somewhere north of Wisbech.

'As I said earlier, the baggage train attempted to cross the estuary while the king travelled to Wisbech. So, where did that ill-fated crossing take place? Of the many theories on this matter, I suggest we concentrate solely on the main ones. We mentioned earlier the possible crossing from Walpole Cross Keys to Long Sutton, a prosperous small town known in those days as Sutton St Mary.'

Rex rapped with the end of his pencil to indicate the two locations on the map.

'Another theory favours a crossing from West Walton to Newton in the Isle,' he continued with more smart taps.

'Then there's the belief that they crossed from Walsoken here,' another tap, 'to Leverington, ah, here.'

A final, loud pencil rap signalled the end of his list of theories.

'Now,' he continued, 'I suggest we take one route at a time and look at its practicalities and, ah, otherwise. Each time we finish looking at a route, we could let Bertle loose with his metal detector...'

Bertle had been dozing in the back row, but he came to at the mention of his name. He grinned broadly.

'Right you are. Ready when you are, sortta thing.'

'Excellent! On then, to our first theoretical crossing; Walpole Cross Keys to Long Sutton.'

'Surely a trifle long?' queried Mark Appledore with a bored expression. He had stretched out his long legs, his trouser legs having ridden up to display socks decorated with small elephants in pink bikinis.

'You have a point, Mark. You only have to glance at the map to see that the crossing would have been about six miles long. Six miles of inter-tidal mudflats and winding, steep-sided creeks. Taking even a small party over such a great distance of perilous terrain would have taken a long time, but when you add the problems of moving a huge wagon train across, the task becomes near to impossible.'

'Absolute lunacy!' said Mark.

'Quite so. But, first of all, if we are to believe, just for a moment, that the baggage train made its crossing from Walpole Cross Keys, how did it arrive at the village?

'Well, on leaving Bishop's Lynn,' he said, indicating with his pencil where King's Lynn was marked on the map, 'they would have had to cross what is now called the River Nar just south of the town. I am using mostly modern river names, you'll note; the waterways have changed greatly over the centuries and many of their original names are long forgotten.

'Having crossed the Nar, the train would then have the far greater problem of crossing the River Great Ouse. There were very few bridges in those days and the nearest crossing point for them on the Great Ouse was at Wiggenhall...here!' Rex's pencil rapped again on Wiggenhall St Germans at the bottom right hand corner of the map. 'In those days, the river there was known as the Wiggenhall Eau.'

'What's an oh?' asked Bertle.

'Not oh, *eau*. French for water,' Bernadette told him. He still looked puzzled.

'Quite so. Thank you, ah, Bernadette,' continued Rex. 'Now, where was I? Ah, yes. Nowadays, Wiggenhall finds itself at the southern end of a nice, straight waterway called the Eau Brink Cut, but this was not constructed until 1821, to by-pass the bend in the river. So, King John and his baggage train, on leaving Lynn, would have had no choice but to travel south along the Great Ouse to Wiggenhall, in order to cross the river. Now, I don't know about you, but...'

'Why, having travelled so far south,' interrupted Archie, 'would the king traipse north again to Walpole Cross Keys? Surely he must have been able to find a more convenient place to cross the Wash?'

Archie had been quiet all evening, but probably only because he was engrossed in what Rex was saying. Monica had to admit that ever since his return from Kenilworth he'd been more attentive. She too had been making more effort and they'd been seeing more of each other. The Jemima situation had given them both a bit of a wake-up call and she just hoped this new situation lasted.

'Precisely Archibald,' Rex was replying. 'Precisely. But some historians maintain that the king and his train travelled to Walpole Cross Keys.'

'Batty,' grumbled Mark. 'No wonder nothing's ever been found at Walpole or Sutton.'

'We'll 'ave a go anyway,' insisted Bertle. 'You never know. Beginners' luck and all that. And trust ol' Bertle. If it's there, Bertle'll find it!'

'Even if it's buried beneath metres of mud?' retorted Mark drily.

'All right, dear people. Let's leave it for tonight. Why don't we meet this weekend at Walpole Cross Keys and take a look at the lie of the land? Bertle can power up his machine and perhaps we could all take a packed lunch? What do you say?'

The general reaction was surprisingly positive and so it was agreed that they would all meet at Walpole on Sunday.

'A day out with Rex,' Bernadette muttered, as she stacked the chairs afterwards. 'What spiffing fun!'

TWENTY-THREE

Sunday 13th November 1216

Rufus made the short journey to Marshmeade on foot. After Mass on Sundays, he was usually free to do as he pleased and today was as good an opportunity as any to visit his old home manor.

He had not been home since the summer, but in truth he hardly missed the place. His life at the castle with its work and responsibilities had eclipsed any sentiment he might once have felt for his old life on the manor with his brutish brother and dominant father.

It was a fine, bright morning, the late autumn sun reflected with a harsh, metallic gleam on the Well Stream, turning the brown water to silver. He passed moored and loaded lighters at the quayside, temporarily motionless as the town took its Sunday rest. Tomorrow, the Barnack Rag limestone blocks would be unloaded from the lighters and pulled to the church on ox-drawn sleds. Extension work was planned for St Peter and Paul's, Rufus had heard. There was always building of some kind going on.

As Rufus continued on his way out of town, he looked down from the bank top into the increasingly sluggish water. The river there, though still no great distance from the estuary, felt less of a tidal pull. Even further upstream towards Welle and March, where the river curved and reeds grew out from the banks in wide sweeping beds, the situation was worse and navigation was becoming increasingly difficult for the many boats which made daily use of it.

The Well Stream, thought Rufus, needed a good scouring out again. Silt, which was constantly washed downstream from inland, was a never ending problem for the Fenland waterways. It built up on river beds, making them ever shallower, and in areas where the lazy rivers snaked their way through the marshy landscape, silt congested whole sections of the waterways, rendering them practically useless to boats.

Once out of town, it was orchards, rather than dwellings, that hugged the river bank. The fruit trees were bare of leaves now, their boughs stripped of pears and apples. Some of the apples had gone to make King John's cider, and not far from here was the walled orchard where his peaches had been grown. Less said about that, thought Rufus, the better. Best to think of the fruit that had gone to make luscious pies and to be stewed with spices for folk who could afford such fancies.

On the river banks, reeds stirred in the breeze, their silvery heads nodding as the wind raised them then let them fall. It was very quiet. Most of the townsfolk avoided this stretch of the river and the reason for that was already coming into view. Just ahead, a haze of wood smoke drifted from a clutch of buildings surrounded by willow trees. Rufus passed the end of an avenue of saplings which led down to the river and he turned his head to look between the newly planted trees. He was rewarded with a glimpse of a high timber gate and the front of the infirmary. The leper hospital.

On the opposite bank of the river, a monk carrying water from a well raised his hand in greeting as he caught sight of Rufus. Over the years, benefactors had gifted land to the infirmary, resulting in a situation where its land was spread along both sides of the Well Stream.

The monks caring for the sufferers of leprosy there always seemed cheerful, disregarding almost the danger to their own health. That horribly disfiguring disease was known to be highly contagious, which was why the hospital, like others of its kind, had been built on the edge of town. It was important to protect the main population from infection.

Rufus kept to the road along the river bank without turning into the manor of Elm, but still he saw people he remembered from his boyhood, hailing them from the bank and exchanging greetings with them. He was walking swiftly now, the end of his journey in sight.

Marshmeade was only half a mile beyond Elm, its pasture land reaching down to the river. A hundred acres of arable land and good pasture surrounded the village and beyond that stretched a great swathe of untamed Fen that also belonged to the manor.

From this wilderness came many riches. Osiers and reeds were harvested and sold for building, while flax and hemp grew readily on the winter-flooded Fen. Flax was especially in demand. English flax was spun and woven on manors everywhere to produce the linen cloth that made garments for rich and poor alike. Marshmeade did so well from its produce that the manor's value equated to one knight's fee. In other words, it was enough in itself to support Sir John of Tilneye, his family and all of his retainers.

Yet life, even on such a prosperous manor, was rarely easy. During times of high rainfall or in spring, when heavy winter snow melted and the river struggled to carry the extra water, the banks had often broken, flooding the land and destroying homes. In really bad years, Rufus' father, Sir John, the lord of the manor, had had to rebuild the village from scratch.

But today the sun was shining and Rufus was making his way through Marshmeade, chatting to villeins and cottagers as he went, all of them fondly remembered from his childhood.

His mother, by some stroke of providence, happened to be standing in front of the low roofed, neat manor house as he approached. She was straightening her back, most likely after spending too long at her weaving. She looked up and saw him, surprise and happiness illuminating her face as she held out her arms in welcome.

'Rufus! What took you so long? It has been forever! How glad I am to see you! Your father and Ralph are out in the west field; some problem on the demesne lands again. You know how it is.'

He smiled ruefully as she continued. As on every manor, much of the land was in demesne, acres held by his father as lord of the manor and worked by his tied peasants, the villeins and cottagers. They accepted their lot with resignation and obedience, renting their small homes and patches of land, as well as working without pay on the lord's land. There would be little point in argument; nothing was likely to change. Sir John, it had to be said, for all his dominance and bluster was not a cruel man. He treated his villeins and even the lowliest cottagers as fairly as could be expected.

In the Great Hall the servants were preparing to serve dinner, the main meal of the day. Rufus could hear them chatting and laughing as they worked. His mother had always run her household well. Though her servants were expected to work hard, she treated them kindly, and as far back as Rufus could remember, there had always been laughter.

One of the older women looked up and saw him as he entered the hall. She let out a cry and rushed to embrace him. The men servants busy with laying the tables greeted him cheerily too. He had known all of them since childhood and in that moment it felt as if time had stood still and he had never left home at all.

An extra place was set for him at the high table on the dais and there he sat with his family, looking down the long hall towards the tables occupied by the manor's many workers. His mother and father were seated at the centre of the high table, he and Ralph at the two ends. Thankfully, therefore, he was as far away from his brother as possible.

His first encounter with Ralph and his father that day had been in the ewery, the anteroom in which they had washed their hands before dinner. It was the first time he had seen either of them since the summer and his father had given him one of his rare smiles and a rough pat on the shoulder. His brother had managed only a sneer.

Though doubtless pleased that Rufus had left home, avoiding any possible future complications in Ralph's manorial inheritance, he still resented what he saw as Rufus' escape from his duties. Ralph could never make up his mind whether Rufus had committed an offence by leaving and, whichever way he thought about it, he was always angry with his younger brother.

Ralph had for some years performed the duties of his father's squire. In time, he hoped to be knighted like Sir John of Tilneye before him, but his lack of knightly qualities was making that outcome increasingly uncertain.

It didn't greatly matter. The manor was clearly thriving, thought Rufus as a huge platter of roasted mutton and a board of the best white wheaten bread were placed on the table. Ralph would be lord of the manor one day, whether or not he earned the title of knight.

Waiting as his father, then as his brother and mother served themselves from the large dishes, Rufus finally helped himself, spooning meat with its dripping, spicy sauce on to his bread trencher.

As he looked down the hall, past the cheerful fire that burned in its grate in the centre of the room and up to the high pitched thatched roof supported by solid wooden beams, a few heads bobbed up from the lower tables to grin or wave at him. He waved cheerfully back, ignoring Ralph's mocking looks.

For the lower tables, there was no roasted meat, but even so it was good food. It looked like boiled fowl in some kind of pale sauce and was obviously going down well, all of the manorial workers tucking in heartily and chewing on great lumps of dark, rye bread. He saw his father's dyke reeve nibbling vacantly on a piece of bread at the high end of one of the long tables. He was a surly man who had seemed old even when Rufus was a boy. He scarcely spoke to anyone, but was diligent in keeping the manor's ditches and banks in order. Such care was essential; a blocked ditch or broken bank could mean ruined crops or the loss of livestock in times of high rainfall.

The land workers, mostly the cottagers and villeins, did not eat in the Great Hall, but out in the fields, where they fed on rough bread and hard cheese. They kept their own simple homes in the village and came to the manor only on feast days or to seek the ear of the lord about a request.

'My dear little brother,' Ralph drawled in his usual lazy way, 'I hear you failed to recover anything of consequence from the king's baggage train.'

Rufus frowned at him. How did he manage to hear so much, stuck out here in the countryside?

'There was no failure,' he replied. 'The seneschal and deputy constable were there to investigate. My duty was to keep records.'

'Well, I hear the king was most displeased, that he...'

'The late king, sir, was too occupied by poor health to be much displeased,' retorted Rufus. He caught a quick glimpse of his father's expression and was surprised to see something there resembling a smile. His mother was looking demurely down at her food, but she too looked pleased. Rufus had grown up considerably since leaving home and it seemed his parents were glad of it.

'Ah, yes, the old king is dead,' sneered Ralph, 'but what about the new king? What about the young Henry III? He is hardly going to rejoice about his losses, is he? I'll wager you haven't heard the last of this, little brother, not by a long way.'

Rufus did not reply. He hadn't thought of that.

TWENTY-FOUR (Present Day)

Complete Detachment

Bertle was picking them up in the Vicarage Car Park. He had insisted. He'd bring the car, he said; there wouldn't be enough room for them all in his work van, not with all the tools and stuff in the back.

Drizzle was rapidly darkening the pavement as Monica and Archie made their way along Nene Quay. The statue of Thomas Clarkson, the early nineteenth century anti-slavery campaigner, peered from the lofty shelter of his memorial, keeping his thoughts to himself as the good people of Wisbech went about their Sunday business.

The couple crossed the road by the Etcetera gift and kitchenware shop and walked around the southern arc of the Crescent. As they turned into Museum Square, the Regency villa known as Wisbech Castle was in full view behind them. The villa was the fourth building to have occupied the site of William the Conqueror's castle and it continued to carry its predecessor's title, proudly celebrating the castle's long history.

Walking through St Peter's Garden past the church, they arrived at the car park and headed straight for the public loos, their prearranged meeting place with Bertle. They'd been there no more than a few seconds when his black Ford SUV swept in and hurtled to a stop in front of them.

'Afternoon,' said Bertle from the driving seat as they fastened their seat belts in the back. 'Have you met me lad, Alfred?'

The twelve year old Alfred, who occupied the front passenger seat, made no attempt to acknowledge their arrival, so Monica leaned forward, craning her neck between the front seats to greet him. He didn't appear to notice.

'The missus wanted to call him Kieran, but I thought nah, that's too arty for us Collinses, so we named him after me granddad, didn't we Alfred?'

As far as Monica and Archie could make out, the lad declined to reply. He didn't look much like an Alfred to Monica. The name made her think of an Edwardian in a tweed suit, smoking a pipe or consulting a fob watch. This Alfred wore a hoodie and a baseball cap, chewed gum and consulted his phone. The fact that it was plugged into both ears may have explained why he seemed unaware of everyone else on the planet.

The other three occupants of the car chatted idly as they made their way along the A47 towards King's Lynn and turned off towards Walpole Cross Keys. The drizzle was gradually strengthening into full blown rain, the sort that rattled on the car windows and necessitated the manic resistance of windscreen wipers.

'Nice day for it,' remarked Bertle. 'Your mate Bernadette coming?'

'I doubt it. She says it'll be a waste of time.'

'It probably will be', agreed Archie, 'but at least we'll get a feel for the place. And a lot of historians believe this was where the baggage train crossed from.'

'Yeah, well, it's their job like, to come up with daft ideas,' replied Bertle as they parked the car in a country lane behind Rex's Mercedes, 'but it don't mean they're right like.'

Rex Monday heaved himself out of the car in front. Pulling on a blue fisherman's hat, he grimaced at the rain and walked to Bertle's car. By the time he had pushed his head through the driver's open window, the grimace had morphed into a welcoming smile.

'Good afternoon, everyone. Really glad you could make it. The, ah, weather isn't being kind to us, but Mark thinks it will blow over in an hour. So, why don't we all eat our packed lunches in the cars and then venture out and see what's what?'

'Fine by me,' replied Archie. 'Can't wait to see what's what.'

Rex retreated to his Mercedes and Monica produced a stack of sandwiches in silver foil from her hessian carrier bag.

'Brought us all some,' she announced cheerfully, though spending a Sunday lunchtime in a rapidly steaming up car with Albert and Alfred Collins of 'Bert'll Crack It (Call Us Anytime for all your Plumbing, Handy-Man and Electrical Needs)' was hardly her idea of a great day out.

Especially since Bertle appeared to have brought the smelliest hard boiled eggs she'd ever been stuck in a car with. He politely declined her offer of a sandwich, proceeding instead to peel his eggs. Alfred was less choosy, snaking one podgy hand around the seat to claim one of her favourite prawn ones. His ear plugs obviously allowed him selective hearing. Handing the other prawn sandwich and a large bag of crisps to Archie, she munched on her cheese and pickle and tried not to notice the eggy pong that wafted like a malignant fog through the car.

Beside her, Archie grinned and opened a window. She was trying not to laugh.

After half an hour of this pleasant dining, the rain showed no sign of stopping. In fact, it was coming down even harder.

'Looks like the weather's cheering up,' claimed Archie. 'Let's have a walk down the lane, Monica.'

She was out of the car in an instant, zipping up her waterproof jacket and pulling up her hood. As they passed Rex's Mercedes, he gave them a jolly wave. Mark Appledore had fallen asleep behind the steering wheel of the car in front, but there was no sign of Bernadette, neither was there any sign of anyone else from the Wisbech Heritage Society. It was all a bit of a washout.

Archie didn't seem to care.

'It's hard to imagine this being the edge of the Wash,' he was saying as they gazed across the acres of cultivated fields. Drainage schemes had long since produced this good agricultural land from the marshy wilderness that remained after the estuary had silted up.

Monica and Archie had walked some distance along the country lane that led out of Walpole Cross Keys and were enjoying the silence that came with the rain. Elder bushes, which in May would be heavy with creamy floral clusters, now dripped bare and mournful at the roadside.

'Sutton Bridge, then, is over there,' remarked Monica, pointing into the distance across the fields.

'That's right. As Rex said, no village would have been there in King John's time because this whole area was under water. There wasn't even a road crossing what was once the estuary until the first bridge was built over the river in the 1830s. Before then, if a traveller heading for Lincolnshire didn't fancy going the long way round, through Wisbech, he had to ford the river. But once the bridge was constructed, travel became easier and Sutton Bridge came into being. Beyond that, of course, is Long Sutton. That was where in the old days, if you'd crossed the estuary here, you'd have ended up on the other side.'

'You know a lot for an incomer, don't you?'

'I've done my homework,' he smiled.

'But what you were all saying at the meeting must be right. A crossing from Walpole Cross Keys to Long Sutton would have been an extremely long one.'

'It would have taken hours,' he agreed, 'hours they didn't have. There would only have been so long before the tide changed.'

Monica slipped her hand in his. For a moment, all was peace and harmony. Things were good again between them. Archie's prolonged stay in Kenilworth seemed a long time ago.

Then, from back near the cars, came the sound of Bertle's voice.

'Right then, Alfred me boy, we'll start over 'ere. Side of the road, like.'

Engulfed in an oversized, yellow high viz jacket, Bertle had appeared at the roadside a hundred metres or so behind them and was shattering the peace with his enthusiasm. Alfred appeared to be making no response.

'Not on the field, not on the field, Mr Collins,' a panting Rex was calling as he ran to catch the father and son up. 'We don't have permission to go on the land...'

Monica and Archie stood and watched from a distance. It was clear that Bertle was taking no notice of Rex and that Alfred was taking no notice of either of them. Bertle was strapping the metal detector to his arm, fiddling with it a bit before beginning to make slow sweeps across the grass verge.

'Come on,' said Archie, 'let's leave them to it for a while. Let's walk a bit further.'

She smiled, linking arms with him and walking along the lane over ground which would once have been beneath the waters of the Wash. They watched the gulls wheeling and chattering above the quiet fields and soon the voices were left behind. As was the bleeping of Bertle's metal detector as it registered every beer can and bottle top tossed away in the last fifty years.

But their peace was not destined to last for long. They ignored the first hollering from the lane, but then there were footsteps, thudding and laboured on the tarmac behind them, and they were obliged to turn round.

Rex, his fisherman's hat askew and his face red from exertion, stood panting in the middle of the lane.

'Ah, much as I hate to interrupt you love birds, Mr Collins, ah, Bertle appears to have discovered something.'

'1970s Party Seven beer can?' asked Archie.

'Possibly, quite possibly, but that machine of his gave a tremendous bleep, I mean louder than all the minor bleeps, and he's digging a hole. Thought you might want to come and see.'

They returned to see Bertle toiling over his spade, piling wet, silty soil around the hole he was digging in the grass verge at the side of the lane. He was sweating profusely, his face patterned with dirt where he'd scratched his nose with muddy fingers. He was so hot that he'd had to remove the high viz jacket which was now held by Alfred. The boy had tucked the coat under one arm, leaving both hands free to rest in his pockets. His round, pimply face, framed by his hood and topped by his cap, was a picture of complete detachment and disinterest as he chewed on his gum. To be fair, though, he had left the phone and earplugs in the car.

'Think I can see sommat,' his father was saying.

Everyone except Alfred crowded round to peer into the hole. There was nothing obvious to see.

'Yep, there it is, soon 'ave that out and Bob'll be yer uncle, like.'

They could hardly wait.

TWENTY-FIVE

Tuesday 29th November 1216

All had been quiet for days on the manor of Wisbech Barton. It was unusual and felt too good to be true.

Rufus made his way down the steep spiral stairway in the keep. As he descended, he steadied himself with his left hand on the smooth stone of the central newel, his feet seeking the broadest part of each step. He had been summoned by the constable regarding a letter which had to be written and despatched immediately, and now his head was full of the instructions he'd been given. Letters of such high importance were normally written by the chaplain, but Rufus had noticed lately how often such tasks appeared on his desk. He supposed it was because of his work in Waltuna and Newton in the Isle.

No wonder Oswy and Egbert were making so many snide remarks about his great pride and big head.

Everyone at the castle was still talking about the news from Gloucester. The new king, nine year old Henry III, had been crowned in the abbey church there. A simple gold circlet, rather than a full crown, had been placed on his young head and very little of the usual royal regalia used on such occasions had been in evidence. Perhaps in the rest of the country this would be understood as being due to his youth; it would have been too much for the child to be weighed down with a full crown, orb and sceptre.

In Wisbech, however, it was seen very differently. Everyone there assumed that the new king's regalia was missing because it had been lost in the Wash.

Was that what King John had meant when he demanded that someone 'just find it'?

At the foot of the stairway, passages led off in two directions, both of them cut into the thickness of the walls. Rufus took the one leading to the Great Hall and the forebuilding. The passage was narrow and dark, lit at intervals by torches held in sconces. The passage, since it was cut into the massive wall of the keep, was entirely of stone, its ceiling smoothly arched like the inside of a barrel. The stone was cold even in the warmer months and in the bitterness of November the chill seemed to hover there, as if nurtured by the stone itself. Rufus was glad when he emerged into the lofty Great Hall and could make his exit via the forebuilding into the frosty open air of the bailey.

How long could this peace last, he wondered? With the seemingly endless conflict with the Welsh, and Prince Louis of France vying to take the English throne for himself, the country was in trouble. No wonder the barons were eager for a capable regent to be found, to guide the boy king.

The crown needed strong guidance, and word was that William Marshal, the Earl of Pembroke, would become regent. He it had been who had knighted the new king before his coronation and he appeared, by all accounts, to be the best man for the role. But who knew what really went on in those far away halls of power? News took so long to reach the Fens. For all they knew, the earl might already be regent.

And meanwhile, in the kitchens of Wisbech Castle, poor Eustace was still fretting about the peaches he had prepared for the king, terrified that someone was going to accuse him of murder. Regicide, actually. No wonder the poor lad was in such a state.

But whenever Eustace brought up the subject, which was often, and whenever anyone else reminded Rufus of all that might have been lost in the Wash, he told them the same thing; there was nothing to worry about.

After all, with the country under threat from foreign powers, who was going to worry about a few lost jewels or some raw peaches? And anyway, as he kept reminding everyone, there had been no sign of the seneschal for weeks. If there really was trouble in store, surely Sir Milo Fulk would have put in an appearance by now?

He had almost reached the office when the seneschal rode in through the gatehouse on his faithful palfrey Merlin.

TWENTY-SIX (Present Day)

An Appropriate Riposte

'What the devil was all that racket?' yelled Mark Appledore.

No one answered, but at least they had stopped shouting now. Mark's uncomfortable slumber behind the steering wheel of his battered Renault had been brought to an abrupt end by all the hollering and cheering. As he roused himself, he caught the stale whiff of his discarded fish and chip papers from his earlier lunch and hastily wound down the misted up window. Unfolding his long legs from their cramped position, he stared out through the rain. Outside, that lot from the Wisbech Heritage Society appeared to be getting excited about something down a hole. He supposed he should get out there and show some interest.

He joined them by the muddy hole Bertle Bodgit had dug in the grass. That dreadful boy was there too, chewing gum and looking vacant. There was also the pompous Rex Monday, Monica Kerridge and that bloke of hers. All of them, apart from the boy, appeared spellbound, waiting with baited breath as Bertle pushed his great fist into the mud and tugged at something.

''Ere we go, 'ave it in a mo and Bob'll be yer uncle, like.'

'Bertle, you've only dug down two feet. There's not likely to be anything of any...' Monica was making a token protest. There was no point. Best to let people like that get on with it.

The rain was coming down even more heavily now. Mark pulled his hood forward on his head, but couldn't stop the rain pelting his face.

'This is ridiculous,' complained Monica's bloke. 'Whatever it is...'

'Bob's yer uncle!' exclaimed Bertle Bodgit in triumph. ''Ave a look at that!'

Rex accepted the muddy lump from Bertle, turning it over distastefully in his bare hands and wiping away some of the dirt.

'It's, well, I'm sorry to say Bertle, it, ah, appears to be...'

'A key!' uttered Mark in disdain, 'it's an iron door key, possibly Victorian by the look of it. Oh, for...'

'Oh dear, yes,' agreed Rex as he stared with obvious disappointment at the large key lying in the palm of his hand. 'It would appear to be exactly that. I do hope no one's still looking for it.'

'Never mind, Bertle,' Monica was saying in that maddeningly kind way of hers. 'Better luck next time, eh? There are still places to look and we might have better weather next time.'

The rest were agreeing with her. Mark snorted.

'And for heaven's sake man,' he snapped, 'leave the verge the way you found it. Someone could turn their ankle in that hole!'

They watched as Mark retreated to his Renault. Bertle shrugged. Alfred blew a bubble with his gum. When it popped it sounded like an appropriate riposte.

'You're right, Monica mate,' stated Bertle philosophically as he began spading earth back into the hole. 'We've only just got started like. I can't wait to have a go in West Walton.'

Rex grunted something. Alfred blew an enormous bubble which burst over his nose.

TWENTY-SEVEN

Afternoon, Tuesday 29th November 1216

Rufus was filled with foreboding. The seneschal had come to the castle after all. Something really was wrong.

He kept an eye on Father Leofric and Sir Milo Fulk as they stood, frowning and talking in lowered tones by the office door. The other two clerks were watching too, though their interest was no more than idle curiosity. Perhaps they even hoped that something was afoot, to liven the place up a bit.

Rufus put his head down again and tried to work, but he couldn't block out the leaden monotone of the men's voices.

'Rufus of Tylneye,' came the seneschal's voice after a pause, 'a word please.'

He rose from his desk and accompanied them from the office, crossing the frosted bailey to the forebuilding. All the time his heart was pounding, his imagination working its way through all the potential horrors of the meeting to come.

The Great Hall was scarcely warmer than the bailey and the three men headed for the large open hearth set into the wall close to the dais. The fire was never very effective in heating the huge hall, the wide flue above it allowing too much heat to escape and letting in too much cold wind. The hall was unable to benefit from the more usual central fire arrangement of the times. With two storeys of chambers above it, there was no thatch for the smoke to seep through, and so the Great Hall's occupants were left to shiver before this huge fireplace and its crude chimney.

'I have just returned from Westminster,' began the seneschal immediately, hardly giving his companions time to settle themselves on the benches before the fire. 'I was summoned there by William Marshal, the Earl of Pembroke, who is to become regent for the young king. He is keen to settle all matters left unfinished by the king's late father. Of particular importance to the earl are King John's calamitous losses in the Wash.'

Of goods or men? Rufus refrained from voicing the question; he was sure he knew the answer anyway.

'It would appear,' continued Sir Milo, as if reading his thoughts, 'that although the great loss of life is much regretted, it is the loss of an item of material wealth which most worries the young king.'

Father Leofric coughed, his opinion of such callousness displayed clearly on his face.

'King John suffered enormous losses that day,' Milo went on. 'Only a few wagons, a score or so of men and a number of oxen and horses survived. It is understood that the wagons which reached the other side contained nothing more than basic supplies. Unfortunately, everything of real value was carried in the centre of the baggage train, where it could more easily be guarded. It would appear that King John had removed many of the crown's greatest treasures from safe keeping at castles such as Corfe in the south, and was keeping them close. Perhaps all the strife in the country made him consider such precautions necessary.'

'And his caution,' put in the chaplain, 'led to the very loss he feared.'

'Exactly,' said Milo with a rueful smile, 'and now the new king would like some of those lost things back.'

Rufus let out a groan.

'But the situation is not, perhaps, as bad as you fear,' continued the seneschal. 'Even the great men of Westminster know that most of what is lost will never be recovered. What hasn't been swept out to sea will be hidden beneath the mud by now. There is one item, however, which the new king is desirous of having returned to him. It was something greatly treasured by his father, something he has graciously requested my help in recovering.'

'Graciously requested?' queried the chaplain. 'By which he means...'

'By which he has commanded that, as Seneschal of the Isle of Ely, I concentrate my powers on finding this thing.'

'And what is this item?'

'It was described to me as a small golden casket set with precious stones. Though the casket itself is of great value, it contains a treasure of such importance that it reduces its container to a shadow in comparison. This treasure is so precious that its description could not be disclosed to me. We must therefore concentrate our search on the casket and hope that it still contains what it is meant to.'

Rufus did not like the word 'we' one bit. He had a terrible feeling about what was coming. Milo was looking at him.

'You, Rufus of Tylneye, benefit from clear thinking and have a keen eye for detail. I liked your work in Waltuna and Newton. Father Leofric has given his leave for you to help me in my search. First of all, I propose we go through the inventories you made of everyone and everything recovered from the mud. It could be that the item was there and we simply missed it. I think, though, that another trip to Waltuna and Newton will be necessary to give us any hope of recovering this treasure.'

Rufus bowed his head in reluctant agreement and made his way back to the office with a heavy heart. He was well aware that failure in a task such as this could bring painful consequences for everyone involved. He wanted no part in it.

And he kept asking himself whether he ought now to tell the seneschal what he thought he'd heard pass between the late king and his baron that night. Yet the more those words, 'Just find it', were replayed in his memory, the more he suspected he had imagined them.

And so he said nothing. Milo Fulk needed his sharp eye, not his wild imagination.

TWENTY-EIGHT (Present Day)

Ancient and Hard Wearing

'We really must decide on what we're doing for Christmas,' announced Monica.

She, Bernadette and Angie were having one of their rare meetings in the Poet's House office. One of the Smutties had jumped on to Monica's lap and she winced as his needle-like claws pierced her jeans in their search for a comfortable snoozing place.

'Are we decorating the place with traditional greenery again, you know, keeping things simple?' asked Angie.

She and Bernadette had come in specially for this Friday morning's meeting, normally working only when the house was open. Angie's job was to look after the catering side of things, while Bernadette took care of reception.

'Yes, we can still do that, keeping the decoration appropriate for a Georgian house, but we need to decide on the main theme. We need something different and special.'

The Smutty was continuing his spiral routine on Monica's lap, his small body vibrating with his purring.

'But I thought we'd already decided to go along with Archie's idea,' said Angie. 'You know, the coffee house.'

'We hadn't decided at all,' retorted Bernadette stiffly. 'It was just one option we were considering. I preferred the Georgian shop idea myself, with shelves of goods and...'

'Yes, that would have been good,' cut in Monica, 'but I think we've left it a bit late for something so ambitious. It's mid November already and we only have three weeks to prepare everything. Perhaps we could do that next year and start planning it a lot earlier.

'I do have to say I like the idea of a Georgian coffee house,' she continued, 'even though it was Archie's suggestion and he's not your favourite person. What I like about it is that we know there were several coffee houses in Wisbech in our poet Joshua's day and that he visited them regularly. Coffee houses played a significant role in Georgian male society, so creating one for Christmas, with silver coffee pots, porcelain coffee cups and tea bowls would be very fitting for this museum.'

'But where would we put it?' Bernadette's voice was still stiff and uncompromising.

'There's plenty of space in reception,' replied Monica, 'and it's not being used to best advantage at the moment. The end of the room farthest from the till could become the coffee house...'

'But that's where the gift shop is! We can hardly get rid of that. We need the income!'

'We wouldn't need to lose it, Bernie. Reception takes up a lot more space than it needs. The gift shop could be moved to that end of the room; there's plenty of space to the right of the desk. That would leave the other end of the room free. Most of the shelves are on wheeled units anyway, so moving the shop wouldn't be difficult and Bertle can deal with the two fixed shelves.'

'So that's it? You've already decided? Are there no other ideas? Why did you bother asking us if you'd already made up your mind?' Bernadette's voice had become petulant.

'Well, *are* there any other ideas?' asked Monica.

'Not really,' admitted Angie. 'It's either that or Mildred Winterbottom's offer to give poetry readings in the evenings, and she does drone on a bit.'

'That certainly settles it,' sighed Bernadette. 'Coffee house it is, then. I suppose we could make space for it where you said, perhaps buy a few antiques; a coffee pot, a few Georgian tea bowls...'

She still sounded reluctant, but already she was warming to the idea, her imagination beginning to take flight. 'But we'd have to serve the coffee and tea in reproduction cups. We could hardly use old ones for that. And how about little snacks on dainty plates? You know, I think our visitors might actually go for that! And we already have the perfect Georgian window at that end of the room. We could set out coffee pots and other bits on the window sill to attract more visitors...'

Monica smiled, caught Angie's eye, but noticed her uncertainty.

'Did you just say *serve* the tea and coffee?' Angie queried nervously. 'You mean it's going to be *real*? I thought the coffee house would just be for decoration! You mean I'd be serving refreshments in reception, instead of in the Garden Room over Christmas?'

'Well, no', Monica replied, 'I hadn't meant it to be a *working* coffee house, Bernie.'

'But it must be!' insisted Bernadette. She was becoming so keen on the idea that anyone would have thought it had been hers to start with. 'Don't you see? It would be a fantastic attraction! Visitors would see it from the street and it would draw in even more local people. A Georgian Coffee House in Wisbech! Perfect!'

'Well, it does sound a good idea,' admitted Monica, 'but it depends on Angie.'

'I'm not sure...'

'Is it the costume that's putting you off?' asked Bernadette with an innocent expression. 'Perhaps having to wear a mop cap and a long skirt isn't your idea of acceptable working conditions.'

'Costume? You mean I'd be serving refreshments in fancy dress?'

'Look, don't worry about it,' said Monica hastily. 'We'll think of something else...'

'No, don't do that,' cried Angie with astonishing alacrity. 'It's a great idea, especially the costume!'

Bernadette smiled. She'd known the dressing up part would do the trick. She'd remembered Angie's excitement a few years earlier when she'd been going through all her options for what to wear to a fancy dress party.

'Well that's excellent!' beamed Monica in surprise. 'And I've just thought. There's an old table in the attic we could use as a counter. If it's a bit scruffy we could sort it out with some polish.'

'And we'll need to bring the tables in from the Garden Room and cover them with something...' Angie added.

'Or just keep them bare and scrubbed clean, with a pewter candlestick on each one,' said Monica. 'We could use those little battery candles; they wouldn't look too bad. Luckily, those tables are like everything else in this building; ancient and hard wearing. They should scrub up perfectly!'

'So, we're giving this thing a go?' smiled Bernadette.

'Looks like it! I'll just need to confirm everything with the trustees and then we can get started. We can shop for the antiques and begin moving furniture.' Monica's mobile began to ring and she ignored it. 'We already have some New Hall and Worcester tea bowls from the right period, but we'll need a silver coffee pot and some other authentic pieces. And then we need to find a supply of decent looking reproduction cups.'

'I'll get on to that!' offered Bernadette.

'And I could make some traditional cakes and other treats. I just need to do some research...' added Angie.

'I'll help!' offered Bernadette. 'And we could have Georgian ices in little cups!'

'I'll phone the trustees straight away,' said Monica. 'Who knows? Our Coffee House might just be successful enough to continue into next season!'

Her phone, having rested briefly from its ringing, started again and she pulled it out of her pocket. She stared at the screen.

'Would you excuse me for a moment?'

She moved the sleeping Smutty gently from her knee on to a chair as she left the office. He looked distinctly put out. Angie and Bernadette could hear Monica in the hallway, muttering crossly into the phone. It wasn't hard to guess who had disturbed their meeting.

'Do you think it'll work?' Angie asked.

'If you mean the Coffee House,' replied Bernadette, 'yes, I think it will. I'm not so sure about anything else.'

TWENTY-NINE

Late Afternoon, Tuesday 29th November 1216

Sir Milo Fulk unrolled the long scroll of parchment and ran his eye down the list set out in Rufus' tiny, neat script. He frowned as he read.

Entry after entry listed broken, mundane objects, all recovered from the tidal mud and no longer of use to anyone. Drenched linen goods, swollen sacks of grain and illegible manuscripts represented the greatest proportion of the items listed. Among them were just a few entries which aroused Milo's curiosity. A jewelled dagger and a golden brooch had been found in a small, iron bound chest recovered in Newton. There had also been a purse containing a few silver pennies which came to light in Waltuna, but there was nothing even faintly resembling a golden casket.

Rufus knew this already. He had written the list out enough times, in order to supply copies for the constable, the bishop, even for the king himself, to know exactly what was written there.

'And so we must endeavour to find this thing,' stated Milo with an air of resignation. 'Be ready and waiting in the bailey at first light tomorrow. The constable will accompany us this time and we'll take two men-at-arms. We shall begin in Newton in the Isle, then cross to Waltuna at low tide in the early afternoon. After that, where we go will depend on what we discover, so come well prepared Rufus. We may well be gone for several days.'

'And if we fail to find this casket?'

The seneschal did not reply.

THIRTY (Present Day)

So Much for That

She had known as soon as her phone began to ring that Archie had gone away once more.

He had gone to stay at Aunt Lizzie's house again. There was, apparently, a worrying lack of interest in the Kenilworth property, and the estate agent had advised them to clear out some of the furniture. The house was too cluttered, making it look smaller and more cramped than it really was. And so, of course, Archie had been called into action, to help with the removal of the offending items.

He had no idea how long he would stay. He'd left immediately after phoning her that Friday morning and had called once at the weekend. At least that was a small improvement on last time's total lack of communication.

He had told her that he and Jemima were making progress and were managing to clear some space in the house. It had been an odd phone call; he'd sounded detached and devoid of humour, as if someone were hovering, listening in the background. He'd seemed like a stranger.

And now it was Monday morning and he was still away, using up more of his annual leave from work, leave that the pair of them had been planning to use for a holiday. So much for that now.

Monica was alone in the silent museum, standing in reception and working out how best to use the available space to create their Coffee House. On Friday, she had phoned Justin Loveridge, one of the museum's trustees, and he'd sounded enthusiastic about the new project. It was, after all, such a good idea; a Georgian Coffee House in a Georgian museum dedicated to a Georgian poet.

Experimentally, she tried pushing one of the wheeled shelving units. It flowed easily, moving without a squeak as she transferred it from the gift shop end of the room to the empty space near the reception desk.

It was always best to stay occupied when too many uncomfortable thoughts crowded her brain. She was losing Archie. Despite all he said, she knew it. The last few weeks had been fairly happy, but he'd seemed preoccupied a lot of the time. He'd said all the right things, paid her plenty of attention, and yet...

She moved the second shelving unit, this time parking it to the right of the entrance door. She stood back to look at the effect and was satisfied. It made perfect sense to have gifts on display close to the till. All she needed now was for the shop table to be moved and the fixed shelves unscrewed from the wall and moved to the other end. That could be done when Bertle arrived later.

When the door bell rang she answered it readily, assuming that her handyman friend had arrived early.

'Ah!' exclaimed Rex Monday, who was wearing his most affable expression. 'Hope this isn't a bad time and all that, but I wondered if I might have a quick word... perhaps *request* might be a more accurate, ah, way of putting it...'

Considering that he had already squeezed his thickset form through the half open door, the possibility of this being a bad time was clearly not of real concern to him.

Monica resigned herself to half an hour of Rex's company, smiling faintly by way of greeting since she couldn't get a word in edgeways anyway.

'I understand you have plans for your kitchen in the basement and I wondered whether I might...'

He was already half way through reception and making for the small door in the back hallway which led down to the cellars. She shrugged and followed. At least this was a diversion for her thoughts.

At the bottom of the stairs they turned left, pulled on the light cord and made their way between stacks of piled up rubbish.

'It's a bit of a mess down here,' Monica began. 'We're in the middle of...'

'Ah, just as I thought!'

'What is?'

'Excellent! Even with your big old kitchen table in the centre of the room, you'll still have plenty of room for the model.'

'The model?'

'Indeed! The model of King John's Wisbech! Some of the members are very keen on making one, you see. I've had a good ring round this morning and quite a few of them, ah, Mrs Cross and a few other ladies in particular, are keen to make a model of Wisbech in 1216 as part of our current project. I do apologise, my dear, you didn't know. I quite forgot! I must announce it at our meeting on Thursday. All are welcome to join in with the model making, of course.

All we'll then need is somewhere to display the, ah, finished article and I thought immediately of your new kitchen project and how you were bound to have plenty of space...'

'But Rex,' she managed to say, 'this is a museum dedicated to Joshua Ambrose, the Georgian poet who lived in this house. It is not a general museum...'

'That's irrelevant,' interrupted Rex dismissively. 'Just think! The plot on which this house was built lies on the bank of the old Wysbeck River. Long ago, there would have been something very different here, perhaps a peasant's hovel, a workshop, a forge... even a dung pile! Who knows? So this museum's ancient history should also be taken into account and it wouldn't...'

'Rex, stop it! My plans to open this house's Georgian kitchen do *not* involve displaying a model of King John's Wisbech!'

'The cellar next door then,' he went on undeterred, scarcely blinking an eyelid. 'What was it? An old wine cellar? You could have it cleaned up, give it a lick of paint...'

'Rex!'

He was silenced at last, but not for long. Half way back up the stairs he started again with his monologue and was still going strong when they reached the door.

'Look,' she conceded, 'I'll have a word with the trustees, just to see if there's any way we can house your model.'

That would fix it, she thought. They would say no and that would be the end of it.

'Excellent. I'm sure they'll see sense. See you on Thursday then! Our meeting this week is all about Walsoken. I'll arrive early to help set up.'

'Yes,' muttered Monica as she watched him walk out on to Nene Quay, 'I bet you will.'

THIRTY-ONE

The Feast of St Andrew, Wednesday 30th November 1216

It was still dark as they set off, torches still lighting the passage beneath the gatehouse. Rufus was grateful for being able to borrow Arnulf again, the good natured rouncey he'd ridden to Waltuna and Newton before, and he gave the horse's neck a gentle pat as they crossed the drawbridge.

There were five riders in the party this time. Sir Hugo de Wenton the constable and Sir Milo Fulk the seneschal rode in front, followed by Rufus, then the two men-at-arms, who went by the names of Drew and Abrecan, at the rear. The soldiers' presence was a sober reminder that their task this time was more than investigation and record-keeping. Their orders now came from the new king, orders which to Rufus made no sense at all. They were going in search of something apparently so precious that its identity was hidden even from them.

As they passed the fields of Sandyland on their way out of town, the sky began to lighten. The morning was chilly but wind still and the sails of the monstrous windmill were motionless. Rufus glanced up at the mill's narrow windows just as the shutters were being folded back. A man with a large, round head, his dark, greasy hair not yet covered with its usual linen cap, peered out and waved cheerfully. Sir Hugo lifted his head and bade the miller a good morning.

Rufus was glad that Giles of Ely was not in their party this time. His haste to declare a matter finished, whether or not it truly was, may have pleased his superiors who received his efficient-looking reports, but his dismissive attitude was irritating and unhelpful to those who had to work with him. The constable, Hugo de Wenton, was a far more reasonable and affable character and it seemed to Rufus that the seneschal also preferred his company, chatting amiably to him as they rode along.

The road along the top of the sea bank was busy that morning. They overtook a considerable number of travellers on foot and met a good many folk who were on their way into town. Some were on horseback, others pushing handcarts laden with sacks of grain, heading for the mill.

The village of Newton in the Isle was vibrant with noise and activity in the fresh morning air. Children squealed as they played in the alleyways between the houses and women chatted as they spread out linen to dry on bushes and the branches of trees. Hens clucked busily behind a patched-up fence and the sights and sounds of industry came from everywhere; the blacksmith in his forge, the carpenter in his workshop and the baker who carried a tray of freshly baked loaves towards the church. This was village life returned to normal, a welcome change from the unnatural quiet that had filled the place the last time the seneschal had visited.

As before, Father Dunstan came out to greet them. He wore the same welcoming smile, but there was wariness too in his look. He had probably hoped to have heard the last of the baggage train and all its misery.

'There are further questions I must ask the villagers,' Milo explained to the priest after the usual greetings had been exchanged. A couple of grooms came from the stables near the church and led the newcomers' horses away.

'But you'll need to eat first,' stated the priest. However reluctant the man may have been to see them, his natural sense of hospitality had not deserted him. They were taken to the same house in the centre of the village where they had enjoyed such excellent pottage before and Rufus' mouth watered at the memory of it. This time, however they were too early for dinner and were brought instead a dish of oatcakes to go with their ale. Rufus ate his share hungrily, mopping up the crumbs with his fingers and thanking the smiling goodwife with obvious sincerity.

Once back outside, the seneschal and constable began their questioning with Father Dunstan. He had very little to add to what he had told them before.

'We sent all the goods recovered from the estuary to Westminster on your orders, my lord,' he confirmed, 'but you saw what poor things they were. I suspect the young king will feel no pleasure in receiving them.'

Milo nodded.

'I must speak to the villagers. Is all the autumn ploughing finished now? The winter rye sown? Are the peasants back from the fields?'

'Indeed, sir. The villeins and cottagers will be working on their own patches of land or can be found in their dwellings. It may benefit you to begin with the blacksmith, however. There's little that goes on here that he doesn't know about.'

Milo turned towards the forge at the western end of the churchyard and told Rufus to accompany him.

'And I'll take the men-at-arms and start questioning the cottagers,' said Sir Hugo. With Drew and Abrecan he set off towards the cultivated strips of land on the outskirts of the village.

The blacksmith did not take kindly to being interrupted and didn't mind showing it. The seneschal's first question hung in the air unanswered as the man continued his work at the anvil, hammering a length of red hot iron. Sweat ran down his face as he laboured, his huge muscles flexing beneath his rough linen shirt and leather apron. He muttered something foul tempered as he went on beating the iron, working it until it was ready to be shaped.

Milo and Rufus waited, the seneschal watching with building impatience as the glowing red iron was transformed into a horseshoe. Rufus didn't mind waiting, however, never having grown tired of watching smiths at work. There was something magical about the transformation of a simple lump of iron ore into a useful item.

Because this was a rural area, the Newton blacksmith spent most of his time in the production of farm implements and horseshoes; the tools of the countryside. It was quite different from the castle forge, which was kept busy with a constant demand for weaponry. There was another obvious difference too; the castle smith was a friendly soul who never minded an audience, quite unlike this surly individual.

The seneschal repeated his question and still he was obliged to wait, his impatience turning to thinly disguised anger. The blacksmith continued to ignore him until at last he was satisfied with the finished horseshoe. Before he began to work on the next, he turned with bad grace towards his visitors and grunted his bad tempered response.

No, he had seen nothing of any goods of any description which may or may not have come from the king's baggage train. He had no interest in such frippery. His workload was heavy and he cared only about delivering his finished goods on time. This morning he had yet to produce four dozen horseshoes before starting on an order for knives, spades and shovels.

This information duly given, the smith turned his back on his callers and started to work on the next horseshoe. It was clear that nothing more could be learned from him.

'So much for him knowing everything that goes on around here,' muttered the seneschal as they left the smithy.

'Perhaps he does,' replied Rufus. 'Perhaps there really was nothing to say.'

The carpenter, baker, cooper and fuller were more cheerful individuals, but their lack of knowledge of goods from the baggage train was equally apparent.

Hugo, on his return with Drew and Abrecan, reported a similar lack of success from speaking to the cottagers and villeins. Women feeding pigs and chickens, kneading dough or brewing ale, men hoeing strips of land or repairing tools ready for spring, had all been questioned. A search of their homes had added to the certainty that they were hiding nothing.

'Hopeless,' admitted Hugo, 'but I have noticed one thing. My deputy Sir Giles told me that in Waltuna you came across reports of rough handling by the Baron de Prys and his men. Here, there has been no mention of the baron, or of anyone else coming to question the villagers.'

'You are right,' agreed Milo. 'It appears that the baron's activities were concentrated in Waltuna. For some reason, they never crossed to this side of the Wash.'

'They must have discovered something which made coming here unnecessary,' replied Hugo. 'And right from the start, it seemed their agenda was different to ours.'

Rufus swallowed hard, knowing that he had to speak, that for too long he had avoided mentioning what he'd overheard after the feast. He had almost convinced himself that he'd misheard or imagined those three small words, but he knew now that he'd made a serious error. He should have told Sir Milo immediately.

'I think it is,' he ventured nervously.

'What?' Milo asked without much interest.

'I believe the baron's agenda is different to yours, sir. Just after the feast held in the king's honour, I overheard his grace speaking to my lord de Prys. I cannot be sure of his exact words, but it sounded like 'just find it'...'

He realised that both men were staring at him. There was a horrible silence that went on for far too long.

'What's wrong with you boy?' growled the constable at last. 'You've kept that to yourself all this time? Even when you were told to list goods as well as men? Did it not occur to you that you were keeping back important information? In future you will tell us everything you see, hear, even suspect. Do you understand?'

Rufus uttered a miserable apology and bowed his head. Milo remained quiet, reassessing the situation.

'So now we know that the baron was seeking something in particular and that he had direct orders from the king,' he said after a pause.

'The golden casket, of course,' added Hugo.

'I presume so. It looks like he was searching for it right from the start and for some reason never looked in Newton in the Isle. He must, however, have failed so far in his search because I have now been called in on an official basis.'

'Now that the trail is cold,' said Hugo angrily, 'now that you stand even less chance than de Prys of finding it.'

'Maybe,' agreed Milo, 'but secrets do not always come to light through rough handling. And we've hardly made a start yet.'

THIRTY-TWO (Present Day)

Cobwebbed

She couldn't believe it. Justin Loveridge the trustee had agreed to Rex Monday's presumptuous idea of putting a model of thirteenth century Wisbech in her Georgian museum!

She'd fully expected Justin to turn down Rex's request, that she'd be able to tell Mr Monday to put his model somewhere else. Yet the trustee had said yes. He'd even been enthusiastic about the idea! Apparently, he'd been racking his brains over what to do with that filthy old wine cellar in time for the start of the new season.

He did have a point. All visitors, as they reached the bottom of the steps on the way to the newly presented kitchen, would have a clear view into the cellar. At the very least, Monica was going to have to tidy up the creepy and cobwebbed room. Otherwise, most of the visitors would take one look and bolt back upstairs.

Justin had come up with a condition, though. He had suggested that, if the Wisbech Heritage Society wanted to use the cellar, they should help to make it ready and pay for the work involved. It would involve a fair amount of labour. Two hundred years before, when the Georgian poet's family had lived in the house and made their fortune as merchants, the cellar had been used to store wine barrels. Ever since then, it had been left to deteriorate.

Monica quite approved of this condition of Justin's. Rex would have to make sure that the society helped with the work and covered the cost. As a result, another room would be opened to visitors without cost to the museum. Justin was craftier than she'd given him credit for.

She ought to be feeling far more positive about the whole thing, but she just couldn't raise the energy. And, as usual, this apathy was Archie-related. Despite all that had been said last time, his communication from Kenilworth had once more faded to nothing. His phone was switched off again.

It was Tuesday now and he'd been away for four days. How long did it take to remove a few boxes and bits of furniture? As the long hours of each day dragged by without contact from him, her heart sank a bit further.

With a deep sigh she picked up the phone to give Rex the good news. She could have done with some herself.

THIRTY-THREE

Afternoon, Wednesday 30th November 1216

It was hard to decide which was the greater peril; crossing the estuary again at low tide or sampling more of the Lamb Inn's culinary offerings.

Rufus was ravenous by the time they reached the inn in Waltuna, but as the mean, gruel-like pottage was slopped into his bowl he could have sworn it was thinner than before. It appeared to consist of nothing more than a few root vegetables stewed to death. At least the bread was fresh this time, but it was of the roughest quality, made of rye flour and a touch of ground acorn, if Rufus were not deceived. And he rarely was, where his stomach was concerned. Despite its indifferent quality, he broke off a piece of bread and wrapped it with a bit of hard cheese in a cloth inside his scrip, to save for later. He knew he would be hungry again before long.

They were not there just to eat though. Between mouthfuls of flavourless swill, Milo began to question the innkeeper. The man didn't appear to mind the interrogation, but gave little away, shaking his head as if trying to recall some distant memory. There'd been the odd rumour, he said, about interesting items showing up where they shouldn't, but he'd heard nothing of any substance.

'Come on,' urged Milo. 'As innkeeper you must have heard plenty. Men talk when in their cups.'

'Alas, that's not always true, my lords,' the man replied with a dismal shake of the head. 'Folk know when to stay tight lipped. If anyone knows anything worth telling, it'll be the priest. You could try the blacksmith, too.'

'Well, it's a refreshing change from Newton,' muttered Milo drily as they left the Lamb. 'There, it's the smith who's supposed to know everything. Here, it's the priest *and* the smith.'

'Perhaps the innkeeper's telling the truth, though,' said Rufus. 'His ale is so weak that, even if they stayed and drank all night, no one would ever be drunk enough to spill their secrets.'

The men-at-arms, Drew and Abrecan, were sitting on a bench against the back wall of the inn, having seen to the stabling of Arnulf, Milo's palfrey Merlin and the other three horses. The men were chomping their way through more of the inn's miserable fare, chunks of rough bread and iron-hard cheese swilled down with ale so weak it looked like it had come straight from the estuary. Milo left them to eat. They would be needed later when the village was searched.

There was no problem in finding Father Anselm. He was returning to the church from the salterns on the edge of the village. Some of the labourers had fallen sick there, a situation which was far from unusual. Their work, tending the fires beneath the giant trays used to evaporate brine to produce salt, was hard and their days were long. The unhealthy, smoky conditions they laboured under often resulted in breathing difficulties.

'Good day to you, my lords!' called the priest with a welcoming smile. 'How may I be of service today?'

Milo explained briefly that certain items belonging to the king needed to be recovered.

'In relation to the recent disaster and the drowning of men, I assume,' said Father Anselm, no longer smiling and reminding them once more of the true nature of the catastrophe.

'You are quite right, father,' replied Milo, his voice expressionless. 'King John suffered other losses that day and our new king is keen to recover certain items.'

'So I was led to believe from my lord de Prys. You are aware that the baron and his men paid us another visit the day after you had taken your leave?'

Milo's stony expression told him that he'd not been in the least aware. The baron, having departed from Wisbech with King John on the morning following the disaster, must have left his side soon afterwards, presumably with the king's blessing to continue his search.

'I assured the baron that everything recovered from the estuary had been sent to Westminster on your orders,' continued Father Anselm, 'but my lord de Prys was far from satisfied. He questioned the villagers again and used the kind of force we are coming to expect from him.'

'Did he question anyone in particular?'

'Many suffered his rough treatment. The knight Edward of Hagebeche was with him again. There was a young red haired fellow too. He must be of some standing, though I never heard his name. He was one of the worst; very handy with his fists.'

Milo frowned, but made no comment.

'You must know who they concentrated their efforts on, though, father,' insisted Hugo.

'Some of the knowledge I have came to me through confession and I am not at liberty to share it with you, my lords, but there is nothing to stop me telling you that the redhead gave the blacksmith a particularly hard time. You may wish to enquire how his mouth is healing after losing several of his teeth.'

The forge was larger than the one in Newton in the Isle, its double doors thrown open to the elements. The weak sun, breaking through the clouds for a fleeting moment, lent the place a cheerful look. It was a veritable hub of industry. Finished items were stacked against the doors; crates of horseshoes, spades and hoes, all of which were being loaded on to a cart by a short and stout yet muscular man.

He turned as they approached and threw them a wary look. His face was still marked with partly healed cuts and yellow from fading bruises. The beating he had suffered over a month ago must have left the man in considerable discomfort.

'A fair morning for your work!' the seneschal hailed him.

'So far,' the smith agreed cautiously. 'I'm hoping to deliver everything and be back before the rain comes.'

'Your injuries can't have helped your labours. My lord de Prys' men have heavy hands, I hear.'

The blacksmith groaned.

'He gave me his word.'

'If so, to my knowledge he has not broken it. Come on fellow, the whole village knows what happened to you. I suggest you tell me everything.'

The man's shoulders slumped. He heaved a bundle of farm implements and a box containing a solid looking door lock and key on to the cart before leading the three men indoors.

'He told me that if I handed over what I'd found, the law need not hear of it. Now, I suppose...'

'Just tell me everything. What did you find?'

The man gave a long sigh and perched himself on the end of a bench.

'It was after all the dead men, God rest them, had been brought up from the estuary. You, my lords, had departed for Newton and the burials were taking place. It had been a long day and I left the forge to take a walk along the sea bank to clear my head. The search for bodies and goods had stopped by then, the tide having turned, but I caught sight of something caught at the water's edge. I know the banks well, know where to tread and where not, and that place was well covered in shrubs. Something was caught up in their branches. I knew it wouldn't be long before the water rose enough to cover the bushes and whatever was there would be washed away. I managed to go down and retrieve it. It was heavier than I expected. It was the broken corner of a wooden chest and tucked inside was something wrapped in cloth. Good quality linen, it was, not the home-spun kind you see around here, so I brought it home and unwrapped it and...'

'Well?'

'Fine things, I knew that. Nothing I could ever fashion in my forge, though I've turned my hand to some pretty things in my time. No, my lords, this...' The man seemed to have forgotten his reluctance to speak, immersed in the memory of his discovery, and he smiled to himself, displaying the gaps in his teeth that would be a permanent reminder of his encounter with the baron's men. 'This was fine goldsmiths' work. Jewellers' work. There were two daggers with jewelled hilts. There were a few smaller, pretty things too, some individual stones and a pendant with great jewels in it. There was an elaborate buckle also and three golden rings with stones as big as robins' eggs, oh, and a box...'

'A box?' cut in Rufus, not able to stop himself. The seneschal sent him a warning glance.

'You too?' laughed the smith bitterly. 'I describe great treasures and all you want to know about is the box. So did my lord de Prys. But that was after his men had exercised their fists on me...'

'Just describe the box,' persisted Milo, his voice low and stern.

'It was of gold. Gold so pure it was like liquid sun, and studded with precious stones of every colour and shape imaginable. It was a small thing, though, no bigger than my fist.' He held out one huge, calloused hand and made a fist thoughtfully.

'Did you look inside?'

'No, my lord, it was locked, its key lost to the waves, but if you shook it you could tell there was something inside.'

The constable exhaled loudly but let Milo continue.

'And the baron took it?'

'No my lord, he was too late. The box had gone by then. The night before his visit, just after I'd found the treasure and closed the forge to have a proper look at my discoveries, two strangers came knocking. Youngsters, they were. Looked harmless enough, though thin and in need of a good meal. One of them said he needed his knife repairing. The blade was damaged and he needed it for hunting, he said. I took pity on them and let them in, but they took me for a fool. They'd seen me out on the sea bank and wanted to know what I'd found.

'It was all right at first; I was just concentrating on the job. I had to use the bellows on the furnace to get it back up to heat and I noticed the boys were eying up the place. The repair was simple, but it took time and one of them started walking around the smithy. I could tell they'd been in the Lamb, could smell the ale on them. They were probably in there when they thought up their tale about the damaged knife, as a way to get in here and snoop around. Well, it was worth their while; they found my treasure, didn't they?

'They found the cloth containing my treasure. Kept leering at me, they did, reminding me to take care when holding on to things belonging to the crown. I told them I had no intention of keeping the treasure, that I was going to hand it all to you, my lord seneschal.'

He glanced at Milo, shame-faced. 'In truth, I hadn't really decided what to do. I told them to get out, told them I'd report them to you, my lord. I thought I saw them put everything back in the cloth, but they were clever. They didn't argue, just paid for the work and left, which made me suspicious. Way too slippery, the pair of them, and too smart for me. It was only after they'd gone that I realised the cloth was much lighter than before.'

'They stole...'

'They took the golden box, my lord, as well as a few smaller things.'

There was a brief silence, heavy and angry.

'It would be asking too much, I suppose, for any knowledge of where this pair was heading from here?' The seneschal's voice was hard, threatening.

'Do you think I gave up my teeth willingly? The boys told me nothing, my lord, but the baron believed me no more than you do, when he came calling the next day. He let his men free with their fists before yelling more of his questions and in the end...'

'In the end?'

'They departed for the Lamb, but not before they'd taken the rest of my treasure. The baron said it would go to the king and that since I'd handed it over willingly there'd be no more said about it. I might even be spared a hanging.'

'So they went to the inn,' Hugo concluded.

'Yes, I'd told them that the youngsters had been drinking in there. I suppose the baron thought the innkeeper might have heard where the lads came from or where they were travelling to.'

As the baron and his men had done before them, Milo, Hugo and Rufus left the blacksmith and walked once more towards the Lamb.

'My lord de Prys assumes the right to threaten hanging in order to get what he wants,' Hugo remarked as they walked.

'It's a method he makes a habit of,' added Milo. 'I find myself wondering how much of the treasure he took from the smith actually reached the king. His actions do not fill me with trust.'

'And what terrible luck,' muttered Rufus. 'The one item we've been sent to recover is the one that was stolen.'

'Thank of it another way,' added Milo with surprising cheerfulness. 'It's the only item of any substance not yet in the baron's hands.'

As far as we know, thought Rufus.

THIRTY-FOUR (Present Day)

Codswallop

'Well, everyone, we've looked at the, ah, Walpole Cross Keys to Long Sutton crossing over the estuary and I think we're all in agreement, ah, about that. It would have been too long, not to mention impractical.'

Rex's delivery was even slower and more ponderous than usual that evening. Bernadette was fidgeting on her hard chair. She wished he'd get on with it. She'd forgotten to fill the coffee machine again and was waiting for a suitable pause to sneak out and do it.

'So, we must ask ourselves, if the baggage train didn't take that route, which one *did* it take?'

He glanced hopefully at his small audience but received no response. The weather that Thursday evening was dreadful. Even above Rex's stentorian tones, the rain could be heard rattling on the old glass of the windows. Quite a few people were missing. Even Ena Cross, who usually looked forward to the meetings, if only for the biscuits, had phoned to say she'd be staying in to watch a repeat of Dad's Army on TV.

November was almost at an end and preparations for Christmas were going well. The small tea room tables had been moved into their new Coffee House setting, squeezing tonight's meeting into a much smaller space than before. It hardly mattered. The seats were only half occupied anyway.

'Well,' continued Rex, 'another theoretical route was between Walsoken and, ah, Leverington. Now, when one considers such a crossing, one immediately thinks...'

'That it's absolute balderdash!' drawled Mark Appledore. 'If the baggage train crossed the estuary so close to Wisbech, it might as well have trailed through the town itself and saved everybody a lot of bother.'

'Ah, some might argue the impracticalities of taking a mile-long train of ox wagons through a small town.'

'Not exactly a breeze to take it across a muddy estuary either,' Mark persisted.

Monica had stopped listening. She was too aware of Archie sitting next to her and apparently paying rapt attention to all that was being said. She was still furious about his lack of communication while he was away in the Midlands.

Even more annoyingly, he knew she was angry and seemed not in the least bit bothered by it. He had turned up for the meeting tonight in his pea green fleece as usual, wearing a bright smile and hugging her as if everything were normal. He had talked about his day at work, going on about the golf club members' complaints about the reshaping of the ninth hole, and hadn't even noticed the incredulous look on her face.

Anyone would have thought that Tuesday night's argument had never happened.

On his return at last from Kenilworth, he'd come straight to her flat. It had been around eight in the evening by then and she'd long since given up on seeing him that day. He'd never switched his phone back on, so she'd had no idea of when to expect him back. Yet, in he had strolled without the slightest hint of apology. Unless, that was, you counted the bunch of drooping chrysanthemums he'd picked up from the filling station and presented to her like a puppy with a stick.

She'd hoped for better than that. An apology might have worked, but there was none forthcoming. Instead, those fading flowers sparked all the pent up misery, worry and frustration from the previous four days into a veritable explosion.

She couldn't remember everything she'd said, but knew none of it had been nice. The neighbours could probably give her chapter and verse if she asked them; her voice had been loud enough.

After that, she hadn't expected to see him again. She hadn't exactly spelled out that everything was over between them, but she may as well have done. He had simply left, looking hurt and a little clueless as to why his four days of absence without communication had been a problem.

But had it just been that? Would she have minded so much if there had been no Jemima in the picture? The woman's name had never been mentioned during their argument. Even in her anger, Monica had managed to preserve a tiny speck of dignity.

Yet tonight, just two days later, in he had walked as if nothing had happened. And here he was, listening avidly to Rex, his arm uncomfortably close to hers and occasionally brushing against it whenever he scratched his nose.

'And what's more,' an eager looking volunteer from the Wisbech and Fenland Museum was pointing out, 'the crossing from Walsoken to Leverington would have been very short. The baggage train would probably have been longer than the crossing!'

Bernadette left her seat and hurried out to make the coffee.

'Precisely!' agreed Mark. 'And how could they have suffered such losses over such a short crossing? Even if the wagons in the middle were swept away, those at the front and back would probably have been safe on solid ground. It's total codswallop!'

'Well,' beamed Rex, 'I see we are still singing from the same, ah, hymn sheet, so to speak. Now, before our coffee break, I have a rather pleasing announcement to make. A few of you have expressed an interest in creating a model of Wisbech in 1216. Following a chat with our delightful hostess Monica, I am happy to confirm that we now have a room in this museum in which to display our model!'

There were a few enthusiastic sounding murmurs. Monica did her best to look keen and benevolent.

'Just one small thing,' continued Rex, 'this museum, like many others, runs on a tight budget and relies greatly on visitor numbers and donations etcetera. Therefore, we have been asked, not unreasonably I hasten to add, to raise a small sum to meet the cost of making the designated room fit for purpose.'

'Which room?' asked Sally Leaming from the bank.

'Excellent question, Sally. There's an unused wine cellar, practically beneath our feet, which could be made ready with a good clean and a lick of paint. I propose that we lend our hands to cleaning the room in the new year and raise the necessary funds between us. Could you please put your minds to that, dear people?'

There were a few nodding heads.

'Count me in with the cleaning,' called out a lady at the back.

'Thank you, my dear. I am also led to believe that Albert Collins, ah, Bertle, is keen to help. He's unable to join us tonight due to a rather nasty cold.'

'And an aversion to Rex's waffle,' whispered Archie. Despite her crossness, Monica couldn't help smiling.

'So I suggest that, starting in the new year, we divide our meetings into two parts. The first half will be dedicated to our discussions about King John's baggage train and, after coffee the second part could be devoted to work on the model. Agreed?'

The general muttered response sounded more or less positive.

'So that brings us to the subject of our Christmas luncheon on the fourteenth of December. I think we should patronise an establishment worthy of our new society. Perhaps we could all put our thinking caps on and decide where we should go, so that I can book it.'

Everyone was already scraping back their chairs, deciding it was time for a break.

'Back in twenty minutes after coffee, everyone!' Rex shouted above the din. 'Mildred has more of her excellent slides, but before we move on, are we in agreement about the Walsoken to Leverington crossing? Should we dismiss it as unlikely?'

Dismiss it? Monica hadn't even given it a thought. She had hardly listened to a word all evening.

THIRTY-FIVE

Late Afternoon, Wednesday 30th November 1216

The innkeeper scowled as the seneschal, constable and clerk walked back into the Lamb. He had finished his daily cleaning and the grey rag he had been using to wipe down the benches now dripped despondently from the rim of a battered wooden bucket.

'You failed to mention earlier your conversation with the two strangers who came here before stealing from the smith.' The seneschal's voice was harsh.

'But my lord,' protested the innkeeper with an innocent look, 'you asked if I'd heard anything about items showing up in the village, not whether...'

'I also asked if you'd overheard anything from your customers which might help our search. You made no mention of the two strangers.'

'Well, now I come to think of it, my lord de Prys was interested in that too...'

'And what did you tell him?'

'I don't remember exactly; it was all weeks ago. It was the day when the bodies were brought up from the water; a grim day. It was close to dusk when the lads came, said they were passing through. I do remember thinking that was a bit of a story because no one passes through here. It's a dead end, unless you want to cross the water, and that costs money. They didn't look like they had much. One of them mentioned the abbey, but there was nothing unusual about that. So much of the land around here belongs to my lord bishop in Ely, as we all know. If the baron hadn't been so keen to hear about the two boys, I would have forgotten all about them. Now, then, more ale, sirs? The goodwife brews a good strong ale which might please you...'

Pity you didn't serve it more often, thought Rufus.

'Please continue,' growled the constable. 'One of them mentioned the abbey. Then what?'

'Nothing much. The other one was going on about the hallow or hallows, something like that, but the goodwife had brought in a batch of new bread and I was unwrapping it, so I didn't take much notice.'

'The hallow?'

'Yes, my lord, I think it was that. That's what I told the baron, and one of his men seemed to understand something from it. Hair like yours, he had,' the innkeeper added, looking at Rufus. 'Fiery red, quite like yours, if I may say so. He said something to the baron and they looked satisfied with what I'd told them. I was just glad when they'd gone and left me in peace.'

'Is that all you told the baron?' asked Hugo.

'Yes, my lord. There was no more I could say about the strangers. I hadn't taken much notice of them. How was I to know they were going to steal from the smith?'

They left him sitting on one of his benches, staring miserably at the stale, matted rushes on the floor.

Milo sent his two men-at-arms to search the village and the salterns on the outskirts. They had orders to search thoroughly, but to avoid the heavy tactics employed by de Prys' men. There was little hope that anything would be found; the baron would already have taken anything of value or interest.

'The hallow,' pondered Hugo aloud as they perched themselves on the stile over the low fence surrounding the churchyard. 'I can't think of anywhere with a name like that around here. It occurs to me, though, that there's a place of some such name near Ramsey.'

'Ramsey?' queried Milo keenly. 'You know the isle well?'

'Reasonably so. An old chaplain I knew once spent some time among the brothers of Ramsey Abbey. There is a hamlet not far out of town called Fen Hallow. The two strangers could have been referring to that place, but of course we don't know whether the innkeeper heard correctly.'

'Or whether the hamlet was where they were heading for, where they'd travelled from, or even where they live. It's all we have to go on, though, so we have to give it a try,' concluded Milo.

'As the baron will doubtless already have done,' added Hugo.

'The redhead too,' added Rufus quietly. He hadn't liked the way the innkeeper had looked at him. Accusingly almost.

'Yes,' smiled Milo, 'there aren't many redheads around here. Perhaps the two of you are related, Rufus!'

Rufus laughed, but something in his memory flagged up a warning. He blocked it hastily.

'I think we need to separate at this stage in our search,' the seneschal continued. 'Tomorrow, my lord, I believe it would be best if you go to de Prys' manor in Lincolnshire. As seneschal, I have no authority in that shire, but as the Constable of Wisbech Castle and lord of several sizeable manors, your authority from the king has no boundaries. You will be able to demand answers. Take Rufus. He can be your eyes and ears in the place while you speak to the baron. Meanwhile, I shall go with my men-at-arms to Ramsey and see what I can discover there.'

Sir Hugo de Wenton nodded, clearly not relishing the task. No one asked Rufus what he thought. He stared at his boots and his spirits sank. Lincolnshire; it was vast and unknown to him, and before they could start on their journey there'd be another night at the Lamb and another crossing of the Wash.

They were returning to the inn when Rufus noticed a boy staring at them from where he sat at the roadside. He couldn't have been more than twelve or thirteen and looked cheerfully dirty. He had just brought the sheep in his care from pasture near the sea bank into the circular pen by the church fence. The afternoon was drawing to a close, the late autumn light already beginning to fade. Though wolves were hardly heard of now in these parts, the sheep were safer overnight within the confines of the village. There was still a multitude of other predators about, mankind and his sheep-stealing habits among them.

Neither of the others had noticed the boy, but there was something about his direct gaze which Rufus could not ignore. After all, he had been told to use his eyes and ears, so he might as well do so. He crossed the road towards the young shepherd and before he had even reached his side, the boy started to speak.

'None of them saw him, did they? I'll wager none of them saw him. They don't notice things the way I do.'

Rufus crouched down in the grass beside the boy.

'Who did you see?'

'Anything to eat? Only I'm always hungry and supper's not for ages.'

Rufus grinned and pulled from his scrip the small wrapper of bread and cheese he'd saved from dinner.

'Here. Have some of this and don't scoff it all.'

The boy broke off a crust and filled his mouth, helping himself to a bit of cheese to go with it. Rufus waited while he chewed his way through the hard bread. By the entrance to the inn, Milo and Hugo were waiting impatiently, but Rufus nodded his head towards the boy and they disappeared inside.

'No one saw him because they have eyes but do not see. The two thieves, the ones who stole from the smith, I saw them too. I saw them leave the village. On foot they were, hurrying and secretive. I could tell they'd done something wrong. They couldn't wait to get away, but they weren't watchful, didn't see the other one.'

'Which other one?'

'The one what followed. On a fine horse, he was. I know one when I see one.'

'Someone followed the two thieves from the village?'

The boy looked at Rufus as if he were stupid.

'That's what I keep telling you. Very sly, he was, kept well back and out of sight. It wasn't easy for him to follow them, there being no cover on these roads. The boys couldn't go all that fast, being on foot. I saw the man on the horse waiting by the last houses there,' he said, chewing and pointing along the road out of Waltuna, 'and he watched a long time before he followed. Daylight was fading by then, a bit like this.' He waved towards the sky to indicate the gathering dusk.

'What did the man look like?'

'Couldn't tell. He had a hood of furs and a big travelling cloak. And gloves. I noticed the gloves. Sort of big, like animals' paws.'

Rufus thanked the boy and left the last of his bread and cheese with him. The seneschal and constable were seated just inside the Lamb and seemed pleased with Rufus' information. Milo searched in the purse that hung from his belt and produced a quarter-cut section from a silver penny. Rufus watched from the door as the seneschal approached the boy and handed him the farthing. Even from that distance he could see the shepherd's eyes light up as he grasped it.

'So it seems I shall be in good company,' said Milo as they sat later by the inn's smoky fire. 'The thieves were followed out of the village by an unidentified horseman, then presumably a day later by our friend the baron. I'll be following the same trail, but a month behind the rest.'

Whichever way he put it, his chances didn't amount to much.

THIRTY-SIX (Present Day)

Sling His Hook

'Needs moving to your left a bit.'

'Better?'

Monica stood back and looked at the large table they were using as a counter for the new Coffee House.

'Yes, I think that's right.'

'Good. Now we can do the interesting bit.'

Bernadette was in a cheerful mood that afternoon, having just returned from the auction in Willingham with a few useful purchases. The two silver coffee pots she had bought would need a good clean, but were just what they needed for their display. They'd really only needed one, but two had come as part of a job lot. One of them was badly dented, but it didn't matter much; if they turned the worst side towards the wall no one would know. She'd also bought a box of pewter items because amongst them were four old candlesticks, which they needed for the tables.

'They've a good shape,' commented Monica as they went through the box. 'More Victorian than Georgian, but they'll pass. We can go online for the rest. Let's get this lot cleaned.'

'Archie coming over later?'

Monica sighed.

'I suppose so. I don't know what's going on with him. I've almost given up telling him I'm angry. He just smiles vaguely and tells me everything is fine. But it isn't fine at all. It's as if he's on another planet.'

'I always knew he was weird. You should tell him to sling his hook. He might get the message then.'

'I thought I had. You can see how well *that* worked.'

They placed the new purchases on the work table in Monica's office and set about cleaning the silver and pewter. One of the Smutties heard their arrival and joined them, tail held high, the tip waving joyously from side to side. His way of smiling and saying hello.

Bernadette picked him up and he soon settled on her knee. Monica wished life could always be so uncomplicated.

THIRTY-SEVEN

Friday 2nd December 1216

Rufus was gradually getting used to the travelling, but he didn't like it any better. It was no fit weather for riding either, the cold easterly wind chilling the travellers to the bone.

Having crossed the estuary once more, he and Sir Hugo de Wenton had ridden northwards, along the top of the sea bank from Newton in the Isle. They had stayed the first night in a run-down inn close to Tydd St Giles. The mattress they had been obliged to share, with its stuffing of rank bedstraw, had been alive with countless small creatures. Their rustlings had kept Rufus awake for most of the night and in no fit state to face another day in the saddle.

Shortly after leaving Tydd St Giles they had followed the high bank road westwards. On both sides of the bank, the marsh stretched bleak and forlorn for miles, host to a seemingly endless sea of bent grasses worn ragged by relentless autumn gales. The road continued along the top of the old Saturday Dyke, then along Austen Dyke. Considering the time of year, the surface was in fair condition and the horses were able to make good progress.

To Rufus' disappointment, they would not be entering the town of Spalding. He had never been there and would have liked to have seen its castle and market close to the banks of the River Welland. Unfortunately, they had to leave the road before the town could even be glimpsed in the distance, in order to reach the home of the mighty Baron de Prys.

The wild expanse of marshland to the east of Spalding seemed an unlikely choice for the home of such a prominent nobleman. Yet, though the baron had other manors in Lincolnshire, it was said he preferred this sad and lonely place.

The manor house was therefore something of a surprise. Built on a slight rise in the land, this handsome range of buildings had the unmistakable air of baronial pomp. Though the land around it must often have flooded in the winter and spring, the baron's residence probably remained dry for most of the time, staying high and safe on its island.

The track that led from the main road towards the house was well gravelled and bordered by young willows. The trees formed an effective wind break, protecting the buildings from the shrieking winds that blew across the Fen. At the end of the track was a sturdy gatehouse built of Barnack Rag, the durable limestone quarried close to Stamford. Though the gatehouse was unguarded, the high stone portal gave the travellers the impression of entering a small castle. The buildings, all of the same creamy limestone with neat, tiled roofs, faced on to a wide courtyard. Directly opposite the gatehouse was the high roofed structure of the Great Hall, the heart of the manor.

The horses' hooves crunched on the gravel, announcing their arrival, and a couple of grooms emerged from the stables. The visitors dismounted and their horses were led away as a huge door of solid oak was opened. A man who, judging from his fur trimmed over-tunic and immaculate appearance, could only have been the steward, stood in the doorway and watched them approach.

The steward, with his smoothly shaven, unsmiling face, appeared to study them carefully before inclining his head in barely perceptible deference. His manner expressed confidence in his own superiority and the importance of the house he represented.

Sir Hugo announced himself and his purpose.

'I regret, my lord, that the baron is away on service to the king. He does not expect to be back for some time. My lady, however, is at home.'

They were taken to the Great Hall through a high arched doorway, the stone carved with an elaborate floral and leaf design which weaved its way around the arch.

The huge hall was light and airy, benefitting from wide, unshuttered windows. The wooden pillars which supported the high roof were slender and graceful, quite unlike the heavy architecture which Rufus was familiar with in the church and castle of Wisbech. The Baron de Prys clearly favoured modern design; elegant and filled with light, the way all buildings would be in the future.

A fire burned brightly in the central hearth and Rufus longed to warm himself by it, to relieve his stiff, cold joints, but they were ushered swiftly past it. The benches and tables arranged around the fire were occupied by groups of men, the baron's Tower device clearly visible on their tunics. They paused in their game of dice to observe the newcomers. A heavy silence filled the smoky air, broken suddenly by the clatter of dice on a board. Someone laughed and it didn't sound pleasant.

Audrey Bottreux, Baroness de Prys was sitting on the dais with her ladies. She lifted her head and observed the men coolly as they approached, resting the needlework she had been busy with on her lap. She responded to the steward's muttered announcement of the visitors with a brief nod.

'My lady,' began Hugo, 'I understand my lord de Prys is away from home...'

'What is it you require of me?' Her voice, imperious and as cool as her look, cut him off in mid-sentence. Her manner was not quite cold, Rufus noted. There was too much life, too much suppressed animation hidden just below the surface, for her to be described as cold, but everything about her was completely devoid of welcome. She did not invite them to sit and offered them no refreshment.

'I was hoping to speak to the baron, my lady, about a matter we are dealing with on behalf of the king. It concerns items carried on the late king's baggage train and...'

'Which were all lost, I understand.'

'That may well prove to be so, my lady, but it would help our investigation if I could speak to the baron. Have you any news of his return or where I might be able to find him?'

'No, Sir Hugo. My husband will doubtless send word when he expects to return, but until then I am as ignorant of his whereabouts as you. Perhaps...' she began, pausing to think. Rufus stole a look at her, as he had done on that seemingly long ago day of the feast, admiring the fine shape of her face, the full lips, dark eyes and strong brows. She caught him looking and dismissed his attention with a glance. It felt like a reprimand and he began to blush like a fool. 'Perhaps,' she continued, 'you should speak to Sir Edward of Hagebeche. He assists with much of my husband's work for the new king. He has a manor near

Holbeach. To my knowledge, he is not with King Henry at present and may be able to help you.'

'Thank you, my lady. We shall do as you suggest.'

She lowered her head again, picking up her needlework and reapplying herself to it with the same lack of emotion.

The steward saw them out, still without offering food or drink.

'Fortunately,' commented Sir Hugo as their horses carried them back along the baronial track towards the bank road, 'there is a half decent inn in Holbeach where we may enjoy a little hospitality.'

After a few miles, they turned from the main road and followed a spur towards the coast, a road which was so narrow in places that they had to travel in single file. The wind blew bitterly from the sea, tearing at their hoods and numbing their faces. There would be snow soon; Rufus could almost smell it.

At last the town of Holbeach could be seen in the distance. Soon, they were following the path around the high, forbidding walls of the local lord's castle, that of the Baron de Moulton, in the centre of town. They rode through the market with its gaily coloured awnings that flapped like gulls' wings in the freezing wind. The stall holders looked miserably cold, rubbing their hands together as they busied themselves with selling their wares. No one seemed to notice the strangers.

'How glad I am not to have to disturb my lord de Moulton on this errand,' said Sir Hugo, glancing towards the castle gatehouse. 'One baron at a time is quite enough to deal with.'

His lady too, thought Rufus.

The castle's high curtain wall blocked much of the wintery light from the streets and dominated the view of the town afforded to the two travellers as they made their way to the Sea Inn.

Wisbech too was dominated by its castle, considered Rufus as they sat in a dark corner of the inn and drank good ale from horn cups and chewed on chunks of fresh rye bread. Because he was used to life in Wisbech, he had never thought of its castle as a domineering presence. He saw it more as a benign stronghold, there to protect its townspeople in times of strife. Here in Holbeach the situation was similar, the houses and market booths gathered around the fortress like children clutching their mother's skirts.

There were, however, a few outlying manors not immediately in reach of the castle's protection, and it was to one of these that the two men made their way as soon as they had finished eating.

After their chilly reception from the baroness, the more cheerful atmosphere of the small manor held by the knight Edward of Hagebeche was very welcome. Though most of the window shutters were closed fast against the bitter wind, the villagers in their homespun clothes were out and about, busy with their various tasks and managing to summon a smile for the strangers.

Grooms came out to take the horses as soon as Rufus and Hugo reached the manor house and they were invited without delay into the Great Hall.

Edward of Hagebeche was seated at the high table on the dais with a number of other men. They had just finished their midday meal and the fine linen table cloth was still littered with sauce splattered trenchers and platters of unfinished food.

The knight looked up, nodding as his steward announced the visitors. He rose to his feet and strode across the rush covered earthen floor to warm his hands by the fire. The visitors followed and behind them a number of male servants began to clear the table on the dais.

Sir Edward shook his head dismissively as Hugo began to speak.

'I fear you will not succeed in your search,' he stated. His look was sober, rather than hostile.

'Then you are familiar with what the king seeks?' prompted Hugo. The knight gave a short laugh.

'So familiar that we chased over most of Norfolk, Lincolnshire and Cambridgeshire in search of it. We found a few trinkets in Waltuna and sent them to Westminster, but there was no trace of King John's most highly valued treasure. My lord de Prys had his orders from the late king himself, but we failed. Despite all our efforts, we failed to find it.'

Rufus thought of the Waltuna blacksmith's injuries, incurred through his encounter with this apparently reasonable knight.

Hugo nodded.

'The casket. And did King John impart what this casket we are all searching for contains?'

The knight laughed with bitter mirth, throwing his head back to display big yellowed teeth in a wide mouth. He looked a bit like a horse when he did that, thought Rufus.

'So the new king has you chasing shadows already? I wish you luck, Sir Hugo, but I tell you again; you will not find what you are looking for.'

THIRTY-EIGHT (Present Day)

What if They Ask for Latte?

'How do I look?' Angie giggled as she gave a little twirl, showing off her full skirt, long apron and cross-over shawl. They had bought three costumes from an online store and after a few alterations they didn't look too bad at all.

'About as daft as I do,' Bernadette grinned, 'but your mop cap is drooping on one side.'

Angie pulled the white cotton cap as straight as she could without the aid of a mirror and stepped primly in her long skirt behind the Coffee House counter.

'Right, so the filter coffee machine is kept out of sight and I use it to refill this nice silver pot, right? But what if they ask for latte?'

'Tell them you've never heard of it. You're a Georgian, remember. They can have tea if they prefer, or hot chocolate. Anyway you'll have Monica to help you.'

'Ready?' Archie came into reception with a wide smile. 'You both look gorgeous!'

Monica laughed as she entered the room behind him, dressed like the other two women. She was still fiddling with her cap.

'I just hope a few turn up.'

There were just five minutes now before the doors opened for the first day of the museum's Christmas Special. The whole place had been decorated with ivy, holly, mistletoe and yew. Understated and very tasteful, as Bernadette had remarked. Of course, the focus for this year's opening was the brand new Coffee House, and the window display looked inviting with its arrangement of coffee beans, antique tea bowls, tea caddies and the two silver coffee pots from the auction. The dented one was placed carefully at the back.

The modern silver plated pot which would be used for serving coffee, conveniently filled from the hidden filter coffee machine, was a clever reproduction. It had come from the same company as had supplied the tea cups and coffee cans. To modern eyes, the coffee cans looked like tiny porcelain mugs, but free refills would be offered to ward off any complaints about short measures.

They had decided in the end not to ask their customers to drink from handleless tea bowls in the Georgian way. To avoid the inevitable confusion and accidents, they were using small cups and saucers instead.

Angie had thrown herself into research for their new project with impressive results. She had found a few eighteenth century recipes and had produced almond custards, apple tarts made with eggs, as well as syllabubs of cream, lemons and white wine served in little glasses. She had arranged them all under glass domes on the counter and they looked truly impressive. She had completed the display with currant buns piled on to large ceramic dishes next to a stack of dainty plates.

Monica had advertised the event almost daily for the last fortnight on social media and both the Fenland Citizen and Wisbech Standard had covered the story. All they needed now were customers.

'Two minutes to go,' Archie reminded them. 'I'll start by helping Bernadette on the till and can help the room stewards later if they need me.'

Behind him, Bernadette pulled a face. Monica ignored it but wanted to laugh. She peered through the window to see if any visitors were coming up the front path. There was no one.

'Don't worry,' said Archie. 'They'll come.' He hugged her, planting a kiss on the side of her face and she smiled. What was the point in being angry with him? He obviously thought things were fine and anyway, she had more important things to think about right now.

'Thirty seconds,' announced Bernadette. 'I'm opening the door. Let's get on with it. Good luck everybody!'

She pulled open the heavy wooden door, wedging it back with an iron door stop shaped a bit like a cockerel. Monica found herself staring at the bird-like object, rather than lifting her eyes to the empty path outside. Her heart was making a nuisance of itself in her chest. She pulled at her mop cap again, feeling extremely silly in it.

And then there were voices outside. There were people coming through the door, purchasing tickets. Children were asking where the three cats were. They always asked about the cats.

Then there were enquiries about the new Coffee House and people were drifting over to where the tables were set out, admiring the counter and its desserts. Admiring the whole thing. Monica and Angie began to serve coffee with a huge sense of relief.

Across the room, Archie sent Monica a smile.

THIRTY-NINE

Thursday 1st December 1216

While Rufus and Sir Hugo de Wenton were crossing the estuary on their way into Lincolnshire, the seneschal Sir Milo Fulk and his two men-at-arms were leaving the Lamb in Waltuna and taking the road back towards Wisbech.

With no better leads to follow, Milo's intention was to make his way to the isle of Ramsey and the hamlet of Fen Hallow. He knew his chances of success were small. The theft had occurred more than six weeks ago and there was little hope now of finding the youths or the treasure they had stolen.

If the shepherd lad had been telling the truth, the thieves were followed out of Waltuna by a man on horseback. A day later, the Baron de Prys had also set out in pursuit of the boys. If neither of these parties had succeeded in recovering the treasure, what hope did Milo have now? This seemed, however, to be his only option.

Milo's journey to Ramsey would be far from easy. Part of the route followed riverside tracks, but at this time of year the waterlogged Fen rendered some of the roads impassable.

Milo and his men could have taken a boat to March from the quayside in Wisbech, but had decided against it. They needed their horses and there were no craft available that could carry the men and their mounts. Besides, if they kept to the road, they were more likely to pick up news of the youths they were following. The boys were unlikely to have travelled by boat; from what had been said, they couldn't have afforded such luxury. They would have had to sell some of their stolen treasure and their chances of doing so while travelling, and quickly enough, were slim.

And so, as the others had done weeks before, Milo and his men-at-arms, Drew and Abrecan, rode along the bank road out of Wisbech in the direction of March.

The December wind was biting, whipping up the dense cloud into an angry mass. Winter was closing in with a vengeance and soon the wind would bring snow. There were few wayfarers along the road, hardly anyone to question about strangers who may have been seen in past weeks. There were no clues. They just had to press on.

Having forded the Well Stream in Wisbech, they followed the western bank of the river to Elm, then to Welle. The narrow bank-top track was thick with mud, the recent frost not sufficiently severe to harden it, but there was good fortune in other ways. The autumn rain had not been heavy and the well restored banks were holding the river at bay.

By the time they reached Welle, the clouds had gathered to form a dark, ominous blanket across the sky. It was not yet noon, but already the manor had an air of dusk about it, the houses and inn well shuttered, the sturdy church silent, its narrow windows dark and its doors firmly closed.

'Snow will be with us before nightfall, sir,' assessed Drew.

'We must press on. The road out of Welle is a good one and we'll soon be able to make better progress,' replied Milo. 'We'll rest the horses here a short while and be in March before the snow comes.'

The innkeeper took his time in responding to Drew's hammering on the ancient timber planks of the door, but he finally consented to rustle up some bread, cheese and ale for the men and to provide hay and water for the horses.

They were soon on their way again. As the seneschal had predicted, the road from Welle was in a better state than most. The high banks bordering the river, along the top of which ran the road, had been recently and well maintained.

At least the wind was behind them now, driving on to their backs and urging them forwards. By the time the town of March came into sight, the first hard, gritty flakes of snow were beginning to fall.

There was a river to be crossed before they could reach the town, but it could easily be forded. For as long as anyone could remember, travellers had been using the ford over the river here.

A swineherd stood by the fording place, well cloaked and hooded, a mantle of rabbit skins protecting his shoulders against the cold. He had brought his pigs back to their shelter earlier than usual that day due to the worsening weather and the animals could be heard grunting contentedly in their sty. The man greeted the travellers with a curt nod.

'Good day, fellow,' called Milo cheerfully as soon as they were across the river. 'You must see plenty of visitors crossing to the town here.'

'That I do. They come with all their noise, disturbing my pigs.'

'Do you happen to remember a baron and his knights coming to the town a few weeks back?'

'Barons? Knights? Why would I remember them? All folk look the same to me.' He spat on the ground to emphasise the point.

'Or a couple of lads keen to make haste along the way? Perhaps looking like they had something to hide?'

'Don't they all? I remember none of them. They're of no interest to me.'

On that less than encouraging note, the three travellers climbed the far bank and entered the town of March.

The snow was falling with intent now, the flakes still small and icy, forced along by the wind. As in Welle, March was closing for the night, its small houses and workshops huddled for shelter around the old church. Here at last, though, was some light, some sign of habitation. Faint candlelight glowed through the narrow church windows and the inn, with its solitary light showing at one half-shuttered window, appeared to be open for business.

The ancient wooden sign above the door of the inn suggested the hostelry was called the Angel. The crevices above the angel's well chiselled sad face and his arching wings were already dusted with snow.

Having seen to the stabling of the horses, Milo and his men went into the inn. The door creaked loudly as they made their entrance, a blast of snowy cold accompanying them. From every corner, faces turned to stare at the strangers and the buzz of conversation dissolved into silence. Their only greeting came from the innkeeper, an anxious looking man in his later years who was pouring ale for the occupants of the bench opposite the door. He gave the newcomers a nod, almost a smile.

'Welcome, sirs. A bed for the night in this biting weather?'

'That would be most welcome,' replied Milo.

There was a sudden raucous laugh from behind them and Abrecan spun round to give the man a warning glare. Perhaps until that moment the cloaks worn by the two men-at-arms had hidden their coats of mail, but as Abrecan turned to face them and the sword he carried at his belt became clear for all to see, the laughter stopped abruptly.

Taking their earthenware cups of ale to a vacant bench in one corner, the three men sat, glad to be out of the weather, however poor the company. There was no fire to warm the room, but gradually the atmosphere thawed, a general murmur of conversation swelling to ease the tension.

Milo took the opportunity to ask the landlord whether he remembered seeing either the youths or the baron and his men. His answer, however, was about as helpful as the swineherd's.

'My lord, you see how busy we are. I can scarcely remember who was in here last week, let alone six or more weeks ago!'

There were three other travellers sharing the single guest room at the Angel with Milo, Drew and Abrecan, so the six occupants had to share the available mattresses, blankets and straw as best they could. Despite the lack of comfort, sleep came easily for Milo and his men, which was just as well, for the following day's travel would be no easier.

By morning, the snow had stopped, leaving only a modest covering on the road out of March. The wind had lost none of its sting, though, and the fallen snow made it harder to seek out the firmest sections of the road.

The countryside they were passing through was still marshy, its endless banks of reeds and rushes tormented and tossed about by the shrieking wind. In some areas, the river which snaked its course across the landscape had overflowed, the floodwater lapping against the foot of the high built-up banks. Reinforced by last summer's maintenance, the banks in most places still held fast, but in others the defences were badly eroded and the path along the top reduced almost to nothing.

Here and there, on patches of higher ground, were hamlets which seemed to cling to their tiny Fen islands like survivors from a storm. March itself was built on one of the larger islands, as were Ely, Ramsey, Whittlesey, Crowland and many other towns and villages. Since ancient times, settlement on the deep Fen had been restricted for most of the year to islands such as these.

The poor state of the roads gave Merlin, the seneschal's palfrey, and the two strong rounceys little opportunity for rapid progress. The journey that day therefore took far longer than they had anticipated. At last, however, the marsh gave way to open water, where reed beds touched with snow fringed the silvery sheen of Ramsey Mere.

All the men needed was a way of crossing it.

FORTY (Present Day)

Kin-what?

In the end, Rex decided to go for the quinoa salad. He seated himself at the head of a long table in the Wheatsheaf, looking as if he were about to chair a meeting. Twelve members of the Wisbech Heritage Society had turned up for their Christmas meal, which wasn't at all bad. Quite gratifying, in fact. It showed that they were still interested in the project and would probably return in January.

He would have preferred a more refined evening at the Rose and Crown, but when Bertle Bodgit had turned up in his old T-shirt and the low-slung jeans he'd been wearing all day for his plumbing, that had ceased to be an option.

At least most of them looked like they were enjoying themselves. There was the normally sensible Monica giggling at Archie's smart remarks at the other end of the table; she'd probably imbibed a few gin and tonics already. Bernadette was sitting next to the couple, throwing them sour looks. Then there was Mark Appledore. Rex was astonished that the man kept showing up; he was always so openly disdainful. Perhaps he was hoping that if he stayed a bit longer he might learn something.

Rex had to admit that so far they hadn't learned a great deal. Monica still hadn't started her research into local buildings with thirteenth century origins. She was promising to start in the new year, though, so perhaps then something new might come to light. In the meantime, they would have to continue discussing what was already known. There was still the next crossing theory to consider; West Walton to Newton in the Isle. That should keep them busy for a bit.

Ena Cross, the dear lady, was chatting to Sally from the bank and a couple of others about the model of King John's Wisbech they were about to start making. Rex caught the words 'balsa wood' and 'super glue', which sounded encouraging.

The pub was getting jolly rowdy now. A group gathered around the big television at the other end of the room erupted suddenly in a great roar. Perhaps some chappy had scored a goal, or whatever they did these days on rugger pitches.

Everyone had their drinks now, and while they waited for their food, Rex thought he ought to say a few words. He found a spoon and clanged it imperiously against his wine glass.

'Well, everyone, thank you for coming along to our Christmas celebration. I think we've made splendid progress with our project and can look forward to new research and, ah, discoveries in the new year. Monica tells me her Coffee House is enormously successful and I sincerely hope that when she opens the museum for the start of the new season, our model of King John's Wisbech will prove to be equally popular.

'So, everyone, happy Christmas! Let us enjoy this convivial atmosphere tonight and...'

'Cor, nah that's what I *call* an All Day Breakfast!' interjected Bertle as his food arrived.

'...and a happy New Year! May it be an absolutely...'

'Yes, happy Christmas,' agreed Archie, holding up his glass so that it almost collided with the plate of fish and chips that was making a rapid descent towards the table in front of him. The smiling member of the bar staff tasked with delivering the food apologised frantically. Archie apologised too, but coolly.

'Absolutely,' added Mark Appledore. 'Now get stuck into your porridge, or whatever it is, before it gets cold.'

'It's quinoa,' corrected Rex, looking slightly miffed.

'Kin-what?'

'It's health food. I am on a diet.'

'Blimey,' commented Bertle. 'Anybody want a bitta my egg?'

Good heavens, thought Rex. The things one puts oneself through for the sake of our local heritage. Some things really were sent to try him.

And he didn't just mean the quinoa.

FORTY-ONE

Friday 2nd December 1216

It began to snow again when they were half way across Ramsey Mere. Milo heard the ferryman's grunted curse from behind him and Merlin shifted restlessly. The palfrey was tethered securely, but the movement of the boat unsettled him as it made its slow way across the water. Milo spoke to him softly, reassuring him for a short while at least.

It had not been easy to persuade the ferrymen to take them across the mere in such bitter weather and the seneschal had been obliged to pay more than double the normal price. Since each man and his horse needed a boat, they had had to wait for three ferrymen to be coaxed from the shelter of their huts. Finally persuaded to take their boats out by the clink of silver coins, they were bad tempered and resentful and in no mood for Milo's questions. Once again he learned nothing.

Rather than crossing the mere, the travellers could have continued along the path that followed the southern shore, but the road was deteriorating rapidly. Ferryboats were a far more practical option now.

The mere was quite shallow, allowing the flat, punt-like vessels to be poled across, in a way similar to crossing a river. Each boat, which was able to carry three or four men or a single horse and rider, steered a course close to the shore, where the water was at its shallowest.

The gentle splash of the pole dipping into the water and the cries of waterfowl were the only sounds in the bleak wintery landscape. At least, that was, while the ferrymen refrained from cursing. A heron winged his stately progress over the grey water while a family of coots scuttled in and out of the thicket of reeds that lined the shore. Now and then, great honking flocks of greylag geese lifted themselves into the white sky, forming ever-changing patterns against the laden clouds.

Before long, the boats reached the mouth of the stream that flowed through the marsh to the isle of Ramsey. There were no other boats on the water, allowing the ferries to make good progress. Even on the bankside path, there was no sign of anyone.

There were a few large boats moored at the quayside, some with masts, but most were flat bottomed lighters used to transport goods around the Fens. Isolated abbeys, like that of Ramsey, relied on supplies reaching them by boat. Grain and other produce not grown on abbey land was brought in from nearby manors, while wax to supplement that produced by the abbey's bees, as well as linen and woollen cloth, came from Bishop's Lynn. Limestone blocks for building were delivered on lighters from the quarry at Barnack in Lincolnshire, though only the abbey and a few other buildings benefitted from such expensive materials.

On the quayside, the wooden crane that was used to unload heavy cargo from boats stood motionless. Were it not for the snow, the crane would doubtless still be working, lifting limestone blocks from the lighters and loading them on to sleds pulled by oxen.

The three ferries were moored without incident, releasing the nervous horses on to the causeway, a solidly built structure of stone, sand and timber. The causeway formed a bridge from the marshy riverside to the town and was strong enough to take the heaviest wagons and sled loads of building stone.

'First of all, an inn, I think,' proposed Milo. After such a journey, the thought of a warm fire was very appealing.

They turned from the causeway on to the town's main street. Houses were squeezed tightly together along the roadside, as if huddled for warmth, the haze of smoke lingering above their thatch an indication of comforting hearth fires within. Even here in the town, there were few folk about; anyone able to do so had retreated inside. At this time of year there were always tools and fishing nets to be repaired, work that could be done indoors, in readiness for spring. Outside some of the houses were small, upturned boats; many of these families relied on fishing for a living and a boat was often their most valuable possession.

As they reached the end of the street, the tall gates of Ramsey Abbey came into view. The place looked welcoming, its gates wide open, and a few Benedictine brothers could be seen moving between the buildings. In front of the abbey stretched a wide, open, grassy space.

This was where, Milo informed his men, the fair was held each July to celebrate the Feast of St Benedict. St Benedict was revered as the father of Christian monasticism and therefore of Ramsey Abbey itself. For three days in July, the whole town flocked to the fair, transforming this tranquil grassy spot into a hub of noise and activity. Booths with goods for sale, entertainers, purveyors of potions and false promises, all of them would light up the town, then be gone again.

Across the lane from the green was the Eel Inn, a well lit hostelry with good stables. Gratefully, the men made their way to it, eager for food and shelter before venturing out of town again.

The innkeeper's wife had an iron pot of good, wholesome pottage cooking over the ashes of her fire. She had just taken new loaves of rye bread from the oven and the dish of mutton pottage with new bread was the best food the travellers had tasted for what felt like weeks. They arranged to return to the Eel for the night, but before their work was done for the day they set out to find the hamlet of Fen Hallow.

The lane followed the high abbey wall on the left before passing through dense woodland to reach the settlement. A large area of hawthorn and scrub had been cleared long ago to make space for this community of fishermen and craftsmen. The land here was lower than where the abbey stood and suffered considerable flooding during times of high rainfall.

In the snow Fen Hallow looked bleak. The smoke from a few peat fires gave the only hint of comfort and the hamlet was swathed in silence. Only the pigs in their sty and the chickens in their coop responded with their restlessness to the arrival of the men on horseback.

Milo hammered with his gloved fist on the door of the house closest to the slumbering timber church. The house was larger than the others and looked moderately well maintained, but the face which appeared in the dark doorway looked far less well cared for. The man's long and matted hair that emerged from his greasy linen cap framed a face that was smudged with soot from the fire.

'How can I help, sirs?' He looked anxious and not at all pleased to have visitors.

Milo explained his role and his search for the youths. He began to give the vague description he'd had from the blacksmith in Waltuna, but didn't have to finish it. The man heaved a great sigh and bade them to enter the house.

The dwelling was lit by a single rush light in one corner and, using this meagre illumination, the man had been busy with the repair of his fishing nets. A woman was crouched over a pot in the ashes of her fire, stirring broth with an aroma considerably less mouth-watering than at the Eel. She gave them a brief nod and withdrew to the darkest recess of the single roomed house.

'I know only too well the boys you are seeking, my lord. One of them you have no hope of finding and the other...' he paused.

'Go on,' Milo said patiently.

'Edwin and Cedric were the brewer's sons. A bad lot, though you won't hear their parents saying so. They were both of an age to help their father, but instead they were always taking themselves off, up to no good. Then one day, round about the Ides of October, the younger lad Cedric was found dead in the lane. His father took it badly, his mother even more so.'

Milo looked down, trying to show some sympathy and hiding his frustration.

'And the older brother?'

'Not seen since. Though the good brewer won't have it said, everyone fears Edwin did away with his younger brother. Edwin was always the worst of the pair, a regular bully, if you ask me. Cedric might have stood a chance of growing up decent and honest if he hadn't always been under his brother's influence.'

'And the manner of Cedric's death?'

'A knife wound, my lord. It was the goodwife herself who found her boy. Later we learned that he'd been struck in the chest. Edwin was always handy with that knife of his.'

'Have you any idea of where Edwin may be now?'

'No, sir. Nor have his parents, or at least that's what they told the law men when they came calling. They've lost one son and, however bad he may be, they won't want to lose a second.'

Milo knew he had to be cautious in his questioning. His authority extended only as far as the borders of the Isle of Ely, not into Ramsey. The isle of Ramsey had, since the long distant times of King Edgar, enjoyed certain rights. It had its own justices and prison and was allowed to keep the fines imposed by its court on tenants who found themselves on the wrong side of the law. It sounded from what the fisherman was telling him that the isle's officials, even the local sheriff himself, had been investigating the murder.

Although Milo was concerned only with the retrieval of stolen goods, his search was bound to cover the same ground as the local men. As a courtesy, he would have to seek permission from the abbot before he went any further with his search.

As the seneschal and men-at-arms left the fisherman's house, the man pointed out the home of the bereaved family.

'Gone away, they have. Gone to the goodwife's sister in the town.'

The silence and the untrodden snow by the door of the wretched house with its badly repaired thatch appeared to confirm what the fisherman said. The place was empty. Even so, Drew pushed open the door and took a brief look inside while Abrecan searched the dark and lifeless brew house in the back yard. They closed the doors behind them as they left. Wherever Edwin was hiding, it wasn't in the family home.

By then, it was mid afternoon and the snow, having fallen intermittently since morning, began to come down with real intent. Mercifully, though, the wind had dropped, taking with it some of the bite from the freezing conditions.

They were leaving Fen Hallow for the abbey when a voice called out to them from a house in the shadow of the trees. Milo turned in the saddle to see the hooded face of an old woman standing beneath the poor thatch overhanging her doorway. Milo dismounted and handed Merlin's reins to Drew.

'You need to find that boy before there's more trouble,' the woman said. 'They went after him and I fear for the boy. He's bad news, always has been, but he'd be no match for them.'

'Them? Do you mean the sheriff's men?' asked Milo in a low voice. The old woman shook her head impatiently.

'No sheriff I've ever seen brings thugs like that. On fine horses, they were, and keen to carry out their threats. Caught me watching and pulled me out of the house, said that since I was so fond of spying on folk, I'd know where the boy had gone.'

'And did you?'

She nodded miserably.

'They made me tell, sirs. They pulled me by the hair and hurt me and I'm ashamed to say I told them. And I'll tell you too, as a true man of the law, in case there's any hope for the boy. He has a hide by the mere; uses it for wildfowling at this time of the year. My son saw him there in the autumn, but few others here know of it.'

Milo thanked her and gave her a coin, leaving her to the peace of her fireside.

'So the Baron de Prys found his way here,' he said as he remounted.

'And it seems he hurts poor old women as well as beating up blacksmiths,' muttered Abrecan.

The abbey gates were closed by the time they had ridden back to town and the seneschal was obliged to knock on the small wicket gate framed within the great double doors.

'Doing a lot of building work here,' observed Drew as they waited. Snow was settling on the shoulders of his cloak and filling the creases in his hood as he stared at the stacks of dressed limestone blocks by the gates. Milo nodded.

'They'll be rebuilding the old timber parts of the abbey with stone. In the old days, only the principal buildings, such as the abbey church and perhaps the infirmary, were stone built. The others were of timber. I see they've already rebuilt the outer walls. I heard the abbot here sends payment of four thousand eels a year to Peterborough Abbey in payment for stone from Barnack quarry.'

'Not sure I'd want payment in eels, sir,' replied Drew. 'Rather have silver any day.'

'Good currency, eels,' smiled Milo as he hammered on the door again, 'though I suspect the good brothers of Peterborough have more than their fill of eel pie.'

At last the wicket gate was opened, but only enough to show part of the nervous face that querulously asked their business. Milo replied curtly and the gate swung fully open.

'Father Abbot has a little time before Vespers,' the lay brother hesitantly informed them, 'so if you would care to wait here I shall enquire whether he is free to see you.'

They were shown to a cheerless, dark and cold timber lean-to close to the infirmary, but were mercifully not obliged to wait for long. A mournful looking novice arrived to take the seneschal to the abbot and to direct the men-at-arms to the refectory. Milo was soon being accompanied by the silent novice through the cloisters and across the snowy courtyard, towards a range of sturdy timber and thatch buildings. Another pile of stone had been deposited there. The spring would bring a time of major rebuilding at the abbey, by the look of it.

Milo had to lower his head to step through the doorway indicated by the novice. He found himself inside the abbot's solar, a surprisingly spacious room. Its thick, solid posts reached high above their heads, joining hefty beams which supported the neatly thatched roof. A good fire burned in the centre of the room. It seemed to Milo a pity that such a well built, comfortable structure would soon be demolished and replaced with stone.

The Abbot Hugh Foliot was small and thin, a quiet man in his middle years, his face studious and intelligent. He was seated in a high backed chair behind a huge oaken desk. A number of scrolls were neatly gathered to one side of the desk and before him was an open document which he appeared to be studying closely.

He looked up and smiled, inviting the seneschal to sit. As Milo settled himself in the proffered straight backed chair, he noticed the abbey seal, Ramsey's mark of authority, placed beside its block of wax next to the scrolls. The responsibility for the whole isle, as well as the abbey, rested on the hunched shoulders of this unworldly looking man with his kind eyes and patient expression.

For Ramsey Abbey was the centre of a great deal of influence. It was enormously wealthy too, with land and manors both near and far and its rights over the banlieu of Ramsey. The banlieu was an area of about three miles surrounding the abbey. Its tenants, both free men and tied peasants, were kept in check with its law courts and it was these villeins and serfs who laboured to keep the manor supplied with its needs. Whether they fished the mere and streams, brewed ale, weaved or fulled cloth, they dutifully paid their rents and tithes to the great mother abbey. In return, the abbey offered them protection, its church providing comfort for their souls, its infirmary healing for their bodies.

This responsibility was reflected in the countless stacked scrolls and leather bound books that filled the shelves behind the abbot's chair, yet despite it all, the solar maintained its air of calm and order.

The seneschal explained his purpose in Ramsey, that he was searching for goods on the king's orders. He also passed on what he had been told about the brewer's two sons. The abbot frowned.

'The boy's death was a very bad business. Of course, you have my leave to carry out your search within the banlieu for my lord king. However, if your investigations lead you to Edwin, the boy suspected of killing his brother, he must be brought back to Ramsey for our own legal processes to determine his guilt or otherwise. You may need more men-at-arms to carry out your search, so I shall authorise two extra men to accompany you.'

'Thank you, Father Abbot.'

'If you ask at the gate tomorrow after Prime, the men will join you.'

'I appreciate your help, and of course the boy will be brought back here, if found.' *After* he'd been questioned and the area thoroughly searched, Milo added mentally. The abbot nodded again, looking him in the eye, as if reading his thoughts.

'Your men will have been given some refreshment while they've been waiting and I am sure you too would benefit from a little ale and bread. I understand you already have accommodation for the night? Come, I'll take you to the refectory myself; I can go that way to reach the church. It is almost time for Vespers.'

The abbot chatted easily as they walked. He was pleasant company and gracious and, from what Milo could see, his was a peaceful, efficient and well disciplined community. From the workshops and bakery came the sound of industry as the brothers working as brewers, tanners and bakers went about their work.

Milo found his men-at-arms sitting by the fire in the refectory. They were steadily eating their way through a huge platter of oat cakes in honey and enjoying cups of good, strong ale. Milo eagerly joined the feast, thinking that the abbot's description of ale and bread hardly did it justice.

It would have been tactless to mention that another meal awaited them at the Eel Inn. This one was far too good to miss.

FORTY–TWO (Present Day)

One Blink

Monica and Archie were driving to Ramsey. It was good to be away from the Poet's House for a few hours, now that it was closed for winter. Now that they finally had a Saturday to themselves.

Another year at the museum had come to a close. The pre-Christmas opening with its Coffee House had been declared a success, bringing in much needed funds. Even the clearing up was finished, Archie being at his most helpful and obliging.

Monica had been surprised by how well things had gone. It appeared that the Coffee House had been just what the town wanted. The children had seemed to like the costumes which she, Bernadette and Angie had worn, and even the adults had played along, ordering the specialities on offer and refraining from requesting a tuna mayonnaise sandwich.

Because of all this, Monica and the trustees had decided to make the Coffee House a permanent feature, starting from the beginning of the new season in March. The gift shop, however, would be moved into the Garden Room at the back of the museum, where the old tea room had been. There really hadn't been enough space in reception to serve refreshments, sell souvenirs and issue tickets. In effect, the café and gift shop would be swapping locations.

They would also have to recruit someone to help Angie in the Coffee House. Monica had too much to do without serving refreshments.

Just too much to do. But at least the museum would be closed throughout January and February, giving her time to get the kitchen and wine cellar ready, cope with Rex and his grand schemes and sort out the recruitment of staff and volunteers.

Monica loved the Fens in midwinter. Miles of dark tilled soil stretched to the horizon in every direction, interrupted only by narrow roads, distant telegraph poles and tired fen grasses that stood sentinel by drainage ditches.

Ditches, dykes and cuts; the vocabulary of drainage. It was as if the engineers behind the seventeenth century drainage schemes had deliberately chosen nouns to discourage sentiment and any hint of romance. Yet, once you knew the Fens you came to understand their wild beauty, their spirit. Not so long ago, the Fens had been a marshy wilderness. Now drained and producing crops, there was still a sense of rebelliousness about them, as if at any moment their patience would snap and they would flood, just for the hell of it.

'So why Ramsey?' Archie was asking.

'No reason. When you suggested a drive out, I just thought of Ramsey, that's all.'

It was hard not to feel close to Archie when he was like this; kind and considerate, warm. Things had been far better lately and he'd been genuinely helpful during the pre-Christmas opening. She supposed the sorting out of Aunt Lizzie's estate was still going on, but she chose not to ask about it and he wasn't volunteering any updates.

They took the lonely Forty Foot bank road out of Chatteris. Constructed in the 1650s, the Forty Foot was one of Sir Cornelius Vermuyden's new drainage channels and the cause of so much anguish for Fenland folk.

Vermuyden, first recruited by King Charles I, later by Oliver Cromwell, undertook the work which would create the agricultural landscape so well known today. Back then, his schemes had been hugely unpopular. The prospect of drained acres for crops meant nothing less to the Fenmen than the utter destruction of their traditional way of life, their wildfowling and fishing.

Nowadays, the Forty Foot, despite its straightness, had claimed its own place in the landscape, its banks softened here and there with reeds and bulrush. From the car window, Monica watched as a swan made its serene way from a fringe of reeds across the rippling water, the wavelets touched with silver as sunlight seeped through the clouds.

Entering the village of Ramsey Forty Foot, the black Nissan crossed the bridge and followed the winding road to Ramsey. On their right was a turning signed to Ramsey Mereside, the village's name a memorial to the great body of water which had once been such a dominant feature of the landscape. It had finally been drained in the nineteenth century.

Before long, they were driving along residential streets and approaching the historical centre of Ramsey.

The handsome parish church of St Thomas á Becket overlooked the part of town it had grown old with. Across the road, by a row of picturesque cottages, were a tussocky green and a horse pond. Horses were rarer visitors to the pond these days, ducks having made the place home as they paddled, splashed and plodded, in and out of the water.

Before the church stretched another green, this one as neat and freshly mown as a well tended lawn. At its far end were the ruins of the ancient abbey gatehouse.

Despite the cars and the usual Saturday morning bustle, there was a sense of peace here. Archie and Monica, having parked the Nissan by the church, strolled across the Abbey Green towards the gatehouse. The sun chose that moment to ease through the clouds once more, flickering briefly across the face of the ancient stone church and smiling on the old abbey gatehouse. For just a few seconds the scene was quite ethereal.

But one blink and it was gone. A car screeched round the corner from the high street and the sun went in again.

'So come on,' chided Archie. 'I know you're dying to tell me the history.'

She smiled.

'I don't know much, other than what I found out the other day from the internet. I promised Rex I'd start looking into the Fenland of King John's time. He keeps nagging and I must make a proper start after Christmas, but at least I know a bit about Ramsey now.'

'Go on then.'

'Well, apparently, the abbey was founded in AD 969 by Duke Ailwyn. Over the centuries it was greatly developed, of course, and the remains of the gatehouse you see here date mostly from the fifteenth century. So, these gates wouldn't have been the ones King John would have seen, had he visited. But, like most abbeys, Ramsey had an infirmary. It would have been quite simple, just a long hall for the patients' beds and a chapel at its eastern end. The building was later extended and developed into the parish church we see here now.'

They turned and looked at the church dedicated to St Thomas á Becket. Its doors were open and a few ladies were walking into it, carrying baskets of flowers.

'Do you mean that the remains of the original infirmary are somewhere within that church? That would mean the church is the oldest remaining part of the abbey.'

'Yes, I suppose you could say that.'

They stood and looked around them for a few seconds, then Archie turned to look again at the abbey gatehouse.

'Any chance we can go in and have a look round?'

'No, unfortunately it's only open once a month during the main season. The National Trust looks after it and I suppose they can't be everywhere, all the time.'

They stepped closer to the ruin, Archie standing beneath a surprisingly well preserved oriel window decorated with detailed carving. A single spike of dead dandelion leaned out from a crevice, a sneaky invader too high for easy removal.

'A pity. I should have liked to have seen it.'

'Come on,' she smiled, 'let's go and get you some fish and chips for lunch.'

He threw an arm around her and they walked back to the car.

FORTY-THREE

Saturday 3rd December 1216

Sir Milo Fulk and four men-at-arms, two of whom had been sent by the abbot, left the isle of Ramsey the next morning at first light.

The Benedictine monks were already well into their long day of prayer, study and work. There must have been some sense of relief amongst them that Church life had at last returned to normal after long years of King John's quarrels with the Pope and what had effectively been the excommunication of the entire country.

During that time, when England had been cast adrift from the Church in Rome, Masses had been suspended, the dead had been buried in unconsecrated ground and payment of tithes to the Church had ceased. For the poor, it hadn't all been bad news. Many must have been grateful for a few years without having to pay the tithes which few of them could afford. Eventually though, the king's quarrel with the Pope had been patched up and Church life had returned to normal. The poor had once more been burdened with tithes and compulsory church attendance had returned to being a way of life.

The five men rode out of town along the causeway. A thick blanket of white covered the path, snow having fallen for most of the night. Already, its crisp surface was spoiled by a mass of footprints, some human, some horse, but the further they progressed along the causeway, the fewer the prints became. The snow had stopped, but the sky was still dark and brooding, promising more. The horses seemed unbothered by it, happy to be on the move again.

The two Ramsey men-at-arms spoke but rarely. Their silence was due more to focus on the task than to ill temper, however, and Milo's own men more than made up for it.

'Seems to me,' Abrecan commented to Drew as they rode along, 'if a man's committed murder, he'll not hang about so close to home. He'll have run by now.'

'As far as he can go on foot,' Drew agreed.

Milo said nothing. Hopeless or not, having been given such a lead, he was determined to follow it up and search around the mere.

The causeway, running alongside the stream for much of its length, eventually came to an end and the men joined the path that led around the southern side of the mere. Here, the pure white covering of snow that passed between reed beds and willow thickets had been disturbed only by water birds. Theirs were the only cries to break the winter hush.

The men, taking nature's cue at last, continued along the path without speaking. Even so, their progress alerted enough of the wildlife to render their stealth almost pointless. On one occasion an entire family of mallards shot off through the reeds with a cacophony of quacking loud enough to awaken the whole of Ramsey.

One of the abbot's men cursed quietly.

The path which wound its way around the mere allowed them in most places a good view of the shoreline. The water's edge was a mass of saw sedge, tall grasses and reeds. Already faded through normal autumnal decline, whole beds of grasses were now flattened by the snow that covered their bent stalks like an uneven, torn blanket. Every so often, the dark shape of a wildfowler's hide, crouched down amongst the grasses, came into view. One such, according to their helpful Fen Hallow informant, belonged to Edwin the brewer's son.

Each time they came to one of these huts, the two Ramsey men dismounted and made their careful way down to it. Usually, there was a narrow path leading to the hide, trodden by countless fishermen over many seasons. The fallen snow helped to mark out these paths, forming neat, white ribbons from the main track to the flimsy structures perched so precariously at the water's edge.

As the morning wore on, the men-at-arms checked and searched each hut they came to. There was no one about; that much was clear from the lack of human tracks in the snow. Had any wildfowler or fisherman been occupying a hut, they would have had to have been there since before the snow had begun on the previous day. Unless, of course, they'd used a boat to reach their hide. Even then, the dilapidated state of most of the hides would have made a prolonged stay extremely cold and uncomfortable. With their badly fitting doors, ill-repaired thatch and miniscule dimensions, these places were not fit to stay in for long.

Any hope of finding their fugitive soon evaporated. Apart from the huts, there was nowhere to lie low. The reed beds, which in summer provided good, thick cover, would be no use at all in their flattened wintery state. Easily penetrated, quickly seen through, the growth around the lake was hiding nothing.

'No one here but dab-chicks, widgeons and godwits,' muttered Drew after a while and the others, even the normally silent Ramsey men, grunted their agreement. The snow had begun to fall again; just a few harmless flakes, but it did not bode well for the rest of the day.

'Nevertheless, we continue,' insisted the seneschal.

They had almost reached the eastern end of the mere when one of the Ramsey men let out a shout.

He had followed one of the narrow paths down to the water and had been looking with jaded expectations inside a particularly scruffy shelter. The four remaining men on the track had watched as he walked around the shack, wrenching open its door and moving a few items. Everything had then fallen silent. He had disappeared from view around the far side of the hut before they had heard the shout.

Milo dismounted hastily, handing Merlin's reigns to Abrecan. Drew followed closely behind him along the narrow path through the reeds, his sword drawn. They edged around the hide, finding themselves immediately up to the waist in the saw sedge that grew on the boggy ground at the water's edge. A grey heron took fright, abandoning his solitary watch on the bank and reaching suddenly, awkwardly for the sky. Both men froze.

But the man-at-arms who knelt amongst the sedge in the oozing mud, the fallen snow around him reduced to sludge, seemed not to notice the disturbance. He was hauling at something, something heavy and awkward caught up in the sedge. He turned at last to Milo and Drew. His face, previously stung pink from the cold, was drained of colour.

'Dead these past weeks, by the state of him,' he said quietly, 'and I doubt he dropped himself into the reeds.'

He moved back on to his haunches then stood, stepping back so that the sad remains of Edwin the brewer's son could be seen. The thick growth at the mere's edge had prevented his body from drifting away from the bank, but only his head was clear of the water. His cap was long gone, leaving his long hair to be tossed about by the wintery wind. Though thickened with mud and darkened by nearly two months of weather, the hair could be seen to be fair in colour. There was little left of the rest of him, fish having aided the inevitable process of decomposition.

Milo stepped back and addressed Drew.

'Ride back to the abbey with the Ramsey men and organise a litter to be brought straight away. Abrecan and I shall stay with the body. Tell Father Abbot I shall accompany the body to the abbey and speak to him then.'

Milo and Abrecan watched as the three men rode away. There was no further need for silence, yet still they felt a reluctance to speak.

'And now we must search this whole area,' said Milo at last. 'When the monks arrive with the litter, the ground will inevitably be disturbed. It's now or never.'

During the search for Edwin, and then with the discovery of his body, they had almost lost sight of their purpose in coming here, but now it came clearly back into focus.

It was highly likely that Edwin had taken the casket when his brother was killed and that he'd brought it with him to this hide. Someone had then killed Edwin and, if the motive had been the most obvious one, that of the desire to possess the treasure for themselves, the casket would be long gone. Gone with Edwin's killer. Milo was weeks too late and his chances of finding the casket were practically non-existent.

Nevertheless, they threw themselves into the search, beginning with the hut itself. They hauled out a small boat and armfuls of nets, laying everything on the ground and checking each fold of net before inspecting every ledge and crevice of the old shed. It appeared from the straw and filthy blanket on the damp earth floor next to the boat, that Edwin had slept there at times. Abrecan hoped it had been in warmer weather.

Milo was still thinking through the possible order of events. Edwin must have fled here immediately after the death of his brother. Whether or not he was Cedric's killer, he must have been planning to move on to somewhere safer. His faith in the legal system, like that of most ordinary folk, was probably very small.

But someone had caught up with him first. Milo agreed with the Ramsey man-at-arms; from the way Edwin's body lay in the sedge, he must have been pushed or dragged there. To Milo, who had seen more than his fair share of death, the body looked like it had been dumped; disposed of. The manner in which he had been killed, however, might remain a mystery. After so many weeks of decay, it would be next to impossible to discern the method used to kill him.

More important to the seneschal, though, was the motive behind Edwin's murder. Had it been revenge? Had someone seen Edwin killing his brother and avenged that death? Or had it been the result of some trouble the boys had made for themselves, something yet unknown to the authorities? According to the residents of Fen Hallow, the lads had made a habit of inviting problems for themselves and others. Or had it simply been because of the treasure Cedric and Edwin had stolen from the Waltuna blacksmith?

Milo and Abrecan found nothing of significance in the hut and they turned their attention to the reeds and sedge surrounding it. A couple of coots, their faces and beaks brightly white against their black plumage, made their busy way out of the reeds, leaving the scene strangely silent.

The snow that had fallen during the night still formed a canopy over some of the reed beds but, the temperature haven risen slightly during the morning, the snowy mantle was collapsing in places, leaving sorry, bent brown stalks. Even where the reed beds had thinned and died back, snow lay thickly between the dark stalks. Anything that may have been lying there would be difficult to spot beneath its snowy covering. For a tediously long time, the two men searched through the grasses and reeds on the firmer ground at the eastern and southern sides of the hut, their boots trampling the snow and their gloved hands clearing what they could of the ground.

'We are just too late, sir,' declared Abrecan after a long and fruitless search, 'if he was killed for his treasure it will have gone weeks ago.'

Milo made no reply, continuing to examine the ground. The monks could arrive at any time now to take away the wretched remains of Edwin, and the seneschal was reluctant to waste any of this opportunity to search undisturbed.

The snow was falling with more intent now, blown by a strengthening easterly wind. As had occurred the day before, its intensity was building and would most likely continue all night. Any hope of success would diminish significantly after that.

The eastern side of the hut was still damp from yesterday's snow, the ground there still covered. The hut had sheltered the ground on the western side, however, the almost inaccessible patch of mud and grass there showing dark against the surrounding snow. Having searched the other three sides, the men pushed their way through the tall grasses towards the sheltered side. The ground there was very wet, sucking at their boots as they squelched through the thick mud. Milo felt icy water seeping into his boots, soaking his toes as he continued cautiously forwards.

He was too busy at first, trying to withdraw his foot from the sticky black mud, to spot the glimmer of gold. It was barely visible in the murk of a shallow pool close to the rough wall of the hut. The seneschal was braced in a precarious position, the mud so thick beneath his feet that any movement might pull him over, yet suddenly there it was, that golden shape in the dark water. He couldn't reach it from where he stood and he was still too far from the hut to use its side for support, but he used his reason. Since the shack was still standing, the ground next to it had to be fairly sound. He back-tracked and tried a more circuitous route, finally arriving close enough to the hut to reach out and lean some of his weight against it.

Abrecan was not far behind him, cursing as he lost one boot in the mud.

'Stay back,' Milo called out. 'No point in us both getting stuck and I think I've found something.'

He was close enough to the pool now to reach into the water and close his fingers around the submerged object. He pulled it out, the disturbed silt instantly clouding the water.

Milo held the long sought for treasure in his muddy hands. It was certainly a wonder, that small golden casket. It had been crafted from the purest, buttery gold and studded with the most glorious gemstones. Even in the falling snow and in its dirty condition, the vivid red of rubies and brilliant green of emeralds shone from it.

Abrecan had reached him now, the state of his boots no longer a concern.

'Woo, that must be worth a king's ransom, sir! No wonder so much fuss was made about finding it! The brewer's sons were playing with fire when they nicked that.'

'And paid for it dearly,' agreed Milo as he continued to examine the casket. 'Look, the lock's been broken. The boys must have tried to find out what was inside. Looks like a knife has been pushed in to force the lock. And that means whatever was inside has either been lost or stolen.'

'Or maybe not.' Abrecan was stooping towards the pool, supporting himself against the hut while reaching into the water with one ungloved hand. The silt was beginning to settle again, the water's former clarity re-establishing itself. With a cry of triumph, Abrecan's searching fingers closed around another bright object and he pulled it out, wiping it briefly between his fingers before opening his palm and displaying his find.

It was a finger ring of the richest gleaming gold. It must have been made for a man of substance; a king. Its broad band divided at the front to form the elaborate setting for the most enormous ruby.

'God's teeth, so *that's* what it's all been about!' breathed Abrecan. 'Not just the casket, but this precious ring inside! This, my lord seneschal, is what your search has all been about. You finally have your prize!'

Milo nodded, opening the box again and examining the lining while Abrecan went on searching the mud with his eyes and fingers. He could find nothing more of value.

'The casket is certainly a fitting container for it,' Milo was commenting, 'lined with the highest quality of silk.'

The crimson silk lining of the box must once have been fine indeed, but it was stained with mud and ruined now. He frowned.

'Why the dismal looks, sir?' Abrecan demanded. 'By God's bones, if I were you, with the king's command heavy on my shoulders, I'd be grinning my daft head off and heading for the alehouse for a long night's drinking!'

Milo smiled at last, placing the ring inside the casket and securing them both in the leather scrip at his belt.

'I may yet do as you suggest, but we haven't finished here yet. For a start, we need to put the wildfowler's possessions back into his hut. By the look of things, his family has very little wealth and now they've lost their sons. Then, when the litter arrives, I must accompany Edwin's body to the abbey and speak to the abbot.'

They made their way back on to firmer ground and began to put everything back into the hut. The small area of mud, no more than an arm's length, between the water's edge and the front of the hide, had been badly churned by their boots. The snow was trodden almost to nothing.

Again, it was Abecan's sharp eyes that brought them good fortune. As he closed the door on the replaced fishing equipment, a speck of gold caught his eye and he bent down to loosen something from the mud. He held it in the palm of his hand while they both examined it. It was a small, lozenge shaped emerald in a plain gold setting.

'Where do you think this came from, sir? Could it have been broken from the casket? Perhaps when the lock was smashed?'

'I doubt it,' replied Milo. 'Though it's clearly a valuable object, it's hardly in the same league as the casket. Besides, it's too small, not even as big as the nail on your little finger. Looks to me more like a buckle decoration.'

'Or perhaps part of a brooch? Maybe it was dropped by the baron, if his search brought him here.'

'Or by the unidentified rider who was apparently following the boys even before the baron set out? The Waltuna shepherd lad seems to have been the only one who saw him.'

'The owner of this stone, then, sir,' summed up Abrecan, 'could well have been Edwin's killer.'

'Yes, but it could also have come from an earlier theft. The brewer's sons seem to have made a habit of thieving and other misdeeds. We'll hold on to it, of course. It isn't our task to find the killer; that's for the local sheriff, but if we're able to help it can only be to the good.'

Abrecan nodded and began to walk back to the horses, giving the ground one last sweep with his eyes.

'When you receive your reward, my lord seneschal,' he said with a grin, 'perhaps I could have some new boots? This pair is pretty well done for.'

'Reward?' laughed Milo. 'I doubt if anything like that will come my way, but you shall have your boots. That much I can promise.'

FORTY-FOUR (Present Day)

Tiny Spark

St Peter and Paul's Church was packed, but then it always was on Christmas Eve. Not only were all the pews occupied, but extra chairs had been set out at the back and down the sides, and people of all ages filled them. Little boys in Santa hats, dads sporting furry Rudolf antlers, women with silver bauble earrings and little girls in tiaras sang with varying degrees of enthusiasm through the programme of carols.

The church was rarely so full, but it seemed that on Christmas Eve, with all the anticipation in children's hearts, there was still something that couldn't be satisfied with television, the internet and staring at month-old Christmas decorations. Whatever it was about this service, it drew families year after year. Perhaps they felt the tiny spark of magic that they needed to fuel them through the next few days of presents, eating and everything that went with it.

There came a moment in the service when the lights in the church were switched off, leaving almost total darkness. The friendly voice of the vicar filled the peaceful shadows and Archie held Monica's hand. She smiled. She was glad he had agreed to join her tonight, having been coming here herself every Christmas Eve for years. Sometimes she attended the Thursday morning healing services too, when her workload permitted it. She found it a comfort.

Around them in the darkness the piping voices of a few excited children asked questions, made comments. All eyes were following the single candle being carried from the chancel. Its flame was transferred to others, then slowly passed from pew to pew until the candles held by every member of the congregation were lit. Gradually, the darkness receded, overwhelmed by the glow of hundreds of small flames.

During one of the carols Monica let her eyes wander around the familiar church. They were sitting in the oldest part of the building, between two solid arcades of columns. The hefty row to her left was part of the original St Peter and Paul's, built around the year 1111, though the arcade to her right was a later replacement, part of the restoration that followed the collapse of the old tower in the early 1500s.

Back in the twelfth and thirteenth centuries, the church with its thick walls and narrow windows would have been a very simple building. Monica let her imagination flow as she looked up at the carved medieval faces that peeped from the stone. She thought of the many generations of worshippers who had walked, sat and prayed in this beautifully atmospheric building. Through flood, plague and destruction, the people of the parish of St Peter and St Paul had brought their hopes, regrets and prayers here.

And continued to do so. Especially on a night like this. When the organ had brought the last carol to an end, everyone spilled out of the church on the wave of a final crescendo, still happy, the children still excited, the whole of Christmas before them.

Archie put his arm around Monica as they parted from the crowd. Opposite St Peter's Garden, the Wheatsheaf was doing even more business than usual. Drinkers were crowding the pavement and every time one of the doors opened a volley of noise erupted on to the street.

'Not bad for six o'clock,' commented Archie. 'Wonder what it'll be like by eleven?'

'Bit the same, but with busier toilets.'

They walked through Museum Square and followed the curve of the Crescent. A few souls were still returning from work, all of them managing to return Archie's insistent 'Happy Christmas'. Monica laughed along with this cheerful version of Archibald Newcombe-Walker. He was fun to be with at the moment; he even ignored his phone when it started squawking in his pocket.

They turned on to Nene Quay, past the Poet's House and around the corner to the entrance of the Victorian building which housed Monica's flat. She was entering a code on the key pad by the door as Archie's phone started to ring again. Once more he ignored it, following her up the stairs to the first floor flat. She went round switching on lamps and putting food in the oven.

Armed with cutlery for the table, Archie noticed the large pile of wrapped presents beneath the glittery artificial Christmas tree in the corner. The tree was showing its age, having been brought into service, according to Monica, for the last fifteen years. He crouched down with an indulgent smile to look at the gift labels. There was a prim, stripy box addressed simply 'to Adela' and huge beribboned ones for each of the two children. He caught the words 'Mum' and 'Dad' too. He was glad. After so many years of avoiding her family, Monica had finally agreed to accept their invitation to spend Boxing Day with them. They'd invited him too and he was pleased to be included.

'So where's mine?' he grinned when he looked up to see her watching him by the kitchen door.

'Hidden. I knew you'd look.' She bent down and kissed him. 'I can't believe you persuaded me to spend a whole day with my family!'

'Yeah, well it was about time. I like them. And you love the two kids, you know you do...'

'True, but my sister and I will end up arguing. We always do.'

'Then try not to for once, if only for the sake of your poor parents. Adela's all right. She's just not as direct as you, tries to see all points of view...'

'Yes, OK, you can stop now.'

He laughed and she left him setting the table while she inspected the contents of the oven. It was going to be a good Christmas this year, she thought. She was gradually feeling more secure about Archie, though still far from ready to consider any sort of living arrangement with him. She knew he was right about her family. They were always reaching out to her; it was she who had always been prickly, who had always held back. Archie was good for her. Because of him she was less brittle, more able to love, even.

She could hear him singing something silly as he set out the glasses, something slightly off-key. Something which was rudely interrupted by the ringing of his phone. She heard him swear. Then there was silence.

She walked back into the sitting room and saw him, phone in hand and listening with undisguised irritation to whoever it was who was disturbing their peace.

As if she didn't know who.

'Well, I'm sure you're right, but did you have to ring and tell me that on Christmas Eve?'

There was another silence while the caller spoke. Archie raised his eyebrows in a display of exasperation for Monica's benefit and she nodded, resigned.

'Of course I'm not! I am not driving over there before New Year...'

Monica uttered an oath not at all suitable for the season of good will. She could faintly hear the woman's voice at the other end. It sounded pleading and sugary.

'Look, Jemima. I will come over on the second of January and no sooner. I don't care how much we need to organise. No workman will even take a call from us over the Christmas break. Just calm down and...'

His impatience turned to mild surprise as she rang off. He stared at the silent phone for a moment before shoving it angrily back in his pocket.

'That woman sometimes...' he muttered. 'Apparently, we've had an offer on Aunt Lizzie's house, but it's conditional on the roof being repaired before they buy. Now Jemima's flown into a panic about getting it all sorted. I told her...'

'I heard. There's nothing you can do over Christmas, but you'll go after New Year's Day. But, Archie, can't you organise it over the phone? Surely you don't need to be there to telephone a builder?'

He looked at her in astonishment, as if such a solution had never occurred to him.

'You're right,' he agreed at last. 'I'll have another word with her, but not until after Christmas.'

'Well, good luck with that. She certainly likes to have her own way. Look, let's forget her, shall we? I have cooked us a fine meal, though I say it myself, and no, it isn't fish and chips, but you'll like it, I guarantee. Also, I have invested hard earned cash in a bottle of champagne. Might not be up to much, but it has a pretty label. Fetch it from the fridge, will you?'

She tried to keep her voice light and to smile as brightly as she'd managed before the phone call. It no longer came naturally.

The champagne was duly brought to the table. It was rare that she splashed out on such luxuries, but she'd been happy and looking forward to this evening.

She had the glasses ready. Archie tackled the cork in a manly fashion and she waited for the loud, satisfying pop.

But instead, the cork came out with a soft, moist pfiff. Which just about summed things up.

FORTY-FIVE

Wednesday 7th December 1216 (First Week of Advent)

The snow had continued to fall as Edwin's body was carried to the abbey. It had gone on snowing all that Saturday night and throughout Sunday and Monday. The seneschal had had no choice but to postpone his return to Wisbech.

He and his two men-at-arms had settled themselves into the Eel Inn, even though the abbot had offered them lodging. Milo preferred to remain independent of the abbey, free to go about his business without the restraint of the many religious offices that shaped the Benedictine day and night.

The snow also delayed Edwin's burial, but allowed ample time for Milo to speak to the abbot. He told him of his suspicions, that the body had been dragged into the reed bed, and showed him the emerald found between the hide and the water. The abbot listened carefully but showed no interest in keeping the jewel, urging the seneschal to take it to the king with the rest of the treasure.

Wash your hands of it, his words implied. Concentrate on the matter of the king's property and leave the murder to be dealt with in Ramsey. Edwin's remains had been examined but declared to be in far too decayed a state for any conclusion to be reached about the method used to kill him. Perhaps, the abbot further implied, it was for the best.

Such a reluctance to seek the truth did not sit well with Milo, but he had no authority in Ramsey and could do nothing about it. He could only withdraw from the abbot's presence with a dignified bow.

He had done as much as he could on the isle, but the weather continued to hold up his departure. The causeway was blocked by snowdrifts and still the snow went on falling. There were no boats either, he was told. In this weather, nothing could persuade the boatmen to leave the comfort of their mereside homes. Milo and his men had no option but to wait.

By Tuesday, when at last it stopped snowing, they rode to Fen Hallow. The narrow lane from the town to the hamlet had escaped the worst of the snow because it was mostly sheltered by woodland. Milo took the opportunity, therefore, to visit the brewer and his wife. Word had come that they had returned to the village.

The seneschal felt that the responsibility of informing the couple of Edwin's death rested on his shoulders. After all, it had been one of the men in his charge who had discovered the boy's body. He was invited into the brewer's humble home, but there was no comfortable way to impart such news. He left out all mention of the theft. There was no point in making the tragedy even more bitter, but still they took the news badly and he was unable to give them any comfort.

At last, by Wednesday they were able to leave the isle. The town was awakening from its slumber, villeins and cottagers going out with shovels to clear the snow from the roads and causeway. As if to celebrate this revival, there was the cheer of the weekly market.

The market was held each Wednesday in an open space leading from the high street. It was always a busy affair, but today the whole town must have been there, glad to be out of doors again, buying and selling, laughing and drinking. The timber booths, with their sturdy roofs and side walls, provided a degree of shelter for the stallholders. Their faces nipped and pink from the cold, they were bundled up in as many layers of clothing as they possessed and their cheerful voices rang out as they sold their bread, eggs, root vegetables and grain. In larger booths, smiling brewers served ale from heavy earthenware jugs to customers perched on rickety benches. The Fen Hallow brewer was absent, Milo noticed. In the end it would probably be hunger that forced that beleaguered family to find its feet again.

Milo, Drew and Abrecan left the market behind as they rode along the causeway in search of a boat. They had agreed that the two men-at-arms would ride back to Wisbech, leading Merlin, Milo's palfrey, and leaving the seneschal free to travel by river. His return would take less time that way. Already much delayed, he needed to be back at the castle; winter was closing in fast and Christmas would soon be upon them. Once he had seen the constable, he would have to depart immediately for Ely and make his report to the bishop.

He had no trouble in hiring a boat this time. The boatmen must have been starting to feel the drop in their income due to the bad weather and were keen to be working again. Drew and Abrecan set off along the road on their rounceys, leading Merlin alongside, while Milo settled himself into the boat.

It was colder than ever on the river, the freezing air seeming to gather in pockets by the banks as the oars moved smoothly through the water. The boatman said little as he rowed and Milo was glad of the silence. He had much to think about.

The casket, ruby ring and emerald were securely wrapped inside his scrip. He knew that travelling alone with such treasure, having given up the protection of his men-at-arms, was risky, even foolhardy, but the sword at his side usually provided enough of a deterrent.

Recovering the casket and ring had brought him great relief, especially when his chances of success had seemed so remote. At last, he had good news for his bishop and king, but still there was something that nagged at the back of his mind, something which had never permitted the celebration so keenly encouraged by Abrecan.

Had it all been just too simple? Despite the inconvenience of it all, the treasure had been found quite easily in the end. He shook his head, trying to use his logic and dismiss his doubts. Once again, he thought through the likely series of events leading up to his discovery of the treasure.

The two lads had stolen the locked casket from the smith and had left the village on foot; that much was certain. If the Waltuna shepherd was to be believed, a mounted stranger had followed closely behind them. But here was Milo's first query. Why had this stranger, who presumably wanted to seize the treasure for himself, allowed them to reach Fen Hallow without taking action? Why hadn't he challenged them along the road? He was mounted, no doubt armed, and the youths had been on foot.

Whatever the reason, the boys had reached their village, where Cedric was murdered. The fact that Edwin had then taken the treasure to the mere suggested that he was his brother's killer. Had the stranger been responsible for the killing, he would presumably have taken the casket and nothing would have been found near Edwin's body.

Edwin, lying low in his hide, already fearing pursuit by the authorities, perhaps heard someone approaching and panicked, throwing the casket into the bank of grasses behind the hut. It was a likely explanation, since the reeds and grasses would still have been close to their summertime fullness at that time.

It would explain why Edwin's killer failed to find the treasure. The emerald may have been torn from the murderer's clothing during whatever struggle took place, or while dragging Edwin's body into the reeds. That small yet precious stone might yet prove to be very useful.

Then there was de Prys. The day after the boys had left Waltuna, Walter Bottreux, Baron de Prys, the knight Edward of Hagebeche and a few heavies had also set off in pursuit. It failed to make sense to Milo how they too had failed to catch up with the boys, despite only being a day behind and having the advantage of fast horses. Perhaps the boys had caught sight of them, evaded them.

It was remarkable that neither the stranger nor the baron had managed to take the treasure they had been seeking.

But despite all his misgivings, the seneschal now had the casket and the ring it had contained. That meant the baron could still be looking for it, perhaps the stranger too.

Perhaps Milo's doubts were based on nothing more than the knowledge that someone as powerful as the baron would hate losing and might choose an extremely unpleasant way in which to show it.

Sir Milo Fulk would be doing no celebrating until the casket and ring were safely delivered to the king.

FORTY-SIX (Present Day)

Terrific Progress

Everyone seemed to have colds suddenly. The miserable damp of early January was getting everyone down and the first Wisbech Heritage Society meeting of the new year was poorly attended.

Bernadette was only there because she was on coffee duty. Her interest in the society was clearly waning, not having been enormous to start with. At least there was no Archie tonight to get on her nerves.

Once again, he was in Kenilworth and Monica was trying to be understanding about it. He had convinced her that he needed to be there in person, to speak to the builder face to face, rather than over the phone. It was also necessary, he'd explained, for him to go up into the attic to show the builder the roof beams which needed to be replaced.

There was no question of Jemima doing such a thing. All that stumbling around in a dusty attic might have spoiled her hair, Monica told herself nastily. So Archie had just had to take more time off work and go there himself.

Monica was determined not to think too much about it this time, though. Christmas had been happy. Even Boxing Day, when they'd visited her parents in Stamford, had gone well. Her older sister Adela, brother-in-law Phil and the two children had been there too, a situation which Monica usually found difficult. Her awkwardness, developed since childhood as a protection against slights, both real and imagined, usually made uncomfortable situations worse.

Adela, with her golden beauty and easy going, generous nature, was the absolute opposite to Monica with her dark hair and eyes and her need for solitude. Even their parents, who shared Adela's outgoing ways, found it hard to understand Monica at times.

But now there was Archie. With his humour and diplomacy, he was able to build bridges even without knowing he had done so. He had a way of dissolving Monica's crossness before anyone else noticed it. Boxing Day, mainly because of him, had been harmonious. She had enjoyed being with the children, especially the three year old Grace who was so uncannily like her. It was funny how genes showed up in families. With their dark, curly hair and brown eyes, aunt and niece seemed to understand each other. And as Monica was sprawled on the floor with Grace, moving bits of furniture around the dolls' house, Monica had caught Archie watching her.

He wasn't looking at Adela, as most men did, but at frosty, plain Monica. And there'd been something in his eyes which...

I must have this wrong, she'd thought, but anyone would think he was in love with me.

So that was why she was making more of an effort now to be understanding.

'And a happy New Year to you all!' Rex Monday was exclaiming. 'We have a thrilling few months ahead of us with so much to explore! I am happy to report that Ena and her team are making terrific progress with their model of King John's Wisbech. They met over the Christmas period, I understand, and have made a jolly good start.

They'll be continuing their work here tonight after coffee and if anyone wishes to join them, I'm sure they'd be delighted.

'But for now, I'd like us to continue looking at the possible routes across the Wash which King John's baggage train may have taken. We have now looked at Walpole Cross Keys to Long Sutton and briefly at Walsoken to Leverington and have, ah, fairly conclusively dismissed them both as unlikely. So now we arrive at the third theory, that of the crossing between West Walton and Newton in the Isle.'

Rex turned to the large A-frame board he had positioned by the door and folded back the blank top sheet of paper to reveal his map of the area in the thirteenth century. With sharp taps of his pencil he drew their attention to certain points on the map, drawing invisible circles around Newton in the Isle and Waltuna, the old name for West Walton.

'The crossing point between these two places has been used for centuries. For a long time it was referred to as a fording place and known as Walton Dam. There are still people who remember cattle being driven across this part of the river in the spring when the tide was at its lowest. The animals spent the summer grazing on the lush pasture of Marshland before being driven back in the autumn to the Lincolnshire side of the river.

'That of course was long after the river was straightened in the eighteenth century and hundreds of years after the tidal estuary, part of the Wash, had silted up. The river we see there now is a mere shadow of the estuary which once dominated the area and it's hard to imagine how different things were when the Wash came right up to our doors.

'Yet, one could say that the spirit of those times lives on in folk memory. Many people in Long Sutton and Walpole Cross Keys strongly believe that the baggage train was lost close to where they live, but equally strong is the conviction of the people of Newton and West Walton that the catastrophe occurred near them. Apparently, during the twentieth century, when graves were being dug in a new part of St Mary's churchyard in West Walton, there were hopes of unearthing a piece of King John's treasure. They had no luck, sadly!

'Back in King John's day, anyone hoping to cross from West Walton to Newton in the Isle was faced with a great stretch of water. Though not as wide as at Walpole, it was still treacherous. Even at low tide, the mud, creeks and gulleys would have presented considerable challenges to anyone attempting to cross them. Arguably, those gulleys would not have been as wide or deep as those closer to the mouth of the estuary, but they still posed a problem. All of the factors which we discussed regarding the longer route would still have been there at Walton, but...'

'It was shorter,' cut in Mark Appledore.

'Quite so. From Cross Keys you would be facing a crossing of about six miles. Between West Walton and Newton, however, it would have been much shorter, about a mile and a half.'

'Bit of a no brainer, then,' remarked Bertle.

'Ah, I suppose one could put it like that, yes. What I suggest is that we go to see both sides of the West Walton crossing place and look at the lie of the land, as we did at Walpole Cross Keys.'

'Nah you're talking my kinda language! Me and the boy'll be there with the ol' machine like, and Bob'll be yer uncle!'

'Jolly good! Now everyone, diaries out please! May I propose that instead of packed lunches this time, we eat at a local pub? That way, we can discuss our observations in a more leisurely and, ah, enjoyable fashion.'

Monica raised her eyebrows, astonished at the obedience with which the dozen or so people present searched in their pockets and handbags for diaries or phones. She was even doing so herself. Bernadette was making no such effort, merely pulling a face and going to switch the coffee machine on. She wasn't in the least interested in wandering up and down country lanes with Bertle and his machine.

They decided to plan their trip for a week on Saturday. By then, Archie would be home and she might even have started her long delayed research into local ancient buildings.

'And now,' Rex was announcing, 'I am delighted to make way for Sally Leaming. Sally, as one of our loyal members, has put together some notes on King John's time. So I shall leave you all in her capable hands as we discover what the people of 1216 ate, how they dressed, etcetera. I am sure we shall find it most entertaining!'

A generous round of applause greeted Sally from the bank, as she was better known. She looked nervous, drawing a deep breath before beginning.

'Yo, way to go, Sally!' cheered Bertle.

For once, the talk was as interesting as Rex had promised. Sally spoke about the different types of food available to the rich and to the poor, going on to describe the way in which each social group dressed. She talked about the Church's influence on the country as well as the castle's central role in Wisbech. There was too much to fit into the half hour she had been allotted, though, and she had to leave a lot out. No one wanted her to finish. Even Bernadette stopped crashing about in the Coffee House and started to listen.

'Could you give a talk next time too?' Monica overheard her asking Sally later as she served the coffee. 'You made tonight almost bearable.'

As the rows of chairs were stacked away, the model makers gathered around their work tables, cups of coffee and stray bits of biscuit hidden beneath scraps of balsa wood and what looked like dried moss from somebody's lawn.

Monica went to look over their shoulders at the heavy duty baseboard they were preparing for their model. About a metre and a half square, its top surface was painted a dull brown.

'It doesn't look much at the moment,' Ena Cross explained between sips of coffee, 'but it'll look better once we've cut out the shapes of the two rivers. The castle and the Norman church will be right here,' she pointed, 'close to the confluence of the Well Stream and the Wysbeck River. Other buildings will be added later; workshops, houses, stables, inns, that kind of thing.'

Monica was impressed. A grey haired man with a wispy beard was working with complete absorption on one of the castle buildings. With its narrow lancet windows and pale stone exterior, she guessed it was a chapel. One of the ladies was applying bits of bristle snipped from a scrubbing brush to the top of a tiny house, giving it an instant thatched roof. The members of the team were obviously happy in their work. It must, she thought, be nice to have the imagination and the talent.

'I could do with some help over here,' yelled Bernadette, 'and we've run out of biscuits again.'

Monica gently replaced the miniature tavern she was looking at on the table and went to find the Hobnobs.

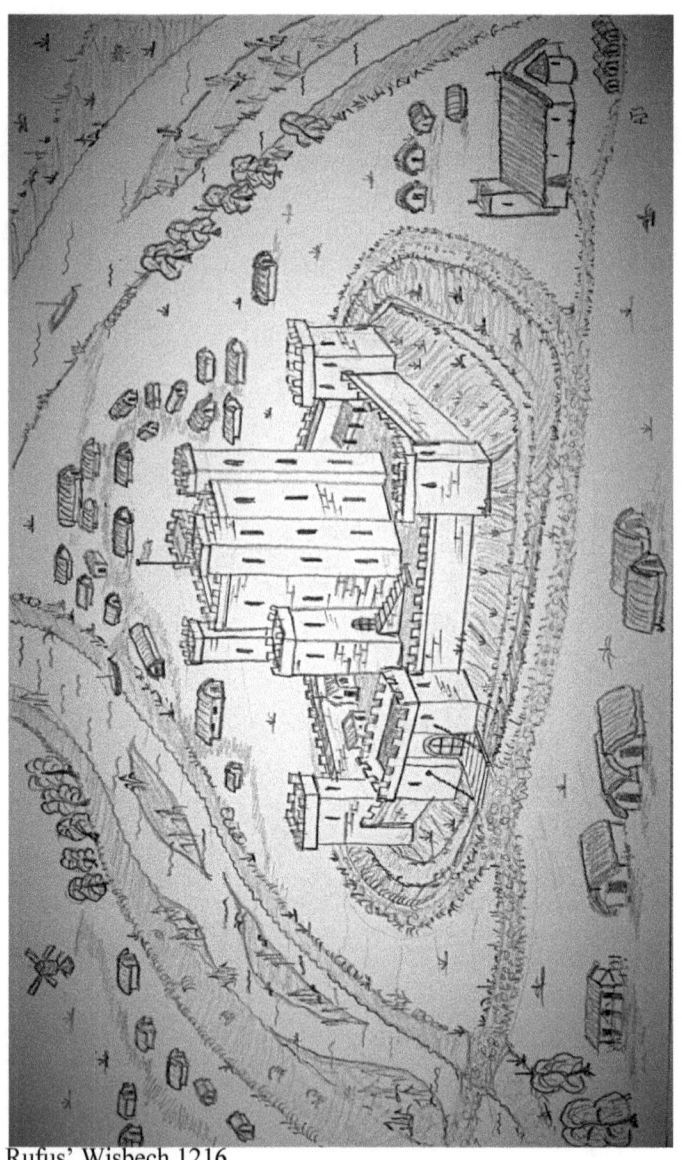

Rufus' Wisbech 1216

FORTY-SEVEN

The Monday after Epiphany, 9th January 1217

January came in clear and bitter cold, and though there had been no snow since before Christmas, the cold was penetrating.

There was little comfort in the chaplain's office for the three clerks who laboured away at their letters and ledgers. Oswy's nose, where it emerged from his oversized fur hood and linen cap, was an unhealthy shade of blue. He'd had what appeared to be a continuous cold since the beginning of Advent and his regular, fulsome sniffing kept everyone in mind of it. Egbert, similarly attired in rabbit fur more often used for travelling than for desk work, expressed his discomfort through a long stream of muttered curses, but only when Father Leofric wasn't around. The fur made him itch and every so often he paused in his work to give some part of himself an almighty scratching.

Rufus' linen cap was almost engulfed in the folds of his woollen tunic which he had pulled up to cover his neck and ears. Though he didn't voice his complaints, he agreed heartily with the others about the cold. It was almost impossible to write neatly with numb fingers. All three clerks longed for mealtimes, when they could warm themselves by the fire in the Great Hall.

Christmastide, with its feasting and merriment, was over now and all that remained was winter. It seemed to Rufus a very long time since Sir Milo had returned from Ramsey and departed almost immediately again for Ely. The constable and seneschal had exchanged reports of their trips to Holbeach and Ramsey and, like the constable, Rufus had felt huge cheer on hearing of Milo's recovery of the casket and ring. The news had made it almost immaterial that he and Sir Hugo de Wenton had discovered nothing in Holbeach.

And so, the seneschal had gone to report his progress to his master, the Bishop of Ely. It had been just before Christmas that word had reached the castle that the bishop had ordered Milo to ride to Winchester and seek an audience with the king.

The young king, it was said, was to spend Christmas and Epiphany in Winchester, and so Milo had set out on his long journey south. He had apparently been accompanied by four of the bishop's men-at-arms; when carrying such treasures he could not afford to take unnecessary risks. From the note Milo had sent, he appeared to be in good spirits. He had succeeded in his mission. He had every reason to be cheerful.

In the wake of such good news and with the fasting and austerity of Advent behind them, everyone at the castle threw themselves into the feasting, frolics and Masses that filled the twelve days of Christmas. The castle and chapel had been decorated with holly, ivy and every other kind of green leaf to be found in the country lanes. There had been plenty of good cider and splendid dishes, such as roasted venison and goose in saffron and butter sauce. On one occasion, there had even been a huge boar's head.

Goodwife Elizabeth too had entered into the spirit of the season. She and Jerome had hosted a feast on Twelfth Night, inviting their three lodgers to share a dish of umble pie, white bread and excellent ale. The lodgers tucked in with pleasure, agreeing that umbles, the offal of venison considered fit only for poor folk, had as fine a flavour as any roasted meat. Rufus savoured each mouthful and tried not to notice how much young Agnes was staring at him from the other side of the table, her face pinker and spottier than ever.

After that, taking advantage of Sunday's leave from his duties, he had gone to visit his family in Marshmeade. It had been good to see his mother and father again and even Ralph had been tolerable, but that was only because he had hardly spoken. He had appeared unusually subdued and, though Rufus cast him a few questioning glances, his brother had ignored him.

Christmastide had given way to Epiphany with its deepening cold. Rufus kept hoping for news of the seneschal. Despite the fact that the treasure had been found and all seemed well, he could not shake off a few misgivings.

He had not forgotten what the knight Edward of Hagebeche had said, that they would never find what they were seeking. Why had he said such a thing? Surely the seneschal had proven him wrong? He had found the casket.

Then there was the ring. Though undoubtedly extremely valuable, it had hardly seemed to justify the effort taken to retrieve it. Perhaps it had unseen value. Maybe it was of sentimental or religious importance to the king. That might explain it and Rufus held on to the thought. Both could be strong reasons for the desire to keep an object safe.

Yet still Rufus' suspicion, that the puzzle had not yet been solved, lingered. And as the days of January passed, still without word from Milo, Rufus' doubts nagged all the more.

He could not shake off the fear that something was wrong.

FORTY-EIGHT (Present Day)

Bumbling Honesty

'I'd had enough by then. I told her I couldn't take any more time off work. I'd spent an hour with the builder on Thursday. He said he'd fit the job in when he can, so all she needs to do is to keep an eye on things...'

'And anyway, why can't the new husband help out?'

'Because, as she keeps reminding me, he's not an executor. And I know I'm being mercenary, but good will can only go so far and she'll be inheriting a hell of a lot of money from Aunt Lizzie, whereas I...'

'You're giving up your time and energy for bugger all.'

'Couldn't have put it better myself.'

Monica and Archie had been driving down the narrow Ferry Lane from the main A1101 towards the high river bank. They parked behind Ena Cross' car, a small white Audi so gleamingly clean it looked like it was left overnight in the car wash.

Weather wise, they had chanced on a far better day this time. It was bright and sunny, though as cold as you'd expect from January. They zipped up their jackets as they walked through a gate at the end of the lane, Monica producing a white woolly beanie hat out of her pocket. She pulled it carelessly on to her head. She knew she looked daft in it, so fussing at the thing while looking at herself in a mirror would have been a waste of time.

They could see the others standing on the top of the high bank and made their way towards them.

What had really happened in Kenilworth? Monica couldn't help but wonder. She hadn't imagined Archie's enthusiasm about his first trips to the Midlands, neither had she dreamed up those furtive little texts he'd exchanged with the wheedling Jemima. So, what had happened to cause this sudden onset of common sense? Had Jemima used her charms to get him to do all the work, then, once convinced that she had him where she wanted him, stopped bothering? Whatever had happened, Archie looked like someone who had awoken abruptly from some cruel illusion.

Mark Appledore was the first to notice their approach and turned towards them with a lazy wave.

'Greetings, Monica Kerridge and friend. Sadly, you have missed Mr Monday's lengthy welcome speech.'

'Ah!' boomed Rex, impervious to any hint of criticism. 'Jolly good! How gratifying to see so many of us here! And what a glorious day we have for it!'

There really was a better turn-out this time. Sally from the bank was there, as was Mildred Winterbottom, several members of Ena's model club, as well as Rex, Mark, Bertle and his son.

'Hello mate,' grinned Bertle. 'Remember me boy, Alfred? He's only 'ere for the fry-up in the pub later, but he... Alfred, I keep bloody *telling* you to stop doing that in company!'

Everybody laughed as Alfred removed his index finger from his nose. Even Rex allowed himself a slight chortle, though he managed to look repulsed at the same time.

'Well, Monica, Archibald, as I was just saying, the area we are looking at now is dominated by the River Nene as it flows out to the Wash. Major work in the eighteenth and nineteenth centuries straightened the river to improve its outflow to the sea and to aid navigation and drainage. The wide estuary which King John would have known had silted up long before that time and it was our Victorian engineers who created the river pattern, bridges and roads which make up the landscape we have now.

'Back in 1216, the estuary was wide even here. Behind us, in the distance, is the village of Newton in the Isle. Facing us, on the far side of the river, way over there,' he pointed with a great flourish, 'lies West Walton. The estuary would have taken up much of the area between the two villages and so, where we are standing now would have been sea bed. This high river bank is, of course,' Rex stamped heavily on the grass, 'fairly new, created as a flood defence after the straightening of the river. Similar banks existed in John's day; they ran along both sides of the estuary. You can still see traces of them on both the Newton and Walton sides.'

'And it would have been about a mile and a half, I believe we said, across the estuary between Walton and Newton,' said Mark.

'Yes, roughly that. Much shorter than between Walpole and Sutton, but still dangerous. Without the help of an experienced guide, a traveller's chances of crossing safely were slim. The likelihood...'

'Right, then. Let's get cracking!' interrupted Bertle as he strode down the grassy bank towards the river. Alfred followed him, hands in pockets. The others watched as Bertle set up the metal detector close to the river, the tall grasses swaying as he moved over the waterlogged ground.

'Shall we go down and see what they're up to?' Monica asked Archie in a low voice. Bertle with his bumbling honesty would be a relief from Rex, however well meaning. Archie nodded.

Alfred, having watched his father assembling the machine, was now having the first try and was sweeping the detector across the ground in slow semi-circles. Bertle, Monica and Archie stood in silence, mesmerised by the detector's rhythmic movements. Up on the bank, the remaining group had broken up. A few of them were walking along the grassy top, enjoying the winter sunshine and getting a feel for the place.

'Wanna break for a snack, lad?' Bertle enquired of his son after long minutes of no action. Alfred, who had soon become bored, answered his dad with a grunt and swapped the machine for a Mars Bar. Bertle had no more luck than his son, however. He moved along the bank, nosing the machine into beds of yellowed grasses, then sweeping it outwards again. There was not a single bleep. Not even from an old tin can.

'Are you sure that thing's switched on?' asked Archie unhelpfully.

Bertle just grunted, sounding a lot like Alfred. After an hour they gave up.

'Never mind!' commiserated Rex. 'We'll drive round to the other side and have a look at West Walton. That should be even more interesting, since it's where the baggage train is likely to have set out from.'

Bertle shrugged and followed the others across the grass. At the gate leading back to Ferry Lane where their cars were parked, they met an elderly man walking a lively

Norfolk terrier. The man spotted the metal detector and laughed out loud, bringing the dog to a reluctant halt.

'Oh, if I had a quid for all the people who've come up here with machines like that! I don't blame you, though. Would probably have a look myself if I had the equipment. We never stop wondering if something will come to the surface one day, do we? Though after all these years and all the tides and mud and...yes, all right, Philip, we'll soon be at the river!'

Philip the terrier, who had been showing his disapproval of the hold-up by straining on his lead, now trotted eagerly towards the river bank, the man just about keeping up. The group watched them go, saying nothing. Philip's owner had not helped their flagging spirits. They were beginning to wonder what they were doing on a muddy river bank in January, but then, as Monica reminded Archie, there was always the pub afterwards.

FORTY-NINE

The Wednesday after Epiphany, 11th January 1217

Dusk descended early on that January afternoon. The sky had been overcast all day, allowing only a meagre level of light to enter the office through its narrow windows. The clerks squinted at their manuscripts for as long as they could, but despite the aid of reed lights, they were soon making more errors than Father Leofric's patience could stand.

He sent them home with a dismissive wave of the hand, gathering up their poor work. Most of the letters and his quarterly report to the bishop would have to be started again in the morning. It was essential that the report was faultlessly set out; it wouldn't do at all for the Bishop of Ely to think his castle in Wisbech Barton was inefficiently run.

Well cloaked and hooded, Rufus, Egbert and Oswy made their way across the bailey. The dense cloud that had dulled the short day was rapidly darkening to night and bringing the first flakes of snow. Before they had even reached the Mote Hall, the snow was coming down thickly and castle servants were beginning to scurry between the buildings. The clerks were glad to be returning to their lodgings; Goodwife Elizabeth always kept a cheerful fire and would have hot pottage ready for their supper.

They were almost at the gatehouse when a clatter of hooves on the stone flags made them draw back. A familiar grey palfrey rode keenly into the bailey, carrying the long-awaited seneschal. The clerks waited as Sir Milo Fulk exchanged a few words with the stable lad who had run out to take Merlin, but the seneschal failed to notice them. They let him pass without greeting and it was more than just his obvious exhaustion that made them hang back.

'God's teeth!' exclaimed Oswy.

'Father Leofric wouldn't approve of such language,' Egbert reminded him pompously.

'But look at him!' insisted Oswy. 'The seneschal looks terrible. Utterly...'

Demoralised, Rufus finished mentally for him as Oswy's words faded to nothing.

Sir Milo Fulk had been in Winchester since before Christmas. Whatever had gone on there had clearly not brought him home in triumph. His appearance seemed to confirm all the doubt and fear that had been building in Rufus' mind over the last few days.

For whatever reason, the treasure found by Ramsey Mere did not appear to have pleased the king. Either that, or Milo's grim looks were merely the results of a bad journey, but Rufus suspected that his first guess had been right.

Things had not gone well with the king.

FIFTY (Present Day)

Queachy

By the time they'd reached West Walton, Archie's stomach was growling. Monica told him he should have had breakfast. He would just have to wait.

The village looked cheerful in the winter sunshine, the high tower of St Mary's standing like a beacon over the surrounding Fenland. Rex's car came to a halt at the kerbside directly opposite the church and the others pulled in obediently behind him.

He smiled benevolently as everyone joined him beneath the great bell tower.

'You may, of course, be wondering why we've stopped in the village of West Walton, rather than proceeding directly to the river bank. But you see, this village is very important if we are to consider that the baggage train crossed the estuary here.'

'And very convenient for lunch,' said Archie, looking longingly at the King of Hearts next door.

'Nah, we need to go darn to the river first,' objected Bertle. 'Me an' the boy 'ave only just got started, like. We can get some docky afterwards.'

'Indeed, Mr Collins, I am inclined to agree with you,' smiled Rex. Bertle raised his bushy eyebrows in amazement.

'For heaven's sake, Archie, go and buy yourself a bag of crisps from the pub,' snapped Monica. He disappeared without argument.

'Now, in the Domesday record of 1086, Waltuna, as this village was then called, was listed as having a fishery, also salterns in which...'

'Salt was produced,' put in Mark Appledore.

'Ah, quite so, and apart from that, it says it had half a church. Whenever we see a fraction used like that in the Domesday record, it means that the church served more than one parish. In this case, of course, 'half' indicates that the church served two parishes. The building you see before you dates to shortly after King John's time, so there must have been an earlier one, probably built of timber.'

'Why is this tower separated from the rest of the church?' asked Monica as she looked across to St Mary's, the church's ancient walls flecked with sunshine.

'I'm not sure,' admitted Rex, 'but I read somewhere that the ground where the tower would normally have been built, at the western end of the church, was too unstable to take such a fine and stately tower, so it had to be built here. Magnificent, though, isn't it?'

He looked up, admiring its impressive architecture, his listeners doing likewise.

'And the Wash?' prompted Mark. 'Were the sea banks near here?'

'Indeed yes. The village names of Waltuna, Walpole, Walsoken etcetera, indicate the presence of a sea wall, or bank, in ancient times. Their names and what remains of the old banks give us a good idea of the width of the estuary.'

Monica waited for Archie beneath the bell tower. By the time he had returned from the pub, his pockets bulging with bags of crisps and bars of chocolate, the others had left for the riverside. They were in no great hurry to join them, remaining by the church and trying to imagine how the village might have looked eight hundred years before.

'Just think,' said Archie as he chewed on a Twix. 'King John's baggage train is thought to have been over a mile long. If it really did come here, its leading wagons, perhaps accompanied by an escort on horseback, would have entered the village to plan their crossing. They would have had to find a guide, consult him on the best time to cross, probably sort out provisions for the hundreds of people travelling with the train, as well as feed for the animals. And all that time, the rest of the long baggage train would have been waiting on the road outside the village. The train was just too long for it all to fit at once into this small settlement.'

'A bit like a long railway train at a short station platform.'

'I suppose so, yes. Come on, let's find the others.'

Back in Archie's Nissan, they followed the narrow lane out of the village. The lane threaded its straight course between fields of fertile, ploughed earth, all of it reclaimed from marsh centuries after the estuary had silted up. They turned on to a private road that ran parallel to the river and parked the car behind the others, walking to the top of the grassy bank that mirrored the one on the far side of the river.

Bertle and Alfred were already busy with the metal detector down at the water's edge. The others were huddled together, watching from dryer land at the foot of the bank. While Archie strolled down to join them, Monica stayed on the bank top, trying to recreate in her mind how this scene might have looked in the time of King John.

In her imagination, the river before her swelled to form the great body of the Wash, swamping the place where she stood. She saw curlews, sandpipers and redshanks, in greater numbers than they were today, and she saw the men. There were over a thousand of them, the poor souls who travelled and would perish with the king's wagons. No different from people living today, most of them were ordinary folk who longed to go home one day, once their work for the king was done. And because of the disaster, few of them would ever do so.

She ignored the shouts and the bleeping detector at first, unwilling to end her reverie. By the time she had turned to look at them, Bertle had produced a spade from the bin liner Alfred had been carrying and had started to dig into the watery mud. The rest of the group was gathering around them. Mark Appledore's sarcastic remarks could be heard, interspersed with Rex's loud instructions. He was warning Bertle about the risk of injury through the incorrect application of a spade.

He'd have it incorrectly applied to his posterior if he didn't soon shut up, thought Monica.

She was still reluctant to join them, wandering along the bank for a short distance before making her way down to the reeds at the riverside. The soil there was so waterlogged that it was impossible to get any closer to the river without soaking her boots. A few words she remembered from a poem written in the seventeenth century by Michael Drayton came to her mind. 'Vast and queachy soyle', was how he had described the Fens of his time. Perhaps less had changed than she'd thought.

Queachy was a good word. It described the ground underfoot better than anything.

'Monica!' Archie was yelling. 'Bertle's found something!'

She headed slowly back towards them. What was it this time? Another house key?

No, it seemed it was not.

'It's silver!' stated Bertle confidently. 'You can tell! I reckon it's a pendant or summat.'

Rex had taken charge of the find and was busily wiping mud from it, using the edge of a once pristine white handkerchief and some river water.

'Jolly interesting,' he acknowledged.

'Yeah, we sortta said, didn't we Alfred, we oughtta look in the reeds coz most people won't 'ave looked where it's wet like. I knew we'd find sommat! I've always loved it round 'ere. Your great granddad came from 'ere, didn't he Alfred?'

Alfred was too busy inspecting his mud splattered white trainers to reply.

'Well done, Bertle,' said Rex. 'Why don't we repair to the pub once we've finished looking round and then we can have a proper look at Bertle's treasure.'

The King of Hearts in West Walton was fairly busy that Saturday lunch time. Bertle and Alfred ordered the biggest mixed grills they could find on the menu and Archie chose his beloved fish and chips. Everyone else satisfied themselves with a mixture of pub classics and salad.

Bertle was in fine form. He had packed away the spade and detector in the car and was eager to have a proper look at his discovery.

Rex had a jewellery loupe in his hand; well he *would* have, thought Monica. He was peering through the lens at a hallmark he'd discovered on the back of the oval shaped item. It was modelled in a similar way to the bowl of a shallow spoon and there was a tiny hole at each end of the oval. Rex tutted to himself, turning the object round to get a better view of it through the tiny magnifying loupe. Perhaps he was trying to look like an expert on the Antiques Road Show.

'A hallmark!' enthused Bertle. 'It's real treasure then!'

Mark Appledore sniggered as he cut into his lasagne. If he could have been bothered, he might have mentioned that Bertle had been wasting his time. He'd been searching too close to the relatively new drainage works and channelled river. If anywhere at all, he ought to be looking much further back, much closer to Newton or West Walton.

'Well,' Rex was explaining, 'you have indeed struck silver, but I'm afraid it, ah, dates from 1973.'

'Nah!' protested Bertle. 'It's a brooch or a pendant. I reckon it's really old!'

'Well it is in a way,' continued Rex in an unusually sympathetic tone. 'It's almost fifty years old. It appears to have been linked to other pieces through these two holes. Perhaps it was part of a necklace...'

'No,' said Ena, 'not a necklace, a belt! My daughter had one like that in the 70s. Used to wear it with her hot pants.'

'Good heavens!' remarked Rex and bit into his nut roast.

'Look, Bertle,' said Monica as she noticed him staring miserably at his mushrooms, 'don't give up. Why don't you and Alfred come back here on your own some time and have another look? Who knows what you might discover!'

He smiled, faintly at first, but then, as he warmed to the thought, the smile widened into a beam.

'You're right mate! Hear that, Alfred, we can come art 'ere at weekends and get searching proper like. Plenty more fish in the sea! That's what I always say!'

'Indeed!' agreed Rex. 'That's the spirit!'

But Bertle said very little more during the rest of the meal.

FIFTY-ONE

The Thursday after Epiphany, 12th January 1217

Rufus had been expecting a summons all morning, but the hours had dragged by in their quiet industry. Only Oswy's regular sniffing broke the monotony of the rasping sound of quills on parchment.

The call finally came just before noon. One of the castle servants knocked at the office door and spoke in an undertone to the chaplain for a frustratingly long time before Father Leofric, with a sober nod, gave Rufus leave to go.

He knew there would be no good news. An ominous feeling hung in the air, mingling with the damp and gnawing cold to create a sense of unease. He crossed the snowy bailey and made his way through the crowd that lingered in the Great Hall after dinner. Reaching the door to the main stair well, he ascended the well-trodden stone steps of the spiral stairway with practised ease. At the top, he paused to straighten his tunic before approaching the constable's door and knocking. The order to enter was curt and business-like.

The tall figures of the constable and seneschal were standing before a pair of narrow windows which allowed a restricted view over the bailey. Sir Giles of Ely, the castle deputy, stood slightly apart from them and gave Rufus a brief nod as he entered.

'I regret taking you yet again from your duties, Rufus,' Sir Hugo de Wenton, the constable, began, 'but you have been involved from the start in this matter concerning King John and his losses. It is fitting that we bring you up to date with events. Sir Milo has just returned from Winchester and I shall let him inform you of the situation we now find ourselves in.'

The seneschal appeared to be in no hurry to speak. His pale blue tunic was badly travel stained and, if Rufus' eyes did not deceive him, torn at the hem. His leather boots, fashionably pointed at the toes, were scuffed and caked with mud. He looked like he hadn't shaved for days and his dark hair hung lankly, reaching almost to his shoulders. Apart from removing his travelling cloak, he appeared to have done nothing to freshen his appearance since riding home the previous afternoon.

'You'll recall that I was sent by my lord bishop to attend the new king at Winchester,' he began at last.

'Yes, sir.'

'The king had settled there with his court for Christmas. I arrived on Christmas Eve and was summoned immediately into the presence of William Marshal, the Earl of Pembroke, the young king's regent. Though in his more senior years, he has lost nothing of his vigour. Nothing of his disdain, either, as I soon discovered when I presented the casket and ring. It seems my doubts about that treasure were well founded. There should have been another item in the casket, the one they most wanted back. Whatever it was must have been removed from its container long before I set eyes on it.'

Rufus frowned. Sir Giles tutted loudly.

'I was ordered from the earl's presence,' continued Milo, 'but was forbidden to leave court. Under such circumstances, it was a long and joyless Christmastide. I found myself wondering at times how much longer my head might remain attached to my shoulders. It was becoming increasingly obvious that my failure to find the most important treasure was seen as much more than incompetence. Apparently, my lord of Pembroke suspects that I have stolen the missing object.'

Rufus stared at him in horror, but said nothing as the seneschal continued.

'I never did see the king himself and was left waiting throughout the twelve days of Christmas. At long last, on the Feast of the Epiphany, I was summoned again by the Earl of Pembroke. He wasted very little of his valuable time with me. I was ordered to resume my search and find the item that had originally been wrapped with the ring inside the casket. I suspect that by then the earl considered I'd be more useful doing the king's bidding than with my head severed from my neck.'

'But, Sir Milo,' Rufus couldn't help interjecting, 'what *is* the missing object?'

'You may well ask,' he replied with something that might have been a smile had the mood been lighter, 'and that's the trick, isn't it? They suspect me of stealing this object and therefore assume I need no further information. I need only recover it from whichever strong box I have hidden it in! We are faced, therefore with the retrieval of an unidentified object. And the trail is no longer merely cold. It is frozen solid.'

We; that word again. Rufus stared at the plaited rushes that covered the floor. The king would surely have the seneschal's head for this. Men had been put to death for lesser crimes than the one Milo was suspected of.

'I have sent my sergeant-at-arms and men to search the area by Ramsey Mere again,' continued Milo, 'also the village of Fen Hallow. My sergeant will seek the abbot's permission, of course, but I see no opposition there. Abbot Hugh Foliot is aware of our quest.'

'It's a fine mess,' grumbled Sir Giles. 'The day that brought this trouble to our castle gates was a cursed one indeed.'

'All the more reason,' retorted Sir Hugo, 'why we must use our greatest efforts to put things right. Our task, to find an object we know nothing about, appears impossible at first sight, but there is one thing we could look into straight away. Sir Edward of Hagebeche told us we would never find what we were looking for. That suggests he had knowledge of the matter. Why did he assume we would never find it? Was it because he knew someone else already had it?'

'That thought occurred to me too, sir,' said Rufus. 'We could make a start with Sir Edward while the search goes on in Ramsey.'

'Go with the seneschal then, Rufus. You'll be leaving first thing tomorrow, with a full support of men-at-arms this time. Sir Giles and I must attend to manorial matters, but our thoughts will be with you.'

Happy the man, said Rufus later to himself, who stays safely at home and sends only his thoughts to help in a crisis.

FIFTY-TWO (Present Day)

Loving Cup

'TREASURE!' boomed Rex dramatically. 'Isn't that what makes King John's connection with Wisbech so fascinating? It happened more than eight hundred years ago, but the story has only become more popular. It has become something of a local legend, enduring mainly because no one knows what happened to all that TREASURE!'

Some of his audience laughed and most of the others managed to crack a smile. They were unusually animated tonight. Perhaps the weather was helping, the sunshine persisting despite the cold. The second Heritage meeting of the new year, held three weeks into January, was quite well attended.

'And of course Bertle, ah, Mr Collins knows more than any of us how the lure of treasure can get to one. There is always that thought, isn't there, Bertle, that you might just be the one to find what has eluded past generations of treasure hunters...'

'Yeah, but we're not done yet.'

'Quite right, quite right, and why should you be? That's what I'd like to make the focus of tonight's meeting. Having established which of the various crossing places over the Wash we favour, ah, definitely the West Walton to Newton in the Isle option...'

'No brainer,' agreed Bertle.

'Unquestionable,' remarked Mark Appledore.

'...I thought it would be fun to look at past documented attempts to find King John's treasure. Then, we have another talk from our own dear Sally Leaming. This time, Sally will be telling us all about the work and homes of our early thirteenth century ancestors. Finally, Ena's industrious team will show us how they are progressing with the model.

'So, then, treasure hunting. Well, of course, people have been trying to find King John's hoard for centuries. Most of these folk left no record of their attempts, but in 1929 an official search programme was launched, meaning that proper records began to be made. The crown granted a licence for four hundred and twenty acres of old estuary land to be searched by a newly formed body called the Wash Committee. They must have had high hopes because in 1932 a Professor James Boone invested £40,000 in the scheme; an enormous sum in those days! However, despite all the digging and the use of divining rods, nothing was discovered. The newly founded Wash Committee went into liquidation.'

'Wotta waste,' commented Bertle.

'Perhaps their hopes were so high because of an occurrence back in 1905,' continued Rex. 'Back then, the Daily Express had published a story about a Wisbech publican who had been digging for clams at Gedney Drove End. That's about six miles north of Sutton Bridge. He'd dug up what the newspaper called a Loving Cup. Though encrusted with mud and in generally poor condition, the publican had thought the cup might be of silver. It measured about twenty centimetres in height and had two handles. He'd taken it home and thought little more about it until a builder arrived to do some work in his house and spotted the cup. The builder must have thought it was of some interest because he'd offered the publican a shilling for it, money which was, ah, gladly accepted.

'Apparently, the builder intended to sell the cup and had examined it carefully before doing so. He'd noticed that it was handsomely chased and weighed two and a quarter pounds. That's just over a kilogram to you youngsters, ha ha, but what had really excited the chap was the date stamped on it. A date of 1162!'

'Blimey! Perhaps we were looking in the right place to start with, sortta thing, when we were in Walpole!'

Rex held up his hand, his eyelids lowered, discouraging any further interruption. He was enjoying the telling of his story and didn't want to lose the flow.

'Of course, news of this find had revived all the old interest in King John's treasure. The Daily Express had clearly believed the cup had come from the king's baggage train. Spurred on by this new hope, a large scale search had been carried out all around Gedney Drove End. Sadly, though, nothing more had been discovered. Even when a new channel was dug during work on the Nene Outfall, nothing had come to light and the public had soon lost interest again.

'But the real anti-climax had come later. A while after the cup had first been examined, it was looked at again. It was found to be made, not of silver, but of pewter. It was also the wrong shape for a cup. It had no lip for a start, and the rim curved inwards. What was worse, the 'date' of 1162 was discovered to be an impressed registered design mark!'

A general 'aaaah' of disappointment erupted from Rex's audience.

'Yes, I'm afraid the discovery of 1905 had nothing at all to do with King John. It was thought more likely to be the bottom of an old moderator lamp, thrown from a ship! And so you see, everyone, Bertle is far from alone in his disappointing finds of a key and part of a belt. King John is perhaps having the last laugh!'

'Must be hilarious for him,' grumbled Bertle.

Sally's talk was as interesting as her first one and Rex settled himself indulgently in the front row to listen and approve. During the coffee break Ena's group set out their model and resumed work on it. Monica was impressed with their progress.

The two rivers, the old Wysbeck and the Well Stream, were now hollowed out from the baseboard and painted a muddy green colour. The rivers converged and broadened into the estuary at the top edge of the board and, positioned close to the confluence of these waterways, was the castle. The model of Wisbech Castle, the largest and most dominant building in the town at that time, measured only about twenty centimetres in diameter, but the detail was impressive. In the centre of the complex of buildings, surrounded by walls and a ditch, was the tall keep. Around it was a variety of smaller buildings; the chapel, stables, workshops and offices, all of them topped with immaculate, tiny thatched roofs.

Next to the castle was the Norman church, the early St Peter and Paul's. Its sturdy little tower wasn't far from the castle dyke and its eastern end was finished with a neatly rounded apse. Between these buildings and the confluence of the two rivers was an open space, painted a dirty brown.

'The New Market,' explained Ena. 'This will have been where most of the houses and workshops were, but we're still working on them. It wasn't a market place as such in those days; the market would most likely still have been held in the churchyard.'

Rex was planning to have the model installed in the cellar of the Poet's House by the end of February, ready for the start of the new season on the first of March. That would mark the conclusion of the Wisbech Heritage Society's project on King John. The group's research and the story of the king's progress from King's Lynn to Newark would be written up and displayed in frames around the walls.

Contributions towards the cost of smartening up the old cellar were landing regularly and generously in the toffee tin provisioned by Rex, and Monica was confident that the cost would soon be covered.

The group had still discovered nothing new. They had never really expected to, but at least they had thought through the various theories and could present their conclusions in a clear and, what they hoped was, interesting way.

Monica sipped her coffee as the rest of the group continued to admire the model. She had hoped that they'd make some new discovery, no matter how small. Simply repeating what everyone already knew was disappointing.

They hadn't finished yet, though, and she hadn't given up.

FIFTY-THREE

The Friday after Epiphany, 13th January 1217

Sir Milo Fulk and Rufus of Tylneye set out the following morning for Holbeach. They were accompanied by four men-at-arms, two of whom were Milo's trusted men, Drew and Abrecan.

So much riding of late had made a slightly better horseman of Rufus. Once again, he had been able to take Arnulf from the castle stables. He and the gentle natured rouncey, with his fawn coloured mane and coat, had become used to each other. Arnulf's calm tolerance of Rufus' inexperienced riding was something the clerk was grateful for. Milo's noble and finely bred palfrey would have been far too lively for Rufus to cope with; the horse's princely name of Merlin suited him perfectly.

The morning had brought no more snow but was windy and bitterly cold, the early sun soon abandoning its sporadic appearances as the cloud steadily thickened. The six riders forded the Wysbeck and rode through the Old Market, taking the bank-top road past Leverington and Newton in the Isle. After Tydd St Giles, they turned on to a lesser used track that followed the line of the high sea bank towards Sutton St Mary.

The sea bank was just one of many constructed over the centuries to protect towns and villages like Wisbech, Sutton, Newton and Tydd from the constant threat of sea flooding. The travellers were kept in mind of the nearness of the sea by the gulls wheeling high above. Their plaintive cries as they circled the wintery sky filled Rufus with foreboding.

The ground, even on the protected side of the sea bank, was marshy in places. Frail, stunted willows overlooked banks of snow-tipped and wind-blown marsh thistle, bulrush and saw sedge and the track steered its course between these outcrops, seeking the firmer ground as it made its way to Sutton St Mary.

The sky had been growing steadily darker, the easterly wind gaining in strength for some time, when the hailstorm burst upon them. They were about half way along the track by then and they pressed forward over the icy, rutted ground as hard as they could. Hailstones pelted the men and horses, rapidly filling every hole and crevice in the road and blurring the way ahead almost to invisibility.

The town of Sutton St Mary, when at last it could be glimpsed in the distance, was a welcome sight. The hail gradually softened to snow and before long the men were making their way between houses and workshops towards the centre of town. Market stalls were set out in the churchyard where most of the morning's business was drawing to a close. Awnings, weighed down and whitened by hailstones, sheltered the vendors as their last few customers, close hooded and keen to escape the weather, hurried to buy their weekly provisions. Everything from flour from the local mill, cheese and eggs, to goose feathers for stuffing mattresses, was changing hands.

'We may as well break our journey here and hope for better weather by morning,' Milo said as they approached the inn. 'This is not one of Hagebeche's manors, but I've heard he's in close alliance with its lord, Edgar de la Haigh. It may prove useful to stay overnight here and see if we can learn anything.'

Sutton St Mary was a prosperous town. Most of its inhabitants looked well dressed and the town was neatly laid out. The Drake Inn stood next to St Mary's Church in the centre, both buildings solidly constructed of limestone. The surrounding buildings were less sturdily built, their timber frames supporting wattle walls and roofed with much repaired, heavy thatch. There was no obvious manor house; Edgar de la Haigh clearly kept his main residence in one of his other manors.

Milo went into the Drake, leaving the rest of his party with the horses who were drinking thirstily from a trough. There was no sign of a groom, but that could have been because the inn was so busy.

The innkeeper was engaged in pouring ale from a great earthenware jug into beakers as Milo entered the crowded room. A group of red faced, sweaty looking men were seated against one wall and more drinkers were huddled around the tables, but neither they nor the innkeeper acknowledged Milo's presence. When at last the seneschal managed to claim the innkeeper's attention, the man informed him in a bored voice, without bothering even to glance up from his task, that both of his guest rooms were full.

'This is clearly a popular place,' commented Milo drily. The man shrugged.

'Folk stop by on their travels. And it's snowing, in case you haven't noticed. You'd better keep moving, unless...' he broke off and grinned, showing his broken teeth and allowing a miasma of foul breath to escape in Milo's direction, 'you want to use the stables. You can stay there for half price. Plenty of straw if you can bear to sink so low for one night.'

Milo could, of course, have given up and ridden further along the road. He and his men were used to travelling in far worse conditions, but his curiosity was aroused.

The innkeeper of the Drake did not want them there. Perhaps he greeted all strangers with the same degree of indifference, but the last few weeks had heightened Milo's suspicions of everyone and everything. Though his authority as seneschal extended no further north than Tydd St Giles, he knew his face was known around here. If he wasn't welcome, it would be a good idea to stay and find out why.

The absence of grooms for their horses was another sign that they were unwelcome, but Rufus, Milo and the men-at-arms were happy to look after the animals themselves. They weren't sure that they would have trusted anyone at the inn with them anyway.

'I'd wager both rooms aren't taken at all,' grumbled Rufus as he began to remove Arnulf's saddle. 'They clearly want us to leave.'

'Which is why I'm determined to stay,' stated Milo.

The four men-at-arms were doing less complaining. They were used to far poorer sleeping conditions. At least the stable was warm, with four other horses already settled in their stalls. The men spoke little as they brushed the horses down, covering the animals' backs with blankets. Arnulf responded to Rufus' care with soft snickering sounds and went gladly into his stall with the promise of sweet scented hay. The inn's lack of space and grudging hospitality fortunately did not extend to their equine guests. There were plenty of stalls and generous supplies of hay and oats.

'Might have to eat oats ourselves if the food's as bad as the lodgings,' Rufus went on complaining, 'and whoever the other guests are, they arrived on only four horses. It's curious that four men couldn't be persuaded to share one room and let us have the other.'

Milo muttered something vaguely in agreement as they headed for the back door of the inn. The place was even more crowded now, wildfowlers coming in from the marsh, their cloaks of rabbit fur dripping melted snow on to the stone flagged floor. They perched themelves on the long benches like rows of pigeons, cloaks spread like wings as they sipped their ale. A couple of them looked up and nodded at the newcomers who had found a free bench in the corner farthest from the fire. Though it was cold there, their seats were almost hidden behind a table and they found they were able to watch the inn's comings and goings without being seen immediately themselves.

There was no obvious animosity from the regulars, but neither was there any improvement in the innkeeper's demeanour. Supper, when at last it came, was almost as bad as Rufus had feared. The crust of warmed-up rabbit pie served to the wildfowlers and the newcomers was so stale that, even when well chewed, it landed in Rufus' stomach like a handful of shingle. The locals made no complaint, washing it down with plentiful supplies of ale. Their hunger after a long day's wildfowling was enough for them to overlook the quality of the food.

That was, until one of them spotted the innkeeper loading his tray with bowls of steaming, aromatic pottage and bread fresh from the oven.

'Hey!' he called. 'How about some of that over here?'

The innkeeper ignored him as he wedged the heavy side door open with his foot and steered himself into the next room. The brief opening of the door gave Milo and his men a glimpse of the cosy room next door, but not of its occupants. They could hear them though. They were roaring with laughter about something and with such good food and warmth, they probably had plenty to be good humoured about. One of them cheered as their supper arrived. As well they might.

'Who are they, then,' mumbled Abrecan to Drew, 'these honoured guests who hog all the sleeping space and the best food and deprive us of grooms?'

'Hagebeche's or the baron's men?' suggested Drew. 'They're certainly being treated like it.'

'It would explain why we're so unwelcome,' agreed Abrecan.

'Didn't you hear me?' persisted the wildfowler as the innkeeper returned with his empty tray. 'How about some of that bread and pottage over here?'

'Sorry, Ned,' the man replied in a tone that suggested he was anything but sorry, 'there's none left. I have a private party in tonight and they ordered the pottage to be made specially for them.' Perhaps reluctant to displease his regular customers too much, he bestowed a toothless smile on them. It wasn't a pretty sight. But then, his was the only hostelry in town. The risk of losing customers wasn't serious enough for him to bother much.

'Let it rest,' muttered one of the other wildfowlers. 'It's of no account. At least we've not gone hungry.'

Bedding down under straw in the stable, with the addition of a couple of shared horse blankets, was not all that different to Rufus' usual accommodation at Goodwife Elizabeth's and he slept tolerably well. He was awoken early, however, by movement and a low murmur of voices outside. It was still completely dark in the shuttered stable and he heard, rather than saw, the men who came in and spoke softly to the four strangers' horses before leading them out, one by one.

Rufus stood up as the last of the four horses was led outside. He brushed the straw hastily from his creased shirt and breaches, hearing his companions stirring around him in the darkness. He whispered a few hurried words and made his way silently outside.

Though the snow had stopped falling during the night, an unbroken canopy of dense cloud held back the daylight and it was hard to make out much about the four men who were mounting their horses by the gate. Rufus kept back, hidden within the shadows of the stable, listening as the men exchanged a few terse comments. It was impossible to distinguish any words, but as one of them placed his foot in the stirrup and swung himself into the saddle, Rufus caught a flash of red hair escaping from a linen cap.

Hair of such a fiery red was rarely seen in that part of the Fens. Folk often remarked as much to him, for his own hair was very similar. The way the man moved, the way he held his head, was familiar too.

The man was the very image of his brother Ralph.

FIFTY-FOUR (Present Day)

A Bucket of White

One of the cats jumped on to Monica's knee as she worked at her desk and she paused from her work to stroke his head. She wasn't at all surprised to see him, having heard Mrs Paynter next door letting the three Smutties out an hour earlier. They had no love of the rain and Monica had heard the thud of the cat flap shortly afterwards as they'd let themselves into the museum.

From downstairs came the reassuring sound of Bertle's electric sander. He was getting on well in the old kitchen now, having already repaired the dresser. No one needed to know that one of its back legs had completely rotted away and had been replaced by a block of new pine. Bertle had also repaired the wall plaster and installed new wiring for concealed lighting. With Monica's help, he had cleaned out the huge fireplace and, with the use of LED lights, cellophane and firewood, had created the illusion of a glowing hearth fire. Monica had then managed to find a large iron cauldron to hang above the mock fire. The kitchen was going to look good.

Meanwhile, she was making a start on the research she'd promised Rex. Using the internet, she was searching for any building, ruined or otherwise, which had been there during King John's reign. A road map was unfolded beside her laptop, showing the areas of Lincolnshire, Cambridgeshire and Norfolk which surrounded the Wash. Every time she found somewhere that fitted into the king's thirteenth century world, she marked it with a small sticky dot. Green ones were used to show places on the route thought to have been taken by the king and the baggage train. King's Lynn, West Walton, Wisbech, Newton in the Isle, Spalding and Swineshead Abbey were therefore highlighted in green.

Other settlements and monastic centres, such as Ely, Crowland, Ramsey, Walpole Cross Keys, Long Sutton, Walsoken and Leverington, were marked with a red dot.

St Mary's Abbey at Swineshead had been included, even though nothing of it remained today. Because its location was known and it was of such importance to the King John story, Monica had rewarded it with a green sticky dot. The abbey had been a stopping place on the king's journey from Wisbech to Newark Castle. At that time, it had been in the ownership of one of John's rebel barons, Robert de Gresley, fifth Baron of Manchester.

Monica wondered whether by the time of John's stay at the abbey in October 1216 the two men had made their peace. Perhaps it was because of the animosity between the king and de Gresley that rumours had later begun about John being poisoned by a monk at the abbey. However, the tales were unlikely to be true because they hadn't started until long after the king's death, when memories of his reign and lost treasure had already merged into myth.

The most numerous red dots on Monica's map marked the parish churches, chapels and shrines that survived from John's reign. There must once have been hundreds of them in the area she was looking at. Some had long since crumbled away as the population moved and changed, and many more had suffered during Henry VIII's purge in the sixteenth century. Stripped of everything of value, including building stone and roofing materials, many religious buildings were destroyed. King Henry had been determined to erase every trace of what he considered to be the idolatrous worship encouraged by the Roman

Catholic Church. Any churches that survived as part of his new English Church were denuded of the decoration he found so offensive.

As for the ancient chantries and chapels, hardly anything remained. Often, all that was left behind these days were a few legends and half-buried walls.

Monica and Archie had been to see a few of the ruined churches in the area, such as the enigmatic remains of St James' at Bawsey near King's Lynn. As a child returning in the car from a day out in Hunstanton, Monica had often gazed at the ruin which stood so romantically on the rise in the land. After so many years, with Archie she'd finally found her way on foot to it, exploring what little remained of the church that had once served a community. It dated from the twelfth century, so may well have been part of King John's world, had he cared to look at it. Bawsey was therefore highlighted on the map with a red sticky dot.

Once she had marked everything of interest on the road map, she would sketch out a map of her own, showing the coastline as it had been in 1216. Her efforts might not look very professional, but she hoped they would attract some interest.

But first there were other ruins she wanted to see. One in particular, which had come to her attention through a local history blog, was the ruin of an ancient chapel on private land in rural Lincolnshire. From the few photographs accompanying the blog, the tiny chapel appeared still to have sections of its walls remaining. More importantly, it was thought to date from the early thirteenth century; John's time. The fact that the owner had written about the chapel for the public domain suggested that if Monica were to ask nicely enough, she might be permitted to go and see it. Frustratingly, there were no contact details included in the information, so a little detective work would be necessary.

In the meantime, she really ought to go down and see how Bertle was getting on in the kitchen.

The cat did not like being moved, snuggling his head persistently into the folds of Monica's sweater. She picked him up gently and placed him on the armchair by the window, but the disturbance was not easily forgiven. As she left the room to switch the kettle on, the Smutty eyed her with obvious disappointment.

Leaving the kettle to boil, she made her way down the narrow stone steps to the cellars. Bertle had replaced the old loose handrail with something sturdier and more compliant with health and safety regulations, as well as improving the lighting. Once the walls had been painted, she hoped the steep stairway would look less intimidating.

Bertle was still busy with his sander on the kitchen's high skirting boards. Damp had rotted them away in places and he'd had to replace sections with new softwood, matching the facias impressively well. He was finishing them off now, smoothing the long sections so that the replaced boards were hardly noticeable. Once they were painted, they would look even better. He looked up over his face mask as he caught sight of her and switched off the machine. He grinned.

'Well Monica mate, Bob's yer uncle and Fanny's yer aunt, may I say?'

'If you must Bertle...'

'Looking good, though, ennit?'

'Yes, it really is. Well done, Bertle and thank you. The decorators are starting on Monday, so everything should be ready in time for opening on the first of March.'

'Got some fancy, la-di-da paint colour again, 'ave they?' he grinned. Bertle never ceased to be amused by the lengths conservators went to, scraping away layers of paint in historical buildings to discover the original colour and then replicating it to be as historically correct as possible.

'It's a sort of taupe or linen colour... something like that. Justin is happy with the shade at last.'

'Oh, how smashing darleengs!' he chuckled, doing a very bad imitation of the trustee, Justin Loveridge. 'He shouldda got a bucket of white emulsion from B&Q and added a bitta muck, blending it in, like.'

'It certainly would have saved a few quid. I'm making tea. I'll bring you a cup down, shall I?'

'Thanks, mate, and bring summa them Hobnobs, will you?'

Monica nodded. She'd bring him the whole packet; he deserved it.

FIFTY-FIVE

The Saturday after Epiphany, 14th January 1217

The innkeeper was in curiously better spirits that morning. He had managed to produce some fresh bread from somewhere, even a piece of sheep's cheese which was surprisingly palatable. His begrudging hospitality seemed to have left with his other guests. He sent his groom out to the stable while Milo's party ate, to make sure their horses were properly fed and watered. He even went out personally to inspect the condition of the road out of Sutton St Mary.

'It's in a poor state, my lord,' he reported sorrowfully to Milo. 'Last night's snow has turned to slush and made the road a sea of mud. You'd better leave while there's a break in the weather; the Holbeach road is always bad at this time of year.'

The seneschal nodded and thanked him. Taking his cue, none of the others said much. They paid what they had agreed then saddled their horses and left.

They did not take the direct route along the coast to Holbeach, however, cutting back instead to the Spalding road. The innkeeper had been quick to assume that they were heading for Holbeach, close to which was Edward of Hagebeche's manor. That assumption had put Milo on his guard.

'If they were Hagebeche's men at the inn, they'll be expecting us this morning,' he remarked once they were safely out of town. 'We shall disappoint them by delaying a little. We'll pay my lord Baron de Prys a visit first.'

'I believe they were, sir,' ventured Rufus, 'Hagebeche's men, I mean.'

'What makes you say that?' asked Milo.

'When I watched them leave this morning, I saw one with red hair. I remember folk in Waltuna mentioning one of the baron's or Hagebeche's men having red hair...'

Milo looked at him curiously.

'You may well be right,' he said, 'and we'll certainly delay our arrival in Holbeach.'

The innkeeper had been accurate in his assessment of the roads. Already, the modest layer of snow covering the ground was melting, watering down the churned mud of the narrow track. The going improved somewhat, though, once they had joined the better maintained road along Saturday Dyke towards Spalding.

Every so often, they passed a stone cross at the side of the bank-top road. These way-markers had been there to guide travellers ever since the old sea bank that ran parallel to the coast had first been used as a road.

Rufus took little notice of them, his thoughts busy as he battled with his conscience. He had omitted to mention to the seneschal how much the redhead had resembled his brother Ralph. He couldn't be absolutely sure of his identity, though, and he told himself that until he was certain, his suspicions were not worth mentioning. But deep down he knew that what really held him back was a stubborn scrap of fraternal loyalty.

As the morning wore on, the clouds grew steadily denser, darker and more threatening. It was no longer cold enough for snow, but some kind of downpour was on the way. The riders met no one on the road now. The wide, flat landscape was as forlorn as it was deserted as they turned on to Austen Dyke and eventually along the willow lined avenue towards the manor house of Walter Bottreux, Baron de Prys.

As they reached the gatehouse, the naked willow branches yielded to a sudden gust of wind. The rain was almost upon them, but any hope of shelter in this place looked as miserably remote as before.

The solidly built gatehouse was still unmanned and no groom, no house servant came out to meet them as they entered the courtyard. The first heavy spots of rain were beginning to fall as Milo dismounted and approached the front entrance. He thumped his fist against the solid oak of the huge front door and waited. Behind him, Rufus and the men-at-arms dismounted and watched.

The door was opened at last by a lad of no more than fourteen years. Judging by his simple clothing and his manner, he was probably a kitchen boy, but he gave no further clues as to his identity. He said nothing, merely bowing and fleeing out of sight again, leaving them waiting on the doorstep, the door half open.

The steward took his time in arriving and regarded them in as superior a manner as Rufus remembered from before.

'I apologise, my lord,' he said in a tone that was completely unapologetic, 'but the baron is away on the king's business.'

Milo had expected nothing more.

'And my Lady Audrey?'

'I regret the baroness is absent also and has left no word of when she expects to return. You will forgive my haste, but I have much to do.'

And with that the steward closed the door, leaving the seneschal still on the wrong side of it. The rain was battering his hood, and behind him his men looked soaked already.

'He's lying,' claimed Drew.

One of the other men-at-arms had disappeared into the stable at the side of the courtyard. He emerged after a moment, shaking his head.

'The horses have gone, sir. Seems the steward was speaking the truth. No one's at home.'

Milo paced over to the stable and looked inside. He beckoned the others.

'Bring the horses in. We may as well shelter here, since we've been offered none by the steward. While we wait, we may even be rewarded by the return of my lord or his lady.'

'The steward will know we're still here,' pointed out Abrecan.

'Possibly, but have you seen how closely shuttered the place is? How is he to watch us without us seeing him? And what can he do about it?' Milo smiled suddenly. 'Let us take this opportunity to feed and water our horses at my lord de Prys' expense while enjoying a fine lunch in this well appointed stable. Then, when the weather improves, we can ride to Holbeach and see what our friendly knight Hagebeche has to say for himself.'

Rufus and the four men-at-arms set about unfastening the horses' bridles. Once the animals were chomping their way through the baron's hay supply, the men delved in the saddle bags to find food for themselves.

'There's nothing to drink,' observed Rufus with an edge of complaint to his voice.

'What do you think the horse trough is for?' laughed Drew. Rufus grinned.

Sitting on stacks of straw and chewing the bread and cheese provisioned by the innkeeper of the Drake, the men kept watch. Their view, through the partly open door and falling rain, of the gatehouse and courtyard, was good enough.

But no one arrived and no one left. The place was as quiet as the grave.

FIFTY-SIX (Present Day)

The Regalia of Kings

'Of course,' Rex was explaining to his audience at the last Heritage meeting in January, 'there are countless theories concerning King John's treasure, but all of them are based on information written down long after the king's death.

'To make things even more obscure, many of the early chroniclers enhanced any facts they had with their own imagination. Over the centuries, fantasy merged with truth, so that no one has a clue any more about what became of the goods carried on the king's baggage train.'

The door opened and Mark Appledore shuffled in, a large red woollen scarf wrapped around his neck and tucked into the top of his tweed coat.

'Sorry and all that,' he snuffled, 'bit of a cold. Dropped off in front of the telly.'

'That's all right Mark, now where was I? Ah yes, the treasure. First of all, the facts, as far as we know them. John, as was usual for monarchs of his era, led a peripatetic life. Though he had palaces at Westminster, Winchester and Windsor, to name but a few, he never stayed anywhere for more than a few weeks at a time. Instead, he and his entourage travelled around the country with a train of wagons containing everything they needed on the road; food supplies, chests of clothes, books, documents, cash and other valuables. Some say he even had his own bath tub.'

'Loved his bath, did King John,' drawled Mark, 'and apparently, he was the first person to own a dressing gown!'

'Really?' queried Monica. 'Where did you get that from?'

'Can't remember where I read it,' shrugged Mark, 'but I know the old boy loved his books and playing chess. Interesting bloke, was John.'

'But what abart the treasure?' persisted Bertle.

'Indeed, Bertle. The crown jewels weren't all stored in one place at that time. They were divided up and kept in castles, monasteries, some with the Knights Hospitaller and some with the Knights Templar. It seems that within a few days of his sealing the Magna Carta, he began to collect some of the jewels from these stores. The main repository in those days was at Corfe Castle in Dorset and it is thought that during the summer of 1216 he removed part of his hoard from there.

'Times were very uncertain for him. His troubles with France were escalating and many of his barons were in rebellion against him. We don't know why he wanted to gather the crown jewels together. Perhaps some were to be used as payment for services and manpower. The war with France was proving to be extremely expensive and the king was short of funds. He'd had to resort to all sorts of taxation schemes which had made him hugely unpopular.

'It's possible that the valuables he recovered from Corfe Castle were later moved to Westminster, but because of all his travelling, collecting and depositing treasure along the way, it is quite likely that at the time his wagons were lost in the Wash, there were still items of treasure carried on some of them.'

'And we know that not all the crown jewels were lost, don't we?' said Monica. 'Because there was some mention of...'

'You are right, my dear. Some of the treasure kept at Corfe Castle had belonged to the Empress Matilda, John's grandmother, and we know that some of it was seen later. When John's son, Henry III, reached maturity a ceremony was held in which the Empress Matilda's regalia was used, so obviously that was not lost. Later on, in 1272 Henry III's son Edward I used Edward the Confessor's regalia, so likewise we know that *that* was not lost.

'However, when Henry III inherited the throne from his father John, he was still a child and was crowned initially with a simple gold band. At the time, it caused speculation about whether the full regalia had been lost, but in all probability the simple band had been used because a full crown would have been too heavy for the boy. Whatever the truth, the crown jewels never again appeared as a whole collection. The Tower of London, which would later become the main repository, apparently has no official record of the items lost by John. It does, however, have an understanding that goes back centuries that around three quarters of the treasure was never returned to London.'

'So, it's still darn there somewhere. We'll keep on looking, me an' the boy,' concluded Bertle.

'Of course you must, Mr Collins. But just remember that, like all modern treasure hunters, you are searching over a layer of silt metres thick which covers a layer of sand and shells. I'm afraid it makes the likelihood of finding anything rather small, but there's no harm in trying.'

Bernadette looked even more bored than usual as she served the coffee. There had been no talk from Sally to liven things up this time, allowing the model makers more time to get on with their work. Most people left straight after coffee, leaving only a small group that lingered in the Coffee House.

'So Rex,' Bernadette was asking, determined to get some value out of the evening, 'what do you think of all the alternative theories? You know, the ones that suggest the treasure wasn't lost in the Wash at all, but flogged off by the king to the highest bidder?'

'What?' he looked confused for a moment as he dunked a ginger nut in his coffee. 'Ah, yes. Well, there will always be people using their imagination to reinterpret events afterwards. I believe you are referring to the suspicion held in some quarters that when John ordered goods to be shipped from Wisbech to Grimsby, the cargo included some of the treasure. These people suspect that he was secretly using it to pay for goods or services. Is that the sort of theory you mean?'

'Yes, sort of. Surely it's possible?'

'Unlikely. If he had sold off some of the treasure and later claimed to have lost it to the waves, the pieces he'd sold would have come to light again before long. You can melt down gold, but what about the jewels? John loved precious stones and those set in the regalia of kings would easily have been recognised. They couldn't have remained hidden forever. Also, to state the obvious, there were no insurance schemes in those days. The king could hardly pretend to lose valuables then lodge a fraudulent insurance claim. No, I've yet to come across a theory of that type which holds water, as they say.'

'But why would there be so many doubts about what really happened to the treasure if there weren't real misgivings about the official version?' Bernadette persisted. 'There are other theories too, such as the king still having his treasure when he reached Newark Castle and its being stolen as he lay dying. Apparently, just after his death in the castle, there were reports of a number of travellers with laden packhorses in Newark. They were all said to be leaving town in a hurry...'

'Yes,' added Sally from the bank, 'and what about all that concerning the Baron Robert de Gresley? He was no friend of the king's, and he was lord of Swineshead Abbey, where John stayed on his way from Wisbech to Newark. De Gresley would have had local knowledge and perhaps the opportunity to cause harm to the baggage train and steal the...'

'Oh come *on*, dear people!' spluttered Rex, nearly choking on his coffee. 'Don't you see? There will always be conspiracy theories! In 1969 man first set foot on the moon, but some people were adamant that the whole thing was a hoax, that even the filmed evidence was suspect. Such doubt is in the nature of mankind. Whenever I look at all the possible versions of an event, all the theories, I think the simplest answer is the most likely to be true. Crossing the estuary would have been hazardous and they made a gross error. As a result, the loss of at least part of the baggage train was inevitable.'

'Well said,' replied Archie who had been quiet all evening. 'Perhaps some of the treasure was recovered at low tide and sold by people who had no business to do so, but we could be here until next Christmas, going round in circles with theory after theory. King John's treasure was lost after an ill-judged crossing of the Wash. It was a bloody stupid mistake, so let's not make it worse by dredging up bloody stupid theories!'

He left the table abruptly, leaving his empty cup behind.

'What's got into him?' grinned Bernadette. It was the best entertainment she'd had all evening.

'Have to say I agree with him,' muttered Rex.

Monica said nothing. She was just glad the evening was at an end.

FIFTY-SEVEN

Sunday 14th January 1217

Before long, the rain eased to a steady drizzle and the six riders left the stable at de Prys' manor and went on their way. From the bank-top road they turned on to the narrow track leading to Holbeach and arrived at Hagebeche's manor around midday.

The same air of cheerfulness that had welcomed Sir Hugo and Rufus before Christmas, now greeted the newcomers. Despite the rain, there was a healthy bustle of activity as the villagers went about their daily work. Edward of Hagebeche, despite the dubious company he kept, must, thought Rufus, be a good manorial lord. Were it not so, his people would not look so positive about their lot in life.

The visitors' postponed arrival looked at first sight to be well timed, for the manor house itself was quiet. Milo's men-at-arms led the horses to drink from the wide trough in front of the stables while the seneschal and Rufus were taken into the house by an obliging servant.

As before, Sir Edward was to be found in the Great Hall. Seated with his steward, his head was bent in discussion over the documents that were spread across the table on the dais. The lord of the manor looked troubled, frowning at the interruption as his visitors were brought into the hall. His eyes were heavy, as if he hadn't slept for a long time.

The steward bowed and withdrew to a trestle table in the far corner, taking the documents with him.

'Still chasing shadows, I hear, my lord seneschal,' the knight said pleasantly by way of greeting. His frown had transformed itself into something like a smile. 'As I told Sir Hugo de Wenton when he was here, I am unable to help you. My part in the search for the late king's property is over.'

Milo ignored his dismissive tone, pulling out a heavy chair and seating himself at the table next to Sir Edward. Rufus, following his lead, perched himself on the end of a bench. The knight gave a wry smile and a servant approached the table with a tray, setting out an earthenware jug and cups before them. Sir Edward nodded and the man poured the ale. The visitors, who had had to make do with water from the baron's horse trough that morning, drank thirstily. The pottery of the jug and cups was of the finest quality, finished with a handsome green glaze and of the type produced in Stamford. It was similar to the wares used in Wisbech Castle and a far cry from the roughly finished home-thrown items used by humbler folk.

Sir Edward and his visitors refrained from speaking until the servant had moved away. In the Great Hall of any manor house privacy was rare. People came and went all day and servants even used the place to sleep in at night.

'Your part in the search is over, you said, Sir Edward?' asked the seneschal once they could no longer be overheard. 'When did it come to an end?'

The knight looked puzzled for a moment, as if wondering whether he'd been thrown a trick question. His face cleared as he delivered his reply.

'In the autumn, round about the Feast of St Martin. My lord Baron de Prys had his knights searching three shires and we managed to recover some of the king's lost treasures. I was given to understand that there was one item yet to be found, but no further orders came. I assumed that more urgent matters had claimed the baron's attention and that of the young king. And God knows there are more important things in this world than the whereabouts of some foolish, vainglorious trinket!'

His smile had long gone and he closed his eyes briefly, as if they hurt. His visitors drank their ale and waited, aware suddenly of movement behind them. A woman in a fur trimmed blue gown had stepped on to the dais. Sir Edward opened his eyes and scraped back his chair, standing and bowing his head. The others rose to do likewise as the Lady Audrey, Baroness de Prys approached the table.

'She is resting, Edward,' she murmured, ignoring the others. 'I have given her more of the medicine the physician left us and she will sleep now. I shall take my leave and let her rest, then return before nightfall.'

'Thank you, my lady. Your kindness has me forever in your debt.'

She smiled the very slightest, stiffest of smiles, but there was warmth in her dark eyes. Rufus was unable to stop himself gazing at her again. He saw clearly the sadness that her pride was trying to hide and the paleness that did nothing to diminish her beauty. Rather, it emphasised it. She was wearing a short white veil over her corn-coloured hair and a few wisps had escaped their plaits, falling across her forehead and on to her slender neck.

'Lady Audrey is nursing Lady Catherine, my wife,' Sir Edward explained once the baroness had left the hall and they had taken their seats again. 'She refused to let any lesser ranking woman attend Catherine and she is tireless in her devotion. Their friendship goes back many years. As a girl, Catherine was sent to attend my lady Audrey, and the two girls remained close even after their marriages. My family has always been in the baron's service, you see...'

His words faded to nothing and for a moment he seemed almost to have forgotten he had company.

'I am sorry, Sir Edward, for Lady Catherine's illness,' said Milo quietly.

'The baroness offers prayers for her daily. She is most devout.'

'An inspiration to us all,' murmured Milo and Rufus' quick glance told him how barely disguised the seneschal's impatience was. As usual, they were getting nowhere, and as tragic as the Lady Catherine's suffering was, they had not come here to discuss the merits of her nurse.

The conversation was clearly at an end, as far as Sir Edward was concerned. He had closed his eyes again and a servant hovered by the dais, waiting to show the visitors out. The seneschal, however, was not yet ready to leave.

'I must ask you, Sir Edward,' he said in a louder voice, 'whether you were given a description of the missing object. I have orders from the king to find it and if you know anything about it, I ask that you tell me now.'

Sir Edward's eyes snapped open. He looked suddenly alert and amused.

'A description?' he asked incredulously. 'Are you telling me the shadow you are chasing still has no form?' His wide mouth opened in a smile, displaying his big teeth, and Rufus came to the same conclusion as he had before. The knight really did look like a horse when he did that.

The seneschal stared at him without a glimmer of amusement.

'Did I really not say before?' the knight continued. 'The thing you seek, my lord seneschal, and which you have no hope of finding, is a very small silver cube.'

He was still smiling when they left.

FIFTY-EIGHT (Present Day)

A Bitta Muck

Bertle hadn't been wrong about the colour. The shade of paint now covering the walls of the old kitchen and wine cellar of the Poet's House really did look like white with a 'bitta muck' blended in. But now the once shabby walls were clean and neat enough to welcome the new season and all its visitors.

The old kitchen was simply furnished, the original, heavily restored table placed in the centre of the well scrubbed flagstone floor. The dresser dominated the longest wall, but the focal point as you entered the room was the huge open fireplace. Monica flicked a switch and the fake fire sprang to life in the hearth, looking hot enough to cook the contents of the great iron pot hanging above it.

Monica had unearthed enough eighteenth century porcelain to fill the dresser shelves and had set a dainty silver tea tray on the table. With its New Hall porcelain tea pot, tea bowls and saucers, the tray looked ready to be carried upstairs to the family sitting room. Most of the porcelain and silver had been useful finds from online auctions. Monica still needed a few more pieces, but they could always be added later. For now, she was happy that the kitchen was ready for the new season.

The old wine cellar next to it, however, was still bare. It had taken ages for the team of volunteers from the Wisbech Heritage Society to clear the room of filing cabinets and the boxes of rubbish that had accumulated over the years. Even Rex had lent a hand, though he'd done more advice-giving than labouring. Yet at last, with its newly painted walls and scrubbed flagstones, the old cellar was ready to receive the model which Ena and her team had been working on for the last few weeks.

Bertle had installed corner lights which could be angled to illuminate the model in the centre of the room. Any day now, Rex was due to bring in the table which would support the model. Then, all the background information put together by the group would be set into frames and displayed on the walls. There would also be Monica's map.

She couldn't add the finishing touches to her map just yet because there were still places she needed to see. She'd been too busy in her Georgian museum lately to pay much attention to her medieval work and she knew she had to find time to chase up emails and plan some visits.

Her mobile started to ring and she removed it from her pocket. Archie.

'Are we going to see a load of old ruins again this weekend?' he asked without any preamble.

'No, I've heard nothing back yet, I...'

'Good, because I've a better idea. How about looking at a far more sophisticated ruin, somewhere King John had some real influence? I need to see the builder in Kenilworth again on Monday morning, so why don't we spend the weekend over there? We can stay in this pub I know, not all that far from Kenilworth, and then spend the weekend exploring. What do you think?'

Monica couldn't believe what she was hearing. He'd been withdrawn and silent for days and now he wanted her to go to the Midlands with him.

'I think,' she said as coolly as she could, 'that it's a perfect idea.'

FIFTY-NINE

Sunday 14th January 1217

'It's a pity he couldn't have been more generous with his information earlier,' muttered the seneschal as they emerged from the Great Hall into the courtyard. 'It might have saved us a lot of trouble.'

'He was deliberately holding back before,' replied Rufus. 'Now, with his lady's sickness, it seems his priorities have changed.'

'Believe that if you will,' replied Milo grimly.

The men-at-arms and a couple of grooms led the six horses into the courtyard. The party was about to mount and go on their way when the individuals they least wanted to see rode with a great clatter through the gate. The men were laughing uproariously, swaggering as they dismounted and carelessly tossing the reins of their sweating horses to the grooms.

A couple of the men threw Milo and his companions hostile glances, but passed them without a word. The redhead walked past his brother, giving no indication that he had noticed him.

Without allowing himself time to think, Rufus handed Arnulf's reins to Abrecan and followed the men towards the house. The man-at-arms nodded calmly. It hadn't been difficult to guess the relationship between Rufus and one of Hagebeche's men. Rufus' obvious reluctance to speak about it had told his companions more than he had intended.

He caught up with the last of the group as he reached the wide oaken door, placing a hand on his shoulder. The man swung angrily round. Anger faded to mild surprise, then to mockery and disdain on the man's face.

'By God's nails! You stupid little fool! You're playing with fire, little brother, creeping around the countryside with that lawman of yours. Take care; I promise you his time is running out fast.'

Ralph was smirking as he delivered his warning, his fleshy face, still pink from exertion, clashing wildly with his red hair.

'Ralph, listen to me. Sir Milo Fulk is the seneschal of the Isle of Ely, the bishop's man. He has orders from the king himself to find an item of the king's property. Whatever your involvement in all this, you need to tell me. And what do you mean about time running out?'

Ralph sighed in a parody of tolerance, relaxing his shoulders as if indulging a slow pupil. The huge door had closed behind the other men and the brothers stood before it, each with his back against a solid timber doorpost. From the courtyard, the seneschal and his men-at-arms kept a close watch. From the manor house, as yet there was no sign of anyone.

'Do you really not know?' Ralph mocked. 'It's your precious seneschal whom the king suspects has stolen his treasure.'

'That,' countered his brother, 'is just pitiful wishful thinking on your part. It isn't a good idea to mess with the law and I ask again, what is your involvement in all this?

In what way are you frittering your time, risking the king's displeasure, when you should be attending to the home manor?'

Rufus knew he was on shaky ground, that at any moment Ralph's companions, even Sir Edward himself, could come crashing through the door, but somehow he held his nerve, staring hard at the older brother who had always taunted and bullied him. From the courtyard came the sound, the very slightest hint, of steel brushing steel. Ralph looked up, seeing that Drew had drawn his sword and that the men-at-arms were moving closer.

'I owed gambling debts to Sir Edward, all right?' Ralph began to gabble, his words tumbling over each other now that he'd decided to speak. 'There was no way of paying them and father refused to help. But then Sir Edward invited me to work for him, pay off the debt that way. Not,' again he gave that smirk of his, 'what you would call nice work, my dear innocent little brother. Intimidation. Getting people to talk. Something I am good at. Sir Edward was pleased with my work and chose me to join his party in seeking out certain items for my lord de Prys. Items belonging to the crown.'

'You beat up the blacksmith in Waltuna,' Rufus stated.

'What of it? He was just a filthy thief and lucky not to hang. We took the things he'd found in the mud, but there was an important item missing. A casket. The old fool told us some boys had taken it. We set off in pursuit of them and, though they had a day's advantage on us, they were on foot, so we soon caught up with them. We found them in the town of March, drinking and making merry with the locals. We couldn't get near them. I reckon they'd sold off some of their loot because the ale was flowing nicely. We stayed the night at the inn, ready to seize the pair of them when they were alone in the morning, but...'

The men-at-arms had moved in even closer now, swords drawn. In front of them stood the seneschal.

'Go on,' prompted Milo, his voice low but full of authority.

'They had gone. They'd paid a boatman and were long gone along the river. Must have left before first light. We set off again, our horses forced to a slow pace by the state of the road and we saw no more of them. We found our way to a hamlet on the isle of Ramsey, a place the Waltuna innkeeper suspected the boys had come from, but by the time we arrived, one had killed the other and the killer had fled with the treasure.'

There was a sound from behind them, from the other side of the door. Soft yet certain, it was the tread of a boot on stone flags. Ralph flinched.

Already he had said too much and must have known that his protection from Sir Edward of Hagebeche had been weakened by it.

Milo took another step forward.

'And then?'

'There was an old woman. The villagers were all wailing with grief over that mean little nothing of a kid and this woman seemed to know something. We didn't need to use much force on her. She told us quickly enough where the killer had a wildfowling hide, so we went to the mere.'

'And you killed Edwin,' Milo finished for him.

'If you mean the kid who killed his brother, I swear we did not.' Ralph's arrogance had not quite deserted him, but he looked afraid now, as if finally aware of what he'd been involved with. 'We found him dead, thrown into the rushes. We didn't even find the casket. We found nothing but an old sack containing a few bits of worthless rubbish.'

'You expect me to believe that?' Milo countered, his voice quieter yet more menacing. Behind Rufus and Ralph the door was slowly opening. Two of Sir Edward's men-at-arms, swords drawn, stood in the doorway. The four visiting soldiers and the seneschal faced them from the courtyard.

Ralph's shoulders slumped. Not one of the men, on either side, would come to his aid now. He was trying to work out where his best options lay and appeared to reach the decision that he'd be better off by pleading his innocence.

'I swear by Our Lady that we killed no one and found nothing. We were glad to get out of that foul place with its stinking mud.' His voice had a slight whining edge to it now.

'Take him,' barked Milo and his men moved forward to bind Ralph's hands behind his back. The soldiers in the doorway made no move.

'As seneschal of the Isle of Ely I am taking Ralph of Tilneye to Wisbech Barton for questioning. Inform your master.'

One of the men nodded and they retreated into the house. Sir Edward made no appearance and when Rufus looked back, the door was closed.

SIXTY (Present Day)

Just in Case

The Bull's Head in Meriden was as pleasant a pub to spend a weekend in as Monica could imagine. Not only was it situated in a perfect Warwickshire village, complete with a Post Office and small shops, but it was right on the edge of Balsall Common.

Being at the very centre of England, there were many places of interest to visit, but once Monica had taken her first steps on the common, once she had climbed its grassy hill and wandered its meadows, fields and copses, she was hooked and didn't really want to go anywhere else.

She and Archie had first met on a common, the wild and beautiful open land that wrapped itself around the village of Corfe Castle in Dorset. This one in Warwickshire was every bit as inviting and, with Archie, she spent the whole of Saturday morning exploring it.

The pub too interested Monica, with her love of all things historical. Dating from the early seventeenth century, the old coaching inn had retained much of its charm, despite its remodelling and renovation. Traces of the inn's long working past were especially easy to see in the restaurant where she and Archie spent each evening of their three night stay. She was happy. She was about as happy as she imagined anyone could be, and Archie, though he would never be one of life's great romantics, was definitely in the mood to be charming.

By the Sunday morning, as they awoke in their room over the bar, he asked, as if thinking aloud, whether they ought to interrupt their idyll and do some visiting. Kenilworth Castle was not far away, he reminded her, and had been one of King John's many residences. Almost before he had finished his sentence, she was in the bathroom, running the shower.

'It *is* open in winter, is it?' she thought to query as she brushed her teeth.

'Weekends only, so we'll be all right.'

And they were. There were few visitors to the castle on that cold yet sunny Sunday in late January and they were free to explore, peeling back the layers of time in their imagination.

The usual vandalism associated with the civil war in the 1600s had made its destructive mark on the once mighty castle, but the years that followed had also taken their toll. The sandstone from which the castle had been constructed was gradually being eroded by the weather. In places, the red stone seemed almost to have melted through centuries of rain and now the ruins needed the help of a guide book to be understood. The basic Norman structure, consisting of the keep, forebuilding and outer walls, had been extended over the years by successive owners, but of course it was King John's influence which Monica really wanted to know about.

Walking past the massive bulk of the keep, they came to what was left of the service wing and kitchens. The remains of fireplaces and ovens could clearly be seen. It was here for a long time that food had been prepared for the keep and later for the more elegant late fourteenth century Great Hall. Sadly, all of this post-dated King John; his kitchens must have been far simpler affairs.

Leaving Archie to read the guide book on the stone steps by an ancient bread oven, she climbed a flight of modern wooden steps to a viewing platform. From here she had a perfect view of the fields and meadows that lay below and it was hard to visualise that this landscape had once been under water, that it had been part of the Great Mere surrounding the castle.

The mere had been King John's work. He had first extended the castle, building an outer perimeter wall. Then he had constructed dams to create the mere which had made an island of Kenilworth Castle. It must once have been truly impressive, thought Monica. The violent times in which John had lived, when he'd had as many enemies in England as in France, had made such defences necessary. Yet he'd created beauty as well as strength and it seemed that the king loved fine buildings as much as he needed security.

Monica reflected on her brief holiday in Dorset almost two years before, when she had first met Archie. She remembered seeing amongst the ruins of Corfe Castle a palace built by King John. Though by his time the castle keep was still the defensive heart of the fortification, John had modernised. He'd insisted on more luxury and elegance than his forebears had enjoyed and had improved his buildings whenever he found time between fighting and his disastrous politics.

It was peaceful up on the wall as she gazed at the quiet countryside. She ignored the cold wind that buffeted her head as she indulged herself with memories. It occurred to her now that the two short holidays she had shared with Archie had featured both a common and a castle. King John had also made his mark on both castles. An odd coincidence.

Sometimes she felt almost fond of the old boy; King John that was.

That she was fond of Archie went without saying. More than fond. But she dared not admit to any deeper feelings, even to herself. She just couldn't trust her luck. This weekend was wonderful, but you could never really tell. Best to stay on the cautious side, just in case.

SIXTY-ONE

Afternoon, Sunday 14th January 1217

Milo did not truly suspect Ralph of Tilneye of murder. He knew that if he and the rest of the baron's men had found Edwin alive they would have taken the casket.

Ralph's arrest had been enacted more as a show of strength and, if the seneschal admitted to having a soft spot, to loosen Rufus' brother from the mess he was in. Not that Ralph would ever see it that way.

They let him go as soon as they reached the road leading back to Wisbech. Perhaps it wasn't strictly necessary to keep his hands tied behind his back and have him escorted to his home manor by two men-at-arms, but Milo considered him lucky to get away with a mild dose of humiliation. He may not have been a murderer, but he'd been acting outside the law for months. And perhaps his worst crime, apart from his tendency to violence, was stupidity.

'So if Ralph and the rest of the baron's men neither stole what we're looking for nor committed murder,' asked Rufus as they continued on their way, 'who did?'

'The unidentified rider who followed the boys out of Waltuna?' offered Abecan.

'Not much to go on, is it?'

The seneschal made no comment. The remaining four men made their way to the Sea, the hostelry in Holbeach. They might perhaps have chosen a different inn had they known how cool their reception would be. The innkeeper neither spoke nor looked at them as he slopped cloudy ale into horn cups and tossed bread and a lump of cheese on to a platter. Word had clearly spread fast that the travellers were no friends of Edward of Hagebeche.

'The ale wasn't this bad last time I was here,' observed Rufus as they sat on a creaking bench in a dark corner, 'nor was the welcome so poor.'

'That's because they know you better now,' grunted Drew as he stuffed a lump of hard bread in his cheek to allow it to soften.

'But where do we go from here?' asked Rufus after a while.

'If Hagebeche was telling the truth,' replied Milo in a low voice, 'we know at last what we are searching for. A small silver cube. He knows more than he's saying, though. He knows where this cursed object is, but we were in no position to push too hard. Even with his favourite thugs out of the way, we were seriously outnumbered by his men-at-arms. He knew that and was laughing at us.'

'But Ralph's arrest must be giving him concern,' said Rufus. 'If Sir Edward knows where this object is, he might wonder how much Ralph knows too; how much he could be telling us.'

'We need to go back there,' agreed Milo, 'use the advantage we've gained through Ralph. Let's drink up and go.'

A sudden cold draught blew through the dark and inhospitable room as one of the locals opened a window shutter. The man was heavily bearded, his face smudged with dirt. His shabby cloak looked like he had slept in it for most of his life.

'Stinks in here,' he complained loudly and it was obvious he wasn't referring to his own unwashed aroma. The man edged past their bench, thumping against Abrecan's shoulder as he did so. Abrecan swore and rose to face him. His broad, muscular form dwarfed the man, but the local merely laughed, backing off in a mockery of terror. The other drinkers burst into a chorus of bellowing laughter.

Rufus had risen to his feet too, throwing a glance through the unshuttered window.

'Time to go,' he announced pleasantly. Drew and Abrecan, still summing up the feeble threat from the drunken locals, signalled for him to sit down again. The seneschal looked up enquiringly.

'No, it really is time to go, sir,' Rufus insisted with as much calm as he could muster. Milo shrugged and stood, the others following his example while throwing evil looks at their adversaries. Their exit from the Sea was interpreted as a victory by the men of Holbeach who cheered accordingly. Hollered curses and inebriated laughter followed them down the street.

'What was that all about?' demanded Milo.

'Lady Audrey. I saw her through the window. She passed the hostelry with two of her ladies and I thought that before going back to see Sir Edward, we could do worse than find out where she's going.'

'You mean your love-sick eyes can't get enough of her,' muttered Drew. Rufus ignored him.

'Come on then,' agreed Milo, 'Sir Edward can wait.'

SIXTY-TWO (Present Day)

Arch

The house wasn't at all what Monica expected. For some unaccountable reason, Aunt Lizzie's house had always been a sweet little cottage in her imagination, its casement windows of diamond shaped panes peeping out from under a perfectly maintained thatched roof.

Now, on Monday morning, having checked out of the Bull's Head in Meriden and driven the short distance to Kenilworth, Monica saw the house as it really was. There was absolutely nothing romantic about it. The image she had been nurturing disappeared as abruptly as the dreamy perfection of her weekend with Archie. Their brief holiday was over and he was back to business, sorting out his ex-wife's family's affairs.

And while Archie and the builder were up in the loft, Monica was stuck downstairs in the 1950s semi without heating and a kettle that was on the blink.

She could hear the murmur of the two men's voices as they discussed the work needed on the roof. Now and then she heard the rafters creaking as they walked around, presumably doing a lot of poking at timbers and sucking of teeth.

Aunt Lizzie had at some point knocked out the dividing wall between the dining and sitting rooms, creating one long, featureless space dominated by a hideous brown carpet. With its nylon sprawl of giant, fern-like shapes and bald patches, it had to date from the 1970s. But at least it picked out the brown of the painted door surrounds and the wall-mounted electric fire.

Monica walked the length of the room as she waited for the kettle to boil, idly peering into the various overstuffed boxes of bric-a-brac that were lined up, ready for disposal. A dusty lamp lay across the top of one of the boxes, its faded, frilly shade giving its 1980s origins away.

The kettle was doing a lot of wheezing and spluttering as she walked into the kitchen to switch it off and make the tea. This room wasn't too bad, having been renovated sometime in the 90s, but some of the cupboard doors were drooping from their hinges and the taps were thick with limescale.

She carried the three mugs up the narrow and uncarpeted stairs. The stair carpet, Archie had told her, was in such a bad state that it had had to be removed. The bare treads were perhaps better to look at than a tatty carpet, but the hollow sound of Monica's footsteps as she climbed the stairs seemed to emphasise the woefulness of the place. Whoever was buying the house had to be pretty brave.

She glanced into the empty, echoing bedrooms, wondering how Archie could so cheerfully have stayed there when he began his executor duties. With furniture, the place must have been marginally better, but his keenness still had to be marvelled at.

She called up into the loft, trying to sound cheery about the tea being ready. There was no reply and she left the mugs on the landing, going to look out of the back bedroom window at the neglected garden below. She sipped her tea and waited.

'Arch!' A voice was calling from downstairs. Monica was sure she had shut the door. It was too cold to have left it open by accident.

'Arch? Arch, are you there?'

Abandoning her tea, Monica made her way back downstairs. As she turned the corner into the narrow hallway, she almost collided with a swiftly moving cross looking woman.

'Who the hell are you?' demanded the woman. With her short pixie-cut dark hair and large brown eyes, this vision of angry loveliness had to be Jemima.

'I said, who are you?' repeated the woman when Monica failed to reply. 'What do you think you're doing in my house?'

Monica smiled, but it was to herself.

'I am Archie's girlfriend,' she said sweetly. 'I am waiting for him to stop wasting his time looking after your affairs. I am waiting so that we can go home and get on with our lives.'

It was Jemima's turn to smile, but her small, dark painted mouth showed more spite than humour.

'Your lives? How can you deceive yourself so easily? From what I hear, you hardly let him into your starchy, corroded life. Don't give me all that sanctimonious 'our lives' stuff. You haven't a hope in hell, lady.'

With that, Jemima trotted up the stairs, her tiny pixie feet hardly making a sound on the naked wooden treads.

Monica was left alone, severely tempted to get into the car and drive away, leaving Archie to get on with it.

And she'd left her tea upstairs. She wasn't going back to retrieve it now.

SIXTY-THREE

Late Afternoon, Sunday 14th January 1217

It was no hard task to follow the baroness and her two ladies through the town. Houses and people provided plenty of cover, but once they had reached the open countryside staying out of sight was a far more challenging concern.

Yet the ladies themselves made their pursuit far easier than expected. At no stage of their short journey did any one of them glance behind. The baroness and her companions were pressing forward on their small mounts as if without a single care. Even from the considerable distance from which the men had to follow, Rufus could tell the women were chatting and laughing together. There was nothing surreptitious whatsoever about their behaviour.

'Completely oblivious,' he heard Milo mutter to himself.

After a while, the road narrowed to a rough track that wound obligingly between small thickets of alder, hawthorn and willow, providing better cover. In some areas, rustling grasses gave warning of marshy ground where the track narrowed even more, threading its way between reed beds. The ladies hardly slowed down in these places. It was clearly somewhere they knew well, though nothing in the landscape offered a single clue about their destination.

At last, after a series of bends that directed the track between shimmering pools of grass-rimmed water, they started to climb. There was hardly anything to it, that slight rise in the land, but enough to create a small island in the marsh. And sitting neatly atop the isle of higher ground, and protected from flooding when it came, was a small stone chapel. The bare branches of a few young willows reached up behind its low roof and a pair of aspens sheltered its eastern end. A narrow path led to its simple door of solid oak.

Milo and his men remained out of sight while the ladies dismounted. By the time the men had arrived at the chapel, only the baroness' two attendants remained outside. They were standing beneath the shelter of a lean-to against the northern wall of the chapel and tethering the three jennets, the small and gentle horses often favoured by women of rank. The ladies looked up as the men approached, clearly unruffled by their arrival. One of the ladies even smiled.

'The chapel is open if you wish to enter, my lord,' she said, addressing Milo, 'or do you come here wishing to speak to my lady? If so, she is busy with her devotions and would prefer to be left in peace until she has finished.'

Milo nodded, handing Merlin's reins to Drew.

'Why does the baroness come so far to visit a chapel?' he asked conversationally. 'Is this place special to her?'

'It is, sir,' replied the same attendant. 'This is my lady's newly founded chapel of healing.'

At these words, an ecstatic beam of a smile spread across her companion's face as she took over the narrative.

'The chapel is dedicated to Saint Ethelreda, the bringer of miracles and healing. My lady has endowed her chapel with land so that it may remain a sanctuary for the healing of souls long after her own time.'

'Indeed she has!' enthused the first attendant to have spoken. She was clearly used to doing most of the talking and she took her time, pausing to stroke one of the jennets' noses. 'Already our blessed saint has graced us with miracles. Only at Michaelmas, a blind woman was given back her sight. She came here to pray to Saint Ethelreda and found she was able to see her way home, without the aid of her groom.'

Milo was scarcely able to disguise his impatience.

'Wondrous indeed, but...'

'If you wish to make your own devotions, my lord, I am sure the baroness would make no objection, so long as you entered the chapel quietly and did not disturb her prayers.'

The seneschal, who was rarely wrong-footed by thugs or villains, felt curiously out-manoeuvred by this gushing sweetness. It was somehow more disarming than knives and possibly more lethal.

Rufus watched as Milo gave the ladies a small bow and entered the chapel.

The door opened to reveal a small yet perfectly proportioned building.

The narrow lancet windows set in the thick walls let in very little daylight. There was radiance enough from the two altar lights, however, for Milo to admire the extravagant decoration which covered the walls.

To his left, a painted Tree of Jesse appeared to grow from the flagged ground, its brown trunk branching to sprout green leaves and golden fruit. The long branches felt their way into the corners, while tendrils embraced the window surrounds, invading every niche. At the end of each branch was a disc outlined in gold leaf which framed a colourful depiction of an ancestor of Christ. Closest to the trunk, the seneschal could see a portrait of Jesse of Bethlehem, the father of King David. On a higher branch he thought he could make out the bearded and wise Solomon. From the Tree of Jesse shone depictions of Biblical characters from each generation and right at the top, framed with lustrous gold, Jesus himself was shown as a child in a manger.

The opposite wall was very differently decorated. Green leaves unfurled, leading the eye towards a niche which housed a small statue of a woman, haloed and veiled. St Ethelreda, Milo reminded himself, sometimes known as St Audrey. He smiled. Lady Audrey was not above a little vanity, then. The saint to whom she had dedicated her chapel was the one after whom she had been named.

The baroness was kneeling before the small, stone altar set into the rounded apse at the eastern end of the chapel. She had not stirred since he'd entered, but the whispering of her prayers brought his attention back to her.

He should not be there. He had no right to disturb her peace.

He turned to go.

SIXTY-FOUR (Present Day)

Corroded and Starchy

Even the tall, spindly grass that in late autumn had risen to engulf the rose trees was spent and listless now. Long, straggling rose stems reached through the jungle of growth, their withered rose hips dripping with moisture.

The path was overgrown and wet from overnight showers, leaving nowhere to walk in this forsaken garden that had once been Aunt Lizzie's pride and joy. Monica could tell that the old lady had cared for the garden for as long as she could. The shrubs which lined the path, though threaded now with grass and weeds, looked like they had last been trimmed in the summer. The neglect was only recent. If Jemima had put in a little care when she inherited the place, it wouldn't look so sad now.

And here, in this abandoned garden, with the washing line that drooped in the centre, a few pegs fastened to it like migrating birds that had forgotten to leave, Monica waited. She waited as she had done in the house, except that now she was angry. Angry and hurt, as well as fed up.

When Archie finally joined her, he looked flustered.

'I'm sorry,' he began. 'I didn't expect Jemima to turn up today.'

'Obviously.'

'I told her I've had enough. I told her that when I've gone to the trouble of coming here to sort something out, I don't expect her to turn up and poke her nose in. And, from now on, she can sort out her own problems because my executor duties have come to an end!'

He finished on a triumphant note, as if he'd just achieved a major breakthrough. When he realised that Monica wasn't cheering or slapping him on the back, he glanced at her curiously.

'What's the matter?' he enquired. 'I thought you'd be pleased. I'm sorry if she wasn't very nice to you. She can be pretty nasty when she wants to be.'

'Except perhaps on that cosy evening when you sat together and shared all the problems you were having with me.'

'What?'

'Archie, you told her about problems between us. That I was 'starchy', oh yes, and 'corroded' was another word I believe she used. What did you do? Share a nice bottle while sitting on Aunt Lizzie's best carpet? Or did you retire to somewhere more comfortable?'

He looked horrified. She could see him thinking hard, remembering, working things out.

'Oh damn it! There was a time, oh Monica, I'm sorry. It was back in the autumn, just after Aunt Lizzie had died and you and I were going through a bit of, well, distance, I suppose you could say. I just found myself telling her. Jemima can be superior and horrible one day, kind and generous the next. That day she was just being a good listener.'

'I bet she was! Well, dear *Arch*, it looks like we're in for another bout of distance. A very long one. Now please get me out of here. I'm just about sick of your old life and have plenty to get on with in my corroded and starchy life at home.'

The journey home was very quiet.

SIXTY-FIVE

Twilight, Sunday 14th January 1217

Rufus didn't wait for long outside the chapel, but it felt like much longer.

The baroness' two ladies had wasted no time in closing in on their fresh audience once Milo had deserted them for the chapel. Lady Audrey's many virtues, graces and goodness seemed to lift her, in their opinion, way above other mortals, and this was made clear to Rufus in tedious detail. He smiled and nodded for as long as he could bear to, but however much he admired the baroness' beauty, he was desperate to escape their unctuous adulation.

Drew and Abrecan had wisely withdrawn to the far end of the lean-to shelter at the side of the chapel. They were busying themselves with brushing down the horses and removing their bridles, leaving them free to feed on oats purloined from de Prys' stable earlier. Rufus knew the men-at-arms were laughing at him. He gave the ladies a brief bow and, muttering something about needing to assist the seneschal, he entered the chapel.

Milo had been on the point of leaving and they met in the doorway. Assuming that Rufus had a specific reason for coming in, the seneschal took a step back and they paused in the entrance, the door closed behind them.

Before the altar, Lady Audrey was rising from her knees. Rufus bowed his head, ashamed that, like the seneschal, he had disturbed her prayers.

From his lowered eyelids, the view of the richly decorated chapel was limited, but he was still able to admire the wall paintings and the statue in its decorated niche. The altar before which the baroness stood was of simple stone; a thick slab supported by two columns. On the altar, spreading their glow throughout the chapel, were two fine beeswax candles in tall and well crafted silver candlesticks, their bases stepped and solid.

'You assumed the right to follow me here, Sir Milo, to interrupt my prayers,' the baroness was stating, her voice cool and steady.

'My apologies, my lady. We were just taking our leave.'

'I turn no one away from my chapel. The blessed St Ethelreda welcomes all and bestows her blessings on everyone who comes here. Many have been cured of their ills. This chapel, you see, is truly blessed and will become the destination of pilgrims for years to come.'

Rufus heard Milo saying something gracious and respectful, but he was no longer really listening. He had raised his head by then; neither the baroness nor the seneschal was remotely interested in him, leaving him free to use his eyes as much as he liked.

Cut into the front of the altar stone, he noticed, was a wide niche protected by two wooden carved doors. The doors were folded back, presumably to display the item nestled in the niche. From where Rufus stood, it looked like a small, rounded silver case, perhaps a reliquary containing a holy relic. There was nothing unusual about a church or chapel holding sacred objects and Rufus' eyes strayed to more interesting things.

Trying not to be too obvious about it, he let his eyes rest on Lady Audrey once more. She was dressed in the same fur trimmed and richly embroidered blue gown she had been wearing earlier. It was well cut, emphasising her slim waist, and draped around her well proportioned hips was a long leather girdle embellished with gold and embroidered linen. Its longer end hung down the front of her gown and was finished in a decoration of filigree gold and emeralds. The emeralds were individually encased in plain lozenge shaped gold settings, about the size of his small finger nail.

There was one such emerald in the seneschal's keeping, one which he had recovered from beside Ramsey Mere.

Rufus lifted his eyes and met Milo's brief, deceptively casual glance. He too had seen it.

Without breaking the genteel flow of his conversation with the baroness, the seneschal walked towards the door. He maintained the same smooth civility even as he opened the door and spoke quietly to someone outside. Returning, he passed Rufus and the baroness, striding straight to the altar. He bowed his head reverently before crouching down to look at the silver reliquary which occupied the niche.

'Please do not touch that, Sir Milo,' came Lady Audrey's voice, still strong and self-assured. 'It is sacred.'

He nodded his acquiescence, using his eyes rather than his fingers to examine the simple chased pattern on the rounded silver case. Rufus had stepped closer to the altar and he too was looking at the design on the case. Tiny, elegant scrolls and the leaf pattern which Lady Audrey appeared to favour framed a central diamond shape on the front surface of the reliquary.

There was a pause. Rufus held his breath. And then Milo did the unthinkable. He seized the case from its niche and examined it closely.

'Don't!' the baroness cried. 'How dare you defile such a sacred thing?'

'Either I do that, my lady, or I give up my search and lose my head. The choice is not difficult.'

Now that Milo held the reliquary, Rufus had a better view of it. The diamond shape had been set into the case and was in fact a diagonally placed square or cube. A silver cube. The thing they had been searching for since October.

The baroness glared at Milo, her expression full of disdain.

'We have plenty of time,' he said pleasantly as he placed the silver case inside his scrip, 'and I would very much like to know how you came by this treasure.'

Outside, Drew and Abrecan, though saved from the two ladies' chatter by their lowly rank, were in for a very long wait.

SIXTY-SIX (Present Day)

Illuminating the Model

'Well, what did you expect? If you ask me, he's always been dodgy.'

'That's not very helpful, Bernie.'

'Well, I'm being honest, which is more than I can say for...'

There was a scraping noise from above as the door to the cellars was opened and Rex began his laboured descent of the narrow stairs.

Monica and Bernadette had spent the morning hanging framed diagrams and information boards on the walls of the old wine cellar and now the central exhibit, the model of King John's Wisbech, was about to make its appearance. It was the first week of February. There were still three weeks before the start of the new season and everything was going to plan. The Wisbech Heritage Society had raised enough money to pay for the renovation of the room and so even the trustees were happy.

'Here we are, ladies,' puffed Rex as he tipped one end of the heavy baseboard to get it through the door. Monica and Bernadette went to help him and together they placed the model on the table in the centre of the room. Behind Rex came Ena Cross and Sally from the bank, both carrying shoe boxes containing the more fragile little houses and other miniature items which they'd been unwilling to subject to Rex's clumsy handling.

'Excellent, excellent!' he declared as the last of the houses and trees were reattached to the model.

Monica smiled. She agreed with Rex for once; it really was excellent. There hadn't been much information about early Wisbech for the model makers to work from, but they had made a very good job of it. Since she had last seen it, King John's Wisbech had been finished with trees, little woodpiles and tiny tracks that led from place to pace. The Old Market had its own cluster of thatched buildings and a windmill.

'*Was* there a windmill?' queried Bernadette.

'No one knows for sure,' came Archie's voice. He must have slipped into the room while the model was being positioned, without anyone noticing. 'We thought, though, that there had to have been a windmill in the town by that time. For grinding grain to make flour of course.'

'Of course! Jolly good thought, Archibald,' said Rex, though no one else commented.

Since *when*, Monica asked herself, had Archie had anything to do with the model? He was getting himself involved with everything. And everybody. She tried to block that last thought.

Everyone was admiring the partly set up exhibition. The new corner lights shone directly on to the model in the centre, making it an island of light in the otherwise dark cellar.

'Only problem is,' observed Bernadette, 'you can't read the information on the walls.'

She was right. Bertle had done such a good job in illuminating the model that he seemed to have forgotten that the walls, and the information displayed there, needed lighting too. Monica had told him right at the beginning, but she had also been responsible for checking the work was finished correctly. It was her fault as much as Bertle's. She'd been far too distracted lately to concentrate on her job.

'Don't worry,' she heard herself reassuring them. 'I'll get it sorted.' Bernadette raised her eyebrows and threw her one of her looks.

'Jolly good, jolly good. Well, I must say, it all looks terrific. All of the information boards read well, as far as one can tell in this dim light, but we're still missing Monica's map, I see.'

'Almost finished, Rex. There are still a couple of places I want to visit, one in particular, but I've been having trouble contacting the landowner. I'll chase him this weekend and...'

'No need,' interrupted Archie. 'I managed to get through to him and we can go over anytime on Saturday.' He was standing in the doorway, looking apologetic. Bernadette raised her eyebrows again, adding a loud tut.

'Well,' he added, 'I was trying to help and knew you hadn't received a reply to your email so I found the phone number and...'

'Excellent!' beamed Rex, unaware of any tension. 'So can we say that the final exhibit, your most informative map, will be added to our display by opening day?'

'Yes,' muttered Monica tersely, 'I'm sure you won't be disappointed.'

She walked towards Archie in the doorway.

'Of course,' he said in a low voice, 'if you'd rather go alone I'd understand. The invitation is open to either or both of us.'

She nodded unsmiling.

'Thanks, no, it was helpful of you. Could we go after lunch on Saturday?'

'Yeah,' he smiled, 'and we can buy fish and chips on the way home.'

SIXTY-SEVEN

Dusk, Sunday 14th January 1217

'I always loathed King John,' said the baroness.

As the last light of afternoon faded to dusk, the glow of the altar candles grew in strength, their soft illumination reaching almost every niche and corner of the chapel.

Audrey Bottreux, Baroness de Prys, lowered herself elegantly on to a bench beneath the wall painting of the Tree of Jesse. The two men remained standing, waiting as she collected her thoughts. When at last she continued to speak, her voice was as cool and apparently in control of the situation as ever.

'I was appalled when John taxed the monasteries, even more so when he had the effrontery to have some of them looted. I know his brother, the late King Richard, had left the coffers all but empty and that John's warring with France had to be paid for somehow, but why punish the religious houses? He cared nothing for the brothers whom his actions made homeless. Some of the abbeys were forced to close because he'd taken so much, their monks left to beg for food and shelter.

'It was at around that time that the idea came to me of building a chapel here, far away from the noise and nonsense of everyday life. I wanted to create a place for prayer and healing and to dedicate it to the blessed St Ethelreda.'

'After whom you were named,' prompted Milo quietly.

'Indeed, yes.' She gave the briefest suggestion of a smile. 'These few Fenland acres came as part of my marriage dowry to the baron, but they were of no use to him. He gave me leave to build my chapel here, since he cared little one way or another. He respects nothing but power.

'My lord baron was one of John's greatest supporters and was often away on the king's service. It was on his return from one such period of service, when he was enjoying the usual surfeit of wine, that I learned of the holy relic acquired by the king. It had come to England long ago, during the time of the first crusade, and John had ambitious plans for it. Despite his love of jewels, he prized the relic above all else, but only because he planned to use it for his own glory. He was determined to carve out for himself a firmer foothold in the Church he had quarrelled with. It was all so wrong. Why should such an impious man, a king who had dared to quarrel with the Holy Father himself, one who had plunged his country into years of darkness through interdict and excommunication, be allowed to hold such a sacred thing?

'But then, all was lost to the waves. Everyone in John's confidence knew that the casket containing the holy relic had been carried on one of his wagons, along with the baubles he called his treasure. When my husband left Wisbech Castle so quickly after the disaster, I knew he'd been sent to search for that one precious thing.'

She paused, one hand rising from her lap to brush a stray lock of hair from her forehead.

'And so...'

'The baron's timing was poor and he failed to find any trace of the casket that day. Meanwhile, I was making my own arrangements. By the time I arrived in Waltuna on the day following the disaster, however, the casket had gone.

Stolen by two foolish boys! It wasn't difficult to find out what had happened. No one notices a humbly dressed and cloaked woman and listening is easy when tongues wag and you are all but invisible.'

Rufus found it hard to imagine such beauty and nobility blending into the background, but such a woman would be clever enough to disguise her appearance well. A plain cloak and hood could hide anyone's identity.

'I followed the boys from Waltuna,' continued Lady Audrey, 'though it was far from easy. They were on foot and I was on horseback. Dusk was falling by then, but long stretches of the road were still open to view from all sides. I had to go slowly, making the most of what little cover there was. I had intended to confront them as soon as darkness fell and we were clear of Waltuna, to relieve them of their stolen treasure, but curiosity overruled my intentions. So did a sense of adventure, I am humbled to confess.

'I admit that I enjoyed the freedom. It is rare that I manage to escape the vigilance of my ladies who, despite all they say, have only my husband's interests at heart. On that occasion, however, I had deceived them with the falsehood that I needed to pray alone in my chapel for the entire day. A lady should never travel alone, but their laziness became my ally. I am known to be so devout, Sir Milo, that my lie must have been easy to believe.'

Again she allowed herself a small smile.

'In the end, of course, I was gone for far longer than a day, but I'm glad to say my ladies suffered no beating for allowing me to slip away. My husband was far too occupied by his own search to notice anything else. By the time he and his men had started out, they were a day behind me and the boys I was following, but he soon caught us up and we were all obliged to spend the night in March. I took great care not to be seen by any of them, being well cloaked and hooded, as a man might be...'

'Your hands thickly gloved too,' added Milo, remembering what the Waltuna shepherd boy had told them. She nodded and continued.

'And while my husband's men drank and caroused, I kept out of sight. The next morning, I was on my way again early enough to catch sight of the boys as they took a boat upstream. I had no choice but to keep to the road; I needed my horse and there was no ferry to take us. This put me at a disadvantage and I lost them briefly in Ramsey, catching up with them only after...' She paused and took a deep breath, her shoulders slumping in the candlelight.

'...I found the body in the lane outside the hamlet of Fen Hallow. The boy was beyond saving. He looked to have been attacked with a knife, but it was hard to tell; there was so much blood. I suppose the boys had fought over the treasure they carried. Riches are ever the cause of strife. The other boy had fled with his stolen treasure and I was unsure of what to do, but my uncertainty did not last for long. As soon as I'd ridden back into town I saw the boy by the abbey. He was clearly in distress, wandering as if in a daze, his clothing stained with blood. There were few other people about and no one else appeared to have noticed him.

'I arranged for my horse to be stabled at the inn opposite the abbey and continued on foot. I soon found the boy again, heading for the causeway. The quayside was busy and following him was easy at first. It was only once we had passed the last of the boats and were on the path leading to the mere that I had to take more care. He was clearly exhausted, his gait slow and laboured, but he seemed to know where he was going. I could tell he needed to rest, to find a place to lie low. He must have known that the authorities would soon be after him.

'At last, I saw him enter a wildfowler's hide by the water's edge. I waited, planning to take the casket from him while he slept. After what I considered to be a long enough interval, I walked down the narrow path to the hide. I made no sound. Even the battered door of the hut opened with surprising quiet and there he was, sleeping a troubled sleep. There was a hessian sack at his side and I reached out, picking it up with extreme care. Still I made no sound and he went on sleeping. But then, just as I was about to open the door again and take my leave, things began to go badly.

The stolen treasures in the sack must have moved against each other because there was a sudden clinking of metal which betrayed me. In an instant, he was alert and angry and ready to defend himself with the very knife he had used to kill his companion.'

'His brother.'

'His brother, then. I reached inside the sack and removed the casket, letting the rest fall to the floor. I told him I wanted just that one thing and that he could keep the rest with my blessing, but he started to lash out with his knife and I acted by instinct and I...'

'Yes?'

'It was not my intention to end his life, Sir Milo, but the door was closed behind me and I could never have escaped with the casket while he had a knife in his hand. I am not certain what happened next, but I think he turned his head. Perhaps he heard something outside. I don't know, but I remember swinging my arm with the casket in my grip and bringing it down as hard as I could on his head. I wanted only to make him drop the knife. I swear it, but I fear...'

Milo nodded. The baroness covered her face with her hands and wept gently.

'I have sinned grievously, I know. I have paid with penance over and over again, but never can I hope for God's forgiveness until...'

'But you left the casket by the hide. You also left a ring that had been contained within it.'

'What did I need of such trifles?' she snapped, angrily wiping away her tears. 'I used the boy's knife to open the casket. I removed the sacred relic and disposed of the rest, threw it into the grasses by the hut.'

'And you dragged the body into the reeds.'

'That was hard. It took all my strength and even now I am not sure why I did such a thing, except that I didn't want to leave him there, sitting like that...'

'And of course, moving the body delayed its discovery, making your escape easier. And the knife?'

'I threw it into the mere. It was an evil thing.'

The baroness appeared to have said all she wanted to say, folding her hands neatly in her lap and lowering her head so that her expression could not be read. They waited. Tension filled the chapel like the deep shadows that gathered in the recesses where the candlelight could not reach.

'So perhaps now you can tell me,' said the seneschal at last, 'what this sacred relic is. This thing which has been the cause of so much strife and bloodshed. It must be small to fit inside such a tiny cube. Part of a saint's finger bone, perhaps?'

'No, Sir Milo,' she replied quietly. 'Far more precious and wondrous even than that. It is a piece of the True Cross. The cross on which Our Lord was crucified...'

Rufus really didn't mean to. Perhaps the tension had become too much for him because he let out a sudden, uncontrolled snort of a laugh.

'You mean a bit of wood? We've been chasing around the countryside since November, searching for a splinter of *wood*?'

She glared at him as if he were a rat emerging from an inconvenient hole. Milo threw him a look and he was silenced.

'I will not tolerate such blasphemy,' she shouted, her voice at last losing its cool. 'This wondrous relic will endow my chapel with the power to heal that is greater even than that of the blessed Saint Ethelreda. Once all the nonsense about the lost treasure is forgotten, I shall make it known that this chapel contains the holiest of relics. Pilgrims will come from afar, bringing enough wealth for an infirmary to be built here. Then the sick can receive healing for their bodies as well as for their souls. Then at last I might hope for God's forgiveness.'

'But first you must answer to a more earthly authority,' Milo said grimly. She looked shocked, as if it had never occurred to her that she might have to account for her actions on this side of immortality.

She watched in horror as Milo opened the door and his two men-at-arms stepped out of the darkness into the chapel.

SIXTY-EIGHT (Present Day)

Just Being

Archie and Monica hardly spoke as they drove out of Wisbech on Saturday morning. The sky was overcast, the day damp and cold after heavy overnight rain. Monica's mood was as dull as the weather.

She could not forget that Archie had discussed their relationship with Jemima, of all people, and in so obviously a disparaging way. She couldn't get his betrayal out of her mind, nor could she rid herself of the image of Archie and Jemima curled up somewhere cosy while discussing things he had no right to mention.

Her imagination was running wild, of course. Perhaps it hadn't been like that at all. His words had probably been nothing but throw-away comments uttered when they were hanging about, waiting to see the solicitor or to do something equally tedious.

Whatever the circumstances, it was the fact that he'd told Jemima about their problems that hurt.

Her mood improved slightly once there was something more immediate to focus on. As they turned off the A17 towards Holbeach, she began to read out directions from the scrap of paper Archie had handed her earlier.

The turning on to the narrow, potholed track that led to the farm was not easy to find. Eventually though, they were navigating their way around the worst of the potholes that had filled with overnight rain to form brown, opaque puddles. They parked well out of the way of the serious looking agricultural machinery that occupied the yard and made their way to the office.

The patched-up glazed door opened with a shudder, its wooden frame swollen with damp, and a man looked up from his phone call. He was sitting behind a counter that looked like it dated from the 1950s, its Formica front faded to a blotchy beige.

'You must be Mr Newcombe-Walker,' the farmer smiled as he finished the call. 'You've come at a good time actually. I was just about to go down to the far field, so I'll walk with you.'

He set off at a rapid pace, his tall frame and heavy duty wellies making light work of the mud and puddles that dominated the track. His companions struggled to keep up. They were wearing walking boots, but they were no match for the mud. Monica thanked him for allowing them to see the ruin and in his amiable way he shrugged off the gratitude.

'No bother. Better that you came at this time of year, when we're less pushed time-wise. I'll tell you what I know about the ruin while we walk and then I'll leave you to make your own way back.

'The farm deeds don't tell us much, unfortunately, but we know that the building was a chapel dedicated to St Ethelreda. It's pretty ancient, founded in the early thirteenth century by Baroness Audrey de Prys. I tried looking her up on the internet a few years ago, but it seems that, apart from her endowing this chapel with land, hardly anything is known about her. I did discover from a library book, however, that the chapel survived until Henry VIII's dissolution of the monasteries in the 1500s. At one time, there was thought to have been a small infirmary here too, but there's no trace of it now.'

Sitting on a slight rise in the land, the ruin was almost engulfed by a tangle of aspens, elder bushes, brambles and the dry sticks of last summer's nettles. Through the sprawl of branches peeped part of an arched stone doorway and the narrow slit of a window. The farmer trod heavily over the brambles and dead nettles to make a path.

'Not much left of the chapel, I'm afraid. I really need to clear the bushes from around the building and get that apple tree out.'

They had made their way through the brambles and were able now to see what remained of St Ethelreda's Chapel. One tall apple sapling had taken root in a crevice between a wall and the floor and last autumn's leaves littered the place in an uneven carpet.

'I'll leave you to it, then, shall I?'

Followed by a volley of more thanks, the farmer left. Monica walked through the rounded arch of a doorway in the narrow west wall. Rather incredibly, the arch was still intact.

'Actually, there's rather a lot of the chapel left,' she said in surprise, 'considering it's been abandoned since the 1500s.'

'Perhaps because it's always been on private land,' said Archie, 'and too far from the nearest villages. Less of its stone would have been looted for recycling into other buildings.'

Monica was exploring quietly. There was a high, well preserved recess in the south wall, which had perhaps once housed a statue. The wall itself was almost complete, but the others had fared less well. There was no tower and no sign that there had ever been one. At the eastern end, the crumbled remains of the wall were curved into an apse.

'Even the altar's still here,' said Monica in astonishment.

'No wonder! It's made of stone and built into the wall. I don't suppose anyone would bother trying to remove it.'

'Even so, I can't believe it's survived so well.'

'It would have been preserved by what was left of the walls. Have you noticed how thick they are?' Archie walked over to the north wall and ran his fingers across the limestone blocks, studying the base of a narrow lancet window.

He was right. The walls were massive, almost a metre in thickness. In contrast, the windows were no more than thirty centimetres wide and would have been unglazed. Set in walls of such depth, they would have let in very little light.

'I wonder whether these walls were ever painted?' said Monica.

Archie wasn't listening. He had turned his attention to the small stone altar in the rounded apse. With the back of his gloved hand he brushed away some of the leaf debris from the top, but could do nothing to shift the moss that had claimed the stone, creating a thick green covering over the years, like a velvety altar cloth.

'There's a hole in the front of the altar stone,' he was saying. 'Monica, look at this!'

She joined him by the altar, placing her fingers into the letter box shaped niche that was carved into the front edge of the deep stone. She looked thoughtful.

'This reminds me of something,' she said, 'something I read once.' She straightened her back and stood still for a moment, as if sifting through half-forgotten notes in the storage files of her memory. 'I remember reading about altar stones being used to house holy relics before Henry VIII's reformation. He'd had everything he considered to be papist destroyed, of course. But before then, if a religious building were lucky enough to house a relic, it would sometimes be placed in a niche in the altar stone and kept safe behind some sort of grille. Very important relics were known to draw pilgrims from miles around. They would come in the hope of cures for their ills and bring generous donations with them.'

'So the relics pulled in the crowds.'

'Certainly.'

Archie was rubbing with one gloved finger at the top of the stone close to the front edge and the niche. There was some sort of inscription there, but it was so badly worn away by centuries of weather that, even with some of the vegetation brushed from it, it made no sense.

''Cruc'...that's all I can see.'

'There's more, look,' said Monica as she rubbed at the moss to the left of the revealed letters. There was more carving there but it consisted mostly of fine, separated lines. Some of them might once have formed letters, but it was hard to tell.

'Could that be 'anc'?' she continued. 'That's all I can make out. The middle bit is completely worn away.'

'If there *was* some sort of relic here,' Archie was thinking aloud, 'it might explain how the place managed to survive for so long. After all, it's tiny and in the middle of nowhere. In King John's time it would have been even more isolated, being so near the coast. Who would have come here? But a holy relic, you say, would have drawn in large numbers of pilgrims and masses of money.'

'Yes, and wealthy people would have endowed the chapel, the infirmary too if there really was one, with land and money. They believed then that giving to the Church would save their souls,' said Monica. 'It would, as you say, explain how this little place stayed intact until good old Henry brought an end to it. I wonder how we could find out...'

'What sort of relic might it have been?' Archie cut in. 'I saw a documentary once about fake relics being sold to gullible people in old times. Folk were only too keen to believe they were buying the real thing. Easy prey for medieval con men. Chicken bones were made out to be the sacred bones of saints. Nothing really changes, does it? Most of the conning just takes place online now.'

'...anc...Cruc...' Monica was trying to decipher more from the inscription.

'Could it have been 'Sanctae Crucis'?' offered Archie. 'It might have been. Look at where the letters are worn away. The Latin term, Sanctae Crucis, is still used today by an Anglican group of priests called the Society of the Holy Cross. This inscription could simply mean...'

'...that the relic was believed to have been part of the Holy Cross. The True Cross,' Monica finished for him.

'Would they really have believed that? It's possible they were taken in, I suppose. All sorts of con men were flogging old bits of wood...'

'Along with the chicken bones,' she interrupted drily.

'Well, there were a lot of fakes about.'

'Perhaps this one was real.'

'Oh, very funny Monica. Don't be silly! But I suppose that if this chapel had a piece of what was *believed* to be part of the cross used for the Crucifixion and brought back from the Holy Land following one of the crusades, it would have become quite an important place. And such a relic,' he continued with a laugh, 'real or not, would probably have been valued in those days more highly than the most precious of King John's jewels!'

She made no reply. She was starting to find Archie's attitude and his sweeping conclusions irritating. She felt a need for stillness, to block him out. Him and all his noise.

She stood in the centre of the leaf-littered floor, thinking nothing. Just being. She had never really done that before, simply standing and, in a way, letting the place come to her.

Afterwards, she could have sworn that the broken chapel, with its mossy altar and memories of candlelight, had in one tiny fragment of a second undergone a change. It was no more than a breath, almost imperceptible, but in that moment the light had altered and the chapel had seemed to glow. It had felt whole again.

'Come on, then,' Archie was pressing. 'Let's go and get some fish and chips.'

She let him go. She continued to stand in St Ethelreda's chapel, absorbing its peace.

By the time she had left the chapel, he was half way down the track.

SIXTY-NINE

Wednesday 1st February 1217

Goodwife Elizabeth waved them away impatiently and disappeared back behind the hen house. Her daughter Agnes, pale face framed by her plain linen cap, watched them go.

'No way to start a day,' moaned Egbert, 'with your stomach groaning with hunger.'

'I blame Rufus,' declared Oswy. 'Even he overslept this morning and we rely on him to wake us up. There was no time to eat and now we'll have to go hungry all morning.'

'However did you manage without me while I was away?' asked Rufus drily. It was always best to make light of Oswy's peevishness. That way it disappeared more quickly.

'We overslept mostly,' admitted Egbert with a grin, 'but we still didn't miss you half as much as that one did.'

'Which one?'

'Agnes. Haven't you noticed how she looks at you? Just now, one glance made her turn as red as the sunset.'

'But she's just a child,' protested Rufus.

'Not any more,' pointed out Oswy, 'but I suppose that compared with certain members of the nobility currently entertained within the castle's more secure quarters, she is very young.'

'Ah, yes, the baroness!' said Egbert. 'Theft of royal property, not to mention murder! But you wouldn't think so now, would you, not when you see the trays of food being taken to our prisoner. Venison and capons, thick with sauce and spiced to perfection. Wouldn't mind being locked up myself if I could eat like that.'

Rufus nodded but added nothing. It was bitterly cold, frost coating thatch and road with a sparkling layer reminiscent of snow. It was still barely light and already they were approaching the castle gates. He was glad of the pause in conversation so that he could lapse into his own thoughts.

It was true what Egbert and Oswy said. Audrey Bottreux, Baroness de Prys was indeed imprisoned at the castle while the higher authorities decided on her fate. Abbot Hugh Foliot of Ramsey, despite his request to oversee justice for the murder of a Ramsey man in his own banlieu, held little sway now. Not now that the killer was known to be the wife of one of the late king's most faithful barons and one who promised that same allegiance to Henry III.

Even Sir Milo Fulk was unable to predict the course of justice in this case. And so, while the seneschal waited to hear when the baroness would be brought to trial, she remained a prisoner in Wisbech Castle. Her chamber, far from being in the darkest of dungeon rooms, was high up in the keep, close to the quarters of the constable himself. Yet for all her fine food and luxurious accommodation, the Lady Audrey was securely confined and could be in no doubt of the severity of her situation.

Rufus felt nothing but embarrassment now about the way he had idolised the great lady. Nothing could have cured him more effectively of that obsession than witnessing her confession. Her ruthlessness had shown itself clearly, making her tears and penance meaningless. Her determination to seize the holy relic for her own chapel, no matter what the consequences, was a cold and unattractive thing.

And then there was his brother Ralph. Rufus wondered how he had settled back into life on the family manor and whether he would ever knuckle down to the responsibilities which one day would be solely his. It was more doubtful now than ever that he would achieve the knighthood he wished for.

One Sunday soon, Rufus knew he should pay his family a visit. He would receive no thanks from his brother for his involvement in severing Ralph's ties with Edward of Hagebeche. Resentment would be all he earned from that. There was never likely to be affection, or anything close to it, between the brothers.

Torches still lit the archway under the gatehouse and the recesses in the stone walls were engulfed in shadow. Even so, everyone was out and about, the castle bailey alive with the usual morning activity. Servants, stonemasons, carpenters, men-at-arms and clerks walked purposefully from one part of the castle to another as they went about their duties.

It was good to be back, thought Rufus. Back to normal.

There was a call from behind and the clerks turned. Agnes, her cheeks pink and her eyes shining, was running hard to catch up with them.

'Mother sent you all some food,' she was calling as she ran, 'since you missed out earlier. There's new bread, straight from the oven, and some sheep's cheese...' The small bundle in her hands was held out in the general direction of the three clerks, but her eyes were all for Rufus. He took the neat, linen-wrapped package of food and thanked her, smiling into her bright eyes. He was wondering suddenly how he had failed so utterly to notice the change in her. How had she grown so quickly from a pimply, awkward girl into such a lovely young woman?

For the first time, he followed her with his eyes. He watched as she ran towards the gatehouse, disappearing into its shadows. Beside him, Oswy sniggered.

Then Father Leofric was striding towards them from the chapel office, exasperation written all over his round face.

'Come on, come on!' he chided. 'What in the world has kept you? I have urgent letters to be dispatched before noon. Get yourselves inside, will you?'

Rufus smiled and obeyed, walking with the others into the small, chilly office that was so familiar. After all that had passed since the autumn, after all the upheaval and uncertainty, the threats and the urgency, it would be good to enjoy quiet times again.

The season of Lent would soon be upon them, with Egbert's daily gripes about the fasting imposed on them all. But then there would be Easter and the spring. And the blessing of summer beyond.

And the peace to indulge in a daydream or two. He had the feeling that Agnes might play a significant part in his.

SEVENTY (Present Day)

A Jolly Good Glass

Rex had purchased a plentiful supply of Bollinger and a large tray of smoked salmon canapés for the opening celebration. If they were going to raise a glass to their new exhibition, he'd said, they ought to do it properly.

Bernadette made her precarious way down the narrow cellar steps with the wide tray, her right elbow bumping against the newly painted stone wall as she descended. Behind her lumbered Rex with his box of champagne, followed by Monica with a cardboard box of glasses hugged closely to her chest.

It wasn't long before the cellar of the Poet's House was full to capacity with members of the Wisbech Heritage Society. There'd been no reluctance to turn up that evening, not when Rex was offering such luxurious refreshments with which to celebrate the conclusion of their first project.

There were a few complaints about the cold because Monica had forgotten until the last minute to switch the heaters on. She seemed to be forgetting a lot lately, but at least she'd remembered to ask Bertle to sort the lighting out. He had managed to rig up some wall lights in addition to the corner ones and at last it was possible to read the information on the walls without a torch.

Of all the members of the society, only Archie was absent. Bertle too had been missing to start with, but he'd clattered down the stairs just as Rex was popping the first cork.

'Sorry I'm late like, but a bloke in Outwell had sommat stuck in his u-bend. No time to get changed or nothing.'

He was still wearing his padded cotton work shirt, the one with the rip in the front pocket and the fleecy lining hanging out, and the jeans that looked specially designed to ride down and display plenty of manly cleavage. He also smelled faintly of drains.

'Absolutely no problem at all, my dear fellow,' declared Rex as he began to fill everyone's glass. 'So now we're all here except for Archibald!'

'That's right,' confirmed Monica. 'I'm afraid he won't be coming.'

Probably because she hadn't told him about tonight. She had decided it would be best if he just stayed away. After their trip to the chapel, she'd had no wish to see him again.

'Well actually,' Bernadette was saying as she accepted a glass from Rex, 'he'll probably be here in a bit. He only found out about tonight a few minutes ago.'

Monica glared at her.

'Look, I'm sorry, all right?' Bernadette whispered as she made her way around the model to join her. 'But I reckoned he deserved to be here. He's been part of this project from the start and...'

'You've changed your tune!' snapped Monica as Rex pressed a glass into her hand. 'I wish you'd stayed out of it!'

'Yes, well, I've been thinking, if you want to know. I don't like the bloke, you know that, but it occurred to me that while he was telling Jemima about you, you were talking to me about *him*. What's the difference really? I know she's his ex and you're as jealous as hell about the woman, but when you think about it, he probably needed to talk to someone. She was just there at the right time. And, after all, it was *you* they were talking about.'

Rex was popping another cork. Monica was feeling flustered.

'And so you decided to interfere and tell him about tonight.'

'Yes, I'm sorry. I think I've been a bit too judgemental about him. And whether or not you're getting on together, he has a right to be here. You don't have to talk to him.'

'Now then everyone, simmer down, simmer down. Let us raise our glasses to the success of our new exhibition!'

Everyone did as commanded, took a sip and cheered.

'Hey, this is good stuff,' said Ena.

'Excellent,' agreed Mark. 'Not every day one enjoys a jolly good glass of Bolly.'

'My sentiments entirely, Mark.' Rex paused before raising his voice to address the room again. 'If I may have your attention for a short while... I hope you are all as pleased as I am about the material we've collected about King John's last visit to our neck of the woods. This marvellous model is bound to attract many visitors when the Poet's House opens its doors for a new season in two weeks' time. I would like once again to thank you all for raising the necessary funds and helping to prepare this room. I'm sure you'd like to join me in thanking Monica for her permission to house our display in her beautiful Georgian museum.'

'Here here!' cried Ena as everyone cheered and applauded.

'I would also like to congratulate Ena and her team for their skilful model making and astonishing eye for detail. I see you have even put tiny people in your medieval town!'

'Made from the tips of matchsticks!' she laughed as she received her own share of applause.

'It would, of course,' continued Rex, 'have been too much to hope that we discovered the truth about John and his baggage train. There are too many theories and too little evidence. I do believe, though, that it was a useful exercise and that we all enjoyed the work.'

A few murmurs of agreement came from his audience. Glasses were emptying fast.

'Sadly, we shall never know the truth. Not unless Bertle builds a time machine to take us back to see for ourselves.'

Bertle, who hadn't been listening and who was holding his champagne flute with one little finger outstretched, grinned as his name was spoken. He looked as if he'd been jolted out of a daydream and had just remembered something, reaching into his bulging shirt pocket with his spare hand.

'Here, Monica mate,' he said when at last Rex's speech came to an end, 'keep meaning to give you this for your museum like. Me granddad reckoned it came from *his* granddad. That means it's gotta be old, so if it's Georgian you might like it for the Poet's House. Don't need it meself and Alfred don't play a lotta marbles these days.'

Monica took the proffered tobacco tin from him, putting down her glass and inspecting it briefly. The old tin was well rusted and dented and looked like it had been in the family for decades. She opened the lid and glanced at the contents.

'Old marbles,' he confirmed. 'Not worth a lot, but might be interesting like.'

'Thank you, Bertle,' she smiled, placing the tin in her jacket pocket. 'I'll look at them properly later.'

They all seemed to be enjoying themselves. Only Bertle looked less than comfortable, his glass the only one still containing champagne. Every so often, he put the glass to his lips but the level hardly dropped and his mouth wrinkled as if he'd inadvertently swallowed a fly.

There was movement in the doorway. Archie had let himself in. She looked at him and nodded. It was the least she could do.

'Ah, Monica,' Rex was saying loudly, 'I see your excellent map has now taken its place on the wall with the rest of our research. Would you like to tell us about it?'

No, she wouldn't. She really wasn't in the mood.

Still holding her glass, she moved closer to the map on the wall and hoped the smile she forced on to her face looked better than it felt.

'What I tried to do with this map,' she began, 'was to show the route we believe was taken by the king and his baggage train. You can see it here, marked with green dots. I've also highlighted a few landmarks from King John's time which still exist today, however ruined they may be. I wanted to give an idea of his landscape compared to ours.'

Everyone was nodding, most of them a bit pink from the champagne. Rex was being very generous with his top-ups.

'You can see that I've drawn the medieval coastline in blue, with the Wash coming in as far as Wisbech. The abbeys are all shown, since they were centres of such importance and wealth at that time; Ely, Ramsey, Crowland and Swineshead. And finally,' she added, feeling a bit red in the face herself, 'I've added some less important sites, chapels mainly, which Archie and I have visited over the last few weeks. I put them in to add colour really, to give a more detailed picture.'

'Ah, and I see you've inserted information about the various locations in the margins. Excellent!'

'Thanks, Rex.'

Archie was smiling at her, encouraging her. Perhaps it was the drink, but she allowed herself to smile back before continuing. Bertle, she noticed, was fidgeting, scratching his nose. The level in his glass had still not dropped.

'Some of the ruins we looked at turned out to date from just after John's time, so I've omitted them, but a few were of interest. There was one which was particularly intriguing, a small chapel dedicated to St Ethelreda on farmland near Holbeach. The farmer told us that the chapel, possibly an infirmary too, had been founded by the Baroness Audrey de Prys in the early thirteenth century. Later, I looked her up and was surprised to discover as much as I did. It turns out that she was the wife of Walter Bottreux, Baron de Prys, one of King John's most loyal barons!'

'Good heavens!' spluttered Rex. 'So there's a connection between that chapel and King John!'

'Yes, though it's a tenuous one.'

There was a gratifying chorus of appreciation. Archie was staring at her in amazement. Perhaps he was feeling peeved too; she ought to have told him about her research. She should have told him that, thanks to the ever-improving information accessible through the internet, she'd been able to find out far more than the farmer had a few years earlier. She'd just not felt like telling Archie, though. She'd been far too angry with him.

He had begun to speak now, his voice carrying easily over the swell of chatter that filled the room.

'That's not all, though is it?' he was prompting. 'Tell them about your theory, Monica.'

She frowned, not quite understanding what he wanted her to say.

'The relic,' he reminded her.

'That was your theory as much as mine.' They were both smiling now.

'I'll say it, then.'

'Jolly good, Archibald, let's hear it,' encouraged Rex.

'Yeah, and then we can get into the cheese 'n' pickle sarnies,' muttered Bertle in the hope of something tasty to go with his unsatisfactory beverage.

'OK, then,' began Archie, 'remarkably, the ruin of St Ethelreda's Chapel still has its original stone altar. We noticed a niche in the front of the altar stone and Monica told me that centuries ago these were sometimes used to house holy relics. Some of these relics were said to be the bones of saints, others, though our modern cynicism no longer allows us to believe it, relics to do with Jesus himself.

'Brought to England from the Holy Land by crusaders, these precious relics were placed in abbeys and churches throughout the country. They attracted pilgrims from far and wide and these travellers brought great wealth to the religious buildings. These relics were therefore very highly valued, and it was only a thought, but...'

'King John's brother, Richard I, was a great crusader,' interrupted Rex, 'as were many nobles and knights in the king's service. Since the Baron de Prys was a loyal supporter of King John, perhaps it wasn't difficult for his baroness to acquire a holy relic for her chapel...'

'And that reminds me of something else,' joined in Mark. 'I've been doing more reading on this subject lately and have learned that it's thought in some quarters that among the items on King John's baggage train was a kind of portable altar. Any altar belonging to the king would have been equipped with the most precious items, some of which may have ended up in the Wash. His closest subjects would have known all about them. They may even have recovered a few of those treasures after the disaster, one of which...'

'...Could have been the relic which ended up in the chapel,' continued Archie. 'And perhaps this one was of particular importance. An inscription we found on the altar suggests that the relic housed there was believed to be part of the True Cross.'

'Oh come on!' protested Bernadette. 'This is all getting a bit far-fetched, isn't it? Are you suggesting that part of King John's lost treasure consisted of relics? Including a piece of *wood*?'

'It's only a theory,' admitted Archie.

'But one that fits darned well,' observed Mark.

'We'll probably never know the truth,' sighed Monica. 'All we've done is to create yet another theory. If anything, we've made the contradictions and myths surrounding King John and his treasure even more complicated.'

'Not at all!' protested Rex. 'This is absolutely marvellous! Bernadette, pass round the smoked salmon canapés, and I'll open another bottle.'

'No cheese 'n' pickle?' asked Bertle forlornly.

'Certainly not, Mr Collins! This is a special celebration and you, my dear fellow, must tuck in and enjoy yourself!'

'I'm sorry I went on about you and Jemima,' Monica said quietly when she reached Archie's side. 'I was jealous. Plain and simple.'

He reached for her hand. From across the room Bernadette gave them a small smile.

'It's all right,' he was saying. 'You have nothing to fear from her and I know I shouldn't have blabbed to her.' He paused, grinning suddenly. 'I do have to ask you, though, what on earth is that sticking out of your pocket?'

She looked puzzled by his change of subject for a moment, then laughed, pulling the tin out of her jacket pocket.

'Bertle gave it to me for the museum. It's a tobacco tin of old marbles.'

She opened it and pushed the coloured glass spheres around with her fingers. Some were clear glass with spiralled centres, others densely filled with bright colour. Most looked well played with, scratched and chipped, others still curiously shiny and bright. There were orbs of brilliant ruby red, turquoise blue, some of pure emerald green. A medley of rich childhood treasures. But among them, especially the very clear red and green and the turquoise ones, were items which looked less like marbles and more like...

'Gemstones,' said Archie. 'Bertle, not all of these are marbles. Where did you say they came from?'

'Me granddad in West Walton. We all came from there. He was the blacksmith; all us Collinses were, as far back as anybody remembers like. Only there's not a lotta call nah for work like that so I did me plumbing and 'lectrics instead. Look, if the marbles are no good, I'll chuck them back in the drawer where they came from. Don't worry abart it.'

'No Bertle, these are really interesting,' said Monica. 'I don't know much about gemstones, but there's something about them which looks pretty old.'

Archie glanced at Rex who was seated in the corner with Ena Cross, giving her the benefit of his wisdom. He was going to have a field-day when he found out about Bertle's tin of marbles.

'Drink up and have another, Bertle,' laughed Archie. 'You deserve it.'

'No thanks, mate,' he replied miserably. 'Don't wanna give no offence or nothing, but has anybody got any beer?'

EPILOGUE

Sir Milo Fulk, the bishop's seneschal for the Isle of Ely, stood alone in the chapel dedicated to St Ethelreda.

The elderly monk who tended the shrine had been in earlier and lit the altar candles. Their flickering warmth kept the brooding shadows at bay and spread their honeyed glow into every niche and corner. St Ethelreda's was still a shrine. It still housed a holy relic that rested safely within its altar stone.

Or at least that was how it appeared. It was all anyone needed to know. Milo was doing his best to make sure of that.

He had arranged for the silversmith in Ely to repair the case he had damaged while removing the fragment of the True Cross. The relic was now in King Henry's possession, but the young king had had no use for the case which protected it. Skilfully repaired, the silver reliquary was back in its niche behind the grille. No one needed ever to know that its contents were missing.

With Lady Audrey awaiting justice in Wisbech Castle, the shrine was left in the reverent care of the brothers of Crowland Abbey. It was something else Milo had taken care of.

As for Audrey's fate, that was largely in the king's hands. Execution would have been the normal outcome, but this was the Baroness de Prys, the wife of one of King John's most loyal barons. No one could tell what the young Henry III would decide, but the baron's allegiance to his late father was unlikely to be completely forgotten.

And so, while her future was being decided in high places, the baroness remained at the castle. By all accounts, she was a quiet and uncomplaining prisoner, spending her days in prayer while she awaited her destiny.

And one day, when the king's justice had been carried out, when all the ugliness and rumours had been forgotten, word of the shrine in St Ethelreda's Chapel would begin to spread. Pilgrims would make their way there in ever increasing numbers, to kneel before a tiny fragment of the True Cross and pray for healing of their sorrows and sickness.

Perhaps then, Lady Audrey's infirmary would be built. Whether or not she survived to see it, her dream would become reality. Through her founding of St Ethelreda's, many might dare to hope for healing of soul and body.

Though containing nothing but the memory of what once was, the reliquary would provide a focus for their faith. And, considered Milo, that was all they really needed.

He bowed his head towards the altar and withdrew, his boots hardly making a sound on the stone flags. He closed the door quietly behind him and Merlin lifted his head in greeting.

Only the rooks, high in the winter-bare aspens, were there to watch the departure of horse and rider. The birds' melancholy cawing followed them along the track and seemed to Milo a fitting appraisal of the fading day. Already, darkness was pooling beneath the trees.

It was time to be moving on.

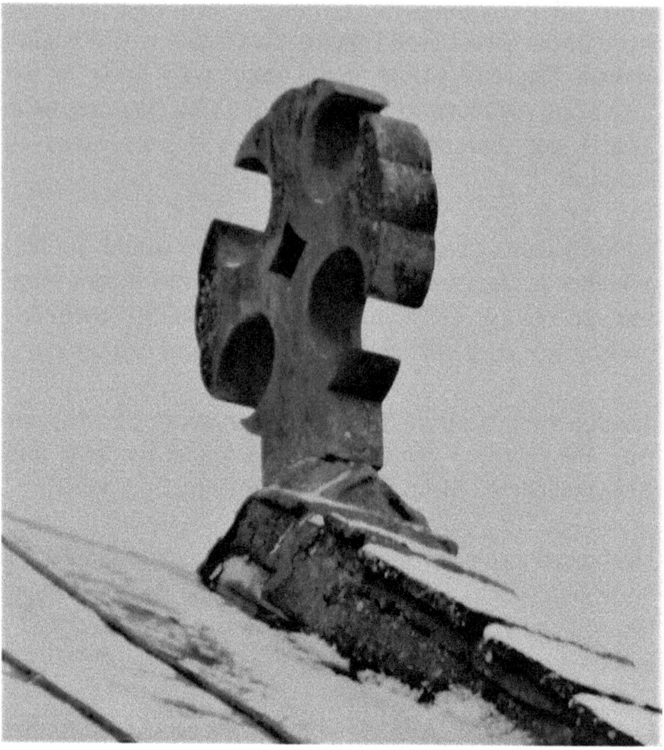

AUTHOR'S NOTES

The loss of King John's treasure in the Wash has become a part of local legend and so it seemed fitting to base a Fenland Mystery on the story.

But nothing is simple, it seems. As soon as I began to work on the plot, I struck an obstacle. Anything to do with medieval peace-keeping usually involves a sheriff, but the Isle of Ely didn't have one!

The Liberty of Ely, thought to have originated around AD 970 through a grant by King Edgar to the monks of Ely for food and clothing, gave the isle certain privileges. By the eleventh century, these rights had developed to allow the isle to keep its own law courts, as well as granting it immunity against any intervention by the county sheriff. By King John's time, the Bishop of Ely was permitted to appoint his own officers for the administration of the Isle. One of these was the 'Seneschallus Insulae Eliensis', or 'seneschal' for easier reference! The status of this officer was of equal importance to that of any county sheriff.

Sir Milo Fulk, therefore, had to be a seneschal, rather than a sheriff. He is a fictional character, though sometimes I find that hard to believe because I've become quite fond of him! Very few of the other characters in the book existed either. Only the kings, the Bishop of Ely, the Abbot of Ramsey, the knight Stephen de Marisco and the barons Robert de Gresley and de Moulton were real people.

I had to invent some of the settings for the story too. Even where using real places, a lot of imagination was called for. For example, although a fair amount is known about later incarnations of Wisbech Castle, little remains to tell us about the original Norman building. I had to use the medieval layout of other castles as a guide, such as those at Kenilworth and Corfe.

The Medieval St Peter and Paul's Church in Wisbech and St Katherine's (now St James') in Newton in the Isle are represented as well as I could manage from the sparse information available.

St Ethelreda's Chapel, the medieval ale houses and inns, the hamlet of Fen Hallow, the manors of the Baron de Prys, the knight Edward of Hagebeche and Marshmeade, Rufus' home manor, are complete fabrications.

The references to medieval Fenland hostelries are meant as no reflection on the good food, drink and hospitality of today's pubs and hotels.

There is perhaps one piece of poetic licence that stands out from the rest. Although I've mentioned a windmill close to Wisbech's Old Market, I have no knowledge of whether or where a mill existed at that time. The manor is known to have had one later in the century, however, and it is likely to have been established for some time before that. The location I gave it seemed a convenient one!

Regarding King John's visit to Wisbech and his lost baggage train, there are so many different versions of the story. No one has ever been able to agree on which route the train took across the Wash, quite when it occurred, or even what was lost. And no one knows what happened to the allegedly lost treasure afterwards.

For the purposes of his book, I had to select one version of the story, and for this I am indebted to the late Beryl Jackson. Her research and theories are logical and very well thought through.

Rex Monday and the Wisbech Heritage Society, of course, do not exist, though there are many excellent societies in the town which enjoy exploring our local history and archaeology.

The role of Rex and his group in the story is to set out the different theories and to provide the framework for the medieval plot as it unfolds.

Sadly, as Rex puts it, we shall never know the truth.

Yet still the story intrigues us. It is one of our most enduring mysteries. While there is a will and a metal detector, we shall go on searching and wondering.

THANK YOU

I have been very fortunate again in the help and advice I have had from kind and generous people. My heartfelt thanks go to:

Bridget Holmes, for bringing Beryl Jackson's research to my attention and for lending me her notes,

Michelle Lawes and Geoff Hill for the loan of some excellent books,

Ben Rickett, Operations Manager of Peckover House who, as before, allowed me the use of his alter-ego,

Wisbech and Fenland Museum,

Wisbech Library,

St Peter and St Paul's Church,

Father David Fysh,

Robert West,

My family, especially Tony for his very patient proof reading and detailed maps, and Aunt Christine for her advice regarding horse behaviour!

And, as always, to everyone who reads this book. I truly hope you enjoyed it.

BIBLIOGRAPHY

'An Historical Account of the Ancient Town and Port of Wisbech in the Isle,' by William Watson

'A Local Historian's Encyclopaedia,' by John Richardson

'Fenland Notes and Queries'

'Food and Cooking in Medieval Britain,' by Maggie Black

'Historical Costumes of England,' by Nancy Bradfield

'King John; England's Evil King?' By Ralph V Turner

'King John,' by W L Warren

'Lionheart and Lackland,' by Frank McLynn

'Ramsey Abbey; its Rise and Fall,' by John Wise MA and W Mackreth Noble BA (1881)

'The Chronicle of Britain and Ireland,' edited by Henrietta Heald

'The Lost Treasure of King John,' by Richard Waters

Lightning Source UK Ltd.
Milton Keynes UK
UKHW011335270720
367245UK00002B/183